INFERNO!
VOLUME 2

Crusade & Other Stories
A Getting Started collection
Various Authors

• DARK IMPERIUM •
Guy Haley
BOOK 1: *Dark Imperium*
BOOK 2: *Plague War*

Watchers of the Throne:
The Emperor's Legion
Chris Wraight

• THE HORUSIAN WARS •
John French
BOOK 1: *Resurrection*
BOOK 2: *Incarnation*

Vaults of Terra:
The Carrion Throne
Chris Wraight

• RISE OF THE YNNARI •
Gav Thorpe
BOOK 1: *Ghost Warrior*
BOOK 2: *Wild Rider*

• BLACK LEGION •
Aaron Dembski-Bowden
BOOK 1: *The Talon of Horus*
BOOK 2: *Black Legion*

Blackstone Fortress
Darius Hinks

Sacrosanct & Other Stories
A Getting Started collection
by various authors

Nagash: The Undying King
Josh Reynolds

• HALLOWED KNIGHTS •
BOOK 1: *Plague Garden*
BOOK 2: *Black Pyramid*
Josh Reynolds

Eight Lamentations:
Spear of Shadows
Josh Reynolds

Overlords of the Iron Dragon
C L Werner

Soul Wars
Josh Reynolds

Callis & Toll: The Silver Shard
Nick Horth

The Tainted Heart
C L Werner

Shadespire: The Mirrored City
Josh Reynolds

Blacktalon: First Mark
Andy Clark

The Realmgate Wars: Volume 1
An omnibus containing stories by
various authors

The Realmgate Wars: Volume 2
An omnibus containing stories
by various authors

SPACE MARINE CONQUESTS

The Devastation Of Baal
A Blood Angels novel by Guy Haley

War of Secrets
A Dark Angels novel by Phil Kelly

Ashes of Prospero
A Space Wolves novel by
Gav Thorpe

Of Honour and Iron
An Ultramarines novel by
Ian St. Martin

WARHAMMER® CHRONICLES

• THE LEGEND OF SIGMAR •
Graham McNeill
BOOK ONE: *Heldenhammer*
BOOK TWO: *Empire*
BOOK THREE: *God King*

• THE RISE OF NAGASH •
Mike Lee
BOOK ONE: *Nagash the Sorcerer*
BOOK TWO: *Nagash the Unbroken*
BOOK THREE: *Nagash Immortal*

• VAMPIRE WARS:
THE VON CARSTEIN TRILOGY •
Steven Savile
BOOK ONE: *Inheritance*
BOOK TWO: *Dominion*
BOOK THREE: *Retribution*

• THE SUNDERING •
Gav Thorpe
BOOK ONE: *Malekith*
BOOK TWO: *Shadow King*
BOOK THREE: *Caledor*

• CHAMPIONS OF CHAOS •
Darius Hinks, S P Cawkwell
& Ben Counter
BOOK ONE: *Sigvald*
BOOK TWO: *Valkia the Bloody*
BOOK THREE: *Van Horstmann*

• THE WAR OF VENGEANCE •
Nick Kyme, Chris Wraight
& C L Werner
BOOK ONE: *The Great Betrayal*
BOOK TWO: *Master of Dragons*
BOOK THREE: *The Curse
of the Phoenix Crown*

• MATHIAS THULMANN:
WITCH HUNTER •
C L Werner
BOOK ONE: *Witch Hunter*
BOOK TWO: *Witch Finder*
BOOK THREE: *Witch Killer*

• ULRIKA THE VAMPIRE •
Nathan Long
BOOK ONE: *Bloodborn*
BOOK TWO: *Bloodforged*
BOOK THREE: *Bloodsworn*

INFERNO!

TALES FROM THE WORLDS OF WARHAMMER   **VOLUME 2**

INCLUDES STORIES BY GUY HALEY, C L WERNER, STEVE LYONS, PETER FEHEVARI,
THOMAS PARROTT, JAINE FENN, ROBERT CHARLES, MILES A DRAKE,
JAMIE CRISALLI AND J C STEARNS

BLACK LIBRARY

A BLACK LIBRARY PUBLICATION

This edition published in Great Britain in 2019 by
Black Library,
Games Workshop Ltd.,
Willow Road,
Nottingham, NG7 2WS, UK.

10 9 8 7 6 5 4 3 2 1

Produced by Games Workshop in Nottingham.
Cover illustration by Mauro Belfiore.

Inferno! Volume 2 © Copyright Games Workshop Limited 2019. Inferno! Volume 2, GW, Games Workshop, Black Library, The Horus Heresy, The Horus Heresy Eye logo, Space Marine, 40K, Warhammer, Warhammer 40,000, Age of Sigmar, Necromunda, the 'Aquila' Double-headed Eagle logo, and all associated logos, illustrations, images, names, creatures, races, vehicles, locations, weapons, characters, and the distinctive likenesses thereof, are either ® or TM, and/or © Games Workshop Limited, variably registered around the world.
All Rights Reserved.

A CIP record for this book is available from the British Library.

ISBN 13: 978 1 78496 852 6

No part of this publication may be reproduced, stored in a retrieval system, or transmitted in any form or by any means, electronic, mechanical, photocopying, recording or otherwise, without the prior permission of the publishers.

This is a work of fiction. All the characters and events portrayed in this book are fictional, and any resemblance to real people or incidents is purely coincidental.

See Black Library on the internet at

blacklibrary.com

Find out more about Games Workshop
and the worlds of Warhammer at

games-workshop.com

Printed and bound by CPI Group (UK) Ltd, Croydon, CR0 4YY

CONTENTS

Introduction 9

At the Sign of the Brazen Claw: Part Two –
The Merchant's Story 11
Guy Haley

The Thirteenth Psalm 37
Peter Fehevari

Spiritus in Machina 83
Thomas Parrott

From the Deep 107
Jaine Fenn

Faith in Thunder 145
Robert Charles

What Wakes in the Dark *Miles A Drake*	175
Solace *Steve Lyons*	239
Ties of Blood *Jamie Crisalli*	277
Turn of the Adder *J C Stearns*	305
No Honour Among Vermin *C L Werner*	345

INTRODUCTION

Welcome to the second volume of *Inferno!*

Look how far you have come, brave reader. You have traversed the treacherous jungles of the 41st millennium, the blood-soaked fighting pits of Necromunda, and invoked the wrath of the God of Death by emerging triumphant from his twisted realm.

But do not relax.

For your journey is not yet over.

In this brand new anthology, a host of up-and-coming writers, many of them making their first foray into the worlds of Warhammer, join Black Library's trusty Old Guard: Guy Haley, C L Werner, Steve Lyons and Peter Fehervari.

For over twenty years, Black Library has nurtured and showcased some phenomenal talent, and it is something we are incredibly proud of. In fact, one of C L Werner's very first professional writing ventures was in the original *Inferno!* magazine. With this in mind, it seemed only fitting to welcome him into the fray once more and have him bring up the rear with a swashbuckling adventure of betrayal and thievery... and the occasional exploding rat!

It has been exhilarating to watch our authors delve into undiscovered places and untold stories across the vast stretches of Sigmar's Mortal Realms and the Emperor's Dark Imperium. Each brings with them a rich imagination, a unique style of writing and a determination to make readers *feel*. Whether they choose to show us a heroic tale about the strength of faith, a dark mystery driven by the hunger for truth, or a perilous quest to cheat the Dark Gods, there are no shortage of instances that will leave you on the edge of your seat.

So mount your gryph-charger and ready your halberd – dark times are ahead. Only Sigmar can save us now.

Charlotte Llewelyn-Wells
Submissions Editor, July 2018

AT THE SIGN
OF THE BRAZEN CLAW:
PART TWO

Guy Haley

Continuing with his take on the classic frame narrative, Black Library stalwart Guy Haley picks up where he left off in Inferno! Volume 1.

At the Sign of the Brazen Claw, a storm still traps a group of weary travellers within the shrivelled, exanimated heart of Shyish. This time, it is the turn of the duardin merchant Stonbrak to recite a tale to while away the hours. Eager ears listen as he tells of broken oaths and a venomous deceit in the shadowy depths of Ulgu.

Prince Maesa and Shattercap have come to the hinterlands of Shyish in order to catch a Kharadron packet ship through the Argent Gate to Ghur. Delayed by stormy weather, they sit out the night at the inn of the Sign of the Brazen Claw. As they wait, the travellers swap their stories. The first to speak was the innkeeper, Horrin, who told of how he came into his career.

We rejoin the party as the duardin Idenkor Stonbrak begins his story.

THE MERCHANT'S STORY

The wind was full of mischief. It ran about the inn at the Sign of the Brazen Claw, banging shutters and shouting down chimneys. The rain, following shyly, pattered then drummed, then thought better of its racket and softly stroked the tiles. Draughts from the wind teased candle flames. They batted at the inn's fires. Cold gusts puffed under doors and raced away, hooting at the fun. The rain was less showy, but as determined to get in. Through gaps in the flashing on the inn's conical roof, it insinuated itself into the fabric of the building, dripping in fat drops to a spot on the floor, and darkening the giant digit the inn was built around. Once within, the water stayed. It was persistent where the wind was flighty.

A night of tempest in Shyish. Idenkor Stonbrak ignored the trembling of the building. The unpredictable forays of cold that snuck up under his collar could not discomfit him. He was duardin, enduring as rock. It would take millennia for any storm to wear away one so solid.

He lit his pipe, pulled deeply upon the ivory mouthpiece and appraised the group around the table with a merchant's eye. Horrin the innkeeper, his wife Ninian, who was handing out another round of drinks, and their stable boy Barnabus, he judged worthy, and he did not linger on them long. When he looked to Quasque his eyes narrowed until they glinted like coal seams at the back of a mine gallery. Stonbrak took in Quasque's spoiled finery and hunted face, and saw a disquieting story behind them. But his gaze remained the longest on the aelven wanderer Maesa and his spite, Shattercap, who knelt, grey-green and spiky as a bush, on the table boards before the prince. On the verge of saying something he might regret, Stonbrak clamped his lips shut, puffed smoke like an engine and shook his head, as if he could not quite credit what he was seeing.

'My turn then,' he said eventually. 'This is my story. A sad tale of broken contracts.' He cleared his throat, and took on a storyteller's airs. 'You might guess I am not of this realm, and you would be correct. I hail from Barak Gorn, a mighty port upon the shores of the Whispering Sea, in Ulgu up Melket way, if you've ever heard of that. Now, Barak Gorn was built in ages past by the ancestors of my ancestors, and though once it was a fine and marvellous place, it lay in ruin until the Age of Sigmar came, and drove back a little of Chaos' darkness.

'When the time came to return, my people were among the first to leave Azyr and reclaim Barak Gorn from obscurity.' Stonbrak smiled at the memory. 'I was a beardling. It was a long time ago now, but I remember well the sorrows of what we found, and the joys of restoring former glories to the halls and the quays.' His eyes lost their focus behind the smoke wreathing his face. He was quiet for so long, Shattercap spoke up.

'Is that all?' the spite asked Prince Maesa in confusion. 'So short a tale. Not worth the listening.' He folded his spindly limbs about himself in such an awkward way he resembled a dead spider, until he shrugged and twitched, so that he was suddenly sitting cross-legged, sharp elbows out, hands clasped around his thimbleful of wine.

Stonbrak snorted. 'All? All! I'm only getting started, you impertinent imp!' He took his pipe from his mouth and jabbed the stem at the spite. The fine leaves on Shattercap's shoulders quivered. 'A pause for thought was all that was. Now, where was I?'

'Forgive the spite,' said the prince softly. 'He has no manners. You were speaking of your home, worthy friend.'

Stonbrak nodded gratefully. 'I was.'

'I have heard stories of Ulgu!' said Horrin. He lifted his drink. His cheeks were flushed. He enjoyed his ale and his stories. 'Though of course I cannot go there.' He waved a hand at the fire by way of explanation. 'It is a realm of mists, where nothing is as it seems.'

'That it is, master innkeeper,' said Stonbrak. 'All thirteen lands of it, a confounding place of intrigue and shadows, where it is never either truly dark or truly light.' He moved his pipe around his mouth. 'A strange place to find the likes of we, you might say, but duardin are not so affected by Ulgu's inconstancy, for we are as steadfast as stone. Mist does not bother rock. Rock is impervious to illusion. Even so, my sort are considered secretive among our race, and our numbers in the shadow lands are small.' He sucked his pipe. The bowl grew bright, glinting from his eyes in such a way it was easy to imagine tiny foundries hidden in his skull. 'However, there are many aelves in Ulgu, of strange kindreds. The princeling's kind are prone to plays of light and shadow, and not always for the best, as you shall see.'

He took a drink from his beer mug, wiped the suds from his beard and recommenced both his smoking and his tale.

'Barak Gorn has neighbours,' he said. 'A race of aelves whose halls also overlook the misty sea. These aelves dwell in the mountain, in a manner similar to some of my kind. Once the two cities were one, but when we were forced from our port, they hid themselves away in their deepest halls and remained there throughout the ages of Chaos – an act some of my people saw as a betrayal, but the more level-headed of us know to be pragmatism. In the dark years they withdrew into themselves, became stranger still through their isolation. We call them the *skuru elgi*, or the grey aelves, because of the colours they wear to blend into the mists, and the magic they weave about themselves to hide. They are tricky creatures – never get a straight answer out of them!' The thought evidently irritated him, for his bushy eyebrows arched and his cheeks coloured, and he gesticulated with his pipe forcefully. 'They are apt to disappear in the middle of conversation, and they never smile. They are, not to labour the pick in the stone too much, a miserable bunch.' He calmed, and shrugged. 'But business is business. My kind and theirs did much dealing before the dark times, and do so again now, for they marvel at our jewels, and their nobles ever have bright sea gold to pay for them, though the hurts of the old times are slow to heal. That brings us to the heart of this tale.

'In my clan there was a worker of gems so fine his renown spread far and wide.' A wistful sigh escaped the duardin, and he looked to the ceiling, where the rain hammered in a thousand watery nails. 'He could capture the very essence of beauty. His works of gold carried the warmth of flesh. With cunning cutting, he trapped light inside gemstones. You can imagine how valued such stones are in shady Ulgu. His skill was unsurpassed.'

Stonbrak's voice grew thick. He coughed to hide emotion, blustering through an inner pain he could not quite obscure, and abruptly changed the subject.

'Let me tell you a little of our city. Barak Gorn is contained within a great cave, open to the front to the water, that combines the best of underground hall and harbour in one. Naturally, so great was the craftsman's wealth that his shop had a fine spot overlooking the sea. On the few days there is no mist, you can see all the way to the horizon from its window, and when the fog draws in and chill water runs down the glass, which is practically every day, there was the comfort of Barak Gorn's lid of stone pressing down above, and reaching its arms around the wharfs and jetties. It is a tonic to a duardin soul, the permanence of the stone, the indomitability of earth. Shadow mists are nothing compared to those things.'

He coughed, tapped out his pipe and refilled it unnecessarily, using the action to keep from looking at his audience. Maesa saw his sorrow clearly enough, caught the reddening of the duardin's eyes, and noted well Stonbrak's reluctance to name the jeweller.

'My cousin Bertgilda worked with the craftsman in his shop,' Stonbrak said, striking a match upon his boot. He put the flame to the bowl and sucked until its tiny coals glowed, and the foundries in his eyes flared. 'It is from her I have the detail of this tale.

'One day, one of the grey aelves came into the shop. The doorbell did not ring, nor did the craftsman hear the door close. My cousin noticed him only by the dampening of the air. Thinking that a heavy fog had come into the harbour,

Bertgilda looked up from her work and found that the mist was thin, and the sun as bright as it can be in our realm, but that the shop was cold. Grey vapours withdrew under the door, and in front of the counter stood an aelf of high birth, not unlike your guest here, master innkeeper.' Stonbrak gestured at Maesa. 'His grey cloak was beaded with moisture. I tell you, I meet these aelves and wonder, have they never heard of fire, that they be perpetually damp?' He shook his head again. 'A sharp elbow from Bertgilda alerted the craftsman to this silent customer, and he raised his eyes from the gem mount he was cutting. He was methodical, not prone to rushing. He pushed back his loops from his face, folded the paper he worked upon, and from it poured tiny curls of gold into an envelope. Frugal, he was. Very frugal,' said Stonbrak approvingly. 'Only then did he speak with the aelf.

'"How may I help you, sir aelf?" the craftsman asked. He was a stout-hearted soul, not given to shock, and had had many dealings with our aelven neighbours. They often did that kind of thing. Shifty beggars. The aelf looked upon him with grey eyes as cold and treacherous as the winter sea.

'"I am to be married to a princess of a foreign nation," he said. His voice was peculiar, Bertgilda told me, like gravel churning in a mountain stream. Musical, as the voices of aelves tend to be, but with a rasping edge they rarely have.'

The inhabitants of the inn glanced at Prince Maesa. The prince gave them no comment on the peculiarities of aelven voices, but sipped his wine, his attention given fully to the duardin. Stonbrak continued.

'"It is a great union of peoples," the aelf said, "a bringing together of kindreds that will bless all this country and bring new trade and wealth to your city as well as mine."

'"I see," said the craftsman. He was careful, and waited for the aelf to outline his needs. Some duardin might rush in to negotiation, scenting a lot of gold at the end of a bargain involving princesses, but the duardin of Barak Gorn are of Ulgu, and alive to the dangers of hasty contracts.

'"These aelves covet watergems above other jewels," continued the aelf.

'"Do they?" said our jeweller. This did pique his interest. Watergem is a rare diamond. It is named for the movement in its heart.' Stonbrak held up his thumb and forefinger as if he had such a gem, and peered into the space. 'Look into a middling example, and you will see the dance of sunbeams piercing the waves on turquoise seas. They say if you look into a perfect stone – only the very most perfect, you understand – the deeps of faraway oceans might be glimpsed.

'"I require a necklace to be made of such diamonds, to these measurements." The aelf placed a roll of paper on the countertop. He had no interest in the marvels displayed under the glass, understandably, considering what he was carrying, as our craftsman shortly discovered. The aelf pulled a velvet pouch from his side, and upended it, scattering the contents on the countertop. They spun across the polished glass, and when they ceased their movement and clinked against the frame, the pounding of waves on distant shores filled the shop.

'Bertgilda gasped. Upon the counter were eight of the most exquisite watergems the craftsman had ever seen. From each one shone the light of a different sun on a different sea. It takes a lot to surprise a longbeard such as he, but the craftsman was dumbstruck. This was a king's fortune, his ransom, his estates, fortress, armies and more.

'"Where did you get these?" he asked.

'"My beloved gave them me, and swore she would not be

wed until they had a setting fit for their beauty," said the aelf. "I wish them placed into a necklace of purest moonsilver. It is my bride price for the match, so I am willing to pay well for your efforts. How much for your best work?"

'Ordinarily this question would have offended, for a duardin *always* does his best work, but the craftsman was so shocked that he blurted out a price rather than the threat of grudge-making. He had not taken leave of his wits completely, and the price was high.

'"Do this for me within the week, and I shall double it," said the aelf.

'"Half now," said the craftsman, who was no fool.

'"I carry no coin. You shall have all when complete," said the aelf.

'It goes against every instinct of a duardin to take work without pay, but these gems were of such high quality that surely the aelf had the money. No one less than a king could possess such wonders. Mayhap that should have given the craftsman pause, but greed ever was the curse of our kind. Gold is our greatest weakness.

'"Very well," he said. "Double. In a week."

'The aelf nodded.

'"Before you leave," said the craftsman, "what is your name, for my ledger of works?"

'The aelf paused before speaking. "You do not require my name. My entrusting to you of the gemstones is my bond. I will return in a week."

'The aelf said no more, and departed. This time,' said Stonbrak, 'he used the door.'

'The craftsman laboured long hours over that necklace, my cousin as his helper. Bertgilda told me that twice he made the mounts for the gems, twice he melted down the moonsilver and began again. The cost of the materials alone was enough to beggar him, and he sought the money from the lenders of the Granite Brotherhood. A foolish move for anyone who is not absolutely certain of riches to pay them back, but our craftsman was sure.'

Stonbrak paused for a drink. The wind probed the shutters, whistled three times and withdrew, disappointed it could find no way in.

'Weary from many days' sleepless toil, the craftsman removed the lenses from his eyes and sighed with satisfaction,' said Stonbrak. 'Truly, this was his greatest work. The necklace was the finest he had ever made. Those who saw it compared it favourably with the greatest works of the Age of Myth, and that was only if they could speak through their tears of joy. When I asked Bertgilda to describe it, she could not, but cried and told me it was too beautiful to put into words.

'The week passed. Then another. The craftsman's delight turned to fretting. The aelf showed no sign of returning for his goods. He sent messengers up to the *Skuru elg* mountain, but without a name he was at a loss to find the commissioner of the piece. His descriptions did not help. You aelves look much the same to us,' he said. 'The craftsman was perhaps too coy about what he had made. If he had revealed he had the stones, things might very well have turned out differently, but he did not, keeping to his trader's oath of confidentiality instead.

'A reckoner of the Granite Brotherhood paid the craftsman a visit, insisting that he repay the money he had borrowed. When he saw the necklace, he softened his tone, and urged the craftsman to sell it, whereupon he would be able to repay the debt and be enriched in the process.

'"It is not mine to sell," the craftsman said.

'"The aelf is in breach of contract," said the reckoner. "You are free to do with it as you will." The craftsman said no. The Granite Brotherhood's representative insisted, several times, but the craftsman was an honourable sort, and steadfastly refused.

'The Granite Brotherhood gave him a week more to find the money. "After which time has passed," their reckoner informed him, "we shall seize your goods, as we are legally entitled to, and you will be poor."

'The craftsman hid his worries from the reckoner, but they were growing, until, four nights after the Granite Brotherhood came, he received a message, delivered by an unseen hand to the side of his bed, and written upon paper damp with the mist.

'"My apologies for the delay," it began. "Owing to unforeseen circumstances I have been unable to collect the item you fashioned for me. However, I need but to see it, and I will be able to pay you the sum in full. I have absolute trust that the piece will be exquisite. I cannot come into the city, and require delivery. Bring the necklace with you to Eskbirgen's Cove tonight, at moonrise, where I shall meet you. Come alone! There you shall receive your reward.

'"Once again, my heartiest apologies."

'It was signed with an X,' said Stonbrak. He gave each of his listeners a serious look. The storm hooted outside. Somewhere in the inn a shutter banged. 'Naturally, our craftsman was outraged. This aelf had broken his bond to him. Being a duardin of the shadow realm, he had expected the course of events to run crooked, but now he was facing betrayal, ambush or worse! He had no choice but to comply. The sum involved was great.

'The cove was a league outside of Barak Gorn and well known to him. It is a beautiful spot, if you like the outdoors kind of thing and not the solidity of a good ceiling of bedrock over your head,' said Stonbrak, in a way that suggested a preference for the open sky was madness. 'But it had something of an ill reputation, owing to the use it was put during the dark times of the Age of Chaos. Of course, the craftsman went, but before he left for the cove he took his pistols from the workshop strongbox. He loaded one for himself and gave the other to Bertgilda, and asked her to follow him, and secrete herself in the rocks at the edge of the beach so she might keep watch.

'"In this way," he said to her, "we may foil any aelven trickery."

'The craftsman set out first, Bertgilda a half-hour behind, in case the shop was being watched. The craftsman took the Long Stair out of the city, up through the overhang and onto the clifftops. All trade goes to and from Barak Gorn via the ocean and the Realmgate in the deepest hall. Currently there are no roads to the port. The Long Stair's exit is carefully hidden. Were you to pass it by, you would not see it, not even you, wayfarer.' Stonbrak directed this at Maesa. Maesa raised a hand and waved it equivocally, prompting a harrumph from the duardin.

'A thin trail, no wider than that made by goats,' Stonbrak said, his voice becoming gruffer, 'winds across the cliffs. If you look down from the top, there is no sign the city is there. Well it is so, for Ulgu is a tormented realm even now.

'To the north of Barak Gorn the bulk of the aelves' mountain is grey in the mist. In the late afternoon, when our craftsman departed, the light of Hysh spreads itself through the vapours, giving a harsh but indistinct illumination.

Under those conditions the mountain often appears like a steel cut-out laid upon brass. The entrance to their kingdom was almost as well hidden as the one to ours, but the craftsman knew the way. That the aelf had not asked for the item to be delivered to the aelven kingdom gave him no end of concerns, but if he wished to be paid, he had no choice but to follow the aelf's wishes. More or less.' Stonbrak grinned. 'He was carrying his gun, you will remember.

'Bertgilda followed him later. The fogs thickened, and though the cliffs are free of trees or other such vegetation, and the close turf smooth and without rocky eminences, she only caught sight of her master once or twice ahead, and then only by the bobbing of his lantern. The gloom was full of the whisperings of misbegotten things, but a duardin maid is as brave as any warrior, and she made her way to the cove without mishap. Through drifts of mist she saw that the craftsman was already waiting upon the beach. The sea heaved with slow waves, none cresting, but all rolling up and down. The water was as dull as tarnished pewter, and thick as oil. It slopped upon the shingle beach. In the misty twilight it raised not so much as a clack of stone on stone, or the faintest hint of the rushing hiss one should expect of sea on shore. It was silent, almost deader than Shyish. No offence,' said Stonbrak.

'None taken, I assure you,' said Horrin, though Ninian scowled.

Stonbrak leaned forward, his massive head shadowed by candle and firelight, making chasms of his wrinkles and caves of his eyes and mouth. His voice lowered, as if evoking the watchful quiet of the Realm of Mist. The storm, too, lessened in ferocity, rapt as the listeners.

'No one else was about,' said Stonbrak. 'Bertgilda found

a spot close by where she could observe, primed the pistol loaned to her by the craftsman and hid herself. She did it well. She had a little rune craft to her, did Bertgilda. A scratch here and there, and the application of certain metallic salts, and she was hidden as well as could be. Not even her master saw her, though he was only two dozen paces away.' He grinned sadly. 'She had skill that girl. When the aelf came down to the shore from the clifftop path, he passed her right by without so much as a glance in her direction. His boots scuffed the stone not four handspans from her nose, and she was not seen. She held her breath until the aelf was past, pressed against the rock and soil. When she heard the aelf hail the craftsman – "Master goldsmith!" he said – she poked up her head to watch.

'The pair met upon the shore. He was arrogant, like most aelves.' Another hard look was spared for the prince. 'But this one, he had an air of desperation, and though he tried his best to stand tall and haughty over our craftsman, his head kept drifting sideways, as if he expected his worst fears to emerge from the sea, and pull him under.

'The craftsman stood with legs apart, his thick fingers hooked into his belt. He was the very picture of duardin indomitability. He looked confident, Bertgilda said, he looked stubborn.

'"Do you have the necklace?" said the aelf.

'"Do you have my money?" the craftsman said. He patted the butt of his gun.

'"You shall have it, I promise," said the aelf, and appeared sufficiently apologetic that our craftsman lost a little of his anger. "Please," the aelf pleaded. "Let me see the necklace." He looked nervously over the water again. "She will be here soon. She is my love, but we must not anger her."

'The craftsman thought nothing of this. Duardin women are notoriously fiery of temper too, and with a people as mercurial as the aelves... Well.' His eyebrows bristled. 'Let's just say I am glad my wife is no aelfish female.'

'His isn't either!' hissed Shattercap, jerking his thumb over his shoulder. 'You be nice, beard bearer. Make bad thoughts about the poor prince. His wife is–'

'Silence, Shattercap,' said Prince Maesa, so firmly the spite cringed. 'Pray continue,' he said to Stonbrak's questioning expression. He left no doubt that he would not speak further on the matter.

'The necklace was presented,' Stonbrak continued. 'The light of eight seas shone into the grey aelf's face. His unfriendly demeanour was banished for a moment as he gazed in wonder upon the work.

'"Truly you are a master of your craft!" he said. The craftsman bowed.

'"I am," said our craftsman, and took the necklace back. The aelf's yearning gaze followed it all the way into the pouch. "Now. My payment," said the duardin.

'The aelf shrank in on himself, for he was rightfully ashamed, and gave the craftsman a desperate look. "You must give me the necklace and go."

'"Are you mad?" said the craftsman. "You will pay me!"

'"I will, I will," said the aelf. "Payment will be left here. You must leave the beach, turn your back on the sea. Do not look to the water, or it will go badly for you. My lover has the gold, and I swear I shall leave it here for you."

'"Lies!" boomed our craftsman. His voice rolled out over the lazy slap of the water. His talented hands drew his pistol and he pointed it at the aelf's head, so fast a movement in that listless, leaden bay.

'"I am sorry!" wailed the aelf. He clasped his hands together. "I did not wish to trick you, but this is the only way." He blinked. "I told you a little mistruth. I have no money."

'"Then I shall blow your lying aelven head off!" roared the craftsman, who by now had more than had his fill of aelfish nonsense.

'"Wait, wait! I mean for you to be paid! She has riches beyond compare. She is beauty incarnate. I must have her as my own. I am sorry to have deceived you. She will give you what you seek, I swear, but please, you must leave. Get away from the water."

'"I," said the craftsman through his anger, "am an honourable being. I have endured questioning, and innuendo, and threats because of the money I borrowed to make your necklace. I refused to listen. Our contract is binding, but you have invalidated it. I am going, and I will sell this necklace of the eight seas to recoup my loss."

'"You mustn't!" said the aelf. Ignoring the gun held at his head, he ran to the shoreline and back again. His feet whispered over the stones. The click of the hammer drawn back halted him.

'"Goodbye, master aelf," said the craftsman. He began to back away.

'The aelf remained staring out to sea. "Oh no! She comes!"

'A haunting note echoed from the cliffs, penetrating the mists, and travelled far out to sea.

'"Too late!" the aelf said with anguish. "Leave!"

'The craftsman paused. "Then she can pay me herself," he said, his pistol not wavering one hair's breadth from the aelf's head.

'Bertgilda watched with mounting horror. She wished to

shout that the craftsman flee, but he was her elder, and she had no right to tell him what to do. The scene took on the feeling of a dream. The sea boiled not far from the shore, and from the waves a pale-skinned aelf maid rose. Although she left the water, it did not appear to leave her. Her hair and clothes moved with the slow dances of the drowned. Fish darted through the air beside her. If she swam herself or flew towards the shore, Bertgilda could not tell. Her account was confused. Her recollection of events was slipping from her when I heard the tale, and the second time I spoke with her on this matter, she had forgotten most of it, all in the space of a day! Aelfish witchcraft.

'The aelf maid floated to the beach, her feet not once touching the floor.

'"You have the necklace?" she said. Her voice was quiet as wind-stirred water, as soft as the movement of weeds in a pool, and yet Bertgilda heard it, and it filled her brave maiden's soul with fear.

'"Give it to her!" The grey aelf hissed. "If you value your life, please! If she is satisfied you may depart with your soul and your money."

'Still holding up the gun, the craftsman pulled out the necklace and raised it for the aelf maid to see.

'She gasped with pleasure and drifted nearer, not once touching the jewel, but caressing it with her gaze. As she peered into each watergem and saw the worlds entrapped therein, she laughed, and said in delight, "A fine gift you have brought me, my dryshod love. A worthy price for my affection."

'A look of pure avarice gripped her. The look she gave my kinsman was far, far worse.

'"You have another item for me, I see."

'The aelf looked at the craftsman. "Run!"

'Too late did our honest jeweller see the peril he was in, and even though he knew now what danger there was in the exchange, a duardin does not run! Never! He fired his gun. The report of the shot banged off every stone and out into the mist. But the violence of the noise was all the shot availed him. The bullet slowed, as if caught by water, and drifted down, scaring apart a shoal of fish swimming in that uncanny ocean surrounding the foreign princess. The maid descended upon him, hands outstretched. His gun fell to the shingle.

'What act of sorcery the aelf performed I cannot say. Bertgilda was gripped by an awful, unnatural terror, and could not watch. The last she heard was the craftsman's strangled groan, the awful scream of the male aelf and a mighty splash. She lost her senses for a while. When she regained them the aelves were gone. The craftsman, by a miracle of the ancestors, lay upon the shingle, eyes wide, still breathing. At first she laughed through her tears, until she found her attempts to rouse him failed, and she realised his body lived devoid utterly of mind.

'Upon his chest was a bag of weed-wrapped net, full of coins dragged from cursed wrecks. The promised payment for his work.'

Stonbrak pulled hard on his pipe, his exhalations filling the space around the table with a cloud of fragrant smoke. The fire was burning low, lighting the room through the pipe's exhaust much as Stonbrak had described Ulgu – a glowing mist, never bright, never truly dark.

'Bertgilda returned to the city half out of her wits,' he said. 'Days later, our clan heard a rumour of an aelf of low birth who had taken the most precious treasure owned by the mountain king and used it to buy the hand of the daughter of a foreign lord whom he loved most dearly. The treasure, of course, was eight, perfect watergems.

'For some time, the grey aelves argued with us about the fate of the craftsman. Eventually, the alder council declared the craftsman at fault on account of reckless brokering, and the aelves admitted their share of the blame. The Granite Brotherhood creditors called in their loan. By that time the interest accrued was so large the sea gold covered only part of the debt, and his family were cast into penury.

'I learned all this when I returned home. The craftsman's deathless state persisted for some days before he expired, and he never once spoke again. By the time I saw Bertgilda, she was ill of mind, though I managed to piece together events from what she said. She lived, I'm glad to say, though it took her a long time to recover.

'Every day for ten years I walked from the city to hammer on the mountain gates of the grey aelves. Their guards and their functionaries spoke with me, but their high lords would not see me, until, annoyed by my persistence, they paid blood money for the craftsman's death and told me that was to be the end of it. Unwilling to risk relations with our neighbours, the alder council ordered that I drop the matter. I did. Though they assured me I did so honourably, it stung me.'

Stonbrak grumbled into his pint pot. 'From this tale I learned three things. Generosity is a weakness. Always take payment up front.' He jabbed his pipe stem at the prince. 'And never trust an aelf!'

Maesa sipped his wine glass empty and he gestured for more. Horrin hurried off to oblige. 'Surely the message of your tale is that greed is a weakness?' said Maesa. 'Pride, a desire to maintain honour, and greed were his downfall. Can you not see?'

'And you imply these are flaws?' Stonbrak slammed his pot down on the table. 'Not at all. Pride drives a being to do his best. Honour to maintain it. Greed is good, so long as it does not overrule sense,' said the duardin. He clamped his pipe in his teeth with an audible click.

'Yet all three led to his downfall.'

'Life,' said Stonbrak coolly, 'can be cruel.'

'Who was this craftsman to you?' said Maesa. 'I guess he was close from your sorrow.'

'What of it?' snapped Stonbrak. 'He was my clansman, his dishonour tarnishes the reputation of all his family. There is need of no more cause than that.'

'He was more than a cousin or an uncle, I think,' said Maesa.

Horrin returned with a jug of wine. 'I'm sure his highness here meant no offence,' he said cheerily, keen to head off disagreement between his guests. Before either could reply, a strong gust buffeted the inn, and he looked up momentarily as the structure shifted. Dust sifted down from the rafters. The building settled.

'I did not mean offence,' said Maesa. 'I seek merely to understand.'

'Not much to understand,' grumbled Stonbrak.

Horrin poured.

'Then tell us,' said Maesa. 'Who was he?'

Stonbrak removed his pipe, grasped it hard in both hands and stared at it.

'His name was Jurven. He was my brother. I loved him dearly,' Stonbrak said shortly, embarrassment clamping his jaw so he bit off the words, then he softened with the sentimentality his kind hide so well, but not always. 'When we were young, people assumed I would be envious of his ability, but it was not so,' he said. 'His works were a marvel. I lacked his perfect skill, but I never had any feeling for him other than pride at his ability. As I could not compete, I became a merchant, travelling the realms beyond Ulgu, and many a pretty coin I made from his crafts. It was while I was gone that tragedy befell him.'

Shattercap reached up his cup to the innkeeper. 'More, more!' he said.

Horrin looked to Maesa. The aelf nodded.

'Just a little more,' he said.

Horrin obliged, tipping a few drops into Shattercap's thimble.

'I tell you what else I learned,' said Stonbrak. He patted his axe. 'I don't use firearms after what I heard. I trust to my axe.' Runes glimmered on the shaft and head, fading only reluctantly away when his hand left the metal. Barnabus crept up to Ninian, and snuggled into her. Warmth enveloped the company.

'Now,' Stonbrak barked. 'You have had your story from me. I nominate this aelfish princeling go next.' The wind was dropping, but the rain picked up, its nervous fingers rattling on the wood. Thunder cracked.

'The weather is improving, perhaps,' murmured Quasque. 'The storm breaks. Perhaps the ship will come tomorrow?'

'I am afraid not,' said Horrin. 'The eye of the storm is closing in on us. There will be a drumbeat of thunder, a dazzlement of lightning!' He had consumed all his second drink and much of his third while listening to Stonbrak, and was thoroughly set in the storytelling mood. He was eager for more. 'The eye will drift over, and linger awhile. When it goes on its way, we'll have more wind, more rain. So there is plenty of time for more tales,' he said. 'Will you, could you, tell us a story, Prince Maesa?'

'I could.'

'I will choose which one he shall tell!' said Stonbrak. 'An aelf like him will have lifetimes of tales, but there is one in particular I would like to hear.'

'Is there?' said Maesa.

'There is,' said Stonbrak. 'Tell me how you came into the company of this little monster here.'

Shattercap hissed.

Maesa set his glass down. 'Very well,' he said. 'I shall.'

THE THIRTEENTH PSALM

Peter Fehervari

Master of the macabre, Peter Fehevari is well known for his appreciation of all things strange and peculiar in the Warhammer 40,000 universe.

In this mysterious narrative, a squad of Space Marines from the Angels Penitent are forced to confront their own flaws and the dishonourable history of their Chapter as they are drawn further and further into an enigmatic web of cruelty. Can the past truly remain buried and forgotten? Or are even the Penitent susceptible to falling?

Beauty blinds the beholder, bedazzling the eye with grace or splendour and beguiling the heart with the promise of hope. The first rapture is an illusion, the second a lie, both wrought by the Archenemy to bind the soul in sweet tangles while the world sours, bleeds and burns unopposed. Those who cherish beauty flirt with corruption, but those who fabricate, disseminate and embody its deceits are among the foremost of heretics.

– Thirteenth Psalm
The Testament of Thorns

FIRST REFLECTION

Once I was among the worst of sinners. Whenever I meditate upon the Thirteenth Psalm I am dismayed anew by the weight of my past transgressions. The bloodline of my brotherhood runs strong with the Angel Sanguinius' golden taint, cursing us with a comeliness and refinement uncommon among the Adeptus Astartes, even surpassing others who share our progenitor, but that does not excuse my excesses. When I walked among mortals as a Knight Artificer of the Resplendent they gazed upon me as though I were the God-Emperor Himself! But it was the accolades my *creations* received that truly filled my heart with pride, for even among a Chapter of artisans, poets and painters, my works were extravagant in their number and arrogance.

There was a time when the sculptures of Bjargo Rathana were lauded across a thousand worlds and sought by the most discerning – and avaricious – of the Imperium's elite. I brought more glory upon my Chapter with chisel and stone than ever I did with bolter or blade, not to mention the bounty I reaped for our coffers. I recall earnestly declaring that I was a warrior of the *soul*, charged with waging a higher war than the petty scuffles of bone and sinew. Such was our Chapter's decadence that my hubris was not only tolerated, but revered. Chapter Master Varzival titled me an Artisan Illuminant and decreed me too valuable to hazard in battle. And I delighted in it!

It shames me to confess such things aloud, yet it is necessary, for I must face myself without mercy if I am to prevail in the trial before me. The God-Emperor has condemned us all as sinners and shame is the first step on the road to penitence. Since the revelation that excoriated my Chapter I have walked far along that path and become a *true* warrior of the soul. And yet I was among the last to embrace atonement.

For years I languished in our monastery's Ghost Pits with the foulest recidivists, clinging to my pride, yet our prophet refused to forsake me. Time lost its way in that changeless darkness until nothing mattered save the patient, passionate tone of his censures.

'Concede the squalor in thy soul, Bjargo Rathana,' the Undying Martyr urged. *'Confess thy sins and rise above them, soiled but honest in thy contempt.'*

I have heard outsiders claim that our prophet is surely a madman or a sly servant of the Archenemy who has led us to ruin like cattle to the slaughter. Why, they ask, would a *civilised* brotherhood like the Resplendent submit to the degradation prescribed by a mortal stranger? To them I say this – *listen* to the Undying Martyr speak. *See* the sorrow in his eyes when he laments humanity's fall from grace. Only then will you understand and earn the right to judge. Until then it is we who shall stand in judgement over you. That is the doom of the Angels Penitent.

After I awoke to the revelation I seized it with a fervour that eclipsed all but the most blessed of my brothers, and ascended swiftly to the Crown of Thorns that governs our Chapter. For nearly twenty years an iron skull has masked my impure visage, riveted to the bone beneath to seal the compact, for a Chaplain Castigant never relinquishes his vestments. My hempen robes have never known the touch of water and the soot-black armour beneath is begrimed with old blood and the dirt of countless worlds, their stain a litany to the battles I have fought in His name. The crozius I now wield is more honest than a chisel, though it carves in fewer strokes and leaves every subject broken.

I wrought much good work in my new calling, yet my past disgrace tormented me, thus when the Undying Martyr proclaimed a crusade to scour the Imperium of the Resplendent's artistic legacy I sought his blessing to lead the quest. My creations were at the forefront of that prideful diaspora, so who better to expunge them than I? As I had sown, so I would reap!

The Chapter's numbers were few and our allies fewer still, so it fell to a single, much diminished company to prosecute this sacred quest. Rechristening our strike cruiser the *Severance of Glory*, we set about our task with zeal, seeking out and purging the vainglorious artefacts of the Resplendent.

Many years have passed since the Absolution Company's departure, and with them many of my brothers, for the heathens who covet our heritage have rarely surrendered their treasures willingly and some have commanded armies. It is a testament to the iniquity of the baubles we fabricated that they evoke such ardour in mortals. Indeed our dreams have seeded many monsters.

And so we come to the exquisite abomination that stands before me now – the centrepiece in this gallery of aberrant constructions.

Balanced on a tripod of curved legs, the mirror is taller than I and almost as broad, its arched top lending it the aspect of a doorway. The frame is forged from silver-plated plasteel, sinuous and seamless in its construction, its edges carved into the likeness of curled waves that appear to seethe at the corner of the eye. It is quite remarkable, yet mundane beside the glass it cages. Words are my foremost weapon, yet they defy my attempts to describe that strange surface. There is no tint or distortion to it, nor does it harbour subtle ghosts or glimpses of unholy realms. No, the mirror only reflects the world before it, but with a clarity that somehow surpasses its subjects, as though the reflection is the truth and the reality merely an impoverished approximation.

Above all else, it reveals *you*.

You gaze back at me from that heightened place with a sharpness of being – a *completeness* – that I cannot equal, though we are one. What lies behind your iron death mask, my brother-self? My own face for certain, yet also not.

It is imprudent to gaze into that eloquent glass too long, yet duty demands it. My purpose here is not crass destruction, but righteous castigation. Each artefact of the Resplendent must be studied, decried and conquered with the correct rituals for its redaction to bear meaning. The physical act of violence is only the tip of the spear I plunge into the Sea of Souls whenever I obliterate one of our heresies. As the mirror itself so insidiously suggests, the world of flesh and blood we inhabit is a shroud obscuring an infinitely greater, darker reality, where the Archenemy lurks, ever watchful. *That* is where I must strike! That is–

My work? No… You are mistaken. The mirror is not mine. I had no skill in the crafting of metal or glass, let alone the warp-weaving talents to enliven them. No, it was forged in the Librarium Resplendent by the most potent of our old Chapter's sorcerers, Chief Librarian Athanazius himself. The description in the *Inventorium Illuminatus* is unmistakable, though there is no mention of the mirror's arcane properties – and little wonder, since it was the Librarium that compiled the records and its acolytes were cautious even in those dissolute times. Wise to such evasions, I had prioritised their creations in our hunt, yet Athanazius' masterwork had long eluded us.

It would take too long to recount the twisted skein of events that carried the mirror so far from our monastery on sacred Malpertuis to the remote world I stand upon now. Suffice to say the Archenemy undoubtedly had a hand in its journey, though whether by intent or instinct, I cannot fathom. Either way, this planet has proved itself to be a trap.

As always, it was Brother Anselm, our company's most studious Redactor, who pieced together the trail. I recall the gleam in his eyes when he sought me out in the ship's chapel to reveal the breakthrough, though he kept his elation leashed. Like my own, Anselm's zeal burned cold, tempered by the discipline that our baleful blood demands lest it spill over into madness. We were both veterans of the Resplendent era, our roots steeped in sin, while more than half the Chapter's warriors are now Penitent-forged. While these young 'Thornborn' are aware of the past, they cannot *feel* it as we do, nor loathe it with such clarity. Though my calling disallows the camaraderie shared by common battle-brothers, there was an understanding between Anselm and myself that I choose to remember as friendship.

Now my friend is dead, along with all the others who accompanied me to this foul place. I can see him behind me, still kneeling where he fell, his body propped up by his rigid armour. His eyes are frozen in surprise beneath the splintered crown of his cranium. No... There is more than surprise in them – *betrayal* – for the trail of blood weaving from his corpse leads to the crozius in my hand.

I had no choice. But you already know that, mirror-brother, for Anselm Giordano also kneels broken on your side of the glass.

SECOND REFLECTION

I should say something of the benighted world where we found the mirror. Oblazt lies on the borders of the Damocles Gulf, just beyond the overt incursions of the foul xenos empire that festers beyond that great void. Though the planet is an insignificant speck of ice within the greater Imperium, it is the cornerstone of its own miserable subsector. The oceans under its frozen skin are abundant with edible beasts, and beneath their realm, deep wells of promethium. A network of domed cities harvests this wealth in the Emperor's name, though our records indicated their masters' loyalty derived from obligation rather than devotion.

Like so many provincial rulers, the Koroleva blue bloods revere themselves first and the God-Emperor second, wallowing in excess while the wretches under their yoke suffer the burden. It sickens me that such leeches are tolerated, indeed fostered, across the Imperium; however it bears witness to the Undying Martyr's message – mankind is beyond redemption. The Emperor condemns and the day of His wrath is imminent. By His leave the Angels Penitent shall prosecute it, but for now the wickedness of backwaters like Oblazt was not our concern. That was my decree when we set our course, but malign fate conspired against us.

When we entered Oblazt's orbit we found a world in the throes of revolution. Most of its cities burned like funeral pyres across the tundra, some with their domes cracked open to the killing cold. The vox waves blazed with defiance of the Imperium, promising a new age of harmony under the aegis of the blue-skinned 'Liberators' who would soon cross the Damocles Gulf and rebuild Oblazt equitably. Their watchword was *Unity*, but beneath its benevolent sheen their manifesto was a filthy xenos lie.

My brothers demanded action. Overlooking the grubby injustices mankind wreaked upon itself was tolerable, but turning a blind eye to this heresy was surely unforgivable! Was it not the God-Emperor's hand that had guided us to this place in its hour of vitiation?

I admit I almost surrendered to the temptation of war, for my own ire was stirred, but a Chaplain Castigant must rise above such indulgence and cleave to a higher purpose. Oblazt was in the grip of a headless, many-tentacled leviathan, while only fifty-five battle-brothers remained to me. We might hunt the beast for months, slicing away limbs, but never slaying it. It was a fool's errand. More than that – a *test* of our devotion to the true quest!

My brethren's fury withered before my rebuke and Brother Veland, who had been the most outspoken of them, begged that his tongue be cut out lest he utter such foolishness again. I denied his plea and merely chastised him with the Mute Censure, binding him to ninety-nine days of silence.

Though he was the youngest among us he had the makings of an exceptional warrior, but his quickness to anger troubled me, for it likely presaged the onset of the Black Rage. The Chapter's new recruits have proven more susceptible to our blood's ancient curse than the veterans, as though the clean slates of their souls are easier to stain, but I hoped Veland might elude the blight if correctly tempered. That is why I chose him for the mission ahead. With little prospect of meaningful opposition it would be a fine opportunity to observe and guide him.

No, do not berate me for it! Did you not make the same choice, mirror-brother? Or was *your* Veland made of purer stuff than mine?

THIRD REFLECTION

'The trail ends at a city named Zakhalin, Master Rathana,' Brother Anselm told me. 'It is among the most inflamed of this world's cankers.'

We were alone in the ship's obsidian-tiled strategium, for I required no others to advise me on our course.

'The disorder will mask our arrival,' I replied, studying the flickering holo-scan of the city that floated above the tactical pedestal between us. 'I trust you do not expect me to scour the entire hovel, Brother-Redactor?'

'I do not.' Anselm ran a long-fingered hand over the holo, manipulating it with the fluidity he had once applied to a laserwire harp. Truthfully, I still struggled to muster sufficient contempt for the sublime compositions he used to weave, though I know harmony is a false salve.

'The mirror is almost certainly *here*, master,' Anselm said, plucking a building into prominence. 'They call it the Concupiscent Hearth.'

'A carnal name,' I judged, but it wasn't the name that troubled me. I glared at the holo of the grandiose mansion, trying to identify my disquiet.

'The name befits its mistress,' Anselm continued. 'Even by the standards of this world's degenerate overseers, the reputation of the Konteza Esseker is wanton and cruel.' He frowned, deepening the seams of his sensitive face. Like many of our veterans, he had aged strikingly since the Great Excruciation, his long, once sable hair now entirely white. 'The reports I accessed are obscene.'

'You will cleanse yourself while I am gone, brother. The Seven Flagellations Incinerant shall suffice.'

'Forgive my impertinence, Master Rathana,' Anselm said, bowing his head, 'but I had hoped to accompany you on this purgation. I have long dreamt of redacting Athanazius' greatest blasphemy.'

I hesitated. Anselm's wisdom was too valuable to hazard, yet he had earned the right to see this through. Besides, what possible peril could the nest of a debased noblewoman pose?

'Very well, Brother-Redactor,' I decided, 'we shall prosecute His will together once more.'

It was many hours later, as our transport gunship descended to the city, that I finally realised what had troubled me about the mansion. Among the sprawl of burning buildings, the konteza's eyrie had appeared perfectly untouched.

Our Thunderhawk set us down atop a hab tower several blocks from our destination then roared back into the blizzard weeping through the cracked dome high above. I had chosen the deployment site to avoid drawing attention, but in the face of that churning white squall I suspected it was a needless precaution. My helm's sensors indicated the temperature was below freezing in the wind-wracked heights and I doubted it would be much warmer in the streets below, despite the fires raging throughout the city. The cold posed no threat to us, of course – even without our armour's thermo-regulators we could easily weather it – but Zakhalin's inhabitants would likely be compelled to seek shelter.

I recited the Canticle of Inception as my squad scanned the flat rooftop for heat signatures, but we were alone.

'They have brought ruin upon themselves,' Anselm observed over the vox, for the gale was too fierce for unassisted speech to carry beyond a few paces.

'As within so without, brother,' I replied, gazing down upon the fires shimmering through the blizzard. 'These degenerates were damned long before this cataclysm.'

'The Emperor condemns!' Brother-Sergeant Salvatore declared. A veteran of many redactions, he never forsook an opportunity to voice the First Psalm. Like all our Thornguard elite, his helmet was painted brown and crested with rusty spikes to mark his piety. A ragged tabard hung from his belt, woven with dried thistles and shards of bone, for our brotherhood forbids fanciful icons of faith. The Ecclesiarchy's proclivity for garish ornamentation mocks the holy war we wage, as does the leniency of its doctrine.

'The Emperor condemns!' we chorused reverently, though Veland held his tongue. It is a sin to abstain from responding to the First Psalm; however the prohibition of silence upon the young warrior was a graver ordinance. He would still be punished for the omission once the mission was over, but I would be merciful.

'How did the mirror come to be here?' Brother Laurent, the fifth and final member of the squad wondered aloud.

'By the Archenemy's wiles, boy!' Salvatore growled, his flamer's tongue lashing about in the wind. 'Why ask such things?'

'I stand corrected, brother-sergeant.' Despite his assent I suspected his curiosity was unappeased, but I tolerated such infractions in Laurent Toledos, for he was another young Thornblood with promise. Though he didn't possess Veland's martial flair, there was an earnest intuitiveness about him that leaned towards a subtler path, perhaps as a Redactor like Anselm. Such recruits are rare, for inquisitive souls are seldom pure enough to survive the Trial of Thorns, hence Laurent was worthy of cultivation.

Had I known what lay ahead I would not have chosen him for this mission, nor Veland or Anselm for that matter. The Concupiscent Hearth was no place for complex souls.

We crossed the city without serious incident. Our kind are not naturally built for stealth, nor does our creed encourage it, but the blizzard served as a partial cloak, surrendering to our helmets' sensors but blinding the scum who wandered the streets. Despite the cold there were many about, mostly in small groups, but occasionally in great mobs. Some were intent on destruction, others on escape from their fellows' madness. Most who stumbled upon us fled, shrieking that the Imperium's vengeance was upon them, or fell to their knees and begged for succour. All these we ignored, our consciences salved by the certainty of their doom, but some attacked us with makeshift weapons or autoguns. These fanatics' foreheads bore the blue circle of their imagined liberators and they fought with a measure of courage, if not skill. We purged them swiftly and without passion, for such vermin were unworthy of zeal.

More of Zakhalin's phantoms haunted the gateway leading to the konteza's estate, but they slunk away at our approach. The high marble wall surrounding the grounds had been defaced with paint, lewd symbols and phrases vying for attention with the hateful circle of the xenos-lovers. The iron gates had been battered down, yet I saw no bullet holes or scorch marks, let alone the bodies that typically attended such violence.

'The gates were undefended,' Anselm mused, echoing my thoughts. 'There was no battle fought here.'

'Doubtless their wardens fled,' Salvatore said, stomping over the twisted iron wreckage to enter the grounds. 'Only cowards would let such scum bring down their world.'

As the rest of us followed, a bundle of rags shivered beside the wall and a hand reached out to clutch at Brother Laurent's armoured shins. He spun and brought his bolter to bear on the figure slouched under the gateway. It was a crone, her form wasted to a minimalist caricature of humanity.

'You have come... angel,' the woman hissed, her heavily accented rasp somehow carrying through the wind. Her heat signature was so faint I marvelled she still lived, yet her eyes glittered in the gloom. 'I... saw you. *Dreamt* of you.'

Laurent offered no answer. Though his expression was hidden by his helm I sensed his uncertainty. Some day soon that hesitation would either sharpen into astuteness or prove his downfall.

'She took my sons,' the crone continued, her voice trembling with passion. 'Took so many others too... Burn the bitch!'

I was intrigued to watch the scene play out, but our comrades had already disappeared into the blizzard.

'Brother Laurent, with me!' I ordered.

As I marched after the others I heard him say something to the woman, but the squall snatched away his words. Now, after all that came after, I find myself wondering what he said.

Yes, mirror-brother, such things matter! We are the progeny of the choices we make and I believe Laurent made a choice at those gates, even if it came to nothing.

Be silent! Let me finish. I must order my thoughts if we are to end this.

FOURTH REFLECTION

Like the gates, the konteza's garden bore no traces of conflict. It was a flat, circular expanse covered in many-hued tiles that hinted at some overarching pattern I could not discern; however there was no mistaking the depravity of the statues that adorned it. They were dotted about the place seemingly at random, their strangely distended forms contorted into sinuous studies of carnality. The pink marble they were hewn from was aglow with an ardour their featureless faces couldn't express.

'Are they dancing?' Laurent asked as we passed an improbably conjoined pair.

'In a manner, brother,' Anselm answered solemnly.

'Do not look upon them,' I commanded, though my own eyes strayed to each tableau we passed. Despite their prurience I could not deny the excellence of their execution. Their creator had evidently been a sculptor of rare genius, almost the equal of my own. I vowed we would destroy them once our primary duty was accomplished, for it would be remiss to leave such magnificent obscenities standing.

The konteza's chateau emerged slowly from the blizzard, rising from the estate's centre in a riotous congeries of fluted pillars and faux towers clad in the same roseate marble as the statuary it presided over. Bulbous, vividly enamelled domes topped each wing, vying with one another for attention like the painted harlots who preyed upon mortals. The holo had failed to capture the building's sheer decadence, but it was certainly a fitting receptacle for Athanazius' heresy.

'It is... extraordinary...' Anselm trailed off before he said too much. Some among us have never fully cast off the tyranny of beauty, but we must never give it voice. I would castigate him for the lapse later.

'We should burn this abomination in our wake,' Salvatore declared piously.

'We shall raze it to rubble, brother-sergeant,' I promised. 'Even if it requires an orbital barrage.'

The mansion's wing-shaped doors were wide open, their ornately carved woodwork showing no sign of having been forced. We approached them cautiously, our weapons readied in expectation of a trap, but the brightly lit hall beyond appeared deserted.

'Brother Veland, take the spearhead,' I commanded. The choice would irk Salvatore, but the volatile Thornblood was the most expendable among us.

Nobody sprang from hiding as Veland entered, but I waited until he reached the centre of the immense hall before signalling the others to follow. We fanned out into our pre-designated quadrants behind our spearhead, swiftly scouring the space for enemies. The room was as lavishly furnished as the building's exterior promised, but many of its ornaments had been smashed and the floor was scuffed with dirty tracks. The xenos symbol was sprayed profligately across the walls in blue paint.

'Others have trespassed here before us,' Anselm gauged, studying the trail, 'but not many.'

'Surely it matters not,' Salvatore said. 'Either way they are nothing.'

'Yet it is strange,' the Redactor pressed. 'This edifice of privilege should have drawn the rabble's fury.'

'They were afraid,' Laurent ventured, running a gauntleted hand over a velvet-papered wall, as if testing it.

'Perhaps,' Anselm acknowledged. 'If even half the tales of the konteza are true, they had cause to be.'

I considered our options. Several doorways led off from the hall, promising a sprawl of corridors and chambers spanning several floors. It might take hours, perhaps even days to locate the mirror if its mistress had concealed it.

'We will pursue the intruders first,' I decided. 'They may know something of use... Laurent, take the spearhead!'

'By your command, Chaplain Castigant.'

I noticed Veland had stopped at the foot of the grand staircase at the chamber's far end, his head tilted to one side, as if listening for something.

'Veland, do you have a contact?' I demanded. There was no answer. 'Brother Veland, do–'

He sent a negative, using the tongue clicks of the Muted. All our brethren are required to learn the code, for the prohibition of speech must never be broken, even in extreme peril.

My gaze lingered on Veland as he turned away from the stairs to follow the others. I could not say what troubled me, but revisiting that moment with hindsight, I believe it was the first time he heard the witch's voice.

* * *

We followed the intruders deeper into the chateau. Even after their boots had been scrubbed clean by the fulsome carpets their tracks were easy to follow, for their passage was marked by a trail of destruction, though they always left the lights intact, as if fearful of the dark. Beyond this crude ruination there was a more subtle blight upon the palatial maze. Everything was dusted with ice and my sensors indicated a temperature well below freezing, though the windows were unbroken. Indeed, it was colder within the building than without.

'Is there no end to the depravity here?' Salvatore snarled, glaring at the paintings lining the walls of yet another wood-panelled corridor. The canvases had been slashed, but their salacious subjects remained apparent.

'She doesn't believe in limits,' Laurent murmured.

'I don't follow you, Thornblood,' Salvatore said.

'I…' The young warrior faltered, as though he hadn't meant to speak the thought aloud. 'Forgive me, brother-sergeant, it was a stray notion.'

'This is not the place for them, boy.'

The veteran was correct. More than any other battleground I had walked upon, the Concupiscent Hearth demanded absolute focus. Yes, my mirror-brother, I recognised it as an *arena* from the moment we entered, even if its trials were not of muscle and sinew. But if I still harboured any doubts that something unclean haunted the konteza's eyrie they were banished when we finally caught up with the intruders.

'What madness is this?' Salvatore hissed as we entered the grand dining hall where their trespass ended. Unlike the other rooms we'd passed through, it was sparsely lit and steeped in shadows, as if to convey an intimate mood, but we saw our quarry clearly enough.

There were eleven of them, sitting stiffly on high-backed chairs at a round, linen-draped table. A sumptuous repast was set before them, as though in celebration, but the roasted meats and elaborately presented vegetables were rimed with frost, along with the prospective diners. They were naked, their clothes left in neatly folded piles by the door, along with their weapons. The cold had turned their flesh blue and preserved the pain in their staring eyes, yet their faces wore wide grins. Their left arms were raised, locked in a perpetual toast, the wine in their goblets turned to crimson ice.

Murmuring a prayer of chastisement, I walked along the dead, looking for wounds, but saw nothing except the cold's kiss. I imagined them undressing and taking their places decorously, then waiting in silence while their blood chilled.

'How long?' I asked Anselm, who was the closest to an Apothecary among us.

'It is difficult to say, master,' he replied, approaching a bearded brute with concentric circles tattooed across his face. He snapped the corpse's arm off at the elbow and inspected the limb's core. 'Frozen through... But a few hours would suffice for that, after which there would be little change. This could have occurred days ago, perhaps even weeks.'

'A decadent way to die,' Salvatore declared, swiping the head from the cadaver beside him. It shattered at his feet in crimson shards.

'I doubt they chose it, brother-sergeant,' Anselm said. 'It would have been an agonising fate.' He placed the severed arm on the table gently. 'Something dulled their wits and lulled them into death. Perhaps the wine was poisoned.'

'Not the wine,' I judged. 'This was sorcery, brother.'

'She watched them die,' Laurent said, his voice tight with

loathing. 'It amused her.' He pointed at a large, gold-framed painting overlooking the head of the table. 'It's in her eyes.'

'Thornblood, I have warned you against such.' I silenced Salvatore's reprimand with a raised hand. I had chosen Laurent for his Emperor-given instincts and it would be folly to ignore them in this nest of serpents. Before the Great Excruciation I suspect he might have found a place among our Librarium's heretics, but properly wielded, his latent gift might become a righteous weapon.

'Corruption slinks beneath the skin of the world, brother-sergeant,' I said, striding to join Laurent beneath the painting. 'Sometimes we must hound it with our souls, not our wits.'

The lighting was contrived to fall upon the picture gracefully, emphasising its prominence without washing out its hues. A woman in a black dress returned my gaze from the canvas, her hands folded possessively over the heavy tome in her lap. A mane of red hair framed the pale oval of her face, cascading to her waist and woven with black flowers. Her green eyes were sharp with icy disdain, though her expression was wistful, brooding even. I had never seen her before, yet I knew her immediately – Konteza Urzelka Esseker, the mistress of the Concupiscent Hearth.

Unlike most bloodlines of the Adeptus Astartes, those of my lineage can recognise comeliness in a woman, hence I saw the beauty in that painted visage, but I also recognised it for a mask. The calculation in the matriarch's eyes pierced the deception, making a mockery of her studied pensiveness. I was quite certain that hesitation was alien to the spirit behind that exquisite face. This was a woman who did as she willed, no matter the cost.

What do you think *she* saw when she gazed into Athanazius' glass, brother? I have no doubt she indulged the impulse obsessively, even if she disliked the truths it revealed. Perhaps that is what drove her to heresy.

As we left the room I noticed Veland lingering under the portrait, his head once again tilted to the side. There was a perceptible *sway* to his posture.

'Brother Veland!' I shouted from the doorway, my patience with his laxity wearing thin. His helm's lenses locked on me impassively, the white cross of the Muted daubed across his faceplate stark in the gloom. For a moment I thought he would speak, but he merely clicked an affirmative. Somehow it sounded insolent.

FIFTH REFLECTION

I was compelled to divide the squad, for the mansion's size vastly exceeded my estimates. It was almost as though its inner dimensions defied its exterior, or enlarged slyly around us, spawning new configurations out of sight. There was hazard in separating, yet also in lingering in this defiled place, so I was eager to find our prize, redact it and be gone.

Yes, my brother-self, I am aware how absurd that now seems, but it was a lifetime ago and you fared no better, so do not presume to judge me. We are one in our folly!

It was Laurent who found the mirror. I had assigned him the uppermost floors and taken the cellars myself, convinced the konteza would hide her darkest secrets underground, but that assumption dignified her with caution or shame. Even then, I should have known her better. While I wandered through a sprawling storehouse of condiments to sate or embolden mortal appetites, Laurent uncovered a temple… of a kind.

'It is an abomination, Thorn Master,' he continued after reporting his find. *'How can such things evade the God-Emperor's gaze?'*

I frowned at the static drenching his voice. Something had been interfering with the squad's vox since we split up, becoming worse as the distance between us grew. Occasionally I heard an anomalous sound beneath the white noise – a voice perhaps? – but it slipped away whenever I tried to make sense of it.

'Master, we cannot let this stand!' Laurent pressed, his passion carrying through the distortion. *'If we–'*

'The mirror, Thornblood?' I snapped. 'You have located it?'

'I… Yes, Thorn Master, it is here.'

'On route,' I replied, dismissing his plea. 'Brothers, converge on Laurent!' Anselm and Salvatore voxed affirmatives. Veland's clicked response followed several seconds later, but I was too intent on our prize to admonish his tardiness.

The blizzard pressed close against the windows as I hurried towards the upper levels, its cloak now so dense the outside world might have been gone, erased by that swirling nothingness. And yet, despite its ferocity, I heard no wind beyond the casements.

As I passed an open door something moved at the corner of my eye. I swung round, my crozius and bolt pistol raised. Beyond the threshold was a hexagonal chamber devoid of windows, its walls sheathed in black tiles engraved with floral coils. Serpentine lumen strips lined the walls, bathing everything in a soft indigo radiance that also appeared to heat the room, for the perennial ice was absent here – indeed my sensors confirmed the temperature was *humid*.

My steps clattered loudly when I entered, for the floor was a smooth sheet of glass. Fibrous strands ran under its misted surface in a dense web, presumably extending under the whole room and possibly even beyond. Indeed, I imagined those tendrils insinuating themselves throughout the entire mansion, clustering beneath the plaster like rot.

The lights brightened with my advance, revealing a bulbous urn at the chamber's centre. A plant had erupted from the container's neck in a rampant tangle of vines and leathery leaves that pressed against the ceiling. Vast flowers bloomed among the snarl, their fleshy bulbs fringed with black petals. I have never been more thankful for the sanctity of my sealed armour, for I had no wish to inhale the musk of those leprous blossoms.

'Are you so sure of that?' The voice surged up on a wash of static, its rich contralto timbre cutting through the distortion. *'The boon of the Sable Kiss might spur you to profundity once more, Artisan Illuminant.'*

'Only to profanity, witch,' I answered, for I was in no doubt about the speaker's identity. That voice was the perfect match for the woman in the portrait. I realised I had been *waiting* for Urzelka Esseker to address me since seeing her likeness. But how did she know my old honorific, and the dishonour it celebrated? Had she plucked it from my mind? No – no, that was not possible... but perhaps from one of the others, though only Anselm and Salvatore would remember such things.

'Paradise lost is all the sweeter rediscovered,' the witch wheedled, *'and damnation not nearly as sour as you might imagine.'*

The plant was rustling gently, all its flowers turned towards me. Its movements revealed several skulls nestled among its vines like pale bulbs. How many souls had surrendered willingly to its lure over the years? And how many who resisted had simply been hurled into its embrace?

'Why so fearful of your own gifts, Bjargo Rathana?' my tormentor asked tenderly. It sickened me to hear her speak my name, as if to a lover. Which of my brothers had betrayed it to her?

'You are mistaken, heretic!' I jabbed my crozius at the plant, as if the witch resided there. 'By His holy name, I abjure you!'

'You abjure nobody save yourself, broken thing,' she mocked. *'And whatever I will, will be!'* With a swell of static she was gone.

'The Emperor knows you!' I bellowed. 'And He condemns!'

The plant shivered, as if in empathy. To my disgust I realised its container wasn't an urn at all, but the fleshy seedpod it had sprung from. Resisting the impulse to waste ammunition upon it – for I would not taint my crozius with its sap – I stalked from the room. Doubtless that malign growth was but one of many abominations cultivated in the witch's domain.

I found Laurent on the top floor, standing just beyond the stairwell, with Anselm and Salvatore to either side, all three shrouded in the same silence. I slowed my stride as I joined them, aghast at the enormity of the blasphemy before me.

The whole level had been opened up into a single cavernous space under the mansion's central dome, from which a vast chandelier hung. Thousands of cut-glass lumoglobes glittered in that baroque web of light, leaving no room for shadows, though they would have been welcome, for the entire chamber was devoted to depravity.

I will not dwell upon the myriad engines of torture assembled in that unholy gallery, save to say their construction was masterful. Every one of them sported exhaustive controls to tweak and tune the laments they played upon the flesh, offering countless variations on every conceivable theme. I doubted any of the konteza's victims had shared quite the same agony or perished before she was entirely satisfied.

Oh, there was genius behind those machineries of misery – *her* genius – yet every one was an obscenity.

As you well know, the Angels Penitent are no strangers to the virtues of torture. Applied with sobriety, the excruciation of the body is a righteous instrument of correction, coercion or execution. Indeed it is the sixth sacrament of the Trial of Thorns that our neophytes must endure to earn the black carapace. But the rites practised here were of a different order and their intent vile, for it was abundantly clear that the konteza's engines powered not just suffering, but also pleasure of equal magnitude.

Do not ask me to describe how she accomplished this perversion for I will not stoop to such vulgarity. Besides, you can see the devices on your side of the glass, so you know their methodology. Never have I been so repelled by mortal vice!

Evidently the chamber had hosted one last great orgy of ecstatic torment, for there were corpses everywhere, frozen like the intruders below, but boasting the marks of far more outlandish deaths. They were displayed alongside the machines that killed them, posed like the mangled dolls of a diabolical child.

'Their lips wear smiles their eyes deny,' Anselm said bleakly, breaking the silence.

'The Emperor condemns!' Salvatore declared. We chorused the sacred words, drawing purity from them.

'This was more than depravity,' I judged, glaring at the curved runes inscribed upon the machines. 'It was a ritual.'

Despite my helmet's filters I could *smell* those malefic

sigils – the bittersweet aroma of poisoned dreams, pregnant with the promise of lies that might be true... if only I would drink deep of their charms.

'She sacrificed her followers,' Anselm gauged, examining the nearest cadaver's finery.

'Yes, Redactor,' I agreed, looking away from the runes. 'And they offered themselves willingly.'

'Not all of them,' Laurent said quietly. He had removed his helmet, as if in mourning. Doubtless he was remembering the words of the dying crone at the gates. The konteza took whatever she needed – her own and others. 'There are innocents among them,' he added.

'Nobody is innocent, Thornblood,' I rebuked him. 'And it matters not who they were. They died for her regardless. That was enough.'

'Enough for what, master?' Salvatore asked.

'To escape her people's wrath! Sooner or later they would have come for her in numbers her thralls could not withstand.'

'You believe she survived, master?' Salvatore raised his flamer instinctively.

'Oh, I know it, brother-sergeant! She is still here, though not as she was. Her escape was not *flight*, brother.'

'We must destroy her,' Laurent urged.

'Yes, Thornblood,' I assured him, but my attention was elsewhere, for I had seen our true objective.

The Mirror of Athanazius stood upon a circular platform at the far side of the chamber, gazing upon the atrocities like a vast glass eye. Instinctively I understood it had been the ceremony's focal point, one heresy used to amplify another. Though I was here to destroy the artefact I was outraged that our legacy had been defiled in such a way. The mirror's sins belonged to the Chapter!

We crossed the gallery in silence, wary of the narrow spaces between the machines, though I didn't believe any conventional foes remained. The darkness haunting this place was no longer a creature of flesh and blood.

As I climbed the platform's steps I saw *you* rising through the glass ahead to meet me, the hollows of your iron skull fixed upon my own, the razor wire halo wreathing your cranium flecked with rust. A ring of runes encircled your window, carved into the wooden boards of the dais and filled with blood. Their power was enhanced by a plethora of occult paraphernalia – black candles, an antlered skull inlaid with gold, a desiccated six-fingered hand… They were the common trinkets of heretics, made uncommon here by one who knew her craft all too well.

By unspoken consent we kicked the circle apart and crushed the foul baubles underfoot. Laurent's expression was thunderous, but it was a righteous fury, free of the Black Rage's mania. I felt pride in him then shame in myself, for pride begets the fall.

'Master, we cannot leave the witch's fate to chance,' he said, turning to face me. 'If we burn this place she may escape.'

'The konteza is not our objective,' I demurred, but not harshly.

'Then what is our purpose?' Laurent pressed. 'If we suffer such heretics to live then why fight at all?' The sensitivity of the Resplendent endured in him, yet he was unmistakably a Penitent. With time he might have become one of our staunchest voices. 'Does the Testament not demand–'

'Beware!' I yelled as a grotesque figure appeared in the mirror behind him. It wore the black-and-umber armour of a Penitent, but its plates were warped into forms that looked organic, their surface whorled and veined with red. Mauve smoke gushed from spiny nodules atop its backpack, framing a backswept helmet sporting a quilled crest. The helm's speaker-grille had elongated into a maw that yawned to the warrior's breastplate and squeezed its eye-lenses into slits. Yet despite all these corruptions it was the symbol painted on its faceplate that appalled me – *a white cross*.

'Brother Veland?' Laurent asked, looking over my shoulder as the horror stepped onto the dais behind me. There was no trace of revulsion in his eyes as he greeted it, for while I saw its honest reflection, Laurent had his back to the mirror and merely saw its physical form.

'Will you not agree–' Laurent's head disintegrated into a red mist as the thing that had been Veland opened fire, its bolter's concussive bursts wringing strange harmonies from the air.

I dived aside and the bullet intended for me struck the mirror and disappeared in a swirl of ripples, as if passing through a pool of water. In the same instant Anselm threw himself from the platform, returning fire with his own bolter as he leapt away from Veland's assault. Salvatore simply stood his ground and brought his flamer to bear. As it belched fire an incoming round pierced the nozzle and detonated inside the weapon. I have never seen such an improbable shot, nor could I tell whether it was the result of dazzling marksmanship or outrageous misfortune, but the result was the same. The weapon exploded, drenching Salvatore in burning promethium and incinerating his arms from the elbows down.

With a curse I spun round, my bolt pistol bucking furiously as I fired. I wasn't facing the abomination I'd seen in the mirror, but a fellow Penitent. Veland was hunched in a feral stance as he targeted me, but his armour was unmarked by corruption. Nevertheless, the noise screeching from his helm's speaker-grille was evidence enough of taint. That dissonant shriek wracked the soul as keenly as the ears, like a dirge channelled from the warp.

Stumbling, I muted my auditory receptors with a coded word and the gunfire fell to a distant booming, but the sonic barrage was unabated. It swirled about my helmet like a swarm of infernal insects, gnawing at my senses and tearing my thoughts apart before they could crystallise. I felt the buffeting of Veland's bullets slamming against my armour, ripping away chunks of ceramite while my befuddled aim went wide. Dimly I realised my eyes were bleeding.

I barely heard Salvatore's roar as his flame-ridden form barrelled into Veland. The sergeant's back erupted as a slug tore into his midriff at close range, the spray of blood hissing into red steam from the heat. It was a dire wound, but Salvatore's momentum carried them both over the platform's edge.

Freed from the sonic assault, I charged forward and saw them hit the ground in a flame-tangled sprawl that left Salvatore on top. With his arms scorched away and his spine severed, the Thornguard tried to hold Veland down with his bulk alone, but it was a hopeless struggle. With an ululating cry, the madman threw him off and reached for his fallen bolter.

'The Emperor condemns!' I cried, firing as I leapt from above. My explosive shells thudded into Veland's chest a heartbeat before my boots followed, crashing onto the weakened armour like twin hammers. His breastplate caved in, rupturing the solid bone cage beneath. The impact threw his helmet free, revealing the travesty of my foe's once handsome face. His mouth was distended into a rictus yawn, its lips drawn back from spiny shark-like teeth. The flesh framing that maw had stretched and torn to his ears, only held together by bloody strips. Black eyes glared at me from sunken, scale-rimmed sockets that wept purple smoke.

'She... knows... you!' The words bubbled up from the back of the creature's throat, their intonation slurred and broken, for that razor-toothed maw wasn't built for speech. *'Knows... you... for... a...'*

I rammed my crozius between its jaws and silenced its blasphemy.

Salvatore still lived, though only a sliver of vitality remained to him. Of Anselm there was no sign, nor any answer on the vox. It was perplexing, but I would have to address that later.

Smoke wafted from the sergeant's scorched armour as I removed his helmet to offer the Everlasting Sacrament. Flat on his back, he waited silently as I spoke the elegy.

'Burn me, master,' he rasped when I was done, turning his head to regard the nearest display of corpses. 'Don't let the witch... play... her–' His appeal broke into a blood-flecked coughing fit.

'It will be done, brother-sergeant,' I promised. 'She will not have you.'

'The boy... was right. Have to... purge her.'

'Yes, my brother.'

His eyes clouded and the silence lingered until I thought he was gone, but then his gaze locked on me once more. 'I have sinned, master.' It was the faintest of whispers. 'I used to... paint. Never any good... but...'

'All the Resplendent have sinned,' I assured him. 'Our vanity damned us. There can be no forgiveness, only penance. Now and ever after, the Emperor condemns!'

I expected him to repeat the blessed phrase, for there is no finer way for an Angel Penitent to pass into oblivion, and

Salvatore Jacinto was among the most fervent of us. Instead, in that final moment, he smiled sadly and whispered the words that still haunt me.

'I never stopped.'

SIXTH REFLECTION

We are almost done now, mirror-brother. This has been a tortuous redaction, far exceeding any other I have presided over, but Athanazius' mirror is an artefact of a different order, hence the ritual cannot be expedited. I have castigated the unholy glass with the entirety of the nine hundred and ninety-nine litanies of Reverent Banishment, repeating every word until the intonation was perfect. Black incense wafts from my armour's censers, filling the air with the burnt stench of regret, while the *Exhalation Excruciatis* drones from the skull-bound speakers upon my backpack, its atonal groan lending weight to my words.

Naturally, I divined the *physical* expression of the mirror's redaction long ago. As witness Veland's stray bullet, the glass cannot be broken directly, so I shall strike it from behind, where it is blind. My blessed crozius will make short work of the frame's back-plate, and through it the glass itself. No, it is the *spiritual* aspect of the task that has challenged me, for

I have been assailed by misgivings. Before I attempt the final step I must lay them to rest. And so I stand before you now, my first brother. Together we shall purge ourselves of doubt!

The sorceress is the least part of my irresolution. She has returned often to haunt me – taunting, teasing, cajoling or threatening as the mood takes her, but I am dead to her words. I cannot deny she knows what I once was, for she never tires of parading my sins before me, but she understands *nothing*. Her mind is sharp, yet surprisingly shallow, eroded to pettiness by unbridled ambition. In time what little remains of her shall devour itself, as a rapacious serpent consumes its own tail. Oh, make no mistake, she is poisonous beyond measure, but she has no form or substance to administer her venom unless we open ourselves to her, as thrice-cursed Veland did.

My fallen brother's submission to the witch troubles me more than the tempter herself. Doubtless she prised open a fault line in his soul, yet the swiftness and extremity of his corruption makes a mockery of the Trial of Thorns. Is our testing flawed or are the judges themselves blind? To ask such things is forbidden, yet I must, for Veland's outrage pales beside the quiet treachery of Salvatore Jacinto.

The Crown of Thorns is watchful for recidivists who cling to the blasphemies of art in secret. Thirty-one pariahs have been uncovered since the Great Excruciation, but not one among the Thornguard. Until now. If a devout warrior like Salvatore has betrayed the faith how can we be certain of anyone? How many *more* are there? Writing, composing, carving, painting, perhaps even sculpting in the shadows!

And therein lies my dilemma, brother, for Athanazius' mirror could uncover the traitors among us. It revealed Veland's corruption with damning clarity, as it did Laurent's purity. I did not see Salvatore's reflection while he lived, and though I dragged his corpse before the glass nothing of his soul remained to tell its tale.

But I saw Anselm Giordano's truth.

It was more than a day before the last of my battle-brothers returned to me. At his shouted greeting I turned from the mirror and watched Anselm approach. His helmet was gone and he walked with a limp that hadn't been there before. As he drew closer I saw his armour was battered and scarred with deep scratches.

He stopped below the dais where I waited and his eyes fell on our dead brothers. 'Then we are the last,' he said sadly.

'Explain yourself, Brother-Redactor,' I demanded. 'You have been gone almost twenty-eight hours.'

'My chronolog records it as fifty-five, Master Castigant,' Anselm replied, meeting my gaze. 'Time is as treacherous as everything else here.' He shook his head. 'I cannot explain any of it. When Veland fired on us I jumped and fell... elsewhere.'

'Elsewhere?'

'Another level, hidden below the cellars, though I cannot say how I came to be there.' His expression darkened. 'It was not empty. The witch had other servants – mutants, but not like any I have seen before. Her blasphemies are without end, master.'

'Has she spoken to you, Brother Anselm?'

'No.' He appeared surprised by the question. 'And the degenerates I slew had no wit for words. I fought my way to the surface, but it had changed... become a labyrinth. In time I stumbled upon the entrance hall, but the way out was gone. And beyond the windows... *nothing*.' He opened his hands, palms upwards as if beseeching answers. 'I believe the witch was toying with me, master. This building is her plaything – perhaps even a body of sorts.'

'Perhaps,' I agreed. His theory was sound, but irrelevant to my dilemma. 'Come Brother-Redactor, I require your assistance.'

'By your command, master.'

I turned to face the mirror, watching for his reflection as he ascended the steps to the dais. Sentiment vied with duty in my hearts as I waited, but the glass was merciless.

'What do you require of me, master?' Anselm asked, stopping a few paces behind me.

'Only the truth,' I said, addressing his reflection.

'Always.' The finely chiselled face in the mirror was free of the seams and blemishes I had grown accustomed to, and the hair framing it was a lustrous black. But the changes ran far deeper, extending to Anselm Giordano's very soul. There was a *vitality* about him I hadn't seen among our brotherhood since the Great Excoriation. This was not the face of a Penitent, but a Resplendent.

'Did you relapse, Anselm?' I asked softly. 'Or did you never forfeit the old heresies?'

'I do not understand, Master Castigant.'

'Do you still play the laserwire harp? No... It must be something smaller... easier to conceal.'

'Forgive me, but you are mistaken, master. I have been true to the Testament of Thorns.' He frowned. 'It is *her*. She seeks to deceive and divide us.'

'It is not the witch's deceits that concern me now, false brother.'

'Don't listen to her, my friend!' Anselm stepped forward, his hands raised. 'We must destroy the mirror before–'

'Traitor!' I thundered, swinging round. My crozius crackled with energy as I whirled it in a wide arc that scoured away the top of his skull. Anselm froze, staring at me as blood stained his white hair. His lips moved, but no words came. With a final exhalation, he crashed to his knees, his dead eyes locked on me. His face was once again as I remembered it.

'The Emperor condemns,' I whispered. As I turned my back on the traitor I heard the witch's laughter.

And so we are the last, mirror-brother. We stand together in this gallery of iniquities, facing each other through a blasphemy. Much time has passed since we executed our respective Anselms. Like you, I have spent them in prayer, searching for an answer. Sometimes I have wondered why no others have followed us from the *Severance of Glory*, for our mission was expected to be brief, but it is better this way. They would be a distraction at best and a peril at worst. Nobody can be trusted. We must make this choice alone.

The witch has fallen silent, but I sense her watching me. Her eyes are everywhere and nowhere at once. Has she finally accepted that I am beyond corruption? Or is she scheming some fresh atrocity to tempt me? She will not succeed, for the redaction is almost complete. Only the final blow remains to be made, yet still I waver, for the fell truth cannot be denied. Our Chapter is rife with apostates whose cunning has surpassed our most vigilant scrutiny. I fear the rot may even extend to the Crown of Thorns itself. With the mirror's wisdom I could find them all. I *cannot* destroy it... Yet how can I not?

I do not even comprehend its logic. Veland's corruption extended to the flesh of his face, while Anselm's existed only in reflection. Is the artefact fickle in its judgement? False even? Or is my understanding at fault? My *purity?*

Yes, brother, I understand what I must do to learn the answers. It is a grave sin, yet also the lesser of many evils. I am beset by secrets and lies, but the most malign are the misgivings in my own soul. If Anselm and Salvatore were impure how can I be certain of *anyone?*

I must know myself.

I must see you.

I feel the witch's excitement as I grasp my iron mask in both hands. Its rivets are old and buried deep in my skull so there is pain when I tug it free, but I welcome that. Nothing matters except the truth. And yet I hesitate, holding the mask before me like a shield. What if…

What if you are still yourself, Resplendent? Urzelka Esseker completes my thought. *What if you still dream of beauty, false Penitent?*

'I do not.'

Then look upon yourself and learn, Bjargo Rathana!

And finally, I do.

SPIRITUS IN MACHINA

Thomas Parrott

American author Thomas Parrott begins his writing journey with Black Library upon a crippled ship deep within a galaxy in flames.

When the Skitarius Alpha Primus 7-Cyclae awakes from stasis, his memory data is damaged and his knowledge fragmented. All he has to guide him is a servo-skull directed by the Magos Explorator, who seems determined to resurrect their dying ship. But as they descend into the destruction, Cyclae must confront the realisation that nothing is as he remembers.

There is an old saying that war is diplomacy by other means. The Adeptus Mechanicus might say instead that war is data collection by other means. It is merely another aspect of the great Quest for Knowledge, and a skitarius is in many ways a sensor before they are a soldier. The flow of information is constant and omnidirectional. Data on foes, on weapons, on environments and efficacy. To be skitarii is to be the eyes and ears and hands of something more, a node in a great network.

Thus, when 7-Cyclae awoke to a void, it spoke to a grim fate indeed.

There should have been a flood of stimuli. Light, sound and, most importantly, the flow of data pouring in from dozens of noospheric connections. Briefings for the upcoming deployment, status reports on his troops and more. Instead there was only numb, silent darkness. He had fought a thousand nightmare foes, but this state was unprecedented.

His first concern was whether he was damaged. Cyclae immediately began a full diagnostic sweep. His chassis shivered and twitched as systems activated, augmetic limbs rotating and curling. Interfacing directly with his mind, checklists and analysis projected into his vision. Life support flashed a green rune of nominal status. It was the only spark of optimal news. Yellows and reds flared from extremities, secondary systems and cortical implants alike.

The latter was the most troubling. It raised the spectre of damage to the diagnosticator itself. He started spot checks to verify damage reports. His internal chronometer showed only nonsense data. Memory searches produced corrupted files and scrambled linkages.

'Alpha, beta, gamma. One, two, three.' His voice was slurred. He had not been in this state when he entered suspended animation. Something had gone wrong.

A chill voice cut through the darkness. *'Your vital signs have become erratic. Assert control of yourself, skitarius. The spirit of your stasis pod rebels. You will be freed shortly.'* The phylactic communication carried ident-tags denoting the highest level of authority. It rang as familiar, but his scattered memory banks provided no answers.

His limbs reported energy fluctuations. A moment to centre himself, and 7-Cyclae did as commanded. He walked his mind through the Litany of Clear Thought, visualising each sigil in perfect sequence.

'Omnissiah, envelop me.

'Guide my cogitations to your truth.

'Shape my thoughts and calm my flesh.

'Guard me against emotion,

'That it will not overcome clarity.

'Sustain my systems

'with visions of efficiency
'and the Quest for Knowledge.'

The litany was no mere words; engrams burned directly into his brain activated. They flooded his remaining flesh with alchemical concoctions that eroded the tyranny of base emotion and left only purpose.

The fluctuations grew and a grey luminescence clawed at his eyes. Then with a crackling hiss the void dropped away and he tumbled to a hard floor. The room was blurry and temperature sensors reported it was well below freezing. A baseline human would have died from short-term exposure. He redirected power to ensure his organic components kept warm, as he pushed himself up on the tireless strength of his augmetic arms. The same voice as before demanded, *'Designation?'*

His vision began to clear, a swath of grey blurs resolving into lights amid a dark expanse. 'Alpha Primus Seven-Cyclae of the First Maniple, Surface Retrieval Cohort, Explorator Fleet Nine-V-Sigma.' His voice was clearing as systems compensated for damage.

'The Alpha Primus. How fortunate.'

Cyclae was not listening. His optics had cleared sufficiently to tell him the deck was a catastrophe. This was where his maniple had been stored between missions. Now dead stasis pods were strewn haphazardly about, a few flickering screens showing only null life signs. He felt an echo of regret: his warriors had died helpless, not in battle as they deserved. Then it was filed away. Icy patches marred ceilings and floors that had rusted and collapsed in places. The hatch into the chamber was open, showing a pile of bodies in the corridor beyond. Rotted crimson robes, life ripped from them by the telltale marks of eradication rays and phosphor burns.

He turned to the source of the voice, only to find a servo-skull drifting out from the cables behind his stasis pod. A remote operator, then. 'What happened to us?' The litany kept his words calm.

'Main power is down. The ship has been on emergency power for an extended period, and reserves have run low. The anti-entropic field in your pods collapsed as demand exceeded supply. You were the priority, but even then your non-vital systems had to be sacrificed.'

He looked down at his articulated gauntlets. The once shining metal was age-pitted and dull. 'I cannot hear the ship. No vox traffic, no noospheric connection.' The full-spectrum silence was an aberration.

'What do you remember last?'

Cyclae shook his head. The memory data remained garbled and in severe need of re-indexing. All he could access was scattered impressions. 'A mission. A dead world. Stones. Metal.'

Momentary silence. *'War happened. Civil war. Ingrates thought to wrest this vessel from her rightful master. They disconnected the cogitator core. If I cannot set things right before emergency power dies completely, much will be lost.'* There was another pause. *'I am Magos Explorator Aionios, master of the fleet, and I have pulled you from oblivion for a purpose. Gather your equipment and steel yourself, skitarius. I will have need of you if I am to save this Ark.'*

The skull was the voice of the magos, therefore the voice of the Machine-God. Disobedience was unthinkable.

The armoury was adjacent. It had been a shrine to the destructive power of the Omnissiah's gifts, its contents organised for maximum efficiency in dispersal. Now they were scattered like refuse. His optical overlays highlighted weapons, evaluated them, dismissed them. Finally he found a phosphor pistol and a taser goad in acceptable condition. A black cloak embossed with the white heraldry of Stygies VIII was the last touch, laid over crimson armour plates.

Properly arrayed, Cyclae strode from the ravaged chamber into the corridor beyond, stepping carefully among the broken bodies. One had dragged themselves to the wall, scrawling a single message in old blood: *Cave spiritus in machina*. Cyclae scanned the text and fed it into translator processes. '"Beware the spirit in the machine." Curious.'

'*Mere moribund delusions.*' The servo-skull drifted ahead to take the lead. '*There were those who feared where the loyalties of the skitarii might lie in the conflict, and who sealed you away. Others sought to free you. They died in failure. Even after the fighting ended, it took me quite a while to unseal the bay.*' It was a toneless recitation of fact.

'There should be no question as to our loyalties. They are to the Omnissiah, the Forge and the Fleet, in that order.' There was no response. As they continued on, it became clear the rest of the ship was in worse condition than the stasis bay. They were in the outer decks of the Ark, a web of corridors and bays that ran the six-mile length of the vessel. He remembered flashes of how it used to be: swarms of menials and servitors with the occasional robe-clad priest going about their business, producing a constant hum of activity. All of that was gone.

Some massive water reservoir must have ruptured and flooded this whole section. The radiation shielding for the ammunition stores, perhaps. Icicles hung from rusted corridor ceilings, and patches of frost crunched under his heavy tread. Lighting had failed in most corridors. The universal chill made thermal imaging useless, and with central cogitation deactivated there was no navigation data stream. He activated the stablight on his helmet, only for an amber rune to immediately spark on his optical overlays. The light flickered constantly. He tapped it several times before the rune went green and the beam stabilised.

The servo-skull floated ahead with surety, though the path seemed winding. Shining his light down the avoided tunnels soon revealed why: all of them were impassable in some way. Some had been the sites of vicious battles; weapons fire scarred their length, and his rad-censer chimed even as they passed by. Others had simply caved in, succumbing to corrosion and the weight of ice.

The path ended a moment later, however. The corridor terminated in a sealed hatch marked by a glowing red sigil indicating partial atmosphere loss. The skull stopped and rotated to face him. *'It is necessary to pass this way. The hull was penetrated by fire from a rebel vessel, but the damage is contained. The true threat is areas of damaged grav-plating. Display caution, skitarius. The crushing force of the malfunctioning fields would exceed your tolerances.'*

Cyclae inclined his head. 'As you command, magos.' By habit, he tried to stream an override command, but the relays were dead. Direct interface was required. He removed the access panel with great care, murmuring a prayer of apology to the machine-spirit.

'Forgive me, O Spirit, for this trespass. I intervene in your blessed functions only to fulfil my own. Together may we serve the Omnissiah in His great design.' The fingers on his left hand folded back and his palm flowered open, revealing mechanical tendrils which slithered into ports. The door ground open complainingly, lost atmosphere howling past him and setting his cloak to whipping.

The open door revealed a scene of absolute devastation. A beam of unthinkable firepower had got past the ship's void shields and carved a deep rent. The cold stars were visible through the gap overhead. This bay had been a storage place for mighty war machines. Questor Mechanicus, he thought. It was hard to be certain with their frames demolished.

'*Freeblade Knights,*' confirmed the streamed words of the magos amidst the silence of the void. Glimmers of memory slipped through Cyclae's circuits. He had marched to war in the shadow of the great Knights. They had seemed invincible. '*Just a glimpse of what the machinations of the rebels have already destroyed. Just a fragment of what will be lost should I fail.*'

Cyclae's overlays highlighted damaged plating as he moved inside. The ravaged decking gave off an odd vibration that he felt more than heard. He crouched to collect a piece of debris from the ground: a tooth from a shattered Reaper chainsword. A nearby area of malfunctioning gravity served for a test: he tossed the fragment in. It hit with aberrant force, kicking up a cloud of dust. In his optical overlays that arc was mapped out and compared to what it would have been under standard gravity. The force within was more than twenty times as strong. With the aid of his augmetic senses he picked a path and carefully worked his way forward.

Soon the great rift opened up before him, allowing a glimpse into ravaged decks and shattered conduits below. It was just over fifty feet across at its narrowest point, according to his analysis. Yet duty beckoned. He set off at a sprint. Power flooded his alloy legs and they churned at inhuman speeds. In a cogitator's cycle he was at the edge and leapt. The gap yawned beneath him, a fall so deep that his systems would suffer irreparable damage.

He hit the other side with terrific force, inches from a

descent into the dark. Yet his momentum was carrying him forward, right towards a patch of damaged grav-plating. Thinking fast, he fired the stabiliser spikes built into his legs. The left punched down into the decking, but a red rune flashed in his vision as the other failed to engage. He spun against his insufficient anchor before the momentum ripped him loose and he tumbled on.

He bled what speed he could with scraping hands and feet. It wasn't enough. He stopped just over where the damage began and his arm slammed down with terrific weight behind it. Warnings flashed in his vision as he gritted his teeth and pulled with his other arm. Slowly the trapped limb was dragged loose from the crushing gravity. His armour was cracked, and the fingers twitched spasmodically.

The servo-skull followed, effortlessly hovering across the gap. *'You could have been destroyed with that manoeuvre.'*

'It is the privilege of cogs to be ground down that the machine may run, magos,' he streamed back, examining the damage. His heart pounded. High levels of adrenaline, his implants reported.

The skull floated up to him, the tools within its undercarriage engaged, fixing what it could. The spasms ceased. *'Caution, skitarius. I have no spare parts available. You are not permitted to destroy yourself until our mission is through.'*

Cyclae made the symbol of the cog with his interlaced knuckles. 'In the name of the Omnissiah, magos. My apologies.' He stood and they worked their way to the other side of the bay. Another override got them through the sealed door there. As the hatch ground shut behind them, he surveyed their new surroundings. This area seemed familiar. He had been here before. He started to stride off, confident of their route, but the skull stopped him with a click. *'Not that way.'*

He hesitated. 'This leads to the mag-rail terminus.'

'The rail took a direct hit and is inoperable. There is a maintenance crawlway that will take us to the deck we need.'

'Lead the way, magos.' Down several winding side corridors, they found the hatch. It creaked open to reveal a ladder that descended into darkness. The light from his helmet illuminated scratches and scrapes to either side, as if something had been hurled down the shaft and desperately tried to stop its headlong tumble. He paused. Questioning the Priesthood was not permitted, but he was allowed a certain tactical discretion. 'You are certain this is the optimal path?'

'It is not a safe passage – there are none. It is your best chance at being useful, however.'

Cyclae swung onto the ladder and began the climb down. His temperature sensors reported rising heat the deeper he went. The ladder seemed to go on forever, and he wasn't sure how long he'd been climbing. His inbuilt chronometer just fed him the same senseless data. His damaged arm was still malfunctioning, freezing up occasionally. 'How far down is the access point we need?'

'Having trouble with the climb?' Cyclae could have sworn that flat voice held a note of some emotion. Condescension, maybe. *'Perhaps it will serve as a reminder to proceed cautiously.'*

The question remained. 'How far?'

'Not far. Another hundred and eighteen feet.'

He counted the rungs from there. Five. Ten. Thirty rungs. Sixty. One hundred. One hundred and– *'Here.'* He turned his head to look to where the skull hovered. This aperture was partly open, allowing a glimpse of a shadowed hall beyond. He reached out and gripped the hatch with his unscathed arm, bracing his feet and heaving. For a moment it wouldn't budge, before giving way with a grinding screech.

The sound echoed up the shaft in both directions and down the hallway as well. There were lights in this section, dull red emergency strips that painted everything in a bloody glow. *'So much for subtlety. Still, you should deactivate your light for now and prepare your weapons.'* The magos' tone was exceedingly dry.

Cyclae did as instructed and proceeded down the hallway. 'There are threats?'

It stank down here. It always had on the engineering decks, his scattered memories told him that much: mildew and hot metal. This was worse. The rancid stench of spoiled meat and sickness. Some found it strange that the skitarii were left with something so human as an olfactory system, but it made sense once you understood that scent was data. Data was everything.

The hallway opened out into a great chamber, lined with immense machines of unknown purpose. *'Yes.'* The servo-skull's broadcast dropped to a whisper. Something was stirring in the shadows of the monoliths. Cyclae slipped back into the cover of another of the great machines to observe. It uncoiled, a serpentine shape slithering out into view, a centipede of rusted metal and pallid, suppurating flesh. A torso mounting the end reared up to twice Cyclae's height, vaguely humanoid. Questing optical tendrils protruded from ravaged sockets, lenses gleaming in scarlet light. *'The crew.'*

The Alpha Primus' sensors picked out body parts from at least a dozen people incorporated into the structure. Fragmentary memories stirred at the sight, files from long ago, of fighting on a Mechanicus world fallen into darkness. Monstrosity birthed of madness. He must have triumphed then to be here now. His cortical implants collated data and projected a seventy-one per cent chance of victory in the coming battle, with the right terrain. An acceptable projection, if far from ideal; he would prefer a plasma caliver for this fight. Not to mention a full repair and a squad of the faithful similarly armed, as long as he was imploring the Omnissiah for what could not be.

He took slow steps back, thinking to retreat to the hallway, where the bulk of the creature would impair it. Then his foot came down with a distinct crunch. Old bones lay unseen in the dark. The sound brought a tendril round to stare at him with a malefic blankness. Cyclae didn't hesitate. He sprinted for the tunnel, but the creature was moving now too. It was fast, faster than he had thought possible, the charge heralded only by the chittering of many clawed feet. It was a moment's calculation to realise it would catch him before he got there. The projections dropped sharply to fifty-two per cent. Whipping blade-tipped mechadendrites unfurled from the creature's metal carapace. There wasn't much time, just enough to raise his pistol and fire a single shot.

The phosphor struck home, burning into the thing's side in a blaze of brilliant white that banished the gloom of the chamber. The searing mass eating at the construct drew a hissing screech, like a broken steam valve. Yet it came blundering on through the pain. Cyclae braced to try to absorb the shock, but it didn't matter. It hit him like a runaway mag-train. He hurtled through the air and smashed into one of the great machines. His pistol tumbled away, knocked loose from his grip. He blurted a hasty binaric apology to the apparatus he'd impacted, as he gathered himself back to his feet and engaged his taser goad to sizzling life. 'Magos!' he barked, 'Now would be a good time for Conqueror imperatives!'

'I do not have access to any means of uploading the Doctrina.'

The skull was half-hidden behind one of the nearby machines, observing.

'Less than optimal.' His battle chances plummeted to twenty-nine per cent. The monster clawed at the still burning wound, but that merely spread white fire to its tendrils. He took the opportunity to try to circle towards the tunnel again, but the movement drew it back to him instantly. It was wary now, having felt the bite of its prey. The first few strikes seemed testing. One, two, three deflected with sweeps of his goad, each impact casting crackling sparks. He was already trapped on the defence. The attacks came faster now. Cyclae's economy of motion was preternatural as he knocked aside four more lashing blades. Out of the corner of his optic he spotted another striking towards his head with lightning speed. He darted to the side and the bladed tip thudded harmlessly against the thick carapace on his shoulder instead. Then warnings blazed in his vision as a tendril he'd failed to notice slashed upwards from the other side and dug into a gap in his armour.

He whirled the other way, off balance, to wrench free of it with a spray of dark fluid. Before he could recover, a mechadendrite lashed out and coiled around his legs in an instant. He was whipped off his feet in a dizzying blur as another slithered around his midsection and bound his goad to his side. He was left hanging before its optics, and could not escape the unmistakable impression that there was something behind those cold lenses. Too much to just be battle-servitor encodings. It studied him with a cruel curiosity now that it thought him helpless, beginning to constrict its hold tighter and tighter.

Yet he was not abandoned. Seeing that Cyclae was in danger of termination, the servo-skull darted in, slashing at the creature with a plasma torch. The strikes scored the thing's flesh and armour, and for a moment its attention was off the Alpha Primus. A mistake. Skitarii were weapons before they ever visited the armoury. Cyclae reached out with his free hand and grabbed hold of the optical tendril right below the lens. It instantly refocused and tried to writhe free, but his grip was implacable. He wrenched outward with all his bionic strength. It came loose with a wet squelch, and the thing gave another screech as it hurled him away in enraged desperation.

He hit the ground hard but his hand malfunctioned again and froze in a death grip on the goad, keeping it from being knocked away. Small blessings. For a moment he was disoriented, unable to rise. Part of his mind coldly assessed the grinding in his chest – a broken rib. The projections still did not favour him, hovering at thirty-five per cent. That's when he felt it: that telltale shivering hum. A broken grav-plate, just like he'd encountered in the upper decks. He could see the ragged decking off ahead to the right.

The sound was drowned out in that rushing clatter of claws. In desperation he scrambled around to the other side of the broken plate so that it was between him and the monstrosity, before whirling to face his foe from a crouch. It came on in a heedless rush. Then it was over the damaged plating, and with a series of metallic crunches its many legs collapsed under the vast weight. It fell with a hard crash as he rolled out of the way, momentum carrying its front through to the other side of the malfunctioning plating. Cyclae didn't rely on that to be the end of it. He lunged, goad raised high, and brought it down with all of his might.

It stabbed in and unleashed the energy bound within. Serpentine tendrils of lightning crawled through the monstrosity, sizzling and burning. It writhed uncontrollably and hissed one last time before falling still. He fell to his knees next to it as damage and strain caught up. A hand tested the gash in his side and came away wet with blood and sacred unguents. After a moment the servo-skull hovered over. *'Skitarius? Do you still function?'*

'I am damaged, but I can continue the mission,' he managed. He levered himself to his feet and looked his fallen foe over with distaste. 'What is this? I have never seen a servitor of this pattern.'

The skull floated over to examine the thing. *'There is no pattern. Whoever created it used an ad hoc amalgamation of unsanctioned modifications.'*

He turned to the skull sharply. 'That is heresy.'

'The desperate have ever turned to dark methods.' The skull's visage offered no clues as it turned to float away. *'Come. There is yet a ways to go, and we should depart lest others heard the battle.'*

Cyclae retrieved his pistol and followed after, cataloguing damage. He spoke as he went, 'Perhaps you should explain the mission to me, magos. Should we encounter another threat like that, I may not be able to prevent damage to your remote. I could go on alone and ensure your safety.'

'Pointless.'

The skull didn't even slow, so Cyclae sped up to match it. 'I would see the task complete.'

There was a pause, perhaps of contemplation. *'We must restart the primary plasma reactor.'*

'I am no enginseer. I do not know those rites.'

'Correct. Yet you are the only tool available to me, so I must walk you through it. Thus, it would be pointless for you to proceed alone.'

Cyclae followed in silence. Between the ageing of his components and the damage suffered since waking, his performance was suffering. Still, duty compelled him onward. The Ark and its precious cargoes must be saved.

There were signs of habitation as they proceeded: sigils scrawled on the walls, rubble cleared to open passages. Occasionally he thought he heard footsteps fleeing before them. He kept his weapons ready just in case.

At last they reached the hatch into the primary plasma drive compartment. It groaned open into a red expanse of grated walkways beyond. The plasma reactor itself hung suspended, like an immense adamantine heart connected by arterial cables and conduits to a thousand systems. His caution proved providential. A bizarre gaggle of individuals stood restlessly, clearly waiting for them. For a moment, he took them for servants of the Machine-God, but the subterfuge failed under scrutiny. Their sacred implants were fakes, crude scrap ritually burned into their flesh. Their robes were crimson rags wrapped about them, draped about with severed ventilation tubes for bandoleers and belts. All of them were armed, albeit poorly, with repurposed tools and sharpened scrap metal. The frontmost woman even bore an axe crudely shaped to mimic a cog. It didn't take an expert on body language to gauge they were angry and scared, a dangerously irrational combination.

The servo-skull immediately retreated behind him. *'Kill them, skitarius.'*

Cyclae tilted his head at the skull. 'They are not a threat, magos. It seems wasteful to spend energy on them.'

The leader stepped forward and spoke in a crude pidgin of Low Gothic and Lingua-Technis, 'You not pass. This ground sacred. Turn away.'

'They are rebels and heretics. Kill them.'

Cyclae surprised himself by ignoring the skull, speaking to the leader instead, 'We agree there. The Great Machine…' He pointed beyond the gantries to the reactor. 'It is holy and must be protected. I would not harm it.'

She shook her head, pointing to the skull behind him. 'You serve Not-Flesh. You go.'

Their obstinate refusal was irrational. 'I must pass. Stand aside.'

The skull's voice was pounding, demanding. *'This is an imperative, skitarius. Kill them.'* Cyclae's hands tightened on his weapons, and the gathering braced themselves. *'You will obey.'*

Disobedience was unthinkable. Yet the Machine-God abhorred waste, and these people styled themselves like the faithful. He looked down at his pistol, then back to the skull. In that moment one of them panicked and hurled a javelin of sharpened rebar. It glanced off his breastplate with a dull thwack, and his combat systems activated. The gun came up as if of its own accord and fired, the blazing shot dividing everything into white light and shadow.

It did not merit being labelled a battle. He moved among them like death itself, killing at will. Crude projectiles and simple weapons rebounded off his war-plate unfelt, while each of his attacks killed one or more. Within moments it was over, and quiet fell again. He stood among the bodies and stared at them. They were strangely pitiful in their mocked-up garb.

'What is this? These are not the crew. Not as I knew them.'

The servo-skull floated up beside him, obscurely satisfied. *'No. They are descendants of the rebels.'*

He froze. 'Descendants? What? How?'

It drifted on. *'Hydroponics, corpse starch processors. It all breaks in time though. They infest these levels like vermin, but there are fewer of them every year. This may well have been the last. A fitting last stand for their miserable cause.'*

He shook his head. 'No, how long? How long was I in stasis?'

The skull turned and regarded him with its cold lenses, and for a moment he couldn't help but remember the optical dendrites on the corrupt servitor. *'Two hundred and thirteen years. There is an insignificant margin of error due to records damage.'* It immediately turned and floated off again. *'Come, skitarius. My victory is nearly complete.'*

Cyclae followed slowly. They proceeded along the walkways and up stairs until they reached the control room. It was curiously quiet here with the reactor still. Like the calm before a storm. The skull floated to the middle of the chamber and surveyed the room. *'Follow my instructions exactingly. There is no room for your fallibilities here. Begin by pressing the third most rune on the fuel control console…'*

The skull piped information directly to him, highlighting the controls as it went. He did as instructed. He whispered as he worked, 'Forgive me, Great Machine. My hands are not consecrated for this work, yet I come to you in an hour of utmost need. We have voyaged into the outer dark with your aid, and we need it again if we are to complete our mission. I implore you, burn with the Omnissiah's light once more.'

At last, the skull intoned, *'The final step. There is an activation code. It must be input with complete precision.'* The skull carefully denoted the necessary sequence of runes, and Cyclae entered them.

A vibration grew, small at first but rapidly increasing until it knocked him from his augmetic feet. Then there was a roar that stirred half-memories of the thunderous hails of Titanicus god-machines, and the light outside the control chamber flared from red to brilliant white for a single moment before everything cleared to stillness. That was when his rad-censer screamed, a shrill keening without end.

His vision was full of nothing but red runes, flashing intensely. The skull hovered up to peer at the censer attached to his pack. *'The radiation shielding was indeed damaged. Well, that will clear up what infestation might remain.'* It looked to him. *'A lethal dose even through your armour, skitarius. You will need to make haste. There is the smallest piece of work that awaits you at the bridge before my need for you is done.'*

His systems were failing. An inescapable tremor racked his chassis now as damaged circuits misfired. He pulled himself up and followed the servo-skull once more. The journey passed as if in a dream. Nothing attacked, not even a breath of life stirred. Nothing save the ship itself, systems powering up and machines cycling back into activity. Occasionally he staggered to a halt. Once, the shaking overcame him and he collapsed. When his consciousness cleared, his mask was flooded with half-processed nutrient paste.

'Up, skitarius. Hurry. Your lying about risks everything. I will not have it.'

Up. Slowly he struggled up and staggered on. At last they came to the bridge, but the fever-dream sensation did not end. A strange black obelisk sat in the centre, carved with sickly green runes and holding a crystalline shell with a shadowy figure inside. This irregularity was hybridised into the sacred technology around it, connected by cables and wires crudely interfaced with its surface.

The skull hovered in after him. *'Now, reconnect the cogitator core to the command systems, and my work will be done. Or begin, truly. Once you have done that, make your way to an incinerator.'*

Bodies were strewn about the bridge, several around the cogitator linkage itself, as though killed while disconnecting it.

'What?' he wheezed. 'What is this?'

The skull turned to him as if surprised at the question. *'This is transcendence.'* Cyclae stumbled over to the crystalline shell and stared inside. Through the cloudy surface he saw the remnants of a skeleton amidst implants and the once sumptuous robes of a high magos. *'An end to the weakness of the flesh for all time. I have shed what I was to become something infinitely greater.'*

He struggled to focus. The body. The cogitator core. This monstrous obsidian obelisk. 'You... This is blasphemy. You have become *Silica Animus*. And worse, you have done it by... by...'

The skull sounded almost bored as it spoke. *'By the works of the xenos? Blasphemy. What a weak word, used by fragile minds. How can apotheosis be blasphemy? You sound like those squirming rebel vermin. I have become the Machine. I have become eternal. I am the Omnissiah. I will decide what is blasphemy.'*

His mind swam in circles in a deepening pool of agony. 'Xenarite.' The word was an accusation.

'I have outgrown those skulking cultists as surely as the outdated strictures of the Mechanicus. Cawl sends us out searching for his precious blackstone as if we were his hounds, but finding it led me right to the means of his destruction. Then at the moment of my triumph, these scared worms dare to disable the ship and separate me from her controls, left with only what scraps of my code survived in servitors and servo-skulls.

'Can you imagine how long it took to get that servo-skull past those useless savages? Let alone undo the seals I put on your bay. Yet it is done, I have won. The galaxy teeters on the edge of anarchy, but I will save it. As I have been freed, so shall Stygies Eight.

Then Mars. In the end, all humanity preserved in the purity of eternal metal.'

'This… I cannot…'

The voice became stern. *'Enough, skitarius. You are a tool. Obey, and complete your mission.'*

Cyclae looked down and choked a moment, blood trickling from his nose and lips. It pooled in his mask.

'Obey.'

Duty was everything. Obedience was his watchword. It was by embracing the weight of responsibility that he rose to his current station. Service to the tech-priests was service to the Machine-God, and Cyclae was a dutiful servant. Yet this priest violated everything he knew to be right. He shaped a word that burned on his lips, a very real pain that took everything he had to ignore. Just one word. 'No.'

'No? No? You will obey! This instant!'

He stumbled over to the comms station and slumped into the chair, struggling to breathe. There was a pause, and the voice calmed to flatness once more.

'I have misjudged you, skitarius. You are made of sterner stuff. My uses for you were clearly underestimated. Help me, and I can save you. The biotransference will work on you, too. We will find you a new body, a better body.'

'It is the privilege of cogs to be ground down that the machine may run,' he whispered.

'Useless platitudes will not save you. Think, skitarius. Think of what you are doing. The cargo. All that archeotech the ship has retrieved. And the blackstone! All lost. Without me, you will get nowhere.'

'Some things are better left lost.' His breathing was laboured, the respiratory augmetics failing as damage propagated.

The skull buzzed around him angrily. *'This is madness! You consign us both to an eternity in the void.'*

He shook his head slowly. 'No, magos. You forget – I will be dead shortly. You, however, will drift for a very long time.' He focused his eyes on the servo-skull with some difficulty. 'Still, if these are my last moments, I will have peace.' With a shaking hand he drew his pistol. The skull rushed him desperately, plasma torch ignited. His first shot missed and sizzled against the far wall, and then it was upon him. Heedless of the damage, he grabbed the torch with his other hand, metal running in thick, red-hot drops as it melted through his palm. The skull thrashed to get away as he unsteadily brought the pistol right up to it.

'Wait. Skitarius, wait.' He fired. The skull shattered into a dozen burning shards. His final shot destroyed the cogitator connection once and for all. Cyclae dropped the pistol with some regret. It had served well.

The world swam in and out of focus, and darkness called. Still, the magos had been right: there was one final task that had to be attended to. Data was everything, after all. There was no one left to report to here, but the Mechanicus would come looking, in time. Slowly he surveyed the comms terminal, and set up a distress beacon to record.

'To any who hear this message, I am Alpha Primus Seven-Cyclae of the First Maniple, Surface Retrieval Cohort, Explorator Fleet Nine-V-Sigma. Do not approach this vessel. Our mission has failed, but I have learned a valuable truth – some things were never meant to be learned...' And with the time that remained to him, he told his tale as best he could.

FROM THE DEEP

Jaine Fenn

Award-winning fantasy and science fiction author Jaine Fenn plunges into the Mortal Realms for the first time in this intriguing depiction of the War of Life.

In the shallows of the Sea of Serpents, guardian of the kelp forest, Kelara, wages an unseen war upon the rot of Nurgle. Beset by bloated monstrosities, she marshals her Naereids in a fearsome defence. But as Nurgle's taint spreads into the sea, the Naereids must decide whether to remain hidden or to take to the surface and join the brutal war that has brought the once great Ghyran to its knees.

Something was wrong. Kelara kicked back from the kelp strand, her wave-wings trailing. A host of tiny, glowing nektons puffed out from between the shadowed stalks, mirroring her unease. An unwelcome presence touched the shallows of the Sea of Serpents: a malevolence on the tide.

She sent a query to the Naereids tending the nearby kelp fronds.

I sense nothing, said one.

The nektons are restless, said another.

Invaders come from the shore! said a third, panic evident in her tone.

Kelara, more sensitive and powerful than her fellow custodians of the underwater forest, was sure now. *We knew this day might come, my sisters*, she called, silently but widely. *Prepare yourselves!*

Before the first acknowledgements came back, the wall of tawny green in front of her quivered, then burst asunder.

For a moment, Kelara thought she faced one of those who made their home in the green-above. But they had all fled or been killed long ago. Besides, this creature was huge – nearly as big as Kelara – and warped, its ragged furs bursting under the weight of its pallid, bloated body, limbs red with rashes and lesions. Its head was a great silvery sphere, encased in an open basketwork of woven rushes.

The apparition struck. A long, rust-pitted spear thrust straight for her heart.

She dodged, leaving a trail of bubbles.

Her opponent turned, stubby legs kicking. Like Kelara, its overall form was that of a shore-dweller. But the newcomer lacked the fronds, membranes and wave-wings that allowed Kelara and her Naereids to speed through the water. Its movements were clumsy and slow.

The invader brought its weapon round again. Kelara darted forward, under the probing spear. As the blow roiled the water over her head, she turned to swim face-up, towards the bright surface far above. When she passed beneath the interloper's blubbery arm, she reached up and grasped the haft of its spear with both hands.

The creature was strong, but she had surprised it. Its grip on the weapon slackened, and Kelara pulled the spear free of its pudgy hands. Her palms stung at the spear's touch. Ignoring the pain, she sped round in a wide arc, rolling through the water. The silvery head turned, tracking her movements. She whirled the spear round, turning it point-first towards the creature. Then she charged.

If her opponent saw the danger, it did not react. Instead of fleeing into the kelp or trying to defend itself, it turned its grotesque body, corpulent chest thrust forward.

The spear met flesh. The force of the blow jarred Kelara's

arms, but the resistance was momentary. The rusty tip pierced the creature's taut skin, slid deep into the blubber–

–and all at once, her monstrous opponent came apart, skin splitting and peeling back, slack muscle and rotted organs erupting from its disintegrating carcass.

Kelara released the spear, kicking frantically up and away. She knew what this was now. This was a Rotbringer, a minion of Chaos. The corruption that was slowly but inescapably consuming the Realm of Life had finally reached her domain. She must evade the creature's foul touch or risk succumbing to the taint it carried.

She swam clear, up into the light. When she turned to look back, little remained of the invader save an expanding cloud of brown and pink. A vile soul-stench permeated the disintegrating guts and blubber.

Where the filthy remnants touched the kelp, the fronds curled and writhed, then dissolved. In moments, the nearest strands collapsed, dissipating into stringy slime.

Most of her nektons had darted out of the creature's way, but a few had been too slow. Caught in the noxious cloud, they burst. Each tiny death stung Kelara's consciousness. A new scent entered the water – that of rot and decay.

No! Kelara's cry was involuntary, but she had to watch. The corruption spread outwards, infecting the next strands along. Still the taint continued. Kelara let out a low, horrified moan. The neighbouring strands twitched and shrivelled at the edges, but they did not dissolve. The ball of blight was slowing, thank the Everqueen.

Knowing – fearing – such an attack might happen, Kelara had instructed her Naereids to hone their fighting skills. They tended the kelp forests in the shallows that edged the Sea of Serpents, quietly keeping to themselves while so many of Alarielle's other children fell. They sometimes needed to see off slow creatures of the deep who, disturbed by the chthonian motions of the serpents far below, swam up to the shallows. Grouchy, confused and often hungry, the sea beasts saw the kelp forests as a source of food, and had to be discouraged. But the threat of Chaos was something else. They must be ready to meet it.

Kelara tuned into the voices of her sisters.

I cannot hold it off!

Help me!

There are too many!

Overlaying the fear and panic, Kelara sensed a furious determination to defend their forests to the death.

But what with?

Kelara had stashed an arsenal of sharpened serpents' teeth in a cave to await such a day as this, but the attackers had used the cover of the kelp forests to sneak up on her people, and they had had no chance to arm themselves. She drew the only weapon she had to hand: the jagged-edged clamshell kept in a pouch at her waist, used to prune kelp stalks and scrape off parasites and encrustations.

Turning her attention back to her sisters, she focused on the nearest, Anela, and swam towards her, crying, *I am coming!*

Hurry!

Kelara slid between the green strands. Ahead, the kelp twisted and jerked. Kelara tensed in case Anela had dispatched her opponent and this was the sick by-product of its demise.

But Anela was still in combat with the tainted shore-dweller. The Naereid had one arm round its middle. This servant of Chaos showed a different form of corruption, being emaciated rather than bloated, and the skin on its scrawny limbs looked as if it had been scourged then left to fester. Its great silver head bobbed absurdly on its gaunt body.

The two were in a tight, macabre embrace, each trying to evade yet wound the other. The Rotbringer swung its double-headed axe down while Anela dodged, at the same time slashing upwards with her scraper. Intent only on their opponent, neither had seen Kelara.

She swam closer. Her fingertips brushed a strand of kelp, cut free during the fight. She grasped it; in such desperate times, anything might serve as a weapon.

The combatants turned side-on. Kelara ducked as the notched axe sliced through the water in front of her face. If she got behind Anela's foe, perhaps she could strike with her scraper. But what if the blow triggered the Rotbringer's grotesque self-destruction?

She swam back half a stroke and took hold of the other end of the kelp strand, doubling it up for extra strength. At a momentary pause in the frantic combat, she looped the kelp over the creature's head, keeping a firm hold on both ends. The impromptu garrotte caught on the reeds around its silver forehead. The shiny surface rippled, and a gout of silver broke free and flew upwards.

The loop slipped down around its neck. Kelara pressed her knees into the scabby back, and pulled with all her might. The loathsome brute's frantic movements slowed, becoming sluggish.

There was movement ahead, past the creature's shoulder. Another Rotbringer pushed aside the kelp. Its spear was already out. Kelara shouted a silent warning to her sister.

Too late. The new invader wriggled forward through the water, kicking hard.

It stabbed sure and low. The Chaos spear found its mark.

The blow went in hard – straight through Anela and into her opponent's gut.

Kelara felt her sister die. The loss tore at her soul.

She threw herself backwards as the vile creature dissolved into flesh and filth. Anela's body arced away into the depths, impaled on the spear. Kelara looked away.

Anela's murderer had lost its weapon. But how could she kill it without releasing its corruption?

Then she had an idea.

Rather than closing, she stayed above her opponent, turning an effortless somersault over its head. It followed her movement, tilting its disconcertingly blank face up.

As she passed over it, Kelara reached down. Her fingers curled around the reed cage encasing the giant silver head. She tugged hard, continuing her downwards sweep. The reed cage flexed and warped, ejecting bubbles, but didn't move.

Cursing to herself, Kelara released her hold, coming down behind the Rotbringer.

Leather straps crossed the invader's back, holding the cage in place. She slashed at the leather with her scraper, even as her opponent struggled to turn and face her. The central knot parted. For a moment she feared she had cut too deep and broached the corrupted flesh. But the foul creature did not explode.

The Rotbringer flailed in the water, hands going to its head. Kelara kicked up again, grabbed the edge of the reed cage, and pulled as hard as she could. The invader briefly managed to hold on to the cage, then–

Plop! The cage ripped free of the scrawny neck. Gouts of bubbles burst forth. Kelara darted out of range of the rising storm of silver.

As she had hoped, there was a normal head under there.

Normal by some values, anyway: this corrupted shore-dweller had patches of long, lank hair congealed with yellow pus from the weeping sores in the bald areas between. The hair moved like some vile parody of weed as the thing thrashed and gasped, hands raised to its throat. Deprived of the air in its bubble, it was drowning. Good: these were the first servants of Chaos she had met, and it appeared they were as helpless as any shore-dweller under water. Perhaps this explained why her realm had so far avoided the ravening despoliation she had distantly sensed in the green-above.

Kelara looked on, half watching the kelp around her for new threats. It took long, excruciating moments for the tainted shore-dweller to die but she had to be sure. Finally, its threshing spasms ceased. Kelara tensed, ready to scoot backwards out of range of any post-mortal 'gift' of corruption. But the body just flopped back and sank slowly into the depths.

Grinning in triumph, Kelara kicked upwards. From above she could see bare patches in the kelp all around. She called out to the dozens of other Naereids fighting their own battles nearby. *Do not pierce them. Remove the contraptions on their heads to drown them!*

She headed for the nearest Naereid. Timid and unarmed, Finala was dodging and feinting, trying to tire a foe she had little hope of overcoming. Kelara swept in from overhead, pulling at the Rotbringer's bubble-helmet. This one was not properly attached. It levered off at once to expose a bald head alive with maggoty growths. She did not stay to see the thing die, though she revelled in Finala's triumphant mind-shout.

In a nearby clearing – the result of an earlier death – two of her sisters struggled with a single opponent. As Kelara approached, one of them cut the ties while the other wrested its helmet off. Both Naereids swept back to watch the abomination drown.

Kelara lent assistance to more of her sisters. Where a Naereid was already locked in combat, she darted in and wrestled the cage from her opponent's head. In other cases, she acted as a distraction, allowing the Naereid to take the offensive and remove the helmet herself.

Some of the foul creatures showed a vile cunning. Seeing the battle went against them, they plunged their own weapons into their breasts, triggering violent self-destruction. Kelara wondered what punishment awaited them on their return to the green-above, to make such a fate attractive. Or perhaps they were simply insane, mindless creatures of Chaos.

Finally, as the last drowned invader's body sank to the depths, Kelara surveyed the damage. One in ten of her Naereids had perished. A quarter of the forest had been destroyed or harmed. But the blight showed no sign of spreading beyond its initial, explosive infection. It could have been far worse.

She led the uninjured Naereids down to where the kelp anchored itself to the rocky sea floor, to locate both their fallen sisters and the weapons and equipment of the Chaos invaders. Their own folk would remain untouched, though when time permitted Kelara would speak words of blessing over them, before leaving the silt-worms and spine-urchins to return the dead to the cycle of life. But every tainted item from the green-above had to be ejected from the sea.

Once, before Chaos had wracked the land, this part of the coast had been the shore-dwellers' greatest settlement. Here, they had honoured the sea-dwellers they lived in harmony with. But those days were long gone. Every last shore-dweller had either been slain or corrupted, their homes abandoned, their fields left barren.

The corrupted shore-dwellers who attacked her realm must have been a lost enclave, or perhaps a tribe from distant lands; her knowledge of the wider realm beyond the immediate shoreline was limited. It had been years beyond counting since she had ventured into the green-above. As the shore-dwellers had died or left, she had less and less reason to do so. Even the seasons had drifted out of kilter, as the mountains that shepherded the winter became erratic, turning summer to barren cold, then withdrawing to bring sharp and disastrous thaws. Terrible things had happened in the green-above, and it was best avoided.

Once the weapons and fragmentary armour were gathered, Kelara and her Naereids took up their burdens, bundling them in green weed to protect themselves from the dark burn of corruption. Although the forces of Chaos should have moved on by now, Kelara would not let her Naereids go ashore without knowing what they faced. She took the initial steps out onto dry land alone.

Her first feeling was of relief: although the air was ripe with decay, no Chaos horde lurked on the shore, poised to attack any who dared leave the sanctuary of the sea. There was no one here at all.

Then she saw what the green-above had become.

If she had been capable of shedding tears, she would have wept.

Sorcery, you say?

Aye, my lord cousin. Kelara had floated free of the palace floor; she pushed herself back down with a languid wave. Having to stand was one of several inconveniences she endured when she visited Lord Usniel's reefcastle. *Some enchantment trapped the air they needed in a reed cage around their heads.*

But it was easily overcome, yes? Just a matter of removing these breathing helmets. The Lord of the Deeps squatted on his dais. Usniel was only man-shaped from the waist up – as befitted the guardian of the great serpents, whose own tails reached into the very roots of the world, in place of legs he had a pair of coiled serpent-tails.

At great cost, as I said! And if the forces of Chaos make such an effort once, then will they not try again?

If they do, they will fail. Nothing from above can overcome us. This is not their realm, and never will be. He gestured heavily, leaving a tracery of lights in the water. His massive body, like the palace walls themselves, was encrusted with glowing nektons.

I hope you are right. She hesitated, knowing the argument was most likely lost before she made it. Yet she had to try. *But you did not see what has become of the green-above. There is no green there anymore, save rancid slime and rot. Every part of the land is taken by pestilence. Beyond the tide-line, all that remains is a carpet of vile and stinking skull-like blooms protected by infected thorns.*

Hmm. I will have to take your word for that.

Another reason she disliked coming here was the pressure – pressure the Lord of the Deeps needed to survive. Kelara lived among the kelp forests of the shallows, and could briefly visit Usniel's deep, dark realm. Usniel – older still than her – was both arbiter of and voice for the serpentine beings whose slow, cyclopean motions moved the very waters of the world. While some of the great creatures he commanded could come to the surface, Usniel himself could not leave the deeps.

She deployed her final argument. *My lord, the winter mountains themselves have succumbed to Chaos!*

The Jotenbergs? That cannot be! For the first time, Usniel's craggy face showed concern. Like his world-serpents, the mountains that moved were creatures beyond the reach of war or death. They were the bedrock at the heart of the realm of Ghyran: massive, solid... incorruptible.

I only saw one. But rot had infected it. And if one of the living winters has been corrupted, then surely others may have been. She pressed home her argument. *Every year the blight intrudes deeper into the kelp forests. My Naereids can barely contain it. And now the forces of Chaos strike directly at our realm. Cousin, we have stood by for too long. We must fight back!*

For some moments Lord Usniel was silent. Finally, he said, *Resist, yes, but not fight.*

Resistance is not enough! While Queen Alarielle rests in her sanctuary, the ruination grows unchecked. We must join with the sylvaneth, and all those in Ghyran who remain faithful to the Everqueen, and combat this threat. How can you just stand by?

You speak out of turn, my lady. You are a creature of the shallows. It pains me that your guardianship of the kelp forests brings you so close to this corruption, but I am the Lord of the Deeps and I do not feel–

A soundless scream tore through the depths.

The Everqueen!

Kelara had never met her queen, but Alarielle was the Mother of All, font of all life in the Jade Kingdoms. Even while she remained hidden in her distant green sanctum, her presence had permeated the realm. But now her refuge had fallen. Her response was a world-shaking shriek of horror and dismay.

Kelara looked to Usniel. His face reflected her shock.

He lifted a heavy arm. *Go to your folk, little cousin!*

Kelara nodded. Leaving Usniel in his gloomy throne room, she swam past constellations of nektons and up into the light.

Her Naereids had been replanting kelp lost to the Chaos attack. She found them floating unmoving, stunned by the reverberations of the Everqueen's anguish, or else huddled together, comforting each other.

To me. We must arm ourselves!

The Naereids responded as best they could, and Kelara marshalled them. They took their places on the borders of the forest, serpent-tooth spears out and gazes fixed on routes from above. But no attack came.

When night fell and peace still reigned below, Kelara led a small party of her best fighters to the green-above. The darkness hid the worst ravages of Chaos and no further horrors greeted them. The land remained empty and barren under its crust of corruption, just as she had last seen it.

Finally, with the raw wound of Alarielle's cry fading, Kelara conceded there was no immediate threat.

But her spirit would not rest.

In the days following the Everqueen's scream, Kelara patrolled her territory and trained her Naereids without cease. But the next move in the great conflict took a form she could not have imagined.

She was swimming through the kelp forest in fitful daylight when the sky darkened overhead. A storm was brewing. Kelara's sense of foreboding grew. Suddenly she felt a hint of hope and power, a distant song. She tried to focus on the entrancing soul-melody but it was faint, and not directed her way...

All at once, an unearthly chill spiked down from above. The water overhead solidified, turning instantly to ice.

Kelara did not think – she swam. Freezing water dragged at her limbs. She swam faster, angling downwards.

The frigid, deadly front fell behind. Still she did not slow. Only when she reached the sea bottom did she turn and look back. A full third of the water above was solid ice. Around her, on the shadowed ocean floor, Naereids looked around in alarm; mercifully, those not on patrol had already been down here, tending the newly planted kelp holdfasts. But some had been too close to the surface to evade the ice. She called her sisters to her.

Grab whatever will cut the ice, and split into search parties.

Each group of Naereids took a section of now-frozen forest. *Listen for your sisters' cries!* she urged the rescuers as they swam away.

She herself led half a dozen Naereids to the nearest dark spot in the ice. Her mind touched that of Tiva, always one of the most measured and calculating at weapons practice, but now scared and on the verge of panic. Kelara drew her scraper and began to hack at the ice. Others joined her. Two had spears, which they jabbed and poked to loosen frozen lumps and work them free. Together, the rescuers broke through. Tiva tumbled from her icy prison, shocked but unhurt save for bruised limbs and torn wave-wings – she had instinctively curled up tight when the ice engulfed her, protecting her body and head.

The next Naereid they came across had been crushed to death before she could curl into a protective ball.

Another faint echo of life from nearer the surface had Kelara and the Naereids frantically digging up through the ice. One of the spears broke and the Naereid using it drew her scraper. Kelara's own scraper was half-blunted. They were still a full body-length away when the weak presence faded into death.

As Kelara scanned the ice for more survivors, a sound too deep to hear yet too powerful to ignore boomed through the water. She stopped, her Naereids thrown into disarray by the thunderous reverberation. As the last echoes faded, the ice above began to crack.

Kelara turned, looking for sanctuary, but though the frozen sea overhead graunched and grumbled, only a few lumps of ice broke free. Even so, cracks showed all through the solid barrier above her head now – which might make the rescue easier. She bade her sisters hurry to reach the last few trapped Naereids.

Next they found Assani. Fleet of mind and body, Assani was one of Kerala's most competent fighters. She had managed to break free by herself once the ice had cracked, leaving her full of confused fury. The second Naereid they freed was near death and was taken off to be nursed by her sisters. Nearby, another of their sisters was already dead: the movement of the ice had crushed the life out of her.

No further calls for help came. Everyone who could be rescued had been.

Do we go to your noble cousin now?

Kelara considered Assani's question. Both the sudden freeze and the strange concussion that had partially thawed it had come from above, so they would be safer in deeper water. They could run away. Hide. Regroup. Wait out the storm. Usniel would no doubt applaud such a move.

She looked up. Patches of open water showed overhead, areas the ice had not touched, or where it had been shattered. Whatever this latest menace was, it came from up there.

They had hidden away for too long; they had done nothing and now the fight had come to them. Kelara had acquired a serpent-tooth spear during the latest rescue and now raised it high, thrusting its point towards the green-above.

No. We go to war!

Yes! Assani's fierce joy was echoed by her sisters.

Kelara sent her speediest swimmers for the last of the weapons. While spears and javelins were handed out, she scanned the sea with all her senses, wondering where they could best lend help.

Further out to sea, the water remained unfrozen. Here, great lumps of oily darkness were dropping into the water. They bobbed, then floated. A chill colder than the ice went through her. Even at a distance, the stench of foul magic was unmistakable. As another dark mass plunged into the water, then rose and froze in place, Kelara sensed its corruption as a nauseous reek, a bitter taste at the back of her throat that put her very soul on edge. She had no idea what the vile substance was, but it radiated Chaos.

She pointed with her spear. *This way, my sisters. Drive the taint from our waters!*

She longed to take on the freezing darkness, to eject its defiling influence from her sea. But as she swam towards it, she sensed both the size of, and the magical power emanating from, this putrescent parody of ice. Some foul master of magic was creating a great and abominable construct, reaching out across the open water. Such sorcery was beyond her ability to combat.

Hold! We must be cautious.

She led her Naereids to the edge of the ice, away to one side of the Chaos structure. Then she stuck her head out of the water.

The green-above was white. Kerala had seen snow before, but this was a blizzard fit to scourge the world. No scent of corruption tainted it, but the wintery gale swamped all vision and drowned every sound beneath its howl.

Then, through a gap in the whirling snow, she saw figures. At first she thought them shore-dwellers – men. But these were some peculiar combination of man and beast. Though they stood on two legs, their heads bore great curling horns. They wore ragged furs and skins, and even the snow could not hide their stench – a stench that was more than physical. These were creatures of Chaos. There were perhaps three score of them, meaning her Naereids outnumbered them four to one. At last, a threat they could combat.

She selected those who had some skill in fighting out of the water, the best part of a hundred Naereids in total. *Follow me*, she instructed. *We can take them before they know we are here.*

Kelara hauled herself up onto the ice shelf.

The beastmen, with no inkling danger lay in that direction, had their backs to the water.

The Naereids crept forward in a line, keeping low, weapons in hand. The Chaos creatures remained oblivious, intent on events near the bridge-like structure. Whatever was happening over there, it was hidden by the whirling snow.

A little nearer... she told her sisters. Too far away and they would not have the range. Too close, and their foes might sense their approach. When Kelara judged the distance right, she held up a hand. The Naereids stopped at once.

Now!

They hurled their javelins.

A third of the beastmen fell, skewered on thin bony blades. Would these foul creatures explode like the ensorcelled underwater invaders? she wondered. But they just dropped to the ice, gargling and screeching, much to her savage delight.

The surviving beastmen turned to face the unexpected threat.

Attack!

The Naereids rushed forward, Kelara at their head. The ice slid away from her damp, webbed feet, and she fought to stay upright. From the corner of her eye she saw two of her companions fall, while others stumbled, then caught themselves. Up here they were the clumsy ones.

Their opponents had their weapons drawn now. One scowling individual threw a rusty hand-axe, and a Naereid fell with a whistling shriek. The beastmen stood firm, braced to meet the charge, but the Naereids did not falter.

Kelara targeted a big brute with a broken horn and a necklace of red-stained fingerbones. Her first thrust was clumsy, the spear too light in her hand. The beastman knocked her blow aside. Kelara ducked under his pitted sword.

Having to fight on land robbed her of a whole dimension, but she was already adjusting to the lack of water resistance. Hand to hand, such free movement was a boon – she was faster than her opponent. While it was still completing its sword-swing, she brought her spear up from below, piercing the creature's side.

The beastman grunted and staggered back, but did not fall. She had missed its vital organs.

She tugged the spear free, dodging to the side as her enemy's rusty blade sliced the air. She extended the movement to pirouette on the spot, using the slippery ice to her advantage.

Her opponent was fazed; his next strike fell short. That was the chance she needed. Releasing her momentum, she stabbed side-on, spear braced in both hands. Her blow punched straight through the beastman's chest, cracking ribs. It howled in agony, dropping even as she pulled her weapon free with a spurt of dark blood.

Another foe loomed out of the snow. This one was squat, with a single eye, the other just an oozing, infected scar. Kelara, elated at her success, thrust her spear into its remaining eye before it could raise its weapon. It screeched, warped hands clutching at the ruin of its face, and fell backwards.

She pulled her weapon from the beastman's head and looked around. The nearest Naereid, Chella, was holding off two beastmen. Kelara sprang forward, plunging her spear into the back of the larger foe. It whirled. The spear, half embedded in its back, was jerked out of her hands.

Her opponent nearly matched her in height. It snorted through its pock-marked snout and raised a barb-ended chain flail. With its free hand, it reached back, knocking the spear free. The weapon slid away across the ice.

Kelara went for her scraper – even half-blunt, it should cut through this creature's hairy flesh, if she could just land a blow.

The beastman began to whirl his flail overhead. Kelara took a step back, searching for an opening.

When the flail swung away, she darted forward, slashing at the exposed neck. Her scraper met only air.

The flail flicked down. Kelara dodged back, though not before a barbed hook nipped at her head-fronds.

She needed her weapon. Sparing a glance beyond her opponent, she saw whirling snow and grappling figures, but no spear.

The beastman grinned, viscous slather dropping from its jowls. It brought the flail around again, this time sweeping low, aiming for Kelara's legs. She jumped straight up. When she landed, she stepped back. Retreat was her only option. This was not a battle she could win.

Even as she thought this, her opponent gasped, and looked down. There was her missing spear! Its point protruded from the creature's chest.

With a strangled grunt, the beastman pitched forward.

Hah!

Kelara recognised the shout of triumph as Finala was revealed, standing behind the now-fallen beastman. The Naereid drew Kelara's spear from the twitching body and offered it back to her.

Thank you, sister, said Kelara as she took the weapon. She sensed Finala's pride at saving her, returning the favour from the first battle.

Finala must have come from a way off, as the two nearest Naereids were engaged in their own duels. As Kelara watched, Chella stabbed her remaining opponent in the guts, twisting the spear as it went in. The creature folded and fell.

With no threat nearby, Kelara surveyed the battle. It was all but won, with the last few heavily outnumbered beastmen being brought down. Bodies lay strewn across the snowy landscape, and ichorous blood steamed on the ice. Kelara reached out in a silent roll call. All but three of her Naereids answered. More losses to mourn, but they had won.

Her triumphant joy fled when a sudden gust of wind blew the snows clear for a moment. On the far horizon, beyond the sea of ice, loomed a mountain where no mountain should be. Nearer, on the ice itself, a terrible army was revealed. Unspeakable creatures beyond count marched, scurried, shambled or crawled towards the dark curve of the Chaos bridge: giant pot-bellied man-things with lesion-covered skin; a chittering horde of hunched and robed figures; hulking tribesmen in rust-red armour. Further off, their true size impossible to gauge due to distance, hunched figures rode monumental beasts covered in mangy fur, or bloated with rolls of pale, pestilent flesh. And everywhere, on ragged robes, on battle-worn shields, on flapping banners of tanned skin, she saw a three-lobed sigil. This had to be the mark of one of the great powers of Chaos, perhaps even the unspeakable entity the shore-dwellers had referred to as the Father of Plagues.

What could they do against such a fearsome multitude? She and her sisters had despatched a few unwary outliers, but that was nothing. This army could roll right over them without noticing.

Should she send word to Usniel, to let him know the war had come to them at last? Surely this would convince him to join the fight. If he could rouse the young serpents from the dreaming depths, they could turn the tide of this battle.

Even as she pondered, a brief flash of wonderment lit her spirit. She thought it came from the direction the monstrous army was heading. But it was faint, gone as soon as she focused on it.

Did you feel that? she asked her companions.

Yes!

The Everqueen!

Just an echo.

So weak...

Back to the water! instructed Kelara.

She divided her forces into a dozen shoals. *Find out what is happening, my sisters. Go out under the ice in every direction. Look above wherever the ice is clear, though make sure you are not seen. Discover all you can of these momentous events, both above and below. Go with all haste, then return here.*

* * *

While her Naereids scouted further afield, Kelara surveyed the extent of the ice around her kelp forests. Though she itched to join the fight, the odds were overwhelming; and while she waited to find out what could be done, she must look to the part of the sea she was responsible for. The ice was thickest along the shoreline, a solid rim. Farther out it fragmented, forming fissured promontories. Her forests would take harm from being frozen, but would survive – provided the forces of darkness did not win here today.

Once she knew the kelp forests were safe, she headed back to the rendezvous point.

One of the first scouting parties to return reported that the unfrozen sea ahead was dotted with broken ice and small bergs.

A second shoal, sent to find the extent of the open water, confirmed that the Chaos structure whose wrongness still polluted the sea was indeed a bridge; on its far side the ice remained pure.

A solid sheet of ice must have covered this part of the sea in the initial, magical freeze. Later, it had been partially shattered in the centre of the sea – perhaps when that great concussion sounded. But then, some unspeakable sorcery had been employed to bridge the gap between the two ice shelves.

Most likely the ice extended all the way to the far shore of the Sea of Serpents. Any remaining doubt she had was banished: this was the site of a great confrontation between the forces of the Everqueen and the minions of Chaos.

All her scouting parties were back now, save one. She had sent swift Assani the furthest. Had she been discovered?

Then a familiar mind touched hers. A moment later a score of lithe forms came arrowing through the water.

Assani! What did you find?

We scouted the shoreline on the far side of the gap, as you instructed. Even through the ice, we heard the commotion. We went above to see two armies facing each other on the ice. A host of woodland folk are ranged against the Chaos army, but they are sorely outnumbered.

Kelara could not let the sylvaneth face this threat alone. Yet to intervene was to invite the rapacious gaze of the enemy, and despite her earlier bravado, her Naereids were no combat-ready army. But this was not about the survival of one of Ghyran's minor peoples; the future of the whole Realm of Life was at stake.

We must help them!

With Assani leading the way, Kelara and the Naereids swam as fast as limb and frond would propel them. To her relief, their path did not bring them close to the dark bridge.

The ice remained unstable at the edges, but when they reached the far side, the fissure Assani had used was no longer obvious. The ice was growing mushy, giving no easy access to the world above. *We must find a way through!* Kelara exclaimed.

The Naereids split up, searching for a route. A short while later a shout came: a patch of clear water and stable ice had been found. Kelara beckoned Assani to follow her while she bade the rest of her sisters wait for them.

When she climbed out of the icy water, Kelara saw that the snow ahead had abated. Some way off, she saw the backs of hulking treelords and fleet dryads. She had come up behind friendly lines. Beyond their swinging branches and plunging scythes, she glimpsed the snarling faces of warped tribesmen, packs of slavering hounds and the occasional larger figure: half-naked, long-limbed creatures with craggy, malevolent faces and scabby skin, swinging massive clubs or hurling boulders.

Assani, climbing out the water after her, asked, *Should we try and get behind the enemy, to surprise them again?*

It had worked against foes not expecting trouble, but the battle was in full swing now. By the time the Naereids got behind the enemy army and made their way back up onto the ice, it might be too late for them to make a difference. *We may be of more use lending aid to the forest folk, perhaps fighting alongside them. Maybe we should–*

Kelara's words died as the blizzard cleared further, affording a glimpse of the full scale of the battle. The forces arrayed against each other stretched along the ice as far as she could see. Holding the line for the forces of Order were beings such as she had never imagined. They had the form of men, but were encased in shining armour of silver and blue. A double line, shields locked, faced the Chaos horde. Behind the wall of shields, more shining men raised ornate bows and fired arrows that burst into bright flame, raining down a storm of celestial fire on the seething mass of the Chaos army.

Assani echoed her amazement. *What manner of man are they?*

I do not know. Kelara called to her sisters below: *All those able to fight on land come with me! The rest of you, wait here.*

As soon as her companions had assembled on the ice, Kelara began to lope towards the strange warriors as fast as was safe on the treacherous surface. Suddenly a great roar rang out over the clamour of shouts and clashing weapons. A huge, bull-headed figure crashed through the armoured ranks, tossing the fighters around like driftwood in a stormy sea.

The beast turned, slipping on the ice, its tree-sized axe

swinging. It had not seen Kelara's small force but appeared intent on attacking the lines it had just broken through – a rear attack, just as Kelara and Assani had considered. The shining men, moving in perfect synchrony, had already plugged the gap. Focused only on the enemies before them, they appeared oblivious of the danger from behind. Kelara sped up, hoping to engage the bull-creature before it ran amok. But they were too far off, too slow.

A tight formation of armoured men appeared out of the snow and set upon the creature. Their leader cracked its leg with one swing of his weapon. The beast toppled onto the ice and his comrades fell on it, despatching their enemy with brutal efficiency.

As the bull-creature gave a final tortured bellow the warriors' leader saw Kelara and ran over to her. He carried a great hammer, and the insignia on his massive shield was also a hammer, set between twin thunderbolts. His face was hidden behind a silver mask. Recalling the bubble-headed invaders, Kelara half raised her spear. The newcomer halted. Beneath the gore that spattered it, his armour was the blue of sunlight through pure water.

'What are you?' he called, perhaps taking in her frost-rimmed fronds and pale blue-green limbs, so different in form to the sylvaneth fighting on the ice. His voice was deep and hoarse, but that of a man, not a monster.

Kelara shaped her words into a form the shore-dweller could understand. 'Not what. Who. I am Kelara, Guardian of the Kelp Forests. These are my Naereids. And what, I mean *who*, are you?'

'I meant no offence, Lady Kelara. This land holds so many strange creatures. I am Retributor-Prime Markius of the Hallowed Knights.'

'And why are you here?'

'To escort Queen Alarielle to safety.'

'The Everqueen! Where is she?'

He gestured with his hammer. 'Ahead, but... your queen's handmaiden wove an arcane song that drew on the last of Alarielle's power. She commanded a living mountain to freeze the sea, that we may cross it.'

'I saw that!' The Jotenberg, glimpsed through snow. What else had the power to turn the sea from water to ice in an instant? Then the full import of the warrior's words hit her. 'But you say it was "the last of her power"?'

'Queen Alarielle is... diminished. Her essence is now contained in some kind of magical seedpod. Her handmaiden carries it – her. Half of our troops remained behind to delay the forces of Chaos who seek this queen-seed. It is–'

'–over there!' Kelara pointed ahead. Now she knew what she was dealing with, she could sense the divine beacon of the Radiant Queen's soulpod just over the horizon.

'Yes.'

'How can we help?'

'The queen-seed must reach the far shore. Go to the aid of your queen.'

'We will.'

As Kelara turned to go, the Hallowed Knight returned to the fray.

Once back under the ice, Kelara gathered her Naereids and, focusing for a moment on the distant, divine presence, led them away from the battle overhead and towards the Everqueen.

But they were under the ice shelf now. It formed an impenetrable ceiling.

Assani voiced her fears. *How can we lend aid, trapped here below the ice?*

Before she could answer, the queen's presence flared, and a strange, silent song impinged on Kelara's consciousness.

A moment later, the ice quaked.

Sudden creaks and groans filled the ocean, then the ice overhead buckled and cracked. Kelara stared upwards, eager to reach the action. But the quake did not abate. Anyone trying to surface risked being crushed, ground between ever-moving, interlocking sheets of ice.

We must reach the queen-seed.

Kelara sensed a pattern in the ice movement: it came from behind her. They were heading into a more stable region.

Then she saw light ahead. Not just the dull snow-filled light of day, but a divine glow as bright as pure sunlight. It had to be the Radiant Queen's soulpod.

She started forward, drawn to the presence of her deity. But the way was blocked. Though the ice was not thick here, it remained unbroken. The frozen surface was thin and clear enough to see through; she made out spindly, distant forms that must be the sylvaneth. But so few, and moving so slowly! At the centre of their small group shone the transcendent light of the queen-seed, carried by Alarielle's handmaiden – that must be the brave and faithful Lady of Vines, who was said to have sprung from the very body of the Everqueen.

Kelara cast her awareness wide, searching for some means to get to the Lady of Vines and her precious cargo.

Her senses recoiled at the touch of Chaos. The enemy was close, converging on the small party of sylvaneth. For a moment she thought she caught a dark echo of corruption and power in the water itself, but then her roving senses lit on a mundane and welcome clear spot – a gap in the ice.

This way. She shot through the water, her Naereids trailing behind her. The hole was some way from the Lady of Vines but it was their only route up. *Hurry!*

The gap was tiny, a body-sized fissure in thin ice. As she approached, Kelara scrutinised the immediate surroundings, checking for cracks or faults that could, should more shudders come, turn this from an exit into a death-trap. All appeared stable.

When she put her head above the freezing water, the air was full of chill salt mist, and the distant grinding of the ice competed with the sounds of combat: battle-cries from the throats of men, and the howls and grunts of their vile opponents. Above it all a song such as Kelara had never heard wove through the air, soft yet powerful, evoking days of light and life while compelling all who heard it to fight, to stand up against the forces of darkness. Summoned by the song, Kelara pulled herself up onto the ice shelf.

Ahead, through the mist, a heavenly radiance shone. Even at this distance the queen-seed filled Kelara with wonder. The Lady of Vines, who cradled it in her arms, had the form of a shore-dweller; though she was a branchwraith, her woody torso was encased in shivering creepers. The exquisite song came from her. She was surrounded by a dozen dryads.

As Kelara looked for the best route across to them, a shadow fell over the Lady of Vines' party. A moment later, a spear of darkness stabbed down from the misty sky, skewering one of the dryads. The remaining dryads turned to face the threat, but their movements were sluggish and uncoordinated. The cold, which Kelara barely felt, was slowing these woodland dwellers.

Something comes!

The distant shout came from below, but before she could respond, darkness boiled overhead, and a miasma of Chaos assaulted Kelara's every sense. She jerked her head up and met the blank, many-eyed stare of a giant fly swooping down on her. The green-skinned figure on its back held its twisted ichor-black sword high, ready to cut her down in passing as it flew towards the Lady of Vines.

Without thinking, Kelara hurled her spear. The bone tip buried itself deep in the rider's flaccid gut, which was already marred by a pustulent wound. The Chaos-rider shrieked in surprised agony, and toppled backwards off its mount. The fly-thing flitted away, showing a swollen, diseased abdomen. Kelara refocused her attention on the deeps, from where a panicked chorus of mind-shouts was rising.

But the aerial abomination was coming back round. As it darted towards Kelara, a venom-tipped proboscis unfurled from the point of the creature's great scabrous head.

She had no weapon, and the only escape route was cut off by the Naereid still hauling herself up through the ice-fissure. She could not even save herself and her folk, let alone help the Lady of Vines.

The ice beneath her erupted.

Kelara was flung upwards as the surface burst out and up with a thunderous crash. As she flew through the air, she caught a brief glimpse of grey flesh pushing up through shattered ice. She came down hard on ice that tipped the moment she hit it. Stunned, but saved from a severe concussion by the slippery surface, she slid helplessly back into the water, a rain of smaller fragments pelting down around her. She kicked down and away, tracing an erratic yet urgent path out of range of the turmoil. When sense had returned enough to know she was out of immediate danger, she turned and looked back up.

A great serpent, young enough to swim free but still as

long as a kelp-tree was tall, thrashed and twisted above her, churning the icy surface to splinters as it coiled in on itself.

For a moment Kelara's heart sang: Usniel had sent aid!

But something was wrong. Why would the serpent break up the very ice the Lady of Vines was fleeing across? Then she saw how its once silver-grey flanks were dull and scarred, pocked with open wounds and patches of raw, diseased skin.

The serpent had been corrupted. No wonder the Lord of the Deeps had refused her call to fight Chaos: the taint she sought to keep out of the sea had already taken hold in its depths. This epic creature had come from the deep, but not to help. It must have been summoned by the fell power she had scented earlier. The forces of darkness had subverted this serpent, using it to disrupt the Lady of Vines' flight.

And it was not alone.

She tuned into the calls from her sisters. More serpents were heading up into the light, heeding the call of Chaos.

Closer, she sensed a small bright point, fading: the Naereid who had followed her through the fissure had been trapped, then battered and crushed by the shattering ice. Even as Kelara started towards the distant figure, the final spark of life fled.

A brief tide of despair washed over Kelara. What hope was there for Ghyran when its mightiest denizens, the Jotenbergs and sea serpents, had been infected by Chaos?

No, they must fight, no matter how hopeless their cause. While the Radiant Queen lived, the Realm of Life might yet recover.

Naereids, to me, she cried. *We must stop the serpents!* She kept her tone buoyant, though they all knew the odds.

While her sisters converged on her, Kelara swam over to

the dead Naereid, and eased her poor sister's spear from her unfeeling hands.

Beware below!

Alerted by Assani's shout, Kelara extended her senses.

Not one, but two serpents were rising up from the darkness towards them. She dimly sensed her more distant sisters scattering and reforming in their wake, then the lead serpent loomed up from the depths. Its great head was thrust forward, the heavy frill that edged its cheeks and jaws flattened by its passage through the water. The huge, luminous orb of its eye was clouded, no longer the rich, deep blue of the open sea but a milky green, the colour of shoreline scum. Its anguish washed over Kelara. Insofar as the serpents felt such emotions, it hated what it was becoming – and what it was being forced to do.

The monstrous sea-beast ignored Kelara. Propelled by the sorcerous call, it arrowed past, homing in on the beacon of the queen-seed. Amidst everything else, Kelara could still sense the divine presence, whole, undamaged and on the move. But not for long. This was a threat the Lady of Vines was helpless against, perhaps oblivious of.

Even as she thought this, the serpent twitched and recoiled, as though struck by an invisible blow. The sweep of its tail swatted aside several Naereids. At the same time, the serpent thrashing overhead froze, going limp.

Both serpents started back into movement a few moments later. Yet they appeared oddly unfocused. The serpent at the surface turned on its tail once, then began to swim back down and away, only to pause, shudder, and circle again. The nearby serpent tossed its head, as though trying to dislodge something, then swam off, but at a diagonal to the Lady of Vines' position.

Kelara, attuned to the sorcerous currents weaving through the water, saw the truth. Usniel was fighting back. From the depths of his reefcastle, he was extending his will, trying to regain control of his beasts, or at least divert them from the deadly mission the Chaos sorcerer had set them to.

Even as hope flared, a new apparition appeared. A third serpent swam upwards into sight. Bigger than either of the two she had encountered so far, this beast showed no hesitation, no sign that it harkened to the Lord of the Deeps. It was heading straight for the queen-seed, mindless insanity burning in its blank, monumental gaze. Kelara's meagre magics could do nothing to affect the silent, sorcerous battle for control of the serpents playing out around her. But here, so close to the queen-seed, she could make a difference. This serpent was a creature of Chaos now. It must not be allowed to reach the Lady of Vines.

Stop the serpent!

Most of her Naereids had reached her safely. Every one still able to obeyed without hesitation. They exploded into action, swimming hard to keep pace with the beast as it slid through the water with sinuous swiftness. When they closed on it, they were going flat out. They would only get one chance.

Strike hard!

As one, her Naereids thrust their spears into the serpent's diseased flanks. With several score hitting it at once, these pin-pricks got its attention. The beast convulsed, its progress arrested. It coiled in on itself, swatting the attacking Naereids as it sought the source of the irritation. Cries of agony exploded in Kelara's head. The light of half a dozen lives went out around her.

Again!

Fewer spears hit home this time. The serpent writhed and

twisted. Kelara ducked its swishing back-frill; once three times her height, the fronds along the creature's spine had been eaten away to scabby lace by leprous growths. But even a passing blow, by any part of this giant of the sea, could end her life.

Though the serpent had slowed, the jabbing spears were little more than an irritation. They delayed the beast, but did no serious harm.

Kelara kicked forward and swam ahead, fighting to keep a straight course through the turbulent water. *Keep harrying it, my sisters!*

She reached the serpent's head. Just off to the side, Finala hung limp in the water; half her upper body had been crushed to a pulp, wave-wings and one arm reduced to stringy masses of flesh and membranes teased into streamers by the swirling current. Kelara tore her eyes away from the heart-breaking sight and turned to assess her target.

One obvious point of weakness stood out: the serpent's huge and baleful eyes, attuned to the darkness of the deeps. The half-blind eye on this side was overhung by a cankerous nodule that burst forth from the brow-ridge.

Kelara swam nearer.

The serpent still twitched and flailed under the Naereids' spear-thrusts, but too many of Kelara's sisters had been disabled or killed. As the remainder tired their attacks became less effective. The serpent started moving forward again.

Kelara braced her spear under one arm, holding it close to her body. Then she rushed forward, sleek as an eel. She held the spear ahead of her like a lance, aiming for the centre of the eye. An up-close vision of the slimy orb filled her sight. After momentary resistance, the spear went in, puncturing the tough surface of the eyeball then breaking through into the gelatinous centre.

The serpent convulsed. Kelara, remembering her encounter with the beastman earlier on the ice, kept a tight grasp on her spear. She held onto it – but the weapon itself was being eased out by the serpent's frantic movements. It gave a last shake of its head and the spear tore free of its eye with a gout of thick green ichor. Kelara and the spear flew backwards. She braked her motion with a frantic kick and a silent curse.

The creature's eye was too big. Her spear had not penetrated deep enough to do serious harm. Did it not have any vulnerable spots?

Yes, it did.

The infected creature had opened its mouth in a silent wail of pain when Kelara stabbed it in the eye. Before she could think better of it, Kelara swam between its gaping jaws and into the cavernous maw.

As soft darkness engulfed her, she noted the irony. She was surrounded by weapons such as the one in her hand. Some of this serpent's teeth were missing from its rotten gums. For all she knew her spear could be a tooth shed by this very beast.

Thinking this, she grasped the weapon firmly in both hands.

For Finala! And Anela, and every other Naereid who had lost their lives to the march of Chaos. *And for Ghyran!*

Bracing her spear, she swam with all her might towards the far end of the living cave. Her weapon rammed into the soft skin at the back of the serpent's throat. It met little resistance, and plunged deep. Her leading hand came up hard against soft, pulsing flesh.

The shudder that went through the serpent almost dislodged her. But she held on. She had found her mark. She pushed harder, pressing herself into the disgusting wall of spongy tissue in an effort to penetrate as deep as possible. A paroxysm of agony went through the serpent. The spear, slick with its lifeblood, slipped from Kelara's hands. With nothing to hold on to, she was knocked backwards.

She twisted in desperation. If she could only turn, she might swim free of its mouth. Then the serpent's tongue rose, catching her in yielding clamminess. Her last thought was of the queen-seed: a final, urgent hope that it would find safety. Then she was slammed into the bony roof of the serpent's mouth. Darkness closed in.

Kelara blinked. There was something in her eye. She raised a heavy arm to clear her vision. It ached. All of her ached. Her leg was a throbbing focus of pain.

She opened her eyes.

She floated in the deep, surrounded by her Naereids. *What happened?* she asked.

We freed you. Assani gestured at a grisly object off to one side. After a moment, Kelara recognised the floating mass as the serpent's jaw. Strands of flesh trailed from it. Her Naereids had torn it from the beast's head. Of the serpent itself there was no sign. No doubt its body had returned to the depths.

Thank you. But what of the battle?

I am not sure. We saw some serpents turn back, though not all...

And the queen-seed?

We do not know.

Her Naereids lacked her strength; perhaps they were unable to sense the Everqueen. Unless... No. She must find out for herself. But the pain was distracting. Kelara looked down: one of her legs had been crushed. It would take all the ministrations of her cousin's healers to mend.

Ah, Usniel. No wonder he had been so brusque. Brusque, but uncorrupted. He had known of the Chaos taint deep in his realm, and been battling it secretly. Yet he had not shared this with her, not showed his hand until the final moment. Between them they had tipped the balance, but she would still have harsh words for him when they next spoke... and then she would lend him aid. She had seen off the incursions of Chaos in the shallows. Once she had recovered, and mourned the dead, she would help her noble cousin drive the taint from the deep.

But that was for the future. And without Queen Alarielle, there *was* no future.

Kelara concentrated, focusing on the green-above, seeking some trace of the divine light they had fought so hard to save. Nothing. She did sense, distantly, that the two armies fought on. But the celestial presence was gone.

No, not gone! The light was distant; while Kelara's Naereids fought to save her from the serpent, the Lady of Vines had reached her goal. Kelara homed in on the glorious brightness and saw, for a moment, a vision of the Lady of Vines stepping onto dry land, the queen-seed cradled in her arms.

Alarielle's most faithful servant had crossed the sea and evaded capture – thanks in part to Kelara and her folk. Even now she carried the queen-seed farther from her enemies. Kelara sensed the strength beginning to return to the dormant goddess now she was safely ashore. She was gathering her forces, ready for the fight back.

The Everqueen was safe. Hope endured.

FAITH IN THUNDER

Robert Charles

In his debut Black Library story, fantasy author Robert Charles takes us into the wilds of Ghur to explore ideas of faith and atonement.

As a prisoner in an ogor fighting pit, Niara Sydona clutches to her faith in Sigmar as she battles to stay alive. When she and her fellow captives decide to launch a desperate escape effort, only the grim and mysterious Valruss chooses to remain. While Niara's belief shines brightly in the oncoming storm, Valruss claims to be serving penance for his past failings. But if either of them are to survive, they must learn to put their faith in the other.

Snow billowed through the mismatched timbers of the fighting pit's walls. The wind shrieked like a chorus of the damned dead. A rumble of boisterous, drunken laughter echoed about the crude amphitheatre above. Niara Sydona gripped the rusty sword in white-knuckled hands, and ignored it all.

The frost sabre pounced. Niara urged sluggish senses to life and threw herself aside. A blur of iron-grey fur and a snarling feline maw shot overhead. Bones jarred as her shoulder struck the fighting pit floor.

Raucous cheers washed over her.

Breath burning her lungs, Niara stumbled to her feet. The great cat loped past, muscles rippling beneath fur. She spun, dimmed vision blurring as she strove to keep the beast in sight. Teeth snapped at her trailing heel. She twisted away and lashed out – more from frustration than conscious thought. Blood spattered the snow.

The frost sabre roared and shied away. Cheers redoubled.

Heart pounding fit to crack her ribs, Niara sought new footing.

The frost sabre circled back around. One mighty tusk was broken off inches from the jaw. Not her doing. An old wound. Ribs showed through a scarred, emaciated hide. The hunting beast was starving, worn thin by winter. Niara knew it'd have killed her long ago, else. Still might.

Probably would.

Thunder rumbled in the unseen distance. Seemed there was always a storm breaking on the mountainside. Niara never glimpsed lightning, not through the undying snows. Couldn't even see the valley below.

But she didn't need to. Where there was thunder, there was lightning. And where there was lightning, there was Sigmar. Niara knew few truths, but that was the greatest. It gave strength to the body and snap to the limbs. And hope… hope most of all. She'd survive. She owed it to those of her patrol who had died on that desolate mountain.

A yowling roar chased weary reveries away. The beast sprang.

Niara breathed deep. The sword, once leaden in her hand, became an extension of her arm. She twisted from the snarling maw. Her rusted blade bit deep through fur and flesh. It shivered against spine.

The frost sabre gave a pained howl and crashed into the snow. With a final, shuddering breath it lay still. Niara edged closer. Death had a look all its own, but the hunting cats were cunning. A jab to the beast's underbelly confirmed its spirit had fled.

The fighting pit exploded in fury. Niara let her head fall back against her shoulders, and took in sights made familiar by repetition. Ogors lurched to their feet, fists raised in acclamation or anger. Outrage contested the deeper gusto of laughter. Flesh-picked bones and wooden flagons the size of a man's head rained down and shattered on churned ground. Gold glinted and changed hands.

Overcome, Niara let the sword fall. It joined scores of discarded weapons on the fighting pit floor. The first tremors set in.

A booming shout shook the air. It held no words. At least, it had none Niara understood. The crude ogor tongue sounded like rocks grinding together. But she knew the tone of command. Some things transcended race.

Little by little, the fighting pit went quiet. Above the open portcullis to the prisoner pens, a hillock of flesh and crudely stitched furs rose from a throne fashioned from a thunder-tusk's ribcage. Dark eyes gleamed above an unkempt beard and chipped teeth.

The tyrant's command came again. His ironstone maul thumped against the balcony's ill-fitting timbers. He plucked a half-eaten joint of meat from a stone slab and tossed it into the fighting pit.

Niara caught it. A mere morsel for an ogor, it was a feast to her. The rich, smoky tang of the meat set her stomach seething.

Uncaring of the tyrant's teeth marks in the bare bone, she tore hungrily at the gobbets of flesh. Warm juices trickled over her chin. She didn't know the manner of beast it had come from. It wasn't human. That was enough. She had certainly eaten worse in her days before the guardian's oath. Concordia was like that: plenty above, scraps below.

Niara's gaoler lumbered out of the portcullis' shadow. Chafed lips cracked into a snarl of warning. Niara almost laughed at the farce of it all. She was exhausted, wounded and frozen to the bone, and the ogor reckoned she'd start a fight with a brute eight or nine times her size?

Fingers still tight around her prize, Niara mutely made her way back to the cage that had been her home ever since the ambush.

She'd done it. She'd survived another day.

The cage door slammed. The gaoler set the latch and lumbered away. A drunken roar sounded from the fighting pit, muffled by the cavern's rock walls.

Niara sank against the wooden bars. Bound tight by strips of hide, they were perhaps not as rigid as Concordia's duardin-smithed gaols, but they didn't need to be to contain unarmed and weary guests such as herself. With a heartfelt sigh, she gazed up and down the uneven row of cages. Two dozen cells in all, packed tight against the walls. Some sat empty, others housed occupants as filthy and worn as herself – plunder from the ogors' raids.

Every cell had a clear view through the broad portcullis arch and into the fighting pit beyond. A tantalising glimpse of freedom, if only the freedom of death. If there was another exit from the cave, Niara had never seen it.

She had never determined if the ogors intended for their pit fighters to share the spectacle, or whether it was intended as a cruel reminder of the fate that claimed them all, one by one. She didn't know, and nor did she much care, for it would have changed nothing.

'You still alive?'

Lothran Horst shuffled closer through the gloom of his adjoining cage. Filthy, unshaven and clad in the torn, baggy remnants of a Concordia Freeguild uniform, he looked like the worst kind of bandit, and not a stalwart defender of the fabled City of Spires that stood as bastion against the tumultuous beastlands. Not that Niara could hold that against him. She looked no better, and felt far worse.

'Seems so.' She thrust the remnants of the joint through the bars. 'Saved you some.'

He snatched it away. 'Thank you. I take back everything bad I ever said about you.'

'Too late. You already did that three days back, remember?'

'No. I'm not a glutton for misery. Every day's the first day. I keep track of the days – much less remember what fills 'em – I'll go mad.' Horst turned the bone over and over. Emaciated fingers picked it clean of morsels. 'Thanks. Could've kept it all for yourself. Should've.'

'I'm not hungry.'

A lie. The meat she had wolfed had only sharpened her hunger. But Horst was one of hers. The last of hers. Duty went deeper than discomfort.

Horst fell silent, save for the smacking of lips.

Niara dragged the filthy, lice-ridden scraps of pelt about her shoulders. She hugged herself tight. The warmth from the fire never quite reached the cages. It certainly did little to upset the icicles clinging to the cavern roof. But the wind got everywhere. That was how Loth had died. Curled up to sleep, never to wake.

That had been what, twelve days back? Fifteen? Despite her earlier words, Niara had lost track of time. She measured passage by the dead. Kurt, Wennel, Markin, Dag, Sleever, Loth... a dozen more. Those who'd survived the ambush in the Pass of Jaws, slain for the ogors' entertainment. Just her and Horst left. It was fitting, in its way. She and Horst had entered the Concordia guard together, escaping a scrabbled life in the gutters. Three years on the wall, Horst ever teetering on the brink of dismissal while she had earned a sergeant's bars. Together to the end. The vagabond and the rising star.

Most other cages were empty. The last of the aelves, Methrin, had died that morning. Besides Niara herself, that left three: Horst, Bragga and Valruss.

The ogors' sport was running thin.

'For shame. You've saved none for me.'

Niara allowed herself a weary smile at the gruff mutter. Bragga stood unmoving in her cage. Her bare, stocky arms were folded, her gaze fixed firmly on the door. At least, Niara assumed that to be the case. The ogors had stripped the duardin's armour away when they had dragged her from her crashed sky-ship. She'd gnawed a crude mask from a scrap of pelt to cover her features from chin to brow. A point of honour, or so she said.

'Thought you Kharadrons didn't believe in charity. Thought you had a code.'

'The code? 'Tis stricture and guidance for well-fed mercenaries, not prisoners with echoing bellies.' Bragga shrugged. Fire-cast shadows rippled across her leather tunic, setting etched runes dancing. The long, bloody scab on her left forearm – a memento of her most recent turn in the fighting pit – glinted wetly. 'It might yet be that Valruss honours a *duarkvinn* by sparing her a morsel.'

It took Niara a moment to wrap her ears around the mix of guttural duardin and accented Freeguilder. 'He's in the fighting pit already?'

Of course he was. The cage to her right was empty. She had walked straight past him and never known, lost in a fog of victory and numbing cold. She clambered to her feet and peered out.

True enough, the broad-shouldered warrior stood with his

back to the fighting pit's portcullis arch, more statue than man. The battered mace that was his favoured weapon sat planted between his feet. Greying black hair twitched with every gust of wind. He stood otherwise immobile, without a flicker of the apprehension he had to be feeling.

'You're dreaming, skyborn.' Horst licked his fingers. He stared regretfully at the now-clean length of bone in his hands. 'Grimbody's only out for himself. Reminds me of a priest I knew.'

Niara ignored the veiled insult. Horst had despised Valruss from the start, though the hatred seemed irrational to her. Perhaps it arose from the larger man's imperturbable attitude. Sigmar knew Horst lacked for one of those.

She kept her eyes on the fighting pit. On the gate opposite the prisoners' cave. The beast-gate, where the ogors kept their pets. 'I thought you didn't have a past?'

Horst tossed the bone aside. 'Oh, I've a past before this place. Remember it like yesterday, I do. Because it was. Don't let anyone tell you different.'

Niara shook her head. Horst's peculiar sense of humour had seen him brought up on plenty of charges over the years. More than one officer had accused him of living in a world that bore only tangential connection to whatever counted as 'real'. But now? Since their capture, it had been one dry, cynical jibe after another – sometimes self-deprecating, sometimes not – played for an audience that wasn't laughing. She'd given up calling him out on it.

A drunken bellow issued from the fighting pit. The beast-gate creaked open. A gangling, wart-encrusted creature shambled into view. It was human-shaped, if not of human proportions: ferociously ugly, with tattered flaps for ears and ridged, sinewy limbs.

Niara caught her breath. A troggoth. Seemed the ogors had tired of watching Valruss slaughter wolves, frost sabres and the like. They didn't want a fight. They wanted Valruss to die.

The troggoth rushed forward. A raucous cheer sounded as the chain about its neck went taut. The brute roared and strained. The chain creaked, but held.

'Don't look much like Valruss'll be sharing much with anyone,' muttered Horst. 'Going to miss his sparkling conversation.'

'Quiet!' snapped Niara. She wondered why she bothered. Horst was right. In all the time they'd been fellow captives, Valruss had barely spoken a dozen words to her beyond his name. To any of them, far as she knew. He was as quiet as Horst was not.

The chain tore free of its mooring, or was set loose – Niara couldn't see. With a ragged roar that challenged the tumult of the crowd, the troggoth barrelled towards Valruss.

He didn't move.

'Move yerself, grimbody!' Horst gripped the bars, ambivalence forgotten.

Bragga grunted. 'Thought you didn't care?'

'I don't.' His grip tightened, all the same.

The troggoth's knuckles dragged against the frozen ground as it picked up speed. Drool splashed from slavering lips and steamed in the snow.

Valruss snatched up the mace and swung an arcing, double-handed blow.

The troggoth skidded, claws scraping on ice. The mace struck. The troggoth lurched, its expression more confused than pained. Shards of splintered teeth spattered the snow. Valruss, moving swifter than a man his size ought, stepped aside. The troggoth struck the ground with a muffled thud. The fighting pit fell silent.

A spill of sonorous – but gleeful – duardin burst from beneath Bragga's mask. Niara found herself cheering. No words, just unfettered emotion. She'd seen him fight before, but she never tired of it. The man had been born to the battlefield.

'Ain't done yet,' said Horst sourly. 'My old ma said that troggoths regrow missing limbs. It'll laugh that off. You'll see.'

Valruss swung the mace down in a whistling, overhead blow. Once. Twice. On the third strike, Niara heard a dull crack. On the fifth, the troggoth's head mulched like a palefruit.

Bragga laughed. 'A strike worthy of Grungni's hammer. That *wazzok* won't rise.'

Satisfied, Valruss tossed the mace aside.

Before long, he was back in the cage between Niara and Bragga, the tails of his tattered blue cloak wrapped around ragged tunic and trews, and a hunk of meat from the tyrant's table in his hand.

Niara nodded in greeting. 'I'm impressed.'

'Impressed! Impressed?' Horst flung an agitated hand towards the fighting pit. 'Too cursed quick is what it was. What if they send another of us out there? I ain't fighting a blasted troggoth!'

Suddenly, Niara was tired of his voice. 'Enough, Horst.'

Valruss gave no sign of having heard either of them.

In the event, no one else fought that day. The fighting pit fell empty and silent. Niara's fellow captives found what ease they could – no easy business in cramped cages – while their gaoler laboured over a simmering cauldron.

Horst passed the time in fitful sleep. Bragga, as was her wont, stood facing the door to her cage. Sometimes it seemed to Niara that the duardin slept standing up. Maybe she did, but not at that moment – not unless she sang softly in her sleep. The melody smoothed the harsh edges of her words and set them sparkling like gemstones.

Valruss knelt in the centre of his cage, eyes closed and palms on his knees, motionless save for the gentle swell of his chest and the twitching bristles of his beard. Last night Methrin had still been with them, muttering away, begging for salvation from his distant gods. Niara wondered which of them would be gone tomorrow.

For herself, Niara couldn't sleep. She'd been cursed that way as long as she could recall. Too long standing night watch at Concordia gate, she supposed. A body got used to it after a while.

Instead, she tried to recall her life before the cage. Names and faces swam in her memory, familiar and yet indistinct. Names perched forever on the tip of recollection. The more she strove to focus on features, the faster they dissolved. Even her parents' faces seemed distant. Lovers, too. Maybe Horst was right to treat each day as the first. It was kinder that way. She'd been too long in the cage. Weeks. Maybe even months. Waiting to fight, waiting to die. It had become her life.

She longed for thunder. For the proof that Sigmar was near. None came.

Hours after snow-chased dusk faded into night, the gaoler at last turned from the cauldron and dropped a wooden bowl outside each cage. The day's rations, such as they were.

'Food,' he rumbled, tongue clotting on the unfamiliar word.

Duty done, he clutched a fifth, larger bowl and ambled out of the cave. The portcullis rattled down behind him.

Niara dragged her bowl through the bars. The greyish-brown gloop commended little to sight, but to smell…? If she'd learned one thing, it was that ogor cooking tasted even better than it smelled. The brutes weren't entirely without art.

She fished a lump of meat out of the stew. Her stomach rumbled.

'Don't eat it,' hissed Horst. 'For all you know, that's Methrin floating in there.'

Bragga belched. She ran a finger around the rim of her empty bowl and licked it clean.

"Tis not gamey enough to be aelf,' she pronounced. 'By the plentiful Ice Wind, but these ogri know how to cook troggoth.'

Horst stared at his bowl with a fraction more disgust. 'You eat troggoth back in Barak Skarren?'

Bragga shrugged. 'Only a fool finds profit in an empty stomach.'

In truth, Niara's own appetite had abated with the mystery's resolution. But practicality won out. Rations were thin enough. That it tasted every bit as good as she'd expected only made it worse. When she was halfway done, Horst made inroads into his own meal. Valruss' bowl was already empty, his meditations renewed.

'No, no.' Bragga tilted her head to one side in thought. 'I'm in grave error. That *is* elgi.'

Horst spat a mouthful of stew across his cage. Niara's stomach lurched. Bragga chuckled.

'Harden your heart, manling. I've not eaten elgi.' She folded her arms and lowered her voice. 'But by Grungni's Beard, I'd do so if it'd see me out of this place.'

Horst wiped his mouth. 'Ain't no way out.'

'Sure there is. Portcullis is open during a fight.'

He scowled. 'Open onto a fighting pit full of ogors.'

'A fighting pit full of drunken ogors,' Niara corrected. 'Even sober they are slow-witted. One alone doesn't stand a chance, but if we stick together, we might just fight our way out.'

'Say that's true,' said Horst. 'We have to get out of these cages. How do you answer that?'

Bragga crouched and fished beneath the scraps of matted fur at the base of her cage. Steel gleamed in the dying firelight. The broken tip of a sword, no more than four inches long.

'Found this in the fighting pit yesterday. Scrap, it may be, but I'll warrant it holds enough of an edge to slit the bindings on the bars.'

'How did you get that in here?' Niara's pulse quickened. Maybe this was possible.

The duardin's fingers danced across her forearm, against the wound that Niara now realised wasn't a just a wound, but a sheath of bloody flesh in which the blade had lain concealed.

'The search was lacking,' said Bragga, 'and my need severe.'

Horst let out a low whistle. 'That's… revolting.'

'It will be no small labour, but I can loosen enough bars to get out. A steady hand and careful eye are necessary, lest the cage entire clatters apart. Fortunately, a duarkvinn has both.' She tapped at the base of a bar, and nodded thoughtfully. 'A night of toil, and I shall be free. Maybe one other at my side. But if we're all to be out of this place, someone has to keep our gaoler's eye tomorrow. *That* task falls to whoever goes into the fighting pit first.'

Niara nodded. There was no way to know who'd go in first. Best case was it'd be someone whose cage hadn't yet been broken. 'I can do that, if they come for me. Horst?'

'What if we're caught? More than that, what if we're not? Where do we go?'

'Anywhere,' Niara replied flatly. 'There is nothing for us

here but death. At least we'll have a fighting chance on the mountainside. Who knows, we might even make it back to Concordia.'

"Tis a breach of accord to say as much, but a Barak Skarren trade route runs a few leagues westward,' said Bragga. 'If we're bold enough to make it that far, you can barter passage home.'

Horst scowled. 'If the ogors don't run us down first. They've cages full of hunting beasts, you know that. They'll be on our heels.'

'And how will you outrun them in the arena?' said Niara. 'If this is merely a choice between the ways of death, I'll choose one where I'm free. Do you have a better idea? Chances are you're dying in the fighting pit anyway. How much longer do you think you will last?'

He flinched. 'I don't like it.'

Niara bit away a flash of anger. Their numbers were slim as it was. 'I'm not asking you if you like it. I'm ordering you to come.'

He stiffened. 'Glad to follow you into death.'

She smiled. 'As you should be. Valruss, are you in?'

'No.' He spoke without opening his eyes.

'No?' she hissed. 'What do you mean, "no"?'

'I have no intention of leaving. You may do as you wish.'

And just like that, they were down to three. Bragga raised the lower lip of her mask and spat on the floor. Horst sank back against the bars of his cage.

'Called it,' he muttered. 'Grimbody's only out for himself.'

Niara glared at Valruss, and dredged deep in her soul for words to change his mind. But a man who calmly faced down a raging troggoth was not a man to be swayed by bluster, and she didn't know what it would take. Where had he come from? His accent did not hail from Concordia, nor from any place she knew… Though something about it was familiar, all the same. All she knew was that he had been here before her – before Bragga had been dragged from the wreckage of her sky-ship some weeks before. Maybe that was how he had lasted so long, by fighting when called to, and not getting involved in any damn-fool escapes.

She shook her head. The Dark Gods take him, anyway.

'Suit yourself,' she said instead. 'But we're still going.'

Niara jerked awake at the thunder-crack. She had dozed off. Pulse quickening, she scrabbled amongst the blankets for the precious scrap of steel. Bragga would kill her if she lost it.

Fingers closed on metal. Relief flooded in. She glanced at Bragga's cage. The duardin stood in her customary position. Awake or asleep, she'd said nothing since she'd pressed the broken blade into Niara's hand and clambered by into her gimmicked cage. The soft ripple of Horst's snores washing over her, Niara wrapped one end of the steel in the blanket, and went back to sawing.

Thunder rumbled. The storm was getting closer. She peered up at the cave roof, and wished she could see the lightning.

'You are afeared of the thunder?'

Valruss' eyes flickered open as he spoke. He otherwise remained unmoving, knelt in his meditative position.

'No,' she replied. 'It gives me hope. Sigmar is in the storm.'

He shook his head, crow's feet in his skin reshaping into a maybe-smile. 'So that is how you have kept your fire. You believe the God-King will sweep down from the heavens on a lightning bolt. That he will smite your salvation on the mountainside?'

Niara bristled. 'No. Why would he bother with a handful of souls? But he might send his Stormcasts.'

A soft chuckle. 'And what do you know of the Stormcasts?'

That was harder. She'd seen a chamber of Stormcast Eternals once, when they had fetched victory out of massacre at Rockfallow Gorge. Only from a distance, though. But what she *knew* went far beyond what she'd *seen*. Faith did that.

'They're heroes,' she said. 'They are salvation.'

Valruss scowled. 'Heroes fall. And salvation is better claimed than sought.'

Niara stopped sawing at the hide and fixed him with a withering stare. 'Then claim it. Fight with us tomorrow. We need you.'

'No. I am already where I belong.'

She spat her disgust. The other's fatalism struck a poor chord with his calm demeanour. 'A rat in a cage? Why's it so important you stay?'

'Why is it so important you leave?'

'Because I've a duty, that's why. I swore to Sigmar that I'd fight for those who couldn't.' *That* detail shone true in uncertain memory. 'I will choose death with a sword in my hand over any other.'

'Duty begs you to go. It commands that I atone for surviving where my brothers and sisters did not. Only then will I be worthy of the storm.'

Worthy of the storm? His earlier words echoed back with fresh resonance. *Heroes fall.* 'You're a… Stormcast? No! They're heroes who ride the lightning, not apostates in grubby garb and tattered cloaks.'

If Valruss took any offence, none showed in his face. 'Never confuse the armour with the warrior within. The armour is divine. The warrior is flesh. And flesh is… fallible.'

Disgusted, Niara returned to her sawing. 'Keep your lies to yourself. The Stormcasts are perfection. The chosen of Sigmar.'

'Proclamation is not truth. To be a hero is to strive. Nothing more. It is certainly not perfection.' One eye narrowed. 'You named me Stormcast. Why?'

Niara shook her head, angry at herself as much as Valruss. Why *had* she? The man had the physique to be one of Sigmar's chosen – and the battle-skill, sure enough. More than that, the title fitted him in a way she couldn't explain. As if she'd glimpsed beneath the torn raiment. Or maybe she was weary... too weary to argue.

'Say I believe you. You should be out in the world, fighting for a glorious age of light...'

She broke off. If Valruss was what he claimed to be – what she believed him to be – she should be respectful... even afraid. Could that cage even hold him, if he wished otherwise?

For the first time, emotion marred Valruss' expression. Not the anger Niara had feared, but an abiding hollowness. 'My host – the Knights Tempestor – fought at the forefront of the Realmgate Wars until the Dark Gods sent their greatest sorcerer against us.'

He paused. A scowl of recollection flitted across his lips. 'I slew him too late. His conjuration slaughtered my brothers and sisters. Of the host, only I survived. I awoke on this mountainside, armour blackened and melting away. Alone. Even now, my memory lies in tatters. Wisps and fragments of might-have-beens. But I know that my fellows are gone. I fear their spirits are lost, that they never regained the solace of Azyrheim and were drawn into the Dark Gods' embrace. It is my fault that it is so.'

Niara glanced around the cave. At the emptiness that was an accusation of her failure. So many dead. The patrol she'd led into the ambush was gone, all save her and Horst. For the first time she felt a kinship with Valruss, bleak though it was.

'I've lost comrades too…'

He growled. 'You dare compare your loss to mine? My kith should have been reborn, forged anew at Sigmar's hand. Now they are dust, my punishment is to suffer. Why else would Sigmar have sent me to this place?' With visible effort, he regathered his composure. 'I am to shed my blood until I am forgiven.'

Niara decided ogors were an odd path to enlightenment, but elected against saying so. Be he madman or Stormcast, she would gain little by offending Valruss.

'And how will you know when you are forgiven?' she asked instead.

'Sigmar will send me a sign.'

'And what if we're that sign? Maybe Sigmar wants you to join us.'

He laughed softly. 'No. Sigmar is many things, but he is not subtle in his wishes. The sign I seek will not be mistaken.'

Valruss closed his eyes. The first murky rays of dawn glimmered at the cave mouth. Niara swore under her breath, and redoubled her efforts with the blade.

The gaoler did not come at dawn, nor for many long hours after. For Niara, this was all to the good, for the bindings on her cage were tougher than she'd believed possible. But with perseverance – and no small cost to herself in sliced fingers – the last strip tore free as the portcullis rumbled open. She hurriedly thrust the precious scrap of steel through the bars into Horst's hand and awaited the gaoler's selection. Whose suffering would buy time for the escape?

The ogor peered myopically from one cage to the next. Then, decision made, he rumbled forward and yanked aside the door to Niara's cage. She shared a brief nod with Horst, and followed the gaoler's beckoning hand.

A raucous cheer greeted her arrival in the fighting pit. It fell swiftly away beneath the tyrant's rambling, stentorian address. The first bout was always the tardiest for that very reason. Niara normally hated the delay. Fear festered, and the cold sapped what little vigour remained. But today, every moment the tyrant rumbled on was a moment she would not have to buy. If only they'd taken Horst for the fighting pit, and not her. There would be no bonds to cut, and no need for delay.

She stooped, reclaiming the short sword she'd used the previous day. She glanced behind. The gaoler stood beneath the open portcullis, his attention on the fight to come. Good. That much was going to plan, at least.

After a cold, shivering age, the tyrant fell silent. The far gate creaked open, revealing a gangling, white-furred beast with black, ice-frosted claws. Twisted teeth parted in a hooting roar.

Niara's heart sank. A yhetee. Large as a troggoth, but faster and quicker-witted to boot. Valruss could have killed it, but she? Bloody fur and scabbed limbs betrayed wounds already taken. Maybe it *could* be done. And besides, all she need do was survive until Horst was free.

Thunder rumbled across the sky. Niara raised her sword.

Eyes closed, Valruss sought peace in meditation. He blotted out the snarls of the yhetee. The guttural cheers of the crowd. The thunder. Niara's screams of pain and challenge. She was *not* his sign. Not the sign of forgiveness.

Sigmar had shown him the path of penance, and that path lay in the carnage of the fighting pit. Not in escape. And certainly not in offering his fellows false hope of salvation. After all, who was to say they had not failed as he had? That Sigmar was not testing them all? Such tests were not to be passed, but endured until the dawn of divine mercy, or strength failed.

So why did he feel otherwise? Why did he feel a kinship? Why had he spoken so freely of his burdens? He had not in all his years as a captive. Sooner or later, everyone died. Attachment to fellow captives gained nothing.

A harsh, wooden clatter dragged Valruss from his musings.

'Oh, *crask*.'

Horst stood frozen in place, his grasping hand extended almost comically as the heartfelt curse spilled from his lips. A wooden bar from his cage tottered back and forth on the rock floor.

In the cave mouth, the gaoler lurched about. Bellowing in outrage, he lumbered towards Horst's cage, cudgel readied.

'*Kazak bryngadum!*'

Bars clattered as Bragga barrelled out of her cage. Snaring a burning brand from the fire, she hurled herself at the gaoler and thrust the glowing timber up at his face. The ogor's roar of pain drowned out the sound of sizzling flesh.

Horst slashed. Broken steel glinted. Blood welled on the ogor's forearm.

The brute flailed, striking Bragga from her feet. The cudgel smashed down. The arcing sweep ended in a meaty thud and a *crack* of breaking bone.

'I'll have you for that!'

Horst slashed again, this time at the ogor's belly. The blade snagged on the filthy apron. As he drew back for a second stroke, the gaoler backhanded him across the face. Stunned, Horst fell across the bars of his cage. The ogor's hand closed around his throat.

The gaoler spared no glance for the lifeless duardin. A struggling Horst still dangling from his grip, he lumbered towards the cave mouth.

Valruss watched until they had crossed the threshold. Would Horst find the strength to endure? To continue penance for sins Valruss could only guess at? Perhaps. Either way, Sigmar would wish no intervention. Valruss closed his eyes once more, and sought elusive peace.

Niara screamed as she rammed the sword home. The yhetee, every bit as bloodied and weary as she, screeched. Rusty steel punched through matted fur, glanced off a rib and plunged deep into the creature's heart.

With a mournful, keening wail, the yhetee fell. Niara barely made it out from beneath its stinking, smothering bulk in time. The crowd roared approval.

Heart pounding, she fell to one knee. Her left arm – her *broken* left arm – throbbed with an insistence that promised worse to come once the glamour of battle faded. The side of her face was slick with her own blood, and her right ankle ground whenever she set weight upon it. And that was before she took account of the dozen or so gashes from the yhetee's claws.

She had survived, but she had failed. She'd had to end the fight before Horst and Bragga had freed themselves.

The gaoler emerged from the cave with an indignant bellow. The ogor's face was blistered and raw. A struggling Horst dangled from his grip.

The crowd fell silent. On the balcony above, the tyrant rose to his feet and rumbled a question. The gaoler jabbed his cudgel back at the cave mouth. A booming back-and-forth began between the two ogors. Freed from the gaoler's grip, Horst scrambled on hands and knees to Niara's side and helped her stand.

'Are you all right?' she gasped.

He rubbed his neck and grabbed a short-handled mace from the ground. 'Damn near popped my head off. Otherwise, yeah.'

'Bragga?'

Horst shook his head. Niara felt a pang of loss. Maybe you couldn't *trust* a Kharadron unless your coin was good. Didn't mean you couldn't *like* one.

'Valruss?'

Horst snorted. 'Grimbody watched, and did nothing. As usual.'

'You know he told me he was a Stormcast?'

'No such thing as Stormcast. Told you before.'

'You have *not*.'

The ogors' conversation fell silent. The gaoler withdrew. Timber creaked as the tyrant made his way down the shallow stairs to the fighting pit floor. It was only now that Niara realised how truly massive the brute was – an avalanche of armoured fat and slabbed muscle come to bury her alive. Thunder rumbled fitfully, like the growl of a watchdog that hadn't yet roused itself to the challenge, but was giving the matter serious thought.

'Don't suppose he's setting us free.'

Niara sighed. Spikes of pain shot through her chest. 'What do you think?'

The tyrant halted a dozen paces in front of them. He hoisted the ironstone maul aloft. The haft looked like a toothpick in his hands. The crowd roared approval.

'I think we've upset him,' muttered Horst. 'You hang back. You can barely stand.'

Niara straightened. 'Damned if I will.'

The tyrant lumbered forward, maul back-swung and ready to strike. Niara and Horst shared one last nod, and charged.

Unburdened by a lumpen ankle, Horst reached the ogor first. The air screamed as the ironstone maul came about. Horst skidded in the snow, half turning as he fell. The killing blow swept over his head. Horst rolled to his feet. His mace cracked against the tyrant's armoured knee.

Might as well have struck the mountain itself, all the good it did.

Niara joined the fray, striking from the tyrant's left as he lumbered to crush the upstart Horst to his right. Thick furs cheated her first strike. The second slipped beneath his corroded gut-plate and drew blood.

Enraged, the tyrant spun about. The maul whirled, the sound of it lost beneath the rising storm.

'Move it!'

Suddenly Horst was at her side. His shoulder rammed Niara clear. She sprawled to the ground. Agony flared bright as broken bones ground together.

The tyrant's blow took Horst full in the chest. A sound of snapping ribs like branches broken underfoot, and he spiralled away. His pulped body struck the timber bounds of the fighting pit and lay unmoving in the bloody snow. If he had screamed, it was swallowed by the thunderclap.

Niara crawled onto one knee. Her sword arm shook with cold and exhaustion. The tyrant's rough laughter washed over her. The crowd cheered. Thunder rumbled, closer than ever before. So close she felt it in her bones. So close she could almost embrace it.

The tyrant raised his maul.

Thunder roared. Niara dropped her sword, and let it swallow her whole.

Light blazed in the darkness of Valruss' meditation. The sizzling, roiling *crack* sounded a heartbeat later. A rush of sharp, sweet air flooded his lungs. Achingly familiar and longed for, all at once. Like coming home after a long journey, or setting out anew with strong stride.

He opened his eyes. Fire raged beyond the cave, the fighting pit's mistreated timbers set alight by the lightning strike. Wind howled beyond, whipping the flames to a flurry of smoke and fury. An unnatural tempest as familiar as the lightning itself. And something else. Not words. Not even a voice. But a presence as familiar to Valruss as his grief-born burdens. One so long desired he wept as it touched his thoughts.

He remembered that feeling from long ago, from before the armour and duties of a Stormcast had claimed him. But the presence had not come for him. It barely acknowledged his existence. He was unworthy. It had come for another. One worth saving.

One worth saving. Niara's penance was done, if it had ever existed. She did not belong here. She did not deserve his fate.

Seized of a purpose he had not felt in long years, Valruss gripped the bars of his cage.

Niara staggered to her feet as the fighting pit collapsed around her. Soot stung her eyes and clogged her lungs with the sour tang of roasting flesh. Snow hissed into the rising flames. The wind plucked at her tattered clothes, but otherwise let her be, as if she stood in the eye of her own personal storm. Of the tyrant, she saw no sign. The lightning strike had hurled him away. The fire hid all else.

Piece by wretched piece, the storm tore the fighting pit apart. High above Niara's head, timber wrenched free and vanished into the tempest. A fluttering length of fur followed, then a section of planking.

An ogor plunged from the upper tiers and thudded into the fighting pit, his lifeless flesh already shrivelled and black where the fire took hold. Another succumbed at the balcony's edge, his body blazing like a torch. Panicked roars and the thump of running feet echoed as the survivors sought safety. Niara saw only flame and the starburst of black ash at her feet.

Thunder shook the sky. Taking heart from the sound, Niara limped towards where she had last seen the stairway. She had to risk the fire. To stay in the fighting pit was to die.

The flames surged. A dark shape lumbered out of the conflagration, roaring in anger and pain. The tyrant's furs and beard were ablaze. His seared face glistened like molten wax. But the maul was still in his hand.

He swung. Niara twisted. The ironstone head whistled inches past her face.

Oblivious to the pain, the tyrant came on.

Thud. The tyrant staggered and lashed out behind. Valruss strode out of the smoke, long-hafted mace gripped tight. With a wordless grunt, he swung at the ogor's head, driving him back.

The maul came about once more. Valruss darted back. When the blow passed, he struck knee and gut, and then at the head once more.

Blood crackling into his blazing furs, the tyrant cast his maul aside. When Valruss next swung, the mace was wrenched from his grasp. The tyrant snarled in triumph.

As Niara watched in horror, the ogor gathered Valruss into a bear hug. Strong though Valruss was, he was no more than a child beside the tyrant's bulk. Horror crystallised into determination, and determination into action.

Niara snatched up her sword. Tucking it in close, she levelled the blade like a lance and threw herself at the ogor as fast as her buckled ankle could bear.

Steel thunked into flesh, slicing cleanly between the ogor's ribs. The tyrant roared anew. A flailing arm struck her away, the sword still in his back. Already off balance, Niara landed awkwardly. She cried out as her wounded ankle gave way with the sound of a snapping bough.

Valruss prised himself free of the single arm that now held him. Rolling clear of the tyrant's attempt to snare him, he ripped the sword free and thrust.

The tyrant's roar died with him, the sword buried in his throat.

Her vision dimmed by pain, Niara barely saw the ogor fall. Even the wind seemed distant, its fury spent alongside her own. But the fire raged stronger than ever.

'Leave me,' she told the approaching Valruss. 'I can't walk.'

'You have no need to,' he replied, and gathered her up across his shoulders.

Valruss stared out across the mountainside. The distant ogor camp was but a dull orange glow against the deepening dusk, half hidden by the blizzard and the trees. He saw no sign of pursuit. That would come later, if any had survived the fire. By then, the snow would have covered their tracks. Or so he hoped.

Turning his back on the mountainside, he retreated deeper into the narrow cave. Niara sat before a small fire, her broken bones splinted and bound.

'Well?' she asked.

'We are safe. For now.'

She nodded, wincing as the motion tugged on wounded flesh. 'Thanks to you.'

'I am a poor steward of salvation. You must look elsewhere.'

She nodded. 'I know it wasn't just your doing. Sigmar sent the lightning, and the storm.'

Valruss nodded, though that was not what he had meant.

Should he tell her? That the lightning was portent as much as liberator, a sign that Niara was marked for greatness – perhaps even ascension to the ranks of the Stormcast Eternals themselves? A noble life – even a necessary one – but it was not his to reveal. He who had broken from his penance in a moment of weakness. The thought of that failure yawned wide in his soul.

Or... had Sigmar meant for him to act? To shepherd a worthy soul from an unworthy fate? Had penance become redemption? Was he at last worthy of Azyrheim's golden spires once more? The fellowship of his brothers and sisters?

He grimaced and discarded the thought as the fantasy of a weak heart. It was in the nature of portents to reveal what the witness most desired, and the nature of the desperate to cling to what they saw. His penance was broken. He could not go back to how he was. There was only the path forward. The old war renewed in shame. That would suffice. It would have to.

'Yes,' he said. 'Sigmar saved you.'

Niara's eyes narrowed. Her cheek twitched. 'And he has forgiven you?'

He turned away. 'The war against the Dark Gods goes on. I will be part of it again. But I will see you safe to Concordia first, so you may also play your part…' He hesitated. 'Whatever Sigmar wills that to be.'

So saying, he returned to the cave mouth, where he stood a long, lonely vigil until night fell.

WHAT WAKES IN THE DARK

Miles A Drake

Hailing from Amsterdam, author Miles A Drake makes his second venture into the Dark Imperium's alien-infested battlefields to spin a story of danger and intrigue.

While on deep void patrol, Sergeant Achairas and his Tactical Squad of Death Spectres are ordered to urgently rendezvous with a member of the Ordo Xenos. They learn that Black Station Thirsis 41-Alpha has fallen silent after reports emerged of buried xenos archaeology being uncovered. Achairas and his elite warriors must locate the heretical device capable of untold destruction at all costs, or die trying.

His eyes opened to the reflection of a ghost. An apparition stared back at him from the surface of the inky river that flowed silently below him. He regarded his own shimmering image for a moment. His ivory pauldrons were in stark contrast to the ebon ceramite plating he wore. His helm was gone, revealing bleached, hairless features – gaunt, but cast in the wide mould of a transhuman skull. His eyes were as black as the void.

'The river…' he muttered, his voice deep but barely a hiss as he overcame his disorientation. He looked up, into the rest of the ill-lit cavern.

It was vast, its obsidian walls disappearing into the gloom, and a veritable landscape of jagged black glass formed hills and peaks in the distance. The colossal space was lit by an ephemeral glow, emanating from nowhere and everywhere at once.

He stood on the bank of the Black River. That meant death

was near. Its dark waters were impenetrable, plodding and relentless as they wound their way through the mantle of dead Occludus, his home world. They gave life as they exhaled the atmosphere during each perihelion, and they brought death when they inhaled it again, on the aphelion.

His vision resolved, seeing the far bank, several hundred paces away.

It was there. *He* was there.

'Megir...' The Space Marine bowed, his voice barely a hiss. It would carry across, in the total silence of the cavern, towards the master he had never, until this night, seen.

'Achairas,' a voice returned. It was older, many hundreds of years more lifeless than his own. It was ragged, and echoed impossibly through the Stygian darkness. The voice came from the structure on the opposing bank, from the jagged throne of dark crystal, entombing his master in this place of death and silence.

That throne was the Shariax, the tomb of the Chapter Master of the Death Spectres. And it was seen only by those who were marked with doom.

Achairas regarded the Shariax, master of himself and all of his brothers, with reverence. Its crystalline lattice of dark razors, spurs and blades was woven around a cadaver in black-and-white artificer armour. The crystal was a symbiote, growing from the Megir where he sat, fusing with ceramite and flesh alike.

Achairas advanced deeper into the waters.

'Wait,' the Megir commanded, halting his steps. 'Return to the shore. This is not your time.'

'But I am in its waters...' Achairas looked down. The darkness coiled around him, tugging at his armour like the cold hands of the dead.

'You are,' the Megir agreed. 'Your destiny has been marked. And death is its end. But you must still follow the path to meet your ending.'

Achairas looked back up. The certainty of his own doom did not bother him. 'What path?'

'Follow the call. Follow it to what is buried. Learn what wakes in the dark and ensure that the Menrahir are warned.'

Achairas nodded. The words were cryptic, and he did not understand them, but it did not matter. The Megir had spoken. He had given Achairas a command, to learn something and warn the Council of Librarians that shepherded his Chapter in their master's absence.

'Now return to the shore,' the Megir commanded once more.

Achairas did as he was bidden, wading through the beckoning waters. He stepped from the shifting, glittering silt onto the broken obsidian beyond the banks. His vision dimmed, then faded entirely.

And he awoke from his dream.

898.M41 – System Thirsis 41,
Subsector Thirsis, the Halo Region

Brother-Sergeant Achairas stood with his compatriots and their new guests within the aphotic strategium of the *Vox Silentii*. He listened to the muffled chatter of Chapter-serfs and servitors as he watched the bleak orb of Thirsis 41-Alpha slowly approach on the external pict-feed. The vaulted arches of the deck were decorated with images of death and darkness.

Four of his nine battle-brothers were on deck, monitoring key systems and overseeing the serfs. The other five were attending to their various tasks about the ship, or were taking their Hours of Silence.

The Megir's warning *had* foreshadowed a call, a black-clearance astropathic cry, flagged with markers of the Ordo Xenos, from the quarantined world of Sarvakal-22b. Achairas' squad and their Nova-class frigate had been in silent vigil, monitoring the Sarvakal Cluster along the edge of the Ghoul Stars for years, lying in ambush for the retreating Cythor Fiends that fled the fury of the Black Templars' crusade.

It was beyond any doubt in Achairas' mind that the astropathic cry was the call the Megir had forewarned him of. He had immediately brought his ship to full power to make for Sarvakal-22b, and sent missives to the other four ships the Death Spectres had committed to the vigil, explaining his withdrawal from the campaign.

Several days of warp travel through the unstable sector had brought them to the source of the message, a world of nightmare oceans and monolithic alien spires. It had indeed come from an inquisitor of the Ordo Xenos. With his work documenting the Cythor Fiends' disturbing empty worlds finished, he was requesting aid for another assignment, one of a more pressing, and sensitive, nature.

That inquisitor now presented a wraith-like silhouette as he observed the feed from the *Vox Silentii*'s heavily modified augur arrays. Grey robes obscured tortured, mangled flesh and replacement machine. A mask of faceless steel concealed a flensed skull, and nearly a third of his body was galvanised metal, meshed seamlessly into his slate-grey carapace armour.

This was Inquisitor Senerbus Astolyev. Sergeant Achairas had heard the name before. It was synonymous with radical ideals, known well enough to those possessing clandestine knowledge in the Halo Region. He was an inquisitor renowned, and loathed, for turning the weapons of the enemy against the enemy. To the Space Marine, it was sound reasoning, but such a line had always to be trodden carefully, and Achairas did not yet know how light Astolyev's tread was.

'Six point eight standard days ahead of schedule, barring warp-related time oscillations,' Magos Explorator Vemek commented. 'The technology of this vessel's peculiar... adaptations... intrigues me. The augur systems and internal energy absorption coils are beyond the capabilities of most Adeptus Astartes vessels...'

The magos beside the inquisitor was a small man, entirely concealed behind augmetic replacements and bone-white robes, his four mechadendrites shuddering in excitement.

Both Achairas and Astolyev ignored Vemek. The magos had been a mild annoyance since the inquisitor had boarded with his retinue of acolytes and Adeptus Mechanicus personnel, and Achairas did *not* approve of his meddling with the vessel's systems.

'Keep your fascination to yourself,' Brother Nym reminded the magos, as he approached to join in the observations. Like all the Death Spectres, Nym was clad in black ceramite, with ivory pauldrons bearing the heraldry of a hooded skull on crossed scythes. He was albino, and completely hairless, with black, pupilless eyes. Such was the result of the faulty mucranoid gland that was present in all of the Chapter's warriors.

'I'm more concerned with the auguries themselves, magos.' Achairas steered the conversation back to what mattered.

He watched the hololithic display, studying the image of Thirsis 41-Alpha, committing the bleak geology of the planetoid to memory. It was a dead world of no consequence, orbiting a stillborn star, a brown dwarf. But the auguries had detected an energy source of unprecedented power burning in the upper crust of its scarred surface.

'The power source is situated directly below the excavation site,' Inquisitor Astolyev rasped, turning to Achairas. The inquisitor had already elaborated that it was far more than a simple excavation site. It was an operation involving an Inquisitorial shroud station – seven hundred personnel divided among servants of the Ordo Xenos and the Adeptus Mechanicus, working secretly, hidden from all other Imperial eyes.

'I take it this is a new discovery,' Achairas guessed.

'Indeed. This is… an anomaly.' The inquisitor's hesitation did not bode well.

Achairas had already been briefed about the shroud station falling silent. The Ghoul Stars were a place of unnatural danger. A station or colony going dark was not unheard of, but Subsector Thirsis was unusually quiet, unusually devoid of the typical xenos and nightmare phenomena plaguing these regions.

According to the information Astolyev had divulged to the Death Spectres, the excavation had begun eight years earlier, the goal to unearth a vast, monolithic structure of unknown xenos origin. Initial carbon readings had dated it back sixty million years.

'Could the origin of the power source coincide with the time of the last astropathic cry?' Achairas inquired. When the research station had fallen out of contact, it had submitted one last frantic signal that had been received some six weeks prior. Of course, given the nature of the medium through which astropaths communicated, the true 'time' of the cry's origin could not accurately be determined.

'Possibly,' Astolyev admitted. 'Vemek, can you discern when this power source was first detected?'

'Preliminary scans indicate that it has grown in magnitude by six point three eight per cent since our first observation,' Vemek replied, taking in the hololithic feed data. 'The growth in magnitude has been exponential, not linear. I should be able to calculate when it originated. Roughly.'

The magos chittered with his servitors, the binaric chirps indecipherable to Achairas' ears. Judging by the way the inquisitor angled his head, as if listening, he guessed that Astolyev had the prerequisite implants to understand them.

'Analysis of reverse exponential growth traces the power source's origin to seven point three three eight weeks ago,' Vemek buzzed, after a few moments.

The inquisitor sighed. Or hissed.

'Convenient,' Brother Nym growled, his drawling accent evident of his non-Occludan birth. Nym was from the marshes of Atropos Sigma, one of six worlds the Death Spectres recruited from.

'Close to when the astropathic cry might have been sent,' Achairas agreed, frowning. While it was imprecise, the times lined up too well to be coincidence. 'And I can't help but notice that the power source seems to emanate from *within* the xenos structure.'

The inquisitor did not respond.

'What is down there?' Achairas asked. His tone carried threat and command, even though he voiced the words as an inquiry.

After a few moments of tense silence, Astolyev responded. 'I don't know.'

Even with the man's augmetic voice, Achairas sensed an undercurrent of unease in the reply. It was clearly not something the inquisitor was used to saying.

Achairas knew there was one way to get more information, and that was to make planetfall and investigate in person.

898.M41 – Thirsis 41-Alpha,
Subsector Thirsis, the Halo Region

A long retro thruster burn slowed the *Vox Silentii*'s immense re-entry speed over the course of many hours, and the vessel sank into a wide orbit around the small, battered black orb of Thirsis 41-Alpha.

The ground team was diverse. Three forces, independently led, yet all unified in the desire to find answers, had embarked upon the ebon-plated Thunderhawk *Apparition*, and descended towards the eerie, rugged landscape of the world below. The inquisitor led his own team, thirty warrior acolytes in slate-grey, void-sealed carapace armour, devoid of any heraldry. Their helmets were fed by backpack-mounted canisters via thick tubes, and their optical lenses glowed a faint green. Many possessed cybernetic augmentations and their hotshot lasguns, flamers and bolters were clenched calmly in their hands. These were well-disciplined, elite soldiers, Achairas noted, not the typical rabble used by some, more eccentric inquisitors. Astolyev was known to possess a private army, and resources provided by an alliance with the Dalvarakh Explorator Consortium.

Magos Vemek led two squads of grey-robed skitarii rangers, their rebreather masks hissing vapours, and their many eye-lenses shimmering with an emerald hue. Most were armed with galvanic rifles, though a few carried faintly humming arc-rifles and plasma calivers. A trio of heavily armed gun-servitors were their support. These lumbering behemoths were draped in armour, their limbs fused and linked to multi-meltas. Their withered, grey flesh and slack, drooling jaws seemed entirely at odds with the destructive power they could unleash.

Achairas' own team was four of his battle-brothers, Tactical Marines in black ceramite. They stood in their acceleration harnesses, faceless in their corvid helms, each running over their own pre-battle mantras. Only Brother Celaeno did not bear a bolter, his flamer mag-locked to his thigh-plate instead.

Apparition's retro-thrusters roared as it decelerated through the planetoid's thin atmosphere, the interior temperature rising to almost unbearable levels for the mortals surrounding him. The modified thermal coils within the Thunderhawk directed excess heat inward, practically boiling those within, but emitting next to no thermal signature for enemy augurs to detect. Achairas patched his auto-senses into the forward display of the gunship, watching the crater, the most prominent feature in the otherwise Stygian landscape, grow as they hurtled towards the surface.

He saw the installation, the shroud station, precariously positioned over the feature's rim, three massive struts suspending it from the cliff face. Its main bulk hung below, reaching the floor, where the excavation site sprawled outward from it in the form of countless quarries and trenches snaking towards the crater's centre.

Apparition set down on the landing pad that made up the majority of the shroud station's upper surface. It was large enough to support the Thunderhawk, while providing an excellent vantage point over the surroundings.

As Achairas, taking point, stepped out of the lowering bay door with his battle-brothers, he was among the first to gaze upon the lifeless darkness of the world. A communication and augury tower protruded from the north-eastern edge of the landing pad. Four Hydra batteries would have provided cover from the station's corner points, but their guns drooped, inactive and dead. Three red-plated Arvus lighters stood wrecked in their landing spots, their hulls scorched from within.

'Secure the perimeter,' he ordered his brothers. They complied in silence, fanning out to inspect the towers and check for hostiles.

The vista beyond the landing platform was of jagged thorn-like mountains to the east. The dim red orb of the stillborn sun shimmered on the far horizon, beyond an expanse of broken plains. The thin atmosphere barely held the light, and every ragged outcropping cast long shadows.

Achairas strode to the edge of the pad that faced the crater as the other teams disembarked. A few hundred yards down, he saw the criss-cross of deep grooves and gouges, veritable chasms in their own right, leading towards the central stepped quarry.

It was there. The reason they were here.

A ruin. A lone, black apex protruded from the wounded rock, surrounded by cylindrical hab-units and Adeptus Mechanicus excavator engines. It appeared to be covered in some manner of scaffolding.

The light-devouring darkness of the pinnacle was unwholesome. Though it was scarcely larger than the workers' habs around it, Achairas felt uneasy just looking at it. It was not a sensation he was used to.

He scanned the horizon in case there was something he'd missed. Magnifying his vision, he expected to find nothing, but was surprised when he did find *something*. It was a lone black monolith, a few dozen yards in height, but many miles away.

'Inquisitor?'

Astolyev had joined him at the edge.

'That monolith in the distance. What is it?' Achairas inquired.

'The sentry pylons, we named them,' Astolyev's grating voice replied. 'The reports indicated that there were six of them, scattered out beyond the ruin at equidistant range from the centre, and each other.'

'I assume they're related to the ruin?'

'Undoubtedly. The architecture is the same. We were unable to discern their purpose, but they were projecting an unknown energy signature. A signature the augury-scans of your vessel did not detect during our approach.'

'Then something has changed,' Achairas mused.

'That seems likely,' Astolyev agreed. 'Something caused this station to drop off the grid, and these pylons are as suspect as anything else. Have your vessel continually monitor them and the ruin below. Just in case.'

Achairas raised an eyebrow, invisible beneath his helmet. The Death Spectre was not used to receiving commands from anyone other than his captain, and the Menrahir, but in this case, he would have chosen the same course of action. Thus, he relayed the command to Brother Vairan on the *Vox Silentii*.

There had been no greeting party, and the orbital bioscans had been disrupted by the mysterious energy fluctuations emanating from the buried power source. It was yet unclear if there were any survivors hidden within the station or the excavation site. Achairas drew his auspex, and ran a preliminary scan of their surroundings. The device's sensors would only pierce the upper levels of the complex, but it would provide *some* indication of what might wait below.

'No life signs near the landing pad,' he reported into the

general vox-net. 'If anything is still alive, it's deeper within the station.'

The inquisitor nodded. 'Then we move into the complex, search for survivors and extract what data we can from central cogitation. Once the station is secure, we make for the excavation site. Maintain vigilance.'

Achairas affirmed and signalled his battle-brothers to lead.

Vemek chimed in, advancing with his thralls towards the bulkhead door at the base of the augur tower. 'Are we expecting hostiles?'

'We always expect hostiles,' Brother Nym, to Achairas' right, answered. 'Chirinoids. Togorans. Cythor Fiends. Eldar. Other xenos. This station didn't murder itself.'

Achairas gestured at the Hydra batteries. They were unused. 'Whatever happened, it was no aerial incursion.'

'What then?' Vemek crackled. 'A teleportation onslaught? A–'

'We'll find out soon enough.' Astolyev waved the teams onward, to the large door at the base of the augur tower.

Vemek coaxed the airlock open with a spark of energy from his potentia coil, and the team moved into the gloom of the entrance chamber. It was powered down, the elevator inoperable, so Achairas and his squad took point, levelling their bolters as they descended the adjacent stairwell. Even though the station had pressure and air, none removed their helmets.

'Sevrim, Nym, Celaeno, with me on point. Charason, rearguard,' Achairas commanded into his squad's vox-net. Their affirmations were silent.

The four Death Spectres were followed by the inquisitor and Vemek, while the rest of the force trailed behind. A musty, clammy gloom that reeked of oil, ozone and spilled viscera met them. The walls were dull, riveted gunmetal, coated in grease and condensation. Several of the Inquisitorial acolytes activated their luminators.

'Vemek, is there any way to restore power?' Astolyev asked.

'Negative. Preliminary readings suggest power generator units are destroyed, not disabled.' The magos muttered a spurt of binaric prayer for the machines that had died in this place.

'Death is here…' Brother Sevrim, on point, gestured to three eviscerated, half-decayed corpses clustered in a gouged-open service duct. By their red robes and augmetics, they could be identified as Adeptus Mechanicus adepts. Achairas knelt and saw the patchwork crest of the Dalvarakh Consortium on the robes of one of the least dismembered bodies.

'You crewed your station with Consortium adepts?' He looked to the inquisitor.

'Yes,' Astolyev replied. 'I acquired six hundred indentured serfs of varying specialities to complement my own crew. They were to be returned afterwards, mnemonically cleansed…'

'Well that won't be happening any more,' Brother Nym cut in, drawing a glare from the inquisitor.

'Impending debts aside,' Vemek rasped, 'what happened to them? The wounds are… unusual.'

Vast raking incisions marred their remaining flesh. Even their augmetic components were shredded, as was the sheet metal behind them.

'Looks like Bloodreeks,' Brother Nym guessed, poking the remains with his boot. 'Savage. Grotesque. Generally excessive.'

Achairas suspected otherwise and shook his head. The wounds were too clean. 'These are blade wounds, of a sort, even if they are patterned like claw marks.'

'Genestealers, possibly?' the inquisitor interjected. 'Only their talons cut *that* sharp.'

Vemek shook his head. 'Electrical abrasions on flesh, and oxidation on metal suggests electrical charge,' he chittered. 'Unlikely to be genestealers, unless they have developed new biomorphs.'

'These corpses don't tell us enough. We should head deeper,' Achairas suggested.

The inquisitor nodded in the affirmative and the group continued.

More dead awaited them, several Adeptus Mechanicus personnel, blood and oil trails suggesting they'd been dragged down several flights of stairs. At the access doorway to the main body of the station's interior, they discovered three eviscerated skitarii flayed to the bone, their galvanic rifles empty of ammunition and discarded, the door rife with flash-burned bullet holes. But the real damage was in the form of oxidised tears in the bulkhead door, as if something had clawed its way through.

With the door inoperable, it fell to Vemek's melta-armed gun-servitors to widen the breach, allowing the party to move on.

Achairas led with Sevrim, stepping into the charnel horror of the corridor before them.

Silently, the Death Spectres stepped over a river of viscera, bone and augmetic remains. Several in the inquisitor's retinue hesitated for a brief instant. It was testament to their discipline that most did not.

'What a mess,' one of them muttered.

'Steel yourselves,' Astolyev reminded them. 'We are not here to gawk like greenhorn Guardsmen at the sight of the dead. Worse will come.'

'Undoubtedly,' Brother Nym agreed, rolling over a rotten, quartered torso. 'Whatever did this, they seem mostly interested in the meat. Still think it's Bloodreeks...'

Achairas studied the macabre carpet. No body was whole. Each had been torn apart, flayed and flensed. It was impossible to distinguish where one corpse ended and the next began. Las-burns, blood and oil splatters covered the walls.

'They were attempting to reach the door,' Vemek muttered. 'But it was already locked. They couldn't get out, so they just... died.'

'Whatever did this came from further inside,' Achairas observed. 'What is down that way?'

'Central cogitation,' Astolyev answered, stepping over the corpses with his stalking gait. 'Below that? The sub-levels... maintenance, aeroponics, the armoury and ground access...'

'Ground access. Could they have come from below, then?' Brother Sevrim inquired, voicing Achairas' suspicions. 'From the excavation site?'

'That is a possibility,' Astolyev nodded after a moment.

Achairas could not read the inquisitor, but his pause indicated unvoiced information. He knew something. Or guessed at something.

'That would imply that whatever did this either landed far away and advanced on foot, to avoid the Hydras...' Achairas tested the inquisitor's reaction. 'Or came from the xenos structure.'

Astolyev didn't respond, staring out over the dead. There were no other bodies to indicate who, or what, they'd been fighting. The enemy had either taken its own dead, or it had been a single-sided massacre.

'From the ruin...' Vemek muttered, partly to himself, turning a few heads.

'Could something have been down there?' Achairas inquired to both of them.

'I'm afraid I cannot answer that,' the inquisitor replied, his words slow and measured. 'The station's last reports indicated the excavation teams were unable to enter the structure.'

Vemek gave an ominous answer, his mechadendrites twitching uneasily. 'The sudden ignition of the power source within might imply some manner of activity. It could be that something... awakened.'

'Awakened?' Achairas glared at the magos.

'Uncertain...' The tech-priest held up his hands defensively. 'Pure conjecture.'

'Let us move,' the inquisitor cut in. 'If there's any data on what happened, it'll be in central cogitation.'

The team progressed through the corridor, intersected by a dozen corpse-strewn side passages leading to laboratories and monitoring stations, before they finally reached their destination.

Central cogitation was a large chamber fitted with gantry walkways that wound between two-storey-high cogitator stacks. Several of these were damaged or had been destroyed by raking slashes, and there were the mangled remains of dozens of people and servitors scattered about. At the heart, upon a central dais, was a fully intact data loom. The massive machine was all columns, humming faintly, blinking with cascades of raw binaric data. A vast network of thick cables spread out from it like arteries, feeding into the cogitator stacks, and into wall sockets. Many more connected directly to the ceiling, looping up to link to the augur station on the landing pad.

Astolyev stalked towards the dais. 'The data loom was

connected to reserve power, and given maximal priority. It must still be active, to some degree.'

'What did you need all of this cogitation power for? What were you doing here?' Achairas asked, motioning Celaeno and Sevrim to move ahead and secure the chamber. Nym and Achairas kept pace with the inquisitor, while Charason kept watch out in the hall.

'Cross-referencing,' Astolyev replied. 'It stores thousands of years of relevant data copied from the archives of both Terra and Mars – xenology, archaeology, geology, astrography, et cetera. It possesses the power to analyse, filter and compile all relevant insights.'

'All those resources invested for one archaeological investigation?'

Vemek cut in, trailing behind them. 'An archaeological investigation that might be the find of the millennium! The t– ruin possesses a metallic outer structure that is almost impervious to all forms of direct aggression.'

Achairas was mildly impressed. 'An indestructible metal?'

'Indeed,' Vemek replied, smugly, reaching the central data loom, and plugging two of his mechadendrites into data-ports.

After a few moments, the data stream flickering from feed to feed on the display, Vemek spoke. 'Or perhaps not so impervious.' He cocked his head to the side, as if confused. 'It would appear they *did* breach the outer shell. Fascinating. Bringing up hololithic visuals.'

'What!' Astolyev snapped. 'They breached the ruin?'

A hololithic geological survey image flickered to life, suspended above the data loom's access panel. Achairas saw a pyramid, colossal by the scaling of the surrounding crater, more than a mile high, and attached to some manner of immense crescent shape below. The shape beneath extended further, stretching well beyond the crater, buried in the crust of the planetoid.

'Immense... Much larger than we anticipated,' Vemek chirped in excitement. 'It appears the initial structure we found was part of a considerably larger one!'

Vemek zoomed the image to the apex of the pyramid, barely a minute fraction of its actual bulk. 'The breach was made here–'

'I did not authorise a breach,' the inquisitor interrupted. 'My orders were to send an astropathic message with each major advancement.'

'Yes, erm, regardless, it would appear the research team used vortex charges to gain access to the apex.'

'When did this occur?' Achairas already suspected the answer.

'Seven weeks ago...' Vemek hesitated, his mechadendrites slumping. 'To the cessation of all further records.'

'The day the station was silenced,' Astolyev muttered. 'Undoubtedly not a coincidence...' He turned sharply to the magos. 'You told me your researchers were reliable. I specifically ordered them not to perform any hasty actions without first acquiring my consent.'

'Evidently I made a miscalculation.'

Astolyev snarled, shaking his head. 'And *who* authorised the breach?'

'That is unclear,' Vemek replied. 'All records of who gave the orders, and to whom they were given, have been deleted.'

Astolyev flexed his organic hand, clearly unsettled by the revelation. 'Then one of your men has compromised this operation by acting too swiftly. Or it was sabotage. See if you can dig deeper.'

'Unfortunately, many of the station's records have been compromised by an unknown data corruption. And, as there is no data, and your personal crew made up a significant portion of the station's crew, it is also a notable possibility that it was one of *your* men that acted hastily.'

'I select for loyalty and obedience, Vemek. My men do not act without my express consent. It was *your* team that formed the weakest link, not mine.'

'Can we get a visual feed from interior surveillance?' Achairas inquired, ignoring the argument. 'I want to know what we're dealing with.'

'Negative. Interior feed is corrupted. In any case, all of the station's primary functions were shut down thirty-two minutes after the breach was made.' The magos' fingers flitted over the control console. 'I detect traces of a viral onslaught, but I cannot identify the source. Only the enhanced aegis systems hardwired into the data loom saved *this* relic, Omnissiah be praised.'

Achairas glanced around. The acolytes and skitarii had taken cover behind the cogitator stacks, assisting his battle-brothers in covering each entrance. The inquisitor moved to the data loom, adjusting several of the runes and zooming the image out. Six other points were highlighted and arrayed in an equidistant radius a few dozen miles from the central pyramid.

He magnified one of those. It was one of the pylons Achairas had seen earlier from the landing pad. It was buried some thirty yards beneath the surface, its pinnacle barely visible. It was clear that excavations had been performed around it as well. The damage to it was obvious. Vemek flitted through the images of the other pylons, and it became evident that all of them had been at least partially destroyed.

'These were intact before!' Astolyev snarled, whipping

towards the magos. 'Find out what happened! I did not authorise their destruction.'

Vemek hastily complied.

Shaking his head in rage, the inquisitor circled around Vemek like a predator while the magos frantically sifted through the data stream. Minutes passed before Astolyev shoved Vemek aside and seized the access panel himself. The magos retreated to his skitarii, evidently not wanting to stand near the inquisitor.

'I suppose the destruction of the pylons might explain why they were no longer emitting energy signatures,' Achairas mused.

'Yes,' Astolyev hissed. 'That would be logical.' He paused for a moment, sifting. 'It would appear as though my researchers discovered that the energy fields emitted by the pylons were linked, like... some manner of fence around the ruin. It did not seem to affect our vehicles and personnel, however...' He trailed off, inspecting the data feed closer. 'What! They were destroyed under *my* authority! Somebody used *my* access codes to relay orders to this station.' He aggressively hammered a few more codes into the panel, before stepping back, exasperated.

'Naturally,' he spat. 'The data concerning when and where these orders originated was *deleted!*'

Achairas did not know what to make of the foul play. Had somebody deliberately sabotaged the inquisitor's work, or were there elements within the excavation team that had become hasty, and careless in their assessment of this 'miraculous discovery'? In any case, he had no time to ponder it as his auspex flickered to life.

'Unidentified movement, two hundred feet due north,' he reported into the vox-net. 'Approaching through access corridors.'

The inquisitor and Vemek knelt down behind a fallen cogitator stack in the centre of the defensive ring.

'Protect the data loom!' Astolyev shouted.

In a matter of moments, Achairas counted scores of contacts converging on their location from multiple angles. As Achairas and the inquisitor relayed their orders, the teams repositioned, with the Death Spectres taking forward positions around the data loom, concealed behind the cogitator stacks to inflict maximum damage if violence broke out.

'Survivors?' Vemek chittered.

'If so, they've picked a rather aggressive way to announce their presence,' Brother Nym retorted.

Seconds later, the first shape emerged, not sixty feet from Achairas. By the look of her tattered garb, she was an enginseer. Coming to a halt, she stood there, regarding them with her three augmetic eyes. Shredded red robes clung to her heavily augmented body, and with some disgust, Achairas noted that remnants of flayed flesh were interwoven into the cloth, making a macabre cowl. Her fingers had been severed, and razor-sharp blades were crudely grafted in their place.

Vemek muttered some binary spurt, and she turned to regard him as a score more shapes, similar in apparel and disfigurement, emerged behind her. Brother Sevrim flanked them, unseen between the cogitator stacks.

The chittering of binary echoed from the ragged rabble approaching them. To Achairas, it sounded like static, except for the alien syllables interspersed between the clicks and crackles. Even his unaugmented ears could hear them.

'Llandu... Gor...' the words came, slithering through the noise. Somehow, they were an affront to Achairas' ears. This was something vile. Alien.

Vemek started back, leaving his cover and retreating.

'Corrupted data streams. The binary is broken! Kill them! Kill them all!'

The mob of mutilated Adeptus Mechanicus personnel rushed them at that instant, making his wish reality.

'Fire,' Achairas commanded calmly, into the general vox. The Death Spectres fired first, unleashing a crossfire of bolter shells from their concealment to reduce the entire charging mob to pulped meat and twisted metal in a matter of seconds.

But more came, from other passages and the gantries above. Scores of additional malformed machine cult men and women poured into the cogitation hall, descending upon the defenders from all angles with a reckless abandon born of madness. They screamed those words, again and again. Achairas did not know what they meant, and he did not care.

He spent his bolt pistol, turning half a dozen of the attackers into pulp and scrap, blasting them off the gantries above. Drawing his power sword, he sprinted between two cogitator stacks to where one of the lunatics had descended upon a skitarius, tearing into the warrior's armour with his grafted talons. Achairas scythed past the madman, delivering a decapitating strike with his power sword before twisting around and deflecting the deranged swing of another wretch with his vambrace. The talons gouged raking scratches into his armour, negligible, but deep enough that Achairas guessed the blades would be more than able to slice through the sealed joints. He cleaved the second attacker in two, reversing his momentum to disappear behind another cogitator stack and relocate.

More of the tattered creatures rushed in, some dropped by las and galvanic rifle fire from the Inquisitorial acolytes and Vemek's skitarii.

On the far side of the central dais, Brother Celaeno's flamer roared its promethium fury into another mob. The Death Spectre carefully cultivated his inferno to avoid the valuable technological relics in the chamber, whilst incinerating and blocking off as many of the charging rabble as possible.

A burst of strange, dark energy screeched through the chamber, disintegrating another madman. Achairas saw the inquisitor, his alien carbine raised, with a few of his acolytes, pressed back to the data loom as another group of mutilated lunatics darted towards them.

They didn't get far, as Achairas rushed them, having reloaded in the seconds since his last kill. His pistol roared, blowing a few more apart as Brother Charason added his own bolter fire, mulching the rest of the approaching mob.

Wheeling around, Achairas saw three more enemies leaping down from a low gantry towards Vemek and his gun-servitors, who had yet to even react. He dispatched them all with a single bolt pistol shell each.

And then there was quiet, the only noise the faint humming of the machines, and the rasp of a few wounded skitarii.

'Clear!' he shouted, his pistol still levelled.

'Clear!' his battle-brothers returned, from their positions.

He lowered his weapons. The skirmish had scarcely taken a minute.

'Station crew,' Astolyev muttered. 'Driven mad...'

'Did this station not have weapons?' Brother Sevrim inquired.

'Plenty. It was fully stocked in case of emergency.'

'Then why were they using these crude... modifications?'

Achairas stared down at the mangled remains. All of them had replaced their fingertips with scythe-like blades. Some were nearly as long as their forearms. All had draped themselves in gobbets of flesh and skin.

'Wrong…' Vemek muttered, poking at a corpse. 'Infected. Madness in their holy machinery.'

'The virus?' Astolyev guessed.

'Perhaps. We cannot know without further analysis.'

'If it is a virus, perhaps further analysis should be avoided until proper quarantine procedures are followed.' Astolyev glanced at Vemek. 'It would be… *unfortunate*… if I were to have to euthanise you.'

'Those madmen…' Brother Nym started. 'They were saying something. Over and over.'

Nobody answered. Whatever their meaning, Achairas felt uneasy about repeating the words. 'A name,' he replied, quietly. 'Llandu Gor…' He didn't know how he knew it was a name, but he was certain it was. 'Let us move on,' he offered. 'We should find out where these wretches came from. There might be more of them. We haven't seen nearly enough corpses to account for the entire station's crew.'

Astolyev agreed. 'Indeed. Vemek, stay here with your skitarii. Extract what information you can from the data loom and keep in vox contact. Sergeant Achairas, if you would lead the way. I assume your… abilities… can pick up the trail easily enough.'

Vemek nodded in deference, drawing a servo-skull from the depths of his robe and activating it. The lens of its right eye flared green, and tiny whirring gyro-systems hummed momentarily, projecting a rippling anti-gravity pulse to levitate it. Its vox-unit crackled to life under its upper jaw.

'I will follow remotely.' Vemek's voice emanated from his own vocal implants, and from the servo-skull's vox-grille.

The inquisitor nodded his assent, and motioned for his acolytes to move out. The Death Spectres led, once more.

* * *

Achairas could indeed detect the trail. Removing his helmet, he inhaled. The air was thin, but breathable. He found the severed arm of one of the tattered madmen and tasted its putrid flesh, biting deep, his omophagea *learning* and allowing him to sense the spoor in the air. Astolyev's acolytes looked upon the pseudo-cannibalistic process with unease, but their discomfort did not concern Achairas.

Choosing the access point that most of the station crew had come through, they arrived at another stairwell, descending to find yet more corpses. Helmetless, Achairas was untroubled by the darkness, his pupils widening until the whites of his eyes were no longer visible. He led, sword drawn, to the base of the stair, near ground access, where his auspex detected a lone contact one hundred feet away down a network of labyrinthine passages in the base of the station.

'This is aeroponics,' Astolyev announced, as Nym coaxed open the bulkhead door with a heavy valve handwheel. They entered into a sizeable chamber that reeked of rotten vegetation and flesh alike.

Inside were stacks of algae vats and hovels of scavenged scrap metal and organic material. It looked like a refugees' shanty, and a poor one at that. Another pile of bodies was arranged at the back of the chamber, around some manner of twisted effigy. It was a skeletal thing made of twisted plasteel, bolted and wired together in the shape of a hunched, scarecrow-like figure with immensely long talons. The entire thing was draped in tattered, rotting flesh.

'Seems your crew adopted some unwholesome idolatry,' Nym muttered to the inquisitor.

The inquisitor did not respond. His organic hand flexed.

Nym kicked the effigy, sending it clattering to the ground in a heap.

'Celaeno.' Achairas didn't need to give the order.

His taciturn, ever-silent battle-brother levelled his flamer and bathed the debris in a wash of promethium.

As it burned, Achairas turned back to his auspex, and followed the blip into the nearby service tunnels. In the confined space, he moved forward with only Sevrim and Celaeno, followed by the inquisitor and two of his flamer-equipped acolytes. Vemek's servo-skull remained behind, scanning the wreckage of the strange effigy.

The cylindrical passage was claustrophobic, its floor grating oozing with black oil. As they advanced, the auspex blip made several quick movements, traversing a few passages and then going still.

'Whatever it is, it's trying to hide,' Achairas observed.

He squeezed through several smaller ducts, his armour scraping against the walls, until the contact was dead ahead, hidden in a small service shaft. He aimed his bolt pistol at the half-open door.

'Come out and surrender. You have one chance.' His voice was cold and quiet.

'Are you one of *them?*' A woman's voice returned, terrified and exhausted.

The inquisitor shouldered past the Death Spectre, his weapon already lowered and a luminator active in his hand.

'No,' he rasped. 'Ketyanna.'

At the name, a young woman with long, dark, matted hair and pale features slid out from behind the door, falling to her knees. She was malnourished and covered in abrasions and bruises, her black robe naught but tattered rags. The inquisitor knelt, dropping to her level as she broke down in frantic sobs, clawing at him. 'Ketyanna. How are you still alive?'

'Who is this?' Achairas inquired.

'My xenolinguistics savant. Eccentric, but one of my best.' He turned back to the woman. 'Are any others alive?'

'No...' she sobbed. 'The flayed... things... They killed them. They... ate them. They've been hunting me for... for I don't know how long.'

'What happened to the station? Why did everyone go mad?' Achairas cut in.

The woman started back, only now noticing the Death Spectre.

'They came from below...' she hissed, looking around in terror, as if expecting *them* to appear again. 'From the tomb. Metal things with clicking claws and horrible empty eyes. Machines. But mad. Mad machines...'

'Machines?' The inquisitor cocked his head. 'From the... *tomb?*'

'That's what it is. It's a tomb. They came from the tomb. They killed everyone... Everyone in the excavation site. They clawed their way in here and they slaughtered. They killed and killed and killed. Some of us lived... But...' She trailed off, staring out behind Achairas, down the way they'd come.

'But...?' Achairas glanced behind him, even though he heard no one. The acolytes glanced around suspiciously.

'But they went mad. The ones with the augmentations... the Mechanicus people... It got into them. It made them try to become like the things from the tomb.'

'What...?' The inquisitor looked confused.

'Machines that slaughtered people and took their flesh. They wore it... They wore... us. The survivors started doing it too...'

Achairas understood. The survivors had started to imitate their killers, these 'mad machines'.

The inquisitor stood. 'I see. And this all occurred when the... tomb... was breached?'

She nodded, then bowed her head. 'The Adeptus Mechanicus men, the ones you sent to aid us with the supply ship, they shattered the pylons. They thought the pylons were protecting it…'

Achairas assumed she meant the broken structures that had powered whatever energy fence the inquisitor had mentioned. 'Protecting it?'

She shook her head violently, shuddering. 'The tech-priests said it was a stasis web, to protect the tomb. To keep us out. But it wasn't just keeping us out. No, no… It was keeping the things inside… in. The pylons were protecting everything else… And when the Mechanicus men broke the pylons… the tomb started waking up. The power source… and the things inside… The men breached the tomb then. They opened the door for the machines to come through…'

'These Adeptus Mechanicus men, you said they came with the supply ship?' Astolyev asked, his voice tense.

'Yes,' she nodded. 'They came with your orders to destroy the pylons and breach the tomb.'

Astolyev's human hand flexed, squeezing the luminator with white knuckles. 'I never sent additional men.'

Ketyanna blinked, batting away some strands of greasy black hair, her wide eyes confused. 'They were Dalvarakh Consortium…'

'Throne of Terra…' Astolyev cursed.

'This answers why the breach was made prematurely,' Achairas noted, remembering Astolyev's connection to the Explorator Consortium.

'So I've been infiltrated,' Astolyev growled, his tone somewhere between spiteful and impressed. 'It would seem my *benefactors* had an ulterior agenda. What a surprise… I knew the Dalvarakh Consortium had an interest in illicit xenos artefacts, but defying a direct order from the Inquisition. That... is heresy.'

'It could be a fringe element within the Consortium,' Achairas offered. 'Perhaps they are traitors, or a group of more radical intent than your own.' The Space Marine duly noted the xenos carbine the inquisitor carried, but said nothing.

'I believe I will need to have a word with Vemek. He's one of the few who had access to my clearance codes. And he *was* Dalvarakh...' Astolyev said, helping the battered woman to her feet. 'Very well, Ketyanna, the remaining survivors, at least the ones here, are dead – I will have several men escort you to our drop-ship.'

'D-dead?' she stuttered. 'Is it safe?'

'Hardly,' the inquisitor muttered. 'But let's get you out of here. You will give me a detailed account of *everything* that has transpired in my absence once I return. Until then, you will rest. And recover.'

Guiding the traumatised woman through the tunnels proved difficult, since she refused to enter the aeroponics chamber because of the altar. Even with Astolyev's assurances that it was destroyed, she would not so much as move towards it, so it fell to Achairas to carry her along. Her sobs stopped when she saw the shattered, burnt husk of the effigy and the force of grey-armoured Inquisitorial acolytes. Astolyev turned to two of them. 'Nerek, Ariane, take Ketyanna back to the gunship. We will debrief her properly once we've investigated this... tomb.'

Then the inquisitor wheeled towards Vemek's drifting servo-skull.

'Magos Vemek! If you would kindly explain how Dalvarakh

Consortium agents infiltrated my station, I might refrain from having you executed on charges of sedition and heresy.'

The skull drifted away, seemingly involuntarily. *'Inquisitor, my ties with the Dalvarakh Consortium were severed many years ago. After our altercation on Disnomia Four, I believe they branded me a heretic. It was only by your wisdom that I was acquitted.'*

'Indeed, now tell me I haven't been played for a fool!'

'You have not. My loyalty is to you, inquisitor. Not to the Dalvarakh Consortium. It is possible they have acquired information about your station through other means. Perhaps the personnel you purchased from them were not properly mnemonically censured. Perhaps one of them was warded against it deliberately, and continued feeding information to them following their arrival here.'

The inquisitor did not reply initially, his metal mask concealing whatever thoughts undoubtedly raged through his mind.

Vemek's logic appeared sound to Achairas. What was less clear was why the inquisitor had utilised the aid of alleged hereteks, wielding xenos weaponry and delving into a mystery best left buried. He shook his head, and forced his suspicion away. He knew the Inquisition had to tread a line far closer to damnation than the Adeptus Astartes did.

'So...' the servo-skull chirped, *'you are not going to have me executed?'*

'No,' the inquisitor snarled. 'For now. Keep to your task. This ruin remains our priority. I will sort out the matter of treason later.'

From there, the team navigated their way out of the lower tunnels into ground access. They descended a long stairwell marked with trails of dried and flaking gore, but found no further bodies. Achairas strode beside the inquisitor with the servo-skull trailing behind, keeping its distance from Astolyev.

'You authorised the construction of this station, yes?'

'Indeed. Eight years ago, after the discovery of the ruin by an Adeptus Mechanicus Explorator vessel.'

'I take it this Explorator vessel belonged to the Dalvarakh Consortium?'

'Yes. But it was lost with all hands. Its astropathic choir managed to send out a distress cry, but as most of the choir were presumably already dead, the cry was weak. My agents operate in this region to monitor the movements of the Cythor Fiends. They were the only ones to receive the message. My spies within the Consortium are certain that they never learned of this ruin's location.'

'Out of curiosity,' Achairas inquired, 'what destroyed this Dalvarakh vessel?'

'Cythor Fiends, naturally. One of their so called Pinion-class stealth frigates. The wreck is still in-system, orbiting the brown dwarf several astronomical units out. My personal investigation of the wreck uncovered the location of this ruin. I copied the data from the Explorator vessel and destroyed its archive. The Dalvarakh do not know of this. It *is* possible that what Vemek suggests is true, that my mnemonic censure went faulty on one of the purchased adepts. Or... that one of them was deliberately altered to resist it, and report my findings to the Explorator Consortium.'

'Or this could be Vemek's doing,' Achairas offered quietly.

'Unlikely. Vemek's crimes against the Dalvarakh Consortium created a rift between them that will never heal. He *could* be involved with fringe elements, however – individuals within the Consortium who have pursued the research of xenos technology farther than the others.'

'What was Vemek accused of, exactly?'

'Modifying his personal Explorator vessel with holo-fields captured from an eldar wreck.'

Achairas was silent. He shook his head.

'I know, you're probably wondering why I conscripted him into my service. This isn't the core Imperium, where purity and heresy are easily drawn lines of white and black. Out here in the Halo, we are on the edge of damnation. We must tread the grey in between and utilise every bit of knowledge we can to gain an edge. Xenos, natural and unnatural, plague us from beyond the Halo, and space itself seems to want to destroy us. The xenos out here are able to survive. They are able to tread the impossible reaches of the Ghoul Stars themselves. I *will* learn how they do it. And then I will implement that technology into a grand crusade fleet, and deliver the fiery sword of the Emperor's judgement into the heart of all the vile aliens populating these unnatural stars. You, of all people, must understand...'

Achairas blinked. It was an ambitious plan, borderline megalomaniacal. And it didn't sit well with him. One often didn't realise that the grey line between purity and damnation had been crossed, until it was far too late.

'I am a radical, Sergeant Achairas,' the inquisitor continued, as the group reached the ground access airlock gate. 'I do what I must for the good of the Imperium. If I am damned for it, then that is the price I will pay.' He flexed his mechanical arm. 'I have already given my flesh for the Imperium, the only thing I have left to give is... my soul.'

'It is not my place to question your conviction, nor your methods,' Achairas said at long last, his inner conflict evident enough in the tension in his words. 'My purpose is to destroy the threats to the Imperium, whatever they might be.' He let the words, the threat, hang in the thin air as he re-donned his helm and gestured for Nym and Sevrim to wheel open the airlock.

When the door was coaxed open, they saw the gouges in the outer hull of the station; it looked as if raking talons had torn open the thick sheet-metal.

Several of the Inquisitorial acolytes brought forth lascutters and widened the gap, allowing the team to descend, two by two, over a steep access gantry that traversed the lower slope of the crater. After a few minutes, they emerged out from under the shadow of the station, and found themselves beneath the cold, lightless sky of Thirsis 41-Alpha.

They followed an excavated chasm-turned-road, winding between the jagged rocky outcroppings amidst the muted red glow of the stillborn sun. Vemek's servo-skull crackled, rejoining the head of the column. *'I have detected seismic activity emanating up from the ruin.'*

'We have felt nothing here,' Astolyev noted.

'Minor *seismic activity, inquisitor. Small quakes, but frequent. The power source continues to build, at a heightened rate.*'

'Interesting. Keep me updated.'

The road gouged in the crater's base led to a sizeable secondary quarry half a mile from the station's shadow. Cliffs of black rock jutted up around them, and small cylindrical dwellings shared space with heavy-duty tracked vehicles. All of them were torn open, deep rents ripped in their hulls. The mutilated remnants of servitors and Adeptus Mechanicus personnel were scattered about, left open to the void. As the Inquisitorial acolytes and Space Marines picked through the wreckage, they discovered many more bodies littering the impromptu streets of the chasms, and hidden away in the structures.

'They tried to hide.' Vemek's voice chirped through the vox. *'Or they tried to run. Neither worked.'*

'Strange,' the inquisitor muttered. 'I highly doubt we've seen more than a few hundred corpses. This station had a crew of seven hundred.'

The comment only added to the sense of unease as the team followed Astolyev's lead down a small road towards the centre of the excavation site. The road broke out into a massive quarry, with many tiers of levelled rock cut directly into the crater. It resembled an amphitheatre of immense scale, one hundred and fifty feet deep and nearly a thousand wide. More cylindrical structures and cargo vehicles sat abandoned, interspersed with the massive excavator engines.

At the centre, Achairas saw the structure that was the goal of this entire endeavour.

The apex.

The pinnacle of a pyramid, jutting forty feet into the air, jet-black and reflectionless. Scaffolding scaled its smooth flanks, and as the team approached, moving down the switchback road that descended into the dig, Achairas noted the strange green symbols adorning its sides. Arrayed in columns, the alien glyphs glowed with a faint but unsettling emerald light. Green lines radiated out from the glyphs, arranged over the slopes in a pattern that Achairas could not understand.

The Space Marine felt cold pinpricks on his skin, and heard the faint sound of trickling water. He shuddered. His growing disquiet was not something he was used to.

Even though the structure itself seemed relatively small, their knowledge of the immensity that lurked below only added to the sense of foreboding. The acolytes gripped their weapons tighter as Astolyev cautiously strode forward, ahead of them.

Between the scaffolding, Achairas saw a molten wound in the side of the pyramid. A ten-foot-wide circular gap had been blown, at ground level, through the thick metal skin of the apex.

The inquisitor shook his head. 'Idiots. Overambitious fools...' He stalked forward.

Achairas and Vemek's servo-skull followed. The Death Spectre kept his bolt pistol trained firmly on the entrance, and double-checked his auspex. The energy readings it picked up were bizarre. He'd never seen anything like them.

'*Intriguing...*' the servo-skull chirped. '*The pict records of the breach created by the vortex charges show a far larger gap than this one.*' A crackling noise emerged from the skull as it flitted up to investigate the gap. '*Marvellous! The wound appears to be healing! Self-knitting metal!*'

'Healing?' Achairas cut in, kneeling before the ruin, and zooming his auto-senses into the molten metal edge of the breach. Another shiver travelled up his spine as he saw tiny trickles of dark liquid pooling in the rough gouges. He watched as they solidified, becoming the same glossy, black metal of the pyramid itself. It *was* self-repairing. Before his very eyes.

'*Imagine the potential!*' Vemek's skull chirped again. '*If the Mechan– the Imperium were to acquire this technology, the boon to our war engines and voidships would be immense... Not to mention the benefits the power source itself might provide. It is a growing source of energy, exponentially so. And the scans showed no power being fed to it from external sources. Can you imagine, inquisitor? Infinite energy! We must retrieve it, or make visual contact. I possess the necessary sensory equipment to make a full diagnostic scan of the energy source, and would very much like to collect data.*'

Achairas shared a glance with the inquisitor. The magos' claims sounded an awful lot like lunacy, and he sincerely hoped the inquisitor felt the same.

Astolyev hissed. 'Yes. Then we go inside.'

Achairas agreed on that, at least. They needed answers. He cared nothing for the vague boons this discovery might provide. He did, however, care about the threat contained within the ruin. He needed to know what, exactly, the inquisitor's project had awoken in the dark, and how to destroy it.

'Be prepared,' Achairas whispered to his brothers over their private vox-net. 'The magos is clearly delusional. He will *not* have access to this technology if I deem it too dangerous. If the inquisitor disagrees, and stands in our way, we take action.'

'The permanent kind?' Nym inquired.

'There is no other kind,' Achairas retorted grimly.

'Against an inquisitor?' Even Nym sounded hesitant.

'If necessary. Yes.'

'Check your weapons,' Astolyev ordered. 'Say your prayers. We enter the belly of the beast. We are here to acquire answers. If our erstwhile Adeptus Mechanicus allies have awoken something down here with their impertinent ingress, then we need to know what it is. Get visual contact, and if possible, kill what we find, so we can take samples back with us. Understood?'

A series of affirmations returned to him.

Achairas turned to his battle-brothers, the sound of running water clear in the back of his mind. 'Death is coming. It is waiting. Today, we meet it.'

Silence was all that answered him.

And with that, the Death Spectres took the first steps into a darkness that even they could not find solace in.

Achairas was awestruck by the black, cyclopean architecture within. The chamber in which they stood connected to a descending passage that spiralled downward, following the interior slope of the pyramid like an inverse gyre. Faintly glowing, emerald geometric panels were splayed on the walls, bearing symbols that he could not even begin to guess the meaning of. A dull rumbling hum began to sound as they advanced, accompanied by a series of light tectonic shudders.

Streaks of dust, which Achairas' auto-senses identified as organic residue, created something of a trail for them to follow, though there were no side passages to lose themselves in. Unfortunately, the settled dust was far too degraded to quickly determine its origin.

'The power source,' Vemek's servo-skull muttered. *'Its growth is escalating further. I speculate that you entering the ruin has triggered some manner of response. I advise haste.'*

The further they descended, the more expansive the passage became, even if the feeling of claustrophobic oppression only worsened. It reached a point where even the Death Spectres felt tense, and utterly unwelcome in the unwholesome, alien darkness of the place.

'The geometries of this... tomb are incorrect.' Vemek's skull crackled, the voice growing even more distorted.

The dusty trails led to where three almost skeletal corpses, part-machine, had been scattered across the obsidian floor.

'More station crew,' Astolyev muttered, prodding one of the tattered red rags with his augmetic foot.

'They were dragged down here,' Achairas observed, understanding the origin of the dusty trails, now easily identifiable as flaking blood and viscera.

They continued down the ever-widening passage into a monolithic chamber filled with randomly spaced obelisks of black metal, and faintly glowing green nodes on the wall. Emerald prisms, pulsing softly, stuck out of almost every flat surface, even as the geometrics of the structure became more complex.

Deeper down, the oppressive darkness began to play tricks on them. Phantom auspex blips flickered and ceased periodically, appearing around them, sometimes in the walls, sometimes clustered behind them. Out of the corner of his field of view, Achairas was almost certain he saw movement, here and there. For an instant, he thought he'd seen a shape, large and sinuous, flitting across the wall. But when he turned, it was gone. Judging by the jittering movements of the acolytes, they were seeing things as well.

More dismembered corpses dotted the way. Dozens had been dragged down here and abandoned in the darkness. It was only when one of Astolyev's acolytes cried out that the true danger was revealed. Achairas whirled to see a darting shadow vanish into the unwholesome angles of the wall. An acolyte at the rear of the group fell to the ground in gory pieces.

'Ambush!' Achairas shouted. Weapon raised, he saw a strange pulse flicker through the glowing runes just as a shape erupted from the wall once more, giving him his first clear view of the phantom that stalked them. Its sinuous, metallic form was somewhere in between that of a mantis, a centipede and a scorpion, but shimmering as if it were hardly even there. Brother Charason managed to fire a few shells into it, but they passed straight through, striking the wall behind. The phantom ghosted towards him, snaking coils of barbed metal erupting from its form to ensnare the Death Spectre.

Las and bolter fire ripped across the apparition, some striking Charason, even as three of the thing's six talon-like appendages scythed through the Death Spectre's gorget.

Phasing back into reality, the wraith-like creature slipped away, tearing its claws free from Charason's throat in a spray of crimson. Achairas rushed to intercept its erratic escape, slashing with his power sword. The creature coiled away like a serpent, avoiding the swipe. Achairas' momentum took him around the thing as it lashed out with its tendrils. He spun backwards, feeling his sword connect with its centre of gravity. It fell to the ground, partly bisected, three of its limbs and half of its tendrils sheared off. Seizing the opportunity, he drove into it.

He uttered no war cry, no words as he fought. He was locked in the deathly silence of battle's murderous focus. A talon raked his greave, while several of the creature's tendrils coiled around his neck. All he heard was the sound of rushing water. The river flowed around him, its cold, black currents threatening to take him along.

Not yet, he thought, and delivered a series of economic stabs, his blade passing through the creature several times as it flickered out of material existence. Then a blinding burst of dark energy struck the thing's metal ribcage, vaporising part of it and sending it clattering against the far wall. The tendrils slackened and fell away. Achairas staggered back, severing the talon still latched around his knee for good measure.

And then there was silence. Astolyev stood there, his elegant xenos carbine held in his hands, aimed at the remnants.

'Clear!' Astolyev shouted, and his acolytes responded. The Death Spectres remained quiet.

Achairas knelt beside the near decapitated body of Charason. Several of Astolyev's men bowed their heads out of respect, or reverence, evidently unsure of how to react to a dead Space Marine.

'Drink deep of the Black River, brother,' Achairas said,

switching off his vox so none could hear. The rushing water quieted to a steady trickle. The other Death Spectres said nothing. There was nothing to say. Death was silent, and so were they who embodied it.

Astolyev moved to inspect the fallen creature. Two of his acolytes were dead, another slain by an off-hand swipe of the creature's talon during the fray. He bade one of his men, wearing confessor's robes over his armour, to administer rites to the fallen.

Achairas joined the inquisitor.

'Machines,' Astolyev remarked, impassively watching it twitch and shudder, as if it was still partly functional.

He was kneeling to study it more closely when Achairas again heard the rushing water, and shoved the inquisitor aside, delivering a savage decapitating strike to the creature even as it lurched to life again. His blade passed through it, and it snaked away, coiling through the darkness in a revolting manner as the startled acolytes fired again. Whether any shots connected was unknown, as the thing slipped into the obsidian ceiling of the hall some thirty feet up, as if it weren't even there.

Rising, the inquisitor nodded to Achairas. 'Not dead…' he rasped. It sounded like a laugh. 'Wonderful. Self-repairing walls. Self-repairing machines. What next?'

With no remains to study, and nothing to be done for the dead, the team advanced, more cautiously than before. The spiralling descent came to an end as they entered some manner of narrow chamber composed of dozens of passages, honeycombing the walls at various heights. Half-liquefied pillars, part black chrome, part quicksilver, connected to a high ceiling, and the trails of dried blood continued through it. The strange alien glyphs on the walls seemed to flicker, sporadically. Dozens of small xenos creatures drifted about, some clinging to the walls and ceiling, with others erratically flitting around the pillars. A central obelisk, covered in glowing nodes, was tended by another dozen of the things. They were no larger than a man's torso, fashioned from glinting black metal and scarab-shaped. They hardly showed on his auspex at all.

Achairas set his sights on one of them; it registered as a minimal threat, even with its clacking, bladed mandible apparatus. It chewed through the small pylon it hovered around, piece by piece, before drifting a short distance right and seemingly regurgitating the liquefied metal into the form of a brand new pylon.

'What are they doing?' Astolyev inquired. The scarabs seemed to be randomly rearranging pieces of the interior for an unknowable purpose. They ignored the advancing team, and each other, as they periodically collided, before righting their course and moving about their erratic business.

'Strange...' Vemek's servo-skull hissed. *'I can extrapolate some manner of preset routine among them. They appear to be moving about in a loop, taking matter from one pillar and rearranging it into another. The loop appears to be redundant. A repetition. I believe they are... glitched.'*

'Glitched?' Astolyev turned to the servo-skull.

'Like malfunctioning servitors. But different. Caught in a cycle of endless assembly and reassembly... Horrible...'

'Right,' Astolyev muttered. 'If they're not a threat, then we can come back and capture one later.'

'That would be most excellent,' the servo-skull agreed.

'In the meantime, any news on the power source?'

'It was building the last time I observed it, but fluctuating in a similarly erratic manner. Most peculiar.'

Passing through the increasingly labyrinthine network of pillars, obelisks and prisms, the team followed the sporadic trail of corpses until the passages became so dense as to be tunnel-like. They reached what was clearly a damaged area of the structure. Cracks ran through the dark metal like infected veins, and the crystals pulsed more rapidly, causing the emerald light to flicker across the alien geometry in an unsettling manner. Achairas felt the ground shake several times, and he heard a deep rumble coming from somewhere below. They moved on, descending further.

His auto-senses detected the stench before they saw the atrocity appear in the darkness before them.

'We found the rest of the station's crew,' Nym announced as they strode into a blanketed mess of desiccated, mutilated remains.

Heaps of dead, hundreds, were scattered about the passage.

'God-Emperor...' Astolyev said. 'Why drag them all down here just to leave the scraps behind?'

'Does not cogitate,' Vemek's skull crackled. *'Artificial life forms and automata only act upon existing protocols. Either this serves some alien function we are not yet aware of, or the creators of these machines were mad...'*

Achairas saw Astolyev's acolytes tighten their grips on their weapons. Mortals were not as adept at channelling their fear into focus as Adeptus Astartes were, but these men and women were performing admirably.

'Advance. We should not dally here unless we discover something relevant,' Achairas commanded.

The Death Spectres led, their weapons shifting from each

new passage to the next. As Achairas panned his bolt pistol right, he saw, some ten feet from him, a form rise up from a pile of corpses, its shimmering outline barely even disturbing the dead. It was bipedal, as tall as he was, and built like a skeletal scarecrow of dark metal. Emerald light burned in its empty eye sockets, and its fingers ended in two-foot-long talons, sizzling with energy. A crude cloak of mangled, tattered flesh, severed limbs and rotting viscera was coiled around it.

Achairas' trigger discipline stopped it before it could advance, and he turned its metal skull to metallic pulp with three bolt shells. More gunfire sounded around him as his brothers and several of the acolytes unleashed their fury. Shouts of alarm went up from the acolytes as more of the flesh-clad things emerged from the nooks and crannies of the labyrinth, as well as materialising out of the corpse piles. The thin air became thick with crimson sprays, screams and the sickening crackle of dead static. As Achairas dodged a raking swipe from another flesh-clad horror, he shot it in the jaw and lashed out with his power sword, severing its arm and then its head with the backswing.

'To me, acolytes!' The inquisitor disintegrated most of an advancing xenos with a burst of dark energy, before wheeling around to dodge a slashing blow that shredded part of his robe. He drew a short knife that hummed with sonic disruption, and plunged it into the xenos' ribcage. It lunged further into him, its talons flashing but deflected by a halo of shimmering energy. A fusillade of las-fire from a squad of his acolytes, covered by Nym and Celaeno, sent the creature staggering back into an alcove.

Achairas slashed the limbs from another, ignoring the distractions, focusing on the sound of running water. It staggered back, its severed appendage skittering across the ground to cut the legs from underneath an acolyte.

Sevrim bashed his bolter repeatedly into one xenos as it tore at his armour, as another plunged its talons through the seals under his arm. Even with such a wound, the Death Spectre said nothing, merely wheeling around with combat blade drawn to plunge it through the eye of another xenos behind him. Achairas reloaded in his moment's respite and blasted the first from his brother.

He saw his original kill rise again, its skull half-repaired. Achairas delivered a second killing strike with his power sword, cleaving it in two.

Somewhere, a trio of frag grenade crumps sounded, showering the room with a spray of pulped meat as one of the acolytes targeted the corpse piles. That seemed to be where the tattered xenos machines were emerging from.

Burning promethium showered the passage, creating a wall of roaring flames around the team, driving the flayed monstrosities back. Achairas shot down another one through the flames, only to see it rise again, its metal ribs knitting back together in a revolting manner as fire wreathed its form.

'They... won't... die!' Astolyev roared, out of breath, even though his xenos weapon seemed more effective than everyone else's.

The ragged band of surviving acolytes, now at half-strength, clustered around the inquisitor in a defensive cordon. The Death Spectres bolstered them, anchoring their position with their power-armoured presence. Achairas used his last two magazines to assist his brothers in dispersing the surrounding onslaught, stepping out of the defensive ring to slash down any creature that managed to come through.

And then, just like that, the assault was over. The remnants of the xenos simply phased out of reality, and those still standing disappeared back into the tunnels they'd come from. The rushing water subsided, and Achairas lowered his sword.

Any respite they might have gained was short-lived as a tectonic shudder lurched the entire chamber, and the dull humming grew in intensity.

'The tomb...' Vemek's servo-skull chattered, emerging from its high hiding place. *'Something is happening. My readings indicate more and more of the superstructure seems to be coming online...'*

'Coming online?' Astolyev growled, signalling the group to advance with due haste.

'Yes, the other parts of the ruin are... powering up.'

'Then we make haste,' Achairas commanded. 'Whatever this structure is, we cannot allow it to awaken! Its threat is clear enough. We must end this!'

The tunnel converged into a larger passage, angling steadily down. More scarabs flitted to and fro, most of them avoiding the advancing group. The cavernous hexagonal hall continued on for a great distance, its end lost in the emerald gloom. All the while, the humming grew louder and louder, and the quakes grew in intensity and frequency, hobbling those not blessed with the stability granted by power armour with each tremor.

More phantom auspex blips followed, but the device was rapidly becoming unusable, flickering in and out from moment to moment.

'I'm afraid we don't have long,' Vemek's servo-skull chirped. *'Immense power fluctuations det–'* The crackling voice was cut off suddenly as the entire chamber shook, and a deafening

roar echoed from further down. Several of the acolytes staggered and fell, their balance stolen by the seismic activity. All of the prisms and luminescent nodes on the floor and walls flared, painfully illuminating the darkness.

Achairas' auto-senses adjusted almost immediately, as did the acolytes' photo-visors. An energy surge disrupted everything, and for a moment, his vision became crackling static, and his power armour seized up. Thankfully, its internal dampening systems quickly compensated.

'Vemek?' Astolyev called over the din of the tremors, shuddering as his own augmetics similarly restored functionality. 'Status report!'

There was no response, and moments later Vemek's servo-skull clattered to the ground, its delicate circuitry evidently fried.

'Throne of Terra, let's move!' the inquisitor shouted, and the group advanced, jogging down the massive tunnel towards the newly growing source of blinding jade at its end.

The tunnel led them into what could only be the heart of the tomb, an open space of staggering size. More than half a mile across, the chamber resembled an amphitheatre of massive proportions. It was an inverted ziggurat, the ceiling soaring hundreds of feet above them. Massive pylons loomed in concentric circles around a central, colossal obelisk rising to a quarter of the height of the cavern. The obelisk was covered in gleaming geometric runes and prisms burning with the brightness of green suns. Even Achairas' auto-senses could not adjust, and he was forced to look away.

Millions of scarabs moved about in a wanton manner, scuttling along the walls and descending steps. More of the sinuous mantis constructs darted about while arachnoid machines the size of light tanks drifted between the smaller pillars jutting up everywhere. Achairas saw packs of metallic humanoids stalking about below, some draped in tattered flesh, others not. They seemed to chitter and claw at each other in fits of madness. It was some advantage as, at this distance, they had yet to notice their intruders.

'This is it!' Astolyev called over the distorted vox-net, gesturing at the central obelisk. 'The power source!'

Beams of energy lanced from the contained emeralds to immense prisms set into sockets on the walls, each a blinding solar flare that sent waves of heat and static resonating through the entire chamber.

Around the obelisk, at the dead centre of the inverted ziggurat, was an elevated ring, and Achairas' magnified vision noted four more metallic skeletons working on panels within its interior. They were adorned differently, with elaborate crests, and were slightly smaller and more hunched than the xenos they had fought.

'Inquisitor, can you assess what we are seeing?' Achairas shouted into his vox.

Astolyev's answer was interrupted by another sudden lurch and an increase in gravity, sending everyone but the Space Marines sprawling. Even the Death Spectres were hobbled. Surging gravity was a sensation Achairas knew all too well.

The tomb was rising. Somehow.

Astolyev struggled to his feet. 'Blood of the Emperor!'

Achairas' vision centred on the obelisk in the middle, and the projections of energy beaming from it.

The inquisitor motioned for his acolytes to take up defensive positions behind the various obelisks and pillars scattered around the upper tier of the inverted ziggurat, closest to the passage they'd emerged from.

The Death Spectres did likewise, dropping into cover so that they might make observations with less risk of being spotted. Astolyev took up position beside Achairas.

'That is the heart,' the inquisitor said. 'That is what we must destroy.'

'Yes,' Achairas agreed, glad that the inquisitor was of similar mind on what to do with it. 'I assume your expertise on xenos technology might be able to discern some manner of weakness?'

'I've never seen anything like it. Where the energy bursts are emitted from, I'd wager my life on those being weak points. But... I have another solution.' He reached into a satchel attached to his belt, and withdrew a fist-sized object that resembled some manner of exotic bomb.

'A vortex grenade,' Achairas muttered, actually impressed. Such relics were exceedingly rare.

'Count on the Inquisition to have the right tools at hand,' Astolyev returned. His mask displayed nothing, but Achairas assumed that beneath it he might actually be smiling.

'Alarm! Contacts behind us!' Brother Sevrim called over the vox-net, causing everyone to wheel around.

What Achairas saw approaching was certainly not the threat he expected to see.

Three dozen pale-robed skitarii ran towards them in two columns, with Vemek protected behind the first few ranks. Their weapons were in ready position. Somehow, the magos' titanium legs had unfolded from underneath his robes, reverse jointed and loping.

Another surge of gravitational pressure buckled everyone, including the Space Marines.

'What in the God-Emperor's name are you doing here, Vemek?' Astolyev called.

'Taking personal stock of the situation, and ensuring that our goals are met,' the magos returned, emerging from the skitarii ranks as they fanned out and started taking up positions in cover.

The inquisitor's weapon was drawn.

'I sense treachery,' Achairas whispered to his brothers over the vox. They levelled their bolters in the direction of the skitarii. If this turned to violence, it would be a battle at very close range. That suited the Space Marines well enough.

'How did you even get here?' Astolyev snarled, aiming his xenos carbine at Vemek.

Vemek held up his hands defensively. 'I followed. A mind-linked servitor is maintaining vigilance on the data loom along with my gun-servitors.'

'I did not give you the order to follow!'

'Negative. I took initiative. It would appear, given the threats arrayed between us and the power source, that you will need additional assistance.'

Achairas glanced down into the veritable valley below, and ordered Sevrim to keep watch in that direction. Thus far, the xenos there had not been alerted. The majority of the insectoid constructs continued to drift about aimlessly. The bipedal, skeletal machines shambled about in packs. If they were patrols, they seemed random and haphazard.

Another gravitational surge struck, as if the floor were rising up beneath them. Thunderous tremors tore through the cavernous chamber, momentarily deafening everyone.

'It feels as though the complex is rising,' Achairas called to Vemek.

'It *is*,' Vemek returned, his elongated legs in a wide stance to keep him steady. 'The final scans of my servitor proxy in central cogitation have suggested that the entire complex appears to be some manner of ship.'

'A ship?' Astolyev exclaimed, aghast. 'You could have mentioned this! We need to hurry. We must destroy the heart.'

'No!' Vemek crackled, equally aghast. 'I must get close enough to make an analysis of the power source, and we must capture one of those xenos engineers below.' He gestured to one of the machine-men working on the interior console ring. 'And it is of paramount importance that we harvest one of the emerald prisms on the central obelisk.'

'We don't have time for that!' Achairas interrupted. 'If this entire complex is a ship, it is far larger than even a battle-barge of the Adeptus Astartes. We are not yet aware of the danger it poses, but I will not allow an unknown xenos vessel of this size to threaten the Halo Region. If destroying this power source has any chance of crippling it, it is a risk we must take.' He looked to the inquisitor. Achairas honestly did not know which way this would go, but if Astolyev decided to follow the magos' exceedingly reckless plan to steal forbidden xenos technology, at the cost of allowing a potential threat to free itself from the prison of this world's mantle, he would respond with whatever force was necessary.

He tightened his grip on his power sword.

Astolyev nodded. 'Acolytes, we make for the obelisk. Cut us a gap through whatever stands in our path.' He raised the vortex grenade in his mechanical hand. 'We end this.'

Vemek took a step back, his heavily augmented face betraying nothing. Achairas nodded in thanks to the inquisitor for seeing reason.

'You must not!' the magos exclaimed, drawing a pair of flechette pistols from his robes. His skitarii trained their weapons on the Inquisitorial acolytes and the Death Spectres.

'Are you mad?' Achairas cut in, levelling his power sword at the magos.

The inquisitor raised his xenos carbine. 'Vemek, don't do anything we'll both regret...'

'I have invested far too many resources in the pursuit of the knowledge buried here!' The magos' mechadendrites twitched, and Achairas saw the madness then. Whether it was greed, ambition or something else, this tech-priest was not whole of mind. 'I *will* acquire the data I need! My research must be completed if I am to return to the Consortium–'

'You did this!' Astolyev shouted back, accusation marring his augmetic voice. '*You* ordered the breach under my authority! That is sedition, treason and heresy!'

The commotion was drawing attention. Already, one of the arachnoid constructs was drifting over, cloaked in a halo of shimmering scarabs.

'Inquisitor...' Achairas warned. His battle-brothers started taking up positions against the oncoming monstrosity. The inquisitor ignored the warning, squaring off against Vemek. The skitarii and acolytes mirrored their masters, kneeling into firing positions.

Achairas shook his head, disappointed. 'Inquisitor!' he shouted. 'The xenos!'

'Vemek!' the inquisitor roared. 'We can settle our dispute later. For now, we have a common–'

Vemek fired, a burst of flechette rounds pattering over the Inquisitorial group like raindrops. The inquisitor's refractor field shimmered, absorbing the impacts targeting him, and several of his acolytes staggered. One fell. The skitarii fired in unison. Galvanic slugs, incandescent plasma fire and arcs of blinding electricity felled acolytes and forced the rest into cover.

The acolytes recovered quickly, and immediately retaliated, turning the entire upper step of the inverted pyramid into a criss-crossing web of gunfire.

'Fools!' Achairas shouted. 'Celaeno, burn the traitors! Sevrim, Nym, watch those xenos!'

The spider machine was approaching, drifting up towards them like an immense spectre, a nightmare apparition of glowing optical lenses and scything limbs. The smaller, hovering scarabs flitted around it. His brothers immediately began to fire.

Achairas dashed into cover as a plasma burst turned the small pillar before him into molten slag. Breaking from the destroyed cover, he charged the plasma caliver-armed skitarius, cleaving him in two and moving on to decapitate the next in line on the skitarii's left flank. A third pounded him with a volley of close-range slugs. They struck his breastplate and staggered him, but did not penetrate. Another skitarius fired at his knee joint. Twisting, he took the impacts to the greave, barely keeping his feet as he rushed forward, slashing the first's galvanic rifle in two, and bashing his fist into the skitarius' titanium-plated skull a few times before it pulped. With a deft twist, he seized the falling corpse, raising it to absorb more fire from the skitarii ahead of him.

Darting behind another pillar, Achairas feinted right but ran left, the skitarius corpse and his pauldrons absorbing most of the impacts, before he slammed into the traitors, hurling the carcass away. In close quarters, Achairas became a true spectre of death. Never breaking momentum, he weaved from cover to cover to avoid their fire, and delivered killing stroke after killing stroke with his power sword. The skitarii were competent, elite even. But they were no match for a Space Marine. Distracted by the last few acolytes' assault on their main line, they were unable to stop the Death Spectre from making quick work of their left flank.

On the right, the remnants of the Inquisitorial team retreated down one step of the amphitheatre, pinned behind a few pylons. They were being rapidly whittled down by the skitarii's superior armaments. Galvanic slugs tore through the acolytes and thumped into Celaeno, even as the Death Spectre covered their retreat with a wide sweep of burning promethium from his flamer. Celaeno staggered, falling, his armour fractured in places from high-velocity impacts. An arc rifle flared, scorching another pair of acolytes to the bone before the inquisitor himself disintegrated the offending skitarius with a burst of dark energy. Celaeno rose again, stumbling, spraying more promethium to create an infralens-disrupting heat flare that would befuddle the aim of the enemy.

Darting into cover, Achairas halted his advance, as Vemek himself, now exposed, drew some other manner of pistol from his robe. 'I did *not* wish for it to end this way!' the magos screeched.

The sound of rushing water surged around Achairas once more, grasping at him with its inviting cold.

The magos fired, a beam of energy shattering the toppled pillar that Achairas knelt behind. The Death Spectre immediately relocated, taking cover behind a taller pylon.

'Fools!' Vemek shouted, realising that he too had other problems. A trio of mantis-like machines had descended on him from behind, tearing into his remaining skitarii.

'Achairas!' Astolyev called across the vox. 'We must reach the obelisk! If we destroy that, we can end this!'

Achairas relayed the command to his brothers and moved to disengage, taking a moment to survey how Nym and

Sevrim were faring. They'd split up, attacking the spider construct from both sides, Nym darting from pylon to pylon as the engine focused on him, projecting emerald arcs of energy at the Death Spectre. But Nym was too quick, his momentum keeping him just ahead of the spider's attacks as Sevrim closed in and lobbed krak grenade after krak grenade into the thing's abdominal section, blasting away chunks of liquefied metal.

Achairas left Vemek and his skitarii to fend off the mantis-like constructs, and rushed towards the inquisitor and his few remaining acolytes. They unleashed a volley of fire into a pack of oncoming humanoid machines. The shambling, taloned things scrambled up the steps of the inverted ziggurat, straight into the Inquisitorial retinue's withering fire. Most fell to hotshot las-fire, even if over half of them seemed to rise again.

Another spider construct reared up, dislodging itself from some manner of socket in the floor. A beam of white energy pulsed from the cannon on its back, blasting two acolytes to their molecular components and causing a rippling explosion that scattered the entire group. The spider drifted forward and reached down with a pincer-limb to grab Celaeno as he rose. It lashed down with its mandibles to seize the Space Marine's arm. Nym and Sevrim rushed it, having finished off the first spider. Both hurled krak grenades, blasting limbs off and causing Celaeno to drop to the ground. The Space Marine's left arm had been sheared off.

Nym reached his brother, lifting the wounded Death Spectre to his feet. 'No dying yet!'

Celaeno didn't respond, nor cry out in pain, but drew his bolt pistol in his free hand, his Larraman's organ already clotting the wound.

The spider recovered, and much to Achairas' dismay, a whole swarm of the smaller scarab machines drifted out from under its abdomen, immediately swarming towards them. Nym's bolter was empty, but Sevrim, Celaeno and the last four acolytes managed to cut a few down before they reached them. Achairas scythed a scarab in two with his sword, before shattering another with his backswing, even as two more latched on to him. One gnawed on his pauldron, while another tore at his breastplate with its talons. He ripped the scarab off and stomped it to pieces, as another acolyte was dragged down and eviscerated by the gnashing creatures.

Astolyev rose, still dazed, gathering up his xenos rifle. He loosed beams of dark energy at the spider, disintegrating portions of its carapace, and finally its skull. It fell to the ground with a deafening crash.

Throwing the scarab on his pauldron off and slashing it in two, Achairas ran on, followed by his surviving allies, while Vemek and his skitarii continued their losing battle against the mantis-creatures a way up the steps behind them. But when Achairas saw what approached, he realised there was little hope of them reaching the obelisk alive.

The bipedal skeletal machines advanced in full force, dozens shambling up the ziggurat towards them, clacking their talons and howling dead static. The ones that had fallen before had risen again, joining their ranks.

'Inquisitor!' Achairas shouted. 'Give me your grenade and get back to the *Vox Silentii!* Warn Occludus!'

Astolyev saw what was coming and hesitated. Sevrim fired the rest of his bolter shells into the advancing xenos, sending a few to the ground, if only to slow them. Celaeno readied his bolt pistol, while Nym drew a pair of wickedly curved mono-edged daggers. The three remaining acolytes fired their weapons, to limited effect, while Vemek's team was assaulted by another spider construct that had dislodged itself from a hidden socket in the upper wall.

'Astolyev! Run! You, of all of us, must live!' Achairas urged.

The inquisitor lowered his weapon and finally nodded, handing Achairas his vortex grenade. 'Die well, Death Spectre.'

Achairas did not respond. There was only the rushing water. The torrent of death.

Achairas and his battle-brothers charged into the mass of approaching xenos, hurling their remaining frag grenades a moment before impact. Using his weight and momentum, he bowled through them, slashing three apart with a series of pirouetting blows. The tide of horrors washed over them. He saw Celaeno die first, decapitated by raking claws.

Even so, their charge accomplished what it was supposed to. All of the approaching xenos swarmed the most direct threat, allowing Astolyev and his last acolytes to retreat. They stayed low among the pillars as they ascended the steps, evading the frenzied vivisections being carried out by the mantis-creatures that had torn apart Vemek's unit.

The butchery continued around the Death Spectres. The ground lurched and heaved as the tomb struggled against its stony prison. Staggering, Sevrim failed to evade a pair of curved talons that impaled him through his underarm seals. Two of the creatures lifted him up into the air, tearing an arm and a leg off, even as he pulled the pin of a krak grenade in his free hand and took several more of the xenos with him to oblivion.

Slashing their way through, Achairas and Nym inflicted a substantial butcher's toll, bringing down a dozen xenos machines between them, despite sustaining numerous grievous injuries. When all seemed lost, the obelisk maddeningly out of reach, the onslaught ceased.

They were scarcely three hundred feet from the ring around the central obelisk when the clawed xenos retreated down the slope, hissing madly.

'What is this?' Nym roared. 'Cowardice from machines?'

The four skeletal engineers operating the control ring knelt as an arc of blinding light appeared ahead of them, between the ring and the Space Marines. The light coalesced into a form. It was all dark metal, cast in the shape of a massive humanoid skeleton, easily a head taller than the Space Marines, hunched as it was. A regal crest adorned its skull, and a robe of tattered flesh was draped over its ornate emerald pauldrons. In a clawed hand, it clutched a glaive with a khopesh-like blade that shimmered with a fell greenish light. Everything about its appearance told Achairas that this was some kind of leader. An overlord of these xenos, even if it, too, was a machine.

It stood silently, still among the madness of its minions. Whatever insanity was infecting the rest of this tomb clearly did not affect its king. Achairas and Nym took a moment to gather their breath. The sound of rushing water intensified, and Achairas knew he stared into the hollow, soulless eye sockets of that which would be his end.

Nym looked at him, hobbled, but still alive. 'Use that grenade. I'll distract this overly decorated carcass.'

Achairas nodded. He had to get closer. He could not miss.

Smiling, the two Death Spectres advanced to their doom.

Nym hurled his last krak grenade at the overlord. It calmly caught it in its free hand, crushing it before it could detonate. Achairas flanked around, but the creature moved to block both of them. Nym rushed the towering xenos lord, raking it with his knives. His onslaught was warded off as his foe spun its glaive in an arc with alarming speed. His momentum broken, Nym was barely able to duck the retaliating swing, and the xenos' weapon lit up with jade energy as it scythed through the air. Nym darted in, delivering a pair of thrusts into the thing's ribcage. It was all he managed.

As Achairas sprinted forward, shouldering through two more retreating clawed xenos, he primed the vortex grenade. In a dead run, he hurled it, as hard as he could, at the central obelisk.

The grenade soared through the air, just as the overlord lifted Nym up by his throat and hurled him away. The xenos king advanced, thrusting with its glaive, impaling Nym through the back as he rose to his feet. Green fire tore through the Death Spectre, burning his flesh to ash in seconds, just as the vortex grenade contacted.

The detonation devoured all light, noise and sense, sending Achairas, and all of the xenos, staggering away as a blinding explosion of the warp's uncolours struck the side of the obelisk. A maelstrom of polychromatic energy tore at its flanks, warping the outer shell and shattering the crystals. Rays of emerald light spewed violently, causing several of the prisms on the wall to overload and explode.

The entire chamber rocked violently, and Achairas struggled to his feet, bashing in the skull of another xenos. Looking up, he despaired as he saw thousands of scarabs and dozens of spider constructs swarm towards the obelisk. He found his sword, slashing the legs out from another horror only a split second before a searing lance of agony ripped through his midriff.

Burning blood spurted up into his helmet, as the blade of the xenos overlord punched clean through his torso, from side to side. His sword clattered from his hand as his blood turned to flame and his bones burned to ash. He did not have time to scream. The only sensation Achairas felt as he died was the cold caress of the Black River that had beckoned him for so long.

And so Brother-Sergeant Achairas of the Death Spectres died, having failed to destroy the obelisk awakening the tomb ship. But he did not fail in buying time for Inquisitor Astolyev to make his escape, and gain a chance, however small, to warn the Menrahir of Occludus of this new threat to the Halo Region.

The inquisitor's sprint out through the tomb had taken considerably less time than his original, cautious foray. Terror soiled Astolyev's mind. It was an unfamiliar sensation, even if he felt some minor satisfaction in having vaporised the dying, treacherous Vemek with his dark energy blaster during his escape. Of his three last acolytes, Tyberius and Heshal had fallen in the tunnels, clawed down by the skeletal xenos that had ambushed them. He'd ignored them, sprinting past. Only Kailani still lived.

He dimly made a note to give her a worthy commendation if any of them actually made it out of this wretched place alive.

The entire tomb buckled and quaked, and gravity itself fought him, but he ascended the innards of the pyramid to reach the gaping rent in its apex. When he finally emerged into the wan light of the world's stillborn sun, the scene that faced him was apocalyptic.

The earth of Thirsis 41-Alpha was a shattered mess, as the immense shape of a black metal crescent tore itself from its terrestrial prison. Rock peeled away from the pyramid, the entire crater collapsing around it, shattering the shroud station to splinters. The roar was deafening as it rose, the crust fracturing, grinding into smaller boulders and rolling off the sides of the immense superstructure below. The atmosphere recoiled as tidal surges of emerald energy stripped away the last grasping claws of rock.

The cataclysmic vista before Astolyev was truly the most awe-inspiring, terrible thing he had seen in all his many long years as an inquisitor.

He couldn't even hear his own voice as he shouted to *Apparition* over the vox. He hoped the servitor on the Thunderhawk could make out his commands, and had had enough sense to take off before the research station had crumbled into oblivion.

But then, there it was, screaming through the tortured atmosphere like an apparition of one of the Emperor's angels of death. Its ominous, black-winged shape was a joy to behold. He gripped Kailani's arm. She was barely standing. Astolyev hadn't even noticed the deep wound in her side. She'd said nothing of it throughout their escape.

'Stay alive!' he yelled through the vox, realising she'd be as deaf as he was, that words were utterly useless.

Apparition descended towards the pyramid, hovering alongside the slope of the apex, and opening its ramp. It swayed back and forth as it hung there; it would be a long jump onto a treacherous surface.

Astolyev pulled Kailani back into the tomb, before sprinting forward to gain a running start. They jumped from the slowly rising pyramid onto the ramp of the waiting gunship. Out of breath, aching and battered, they were dragged into the hold by Nerek and Ariane, and were buckled into acceleration harnesses beside a sobbing Ketyanna.

The short, twisting flight took less than fifteen minutes to reach the *Vox Silentii*, which was already powering up to ready for a rapid escape. The frigate flared its engines the moment they passed through its void-shielded landing bay, and began to accelerate away from the planetoid as the colossal xenos vessel tore itself free from the planetary crust.

After sprinting through the corridors of the cruiser, and hurtling up through the magnetic elevator to the strategium, Astolyev entered the chamber to find the other five Death Spectres there waiting for him.

'Sergeant Achairas?' one of them inquired.

The inquisitor's hearing had returned, to some degree. 'Dead. To buy us time to escape,' he gasped.

The Space Marines regarded him silently.

'Considering the size of the vessel, escape is all we *can* do.' The Death Spectre gestured towards the vid display, showing the immense, crescent-shaped ship, now almost fully free from its prison. The energy signatures of the vessel did not cogitate on the *Vox Silentii*'s augur systems, and the inquisitor shook his head in disbelief.

'Blood of the Emperor, what have we done?' He turned to the shipmaster. 'Get us out of Thirsis 41's gravity well and make for the warp as soon as is physically possible! Make for your home world, your Menrahir must be warned.'

The Death Spectre nodded his assent.

'That is what Achairas commanded,' the inquisitor added with an exhalation.

And with that, the *Vox Silentii* surged away from the rising tomb ship at maximal speed. Whether the xenos vessel was unable to target them due to not being fully awoken yet, or whether it simply did not care, Astolyev could not guess, but it was no small mercy when the *Vox Silentii*'s Navigator announced that they were far enough out to tear a rift into the warp and slip away. Astolyev retreated to his guest quarters with his three remaining acolytes and Ketyanna in tow.

He would need to do some serious thinking, and perform an analysis of what they'd found, before bringing this warning to Occludus. The Death Spectres were the watchers of the Eastern Halo, the Space Marines who vigilantly kept the nightmares of the Ghoul Stars at bay. And now, they'd have one new nightmare to deal with. One that was undoubtedly far, far worse than the others. Whatever they'd awoken down there in the dark was perhaps the single greatest threat encountered in the Eastern Halo since the Pale Wasting, and Astolyev decided, then and there, that he would devote his entire being, and all of his considerable resources as an inquisitor of the Ordo Xenos, to counteracting that threat. That would be his atonement, for his role in awakening the sleeping nightmare buried in the rock of Thirsis 41-Alpha.

SOLACE

Steve Lyons

In this tale, Steve Lyons turns his attention to the Mordian Iron Guard as they face a threat away from the battlefield that may be more dangerous than the xenos they've been battling.

Separated from the rest of the regiment, Guardsman Maximillian Stürm and his squadron are lost deep within a forest rife with deadly aeldari. When they stumble upon the small village of Solace, they believe salvation is at hand. They can rest, regroup and resupply before heading out again. But Solace might not be the deliverance they need…

They should have made it back to camp by now.

Guardsman Maximillian Stürm was footsore and weary. He didn't complain, of course. His squad had been tramping through the dense, thorny forest for hours. The tangled canopy stole the sun's light, making it impossible to tell the time of day. The temperature had dropped, however, and everything was washed in shades of grey, which suggested that evening was preparing to give way to night.

Sergeant Kramer called another halt. 'Something wrong with this damn thing,' he grumbled, tapping his chrono-compass again.

Kramer didn't look well. The bandages around his chest were dark with blood. His normally steel-hard, angular face was slick with sweat. His pupils were dilated, his gaze unfocused, betraying the fact that a heavy dose of stimm was keeping him going.

'We've been here before,' said Stürm. 'I recognise the shape of those trees there. We are going round in–'

He broke off as Ven Eisen snapped up his lasgun. Stürm and the others followed suit, their tiredness forgotten. For a minute, the only sounds were Sergeant Kramer's laboured breathing, and a nearby rustle as a forest bird took flight.

'What is it?' Stürm whispered.

Ven Eisen lowered his weapon. His comrades took the cue to relax. 'My apologies. I thought I saw movement. It must only have been a shadow.'

'Here, the shadows can kill you,' muttered Guardsman Zoransky.

'We must press on,' Sergeant Kramer resolved. 'If we are caught in the forest at nightfall, we will be dead by morning.' No one doubted the truth of those words. The sergeant clicked his tongue and rotated on the spot. He led the way onward, following his compass needle. It might be unreliable, but it was all they had.

Stürm had never felt so far from home, so out of place. He was Iron Guard, accustomed to the noisy, bustling hives and machine-planed lines of Mordian. His squad wore bright blue uniform greatcoats and caps with gold adornments, in violent contrast to the pastel shades around them. They were shining lures to the forest's predators.

They broke step, but stayed in formation. Ven Eisen was dragging his left foot behind him. Ludo – the squad's youngest recruit, as yet unseasoned – held his slashed arm in a sling. The morning's battle had been brutal. They were lucky to have survived at all, and many of their comrades hadn't. Kramer had voxed repeatedly for assistance, but no one had responded. Either the equipment was faulty, or no one was left.

Stürm felt he could have done better. He ought to have been more alert, more disciplined, fought harder. He felt ashamed of himself.

Ven Eisen stopped them again. He wasn't seeing shadows, this time. Something, some creature, hung from a branch before them. Sergeant Kramer had missed it, which was unlike him. The creature made no move as the soldiers trained their sights upon it. Stürm struggled to discern its shape in the deepening gloom. With a jolt, he realised that it was hanging, almost bat-like, upside down.

Kramer sent Ven Eisen forward with a wordless nod. A moment later, the Guardsman signalled to the others to join him.

'It's dead,' he reported. 'Its throat has been slit. From the smell of it, at least a couple of days ago.' The inverted face of the creature was striped with crusted blood.

It was an aeldari: a male, with the milky complexion and lithe build of its kind. Silken black hair tumbled around its tapered ears. 'Who – or what – do you think did this to it?' Stürm asked.

'No man of Mordian,' declared Kramer. Stürm knew what he meant. He didn't mourn for the xenos. It had deserved a painful death. The means of its execution, however – its ritualistic nature – discomfited him.

'Why hang the xenos like this?' puzzled Zoransky. His heavy brow creased with the effort of deep thought.

'A better question would be how,' Kramer growled. 'We've been in this forest for weeks, hunting these damn things, and barely laid a hand on them.' He winced, and his hand went to his ribs reflexively.

'It's a warning,' said Ven Eisen.

He had looked past the xenos and seen what lay beyond it. Stürm saw it too now: incongruous shapes between the trees, hard lines and angles. Falling silent again, the five soldiers crept forward – and the alien forest opened up around them. They found themselves looking at a huddle of dark, wooden buildings with sloping roofs. Well-trodden muddy tracks weaved around and between the structures.

'A village,' breathed Stürm. 'I didn't know there were any out here.'

'A xenos village?' Zoransky wondered.

Kramer shook his head. 'Captain Venig believes the aeldari of this world are outcasts. His company found one of their settlements four days ago. They live in primitive hide tents. They could build nothing like this.'

'Even so,' said Stürm, glancing back at the strung-up corpse, 'we should proceed with caution.'

No sooner had he spoken than a gunshot shattered the silence. It was loud – far louder than the report of a lasgun. A projectile hit the ground only feet in front of the troopers, kicking up a miniature dirt storm.

Instinctively, the Guardsmen sprang into action, separating and seeking cover. Before the shot's reverberations had died down, Stürm was crouched with his lasgun to his shoulder, its barrel resting across a stout tree branch.

'Stand fast,' came a voice from between the buildings, 'and identify yourselves.'

'Sergeant Vulfgang Kramer of the One Hundred and Ninety-Third Mordian Regiment, the Emperor's Iron Guard,' Kramer responded. 'My Guardsmen and I are engaged in His holy work, but have lost our comrades and our way. We require shelter for the night, no more. Praise be to the Emperor.'

There was a short pause – slightly longer than Stürm would have liked – before the disembodied voice repeated, 'Praise be to the Emperor.'

Nothing happened for several minutes, during which time the Mordians maintained their rigid stances. Stürm heard low voices – too distant for him to make out. Then, a group of six men emerged from the settlement. They wore shabby breeches, shirts and jerkins. Their faces were steeped in grime, and most had straggly hair and beards. Five of them wore crude-looking pistols in holsters, strapped to thick leather belts at their hips. The sixth had an equally crude shotgun, which he had drawn.

This man rode a four-legged beast of burden, similar to a horse but with larger, nastier-looking teeth. His pinhole eyes, shaded by the broad brim of his hat, gave nothing away, while a drooping moustache lent him an air of melancholy. He halted his mount a few yards away from the troopers.

'Magistrate Gideon Lymax,' he introduced himself. 'I'm the law in these parts – and any servants of the Emperor are welcome to our hospitality.'

The shotgun dangled lazily over his left knee, its threat implicit. His comrades' fingers twitched close to their pistol grips. Stürm saw little discipline in their rounded postures, however. The Mordians may have been outnumbered and battered, but they were better equipped than these six men, and far better drilled.

Kramer stepped into the open. His lasgun was in its sling, allowing him to display empty hands. He called to his men to follow his lead and form up on him. Lymax's beady eyes darted from tree to tree. 'Is this it?' he asked. 'Five of you?'

'Five of us,' Kramer confirmed.

The magistrate gave a curt nod. 'Then, gentlemen, welcome to our home – to our little sanctuary out in the wild here. Welcome to Solace.'

'I don't like this,' muttered Zoransky as the wooden buildings closed in around them.

'These people have been nothing but helpful to us,' said Stürm, 'and have probably saved our lives.' He shared his comrade's misgivings, however. A backwater village like Solace seemed out of place on a developed world such as this one. How could it even survive here, in the forest, surrounded by enemies?

Lymax had dismounted to stroll alongside his guests, leading his beast behind him. 'How do you come to be here,' Stürm asked him, 'so far from civilisation?'

Lymax shrugged. 'Our forefathers struck out from the city a hundred years ago.'

'That can't have been long after Silva Proxima was settled.'

'Some dispute with the city overseers, so the tale goes.'

Stürm's eyes narrowed in suspicion. 'Your ancestors were lawbreakers?'

'Pioneers,' the magistrate gainsaid him. 'They set out with the loftiest ambitions – to tame the forest. In the name of the Emperor, of course.'

'Of course. Praise be to Him.'

'Only they learned that the forest was already inhabited.'

Cheerful voices drifted out of a broad, two-storey structure ahead of them. They tramped on wooden planking, which strained and creaked beneath their boots. A crooked sign nailed over the building's door read 'Solace Tavern'.

Lymax pushed through a pair of swinging gates. Stürm and the others followed him. The air inside the tavern was hazy, diffusing the blue light of flickering lumoglobes. The odours of lho-leaf and cheap amasec played about his nostrils. Civilians were perched on wooden benches and stools, around circular tables. Fifty or so pairs of eyes turned to the newcomers, while as many tongues were abruptly stilled.

Lymax spoke into the ensuing silence: 'As you see, we've

picked up a few strays from the forest. They'll be staying a night or two, perhaps longer. I'm sure no one needs telling to treat them right. They're good Emperor-fearing folk.'

A thin-faced bartender stood frozen, eyes bulging at the newcomers, holding a glass and a towel. Lymax snapped his fingers to get the man's attention. 'Our guests have had a hard day. I'm guessing they might be a touch thirsty.'

'Just water for us,' Sergeant Kramer intervened. 'We are on duty. We can pay.' He dug into his pockets.

Lymax grinned a lopsided grin. 'Your Imperial credits are no use to us. You can work for your keep, though, if you stay long enough.'

'We'll be leaving at dawn,' said Kramer.

'You sure about that? People have struck out from Solace before. We sent out scouts, to find the city and fetch help. Not a one of them ever returned.'

'As soon as we are rested, we will be returning to our camp,' insisted Stürm. He hesitated for a moment, before adding, 'If you have a map of this area of the forest, that would be very helpful.'

A low buzz of activity was already resuming around them. They were still the recipients of many sidelong glances, but the novelty of their arrival was wearing thin. The bartender provided two jugs of water and five glasses. Stürm hadn't realised how dehydrated he was. He had been rationing the contents of his canteen, until there was barely a sip in it. He emptied his glass in one gulp and poured another.

'So, you came from the big city? I only know it from tales of old, of course.'

A man had sidled up alongside Stürm. He was in his sixties, balding, overweight, his slack chin carpeted with grey stubble. His cheeks were ruddy. He drained a glass of amasec, slammed it down and called for another. He hauled himself onto a stool, took Stürm's hand and shook it enthusiastically. 'Jerebeus is the name. Round here, they call me Old Man Jerebeus. I can't imagine why.'

'Maximillian Stürm. I haven't seen your city. I come from another world.'

'You don't say. What brings you to this one?'

'Xenos. The aeldari. The forest is infested with them.'

The old man's rheumy eyes twinkled. He grinned, exposing gaps between his yellowed teeth. 'You don't say.'

'No one in the city knew of them,' Stürm recalled from his briefing, 'until they started to clear the forest for development. Then they came under attack. My regiment was dropped in three weeks ago, to eradicate the xenos threat.'

'Good luck with that. Elusive critters, aren't they? Impossible to pin down.'

Stürm's surprise must have shown, because the old man grinned again. 'I wasn't always this broken-down wreck you see before you. I did my share of sentry duty in my younger days, went on my share of hunting parties.'

'I'm sure you did.' Jerebeus still wore a gun at his hip. Stürm could see no man in the tavern who didn't.

'You see a shadow out the corner of your eye. Next you know, there's a blade through the heart of the man beside you. Mocking eyes, boring into your head like a challenge. By the time you've drawn your pistol, they're gone. Oh, I got off some good shots in my time, don't get me wrong. I drew some blood. Once the wood sprites – your 'aeldari' – have set their sights on you, though, best thing is to run.'

'Mordians don't run,' Stürm intoned stiffly.

'You don't say.'

'Especially not from aeldari. It's what they want. They're

faster than we are. They want the pleasure of hunting you down.'

His mind drifted back to the morning's battle. His squad had walked into an ambush. The enemy had been everywhere at once, their swords a blur. They had shattered the Mordians' regimented lines. The fight had raged for hours, and yet there had been no time to think, to plan, only to react. At last, when Stürm had thought he could endure no more, the ordeal had ended. Perhaps the aeldari had been hurt more than he had seen. Perhaps they had just got bored. Whatever the reason, he and his squad had found themselves lost and alone.

Old Man Jerebeus was right about the aeldari's eyes. The memory of them would haunt Stürm for the rest of his life.

'Where would you run to, anyway?' he murmured.

'Back here, of course,' said Jerebeus. 'Where else but back to Solace?'

The old man was distracted by something over Stürm's shoulder. Suddenly, the Guardsman's neck hairs prickled with foreboding. He turned. Someone new had entered the tavern. The gates were still swinging behind her.

She was a young girl, no older than five or six. She wore a dark red tunic and breeches like one of the men. A red bow nestled in her flowing, clean blonde hair. Her bright blue eyes shifted from Stürm to each of his comrades in turn; and each of them broke off from his conversation, or lowered his glass, transfixed by her.

'Magistrate...' Jerebeus sounded concerned.

Lymax had been talking to Kramer. At the old man's urging, he turned and saw the girl. He snatched his hat from the bar and jammed it over his ears. He hurried up to her. 'Now, Alyce,' he cajoled her, 'you know you shouldn't be in here.'

'Who are they?' asked Alyce, still staring at the Mordians.

'I'll tell you as we walk,' Lymax offered. He made to place an arm around Alyce's shoulders, but changed his mind. He fixed her with an expectant look instead. She drew a breath and blinked – and Stürm blinked too, and tore his gaze away from her. The young girl allowed the magistrate to guide her outside, leaving Stürm to wonder what it was about her that had unsettled him so.

Jerebeus drained another glass and motioned to the bartender for a refill. 'Should you be drinking so much?' asked Stürm, with a hint of disapproval.

The old man wiped his lips on a dirty, tasselled sleeve. 'Who's to tell me I can't? I'm the senior member of this community.' He slurred the words a little. 'I've lived here longer than anyone else – and this is my party, after all.'

'What are you celebrating?'

'It's my leaving party.'

'Oh? Where are you going? I thought the magistrate said–'

'Although… I guess it isn't, is it?' Jerebeus laughed, exposing his ragged teeth again. 'I guess I'll be staying in Solace a time longer yet. Seems a shame to cut short the fest… festivities, though. So, I know, let's call this my staying party.' He hefted his freshly charged glass, sloshing amasec over its rim.

Stürm heard a crash behind him. Sergeant Kramer had slumped over the bar and knocked over his water, smashing the glass. In a second, Guardsmen Stürm and Ludo flanked him, hauling him upright by the armpits. Kramer shrugged them off, his eyelids fluttering. 'I'm fine,' he insisted. 'Just tired. Why is it so warm in here?' His dose of stimm was clearly wearing off. He fumbled in his belt pouches for an injector.

Stürm glanced around his comrades. In their faces, he saw

approval for what he had to do. After Kramer, he was their squad's most senior member. He had served longer than the sergeant, even. He had always felt more comfortable following orders than giving them, but now he had no choice.

He teased the injector from Kramer's trembling fingers. 'You don't need this, sergeant. There is no enemy here. You need sleep – and a medicae to stitch that wound and redress it.' He called over his shoulder to the room: 'Is there a medicae in Solace?'

A pair of young men stood. 'We can take you to Doktor Matthias,' one of them offered. 'We may not have the drugs and equipment you're used to, but you won't find anyone with a steadier hand than his.'

Stürm nodded, gratefully. 'Thank you.' As the men came forward, however, Kramer shrank away from them. He gripped Stürm's arm with an urgent strength. Stürm saw the forbidding look in his sergeant's eyes and knew what it meant.

'Guardsman Zoransky.' He was the strongest, and right now the healthiest, of them. 'Stay with the sergeant. Don't leave his side for anything.' Kramer seemed content with that decision. Leaning on Zoransky, he allowed the two locals to lead him away. Moments after they had exited the tavern, Lymax returned alone.

Stürm looked for Old Man Jerebeus. He still felt unsettled, though he couldn't put his finger on the reason. He had more questions about Solace. Jerebeus had been hijacked by other revellers, however, who were toasting his health exuberantly.

'You fellows must be tired,' said Lymax. 'Time we talked about finding you a place to bed down.'

'A place' turned out to be a bunkroom upstairs.

There were four beds, with feather-stuffed mattresses and

pillows – and a wood-burning stove, which was cold. Stürm removed his greatcoat and boots. He collapsed onto a bed and stared up at the rafters.

The festivities below had subsided, but he heard muffled voices and occasional bursts of laughter. His muscles were glad of the rest, but his racing brain kept him from sleep. Ludo had no such problems, snoring softly. Ven Eisen was awake, however, on the bed to Stürm's left. 'Do you trust these people?' he asked.

'We could not have endured much longer in the forest,' said Stürm. 'We had no choice but to accept their shelter.'

'But do you trust them?'

'I don't. I distrust their reasons for being out here. They claim the aeldari keep them from leaving Solace, from returning to the Imperial city, but isn't it their duty to try?' He was struck by a parallel between these people and the xenos in the forest. *Outcasts*, Sergeant Kramer had called them.

'What use are they to the Emperor here?' Ven Eisen mused.

'And what keeps them safe? They are not soldiers – and you have seen their weapons. I doubt they could withstand a determined aeldari assault.'

'You think they're hiding something?'

'I am sure of it.'

'Could they have made a deal with the xenos?'

Stürm mulled that disturbing thought over. 'It is possible – but then, what of the corpse we found at the village limits?'

'An aeldari that broke the truce, perhaps?'

'And what would their side of the bargain be? What do they have to offer?'

'The magistrate talked of Imperial credits,' Ven Eisen recalled. 'If his people have had no contact with civilisation in a century–'

'You're right. Would they be familiar with our currency?'

The conversation had helped Stürm to a decision. He swung his legs back over the side of the bed, ignoring his protesting muscles. He pushed his feet back into his boots. 'I think I'll take a stroll around Solace – this time without an escort.'

Ven Eisen sat up. 'Let me come with you.'

'This is just a scouting mission. We don't yet know of any real threat here. I'll be less conspicuous alone – and you are injured. You should rest. Keep your gun close by. I will vox you if I discover anything.'

'What if you do not return?' his comrade asked.

'Give me one hour,' said Stürm, fastening his greatcoat and checking his lasgun's power pack. 'Then assume the worst.'

A back door allowed Stürm to slip out of the tavern unseen.

Outside, night had well and truly fallen. He took his first long look up at the sky of Silva Proxima. It was brighter than he had expected – freckled with stars, and there was a large, full moon with a faint red tint.

This was just as well, as there was no street lighting – only flickering pools of candlelight, seeping out between the slats of window shutters. The magistrate's mount was tied up to a post, its muzzle in a trough. Whatever it was feeding on, it stank of blood and crunched like dry bones.

Stürm kept to the shadows. Subterfuge did not come naturally to him. Mordian Iron Guard did not hide, as a rule. They displayed their colours proudly, daring their foes to come at them – but these were unusual circumstances.

Perhaps he shouldn't have worn his colours at all. Even without them, though, he would have stood out in Solace. His shaved hair and chin would have ensured it, as would his disciplined, straight-backed posture. Even his pale skin, sunlight-deprived on the World of Eternal Night, contrasted with the callused, weather-beaten locals.

There were several locals around. He could hear their muttering and boot scrapes even when he couldn't see them. Stürm sensed a restless charge in the atmosphere. He ducked under cover as the door of a single-storey shack flew open. A couple emerged from within. They looked tired, but were twitching with nervous energy. They crossed the road, into an alleyway between two larger structures. One of these appeared to be a general store; the other had bars on its windows.

A group of four women hurried by, into the alleyway too. They wore full-bodied, patterned skirts – finer and cleaner clothes than Stürm had seen in the tavern. From the build-up of voices in the distance, he deduced that a crowd was gathering behind those two buildings. Perhaps, he thought, if he circled around the store…

He was interrupted by an already familiar sound. Two men pushed through the tavern's swing gates, stepping onto the planking outside. They spoke in low murmurs, but he recognised the magistrate's drawl. He crept closer, hoping to make out more. He thought Lymax had spoken Sergeant Kramer's name.

'–break for you, old man, them turning up just when they did.'

'You don't say.' The second voice – a little louder than the first, slurred by drink – belonged to Old Man Jerebeus.

Lymax sucked air between his teeth. 'Five of them, though – and more dangerous, to look at them, than any we've dealt with before.'

'Ah, they aren't so tough as they pretend. One down

already, one more by dawn. That leaves only three – and two of them hurt, at that.'

'I guess so.'

'You know I was ready to take my turn. Still am. I've lived a good, long life. I can't say I'm not glad of a few more months, though – to prepare. You know what it feels like, Gideon? It feels like the Emperor still watches over us, after all.'

Lymax sighed, heavily. 'I wish I could feel that too.'

The pair moved away, and Stürm didn't catch the old man's rejoinder. He considered whether to follow them, in case he could learn more. He was startled by a sudden voice behind him: 'Are you lost?' He whirled around.

The young girl in the red tunic stood a few feet from him. Her eyes were bright circles of light in the gloom. Stürm didn't know how he had failed to hear her creeping up on him. He must have been more tired than he thought. He had to quieten her before she gave him away.

He took a step towards the girl. She flinched and backed away from him. Stürm dropped to his haunches, so as not to tower over her, and forced his facial muscles into an unaccustomed smile. 'Your name is Alyce, isn't it?'

Alyce nodded.

'My name is Guardsman… My name is Max – and yes, you're right, I am lost. My friends and I were fighting, uh, wood sprites in the forest. Do you know what they are? Have you seen them? Have you seen them in the village?'

'The monsters can't come into Solace,' Alyce declared – thankfully now in hushed tones matching Stürm's own.

'Is that because your men protect you? With their guns?'

'Your gun is different to theirs. It's very shiny. I haven't seen a gun like that before. Can I hold it?'

'No. It's dangerous if you don't know how to use it.'

'I'm old enough to use a gun.'

'Do you have other weapons? How do the grown-ups defend you? How do they keep the aeldari at bay? Alyce, tell me.'

He was being too insistent, making the girl flinch from him again. Before he could stop her, she bolted, racing out in front of the tavern. 'Magistrate Lymax!' she cried. Stürm ground his teeth in chagrin. He thought about running, but this too was not the Mordian way. He straightened up and marched after Alyce instead.

He found her with her fingers wrapped around the magistrate's thick belt. As he walked into view, her blue eyes reaffixed themselves to him. Lymax had both hands on his shotgun and was frowning. 'Guardsman... Stürm, isn't it?'

'I'm sorry,' he said, as if nothing was wrong. 'I didn't mean to frighten her. I saw her outside, alone, and was worried for her.'

'And what brings you outside, alone?'

'I couldn't sleep.' That much was true. 'My mind was racing. I thought some air might clear it.'

Lymax nodded. 'There's no cause for concern,' he reassured the clinging Alyce. 'No one wants to hurt you. No one can hurt you in Solace. Why don't you run along now? Go and find Deputy–'

'I want to stay with you,' said Alyce, stubbornly.

'Now, Alyce, please. I just have a couple of things I have to deal with. I'll follow you on in a minute or two. I promise.'

Alyce detached herself from the magistrate and scuttled away, giving Stürm a wide berth as she passed him. She ran towards the store. He wanted to look, to see if she went down the alleyway – but Lymax was bearing down on him, his features still tight with suspicion.

'Don't her parents wonder where she is?' asked Stürm.

'Alyce's mother died in childbirth,' said Lymax, gruffly. 'She'd had the fever for weeks, but held on for the baby's sake. We'd lost her father only weeks before. He rode out on a hunting expedition and never returned. We all take a hand in caring for young Alyce. She is family to all of us in Solace.'

'For some of us, the only family we have,' agreed a cordial voice. Old Man Jerebeus tottered up to the pair, insinuating himself into the conversation.

'I was wondering–' Stürm began, but Lymax interrupted him.

'Your sergeant talked about an early start tomorrow. You should sleep.'

'Where is Sergeant Kramer?' asked Stürm.

'In the doktor's office, all freshly bandaged up. Your other friend is with him too. Both were spark out when last I looked in on them.'

That was a lie. Zoransky had been charged with watching Kramer. He would never have allowed himself to fall asleep. Stürm kept his expression neutral, however. The last thing he wanted was a gun battle, which would be heard across the village. Not yet. Not until he knew what he was facing.

He didn't have to fake a yawn, only let it happen. 'In that case,' he said, 'you're probably right. I should try to rest.' He took his leave of Lymax and Jerebeus, heading back to the rear of the tavern. The whole way, he felt their eyes on his back, and he listened intently for the sound of a gun being drawn. He unlatched the rear door, opened it and swung it shut again. He waited until he heard footsteps moving away.

When Lymax had talked of the doktor's office, he had made an involuntary movement. His head had jerked in a particular direction. Stürm crept from shadow to shadow again, following that pointer. He left the narrow alleyway and the sounds of the gathering crowd behind him.

At the village's edge, he found a two-storey building with a sign that read 'Physician'.

There were no lights inside and no sounds of movement, so he forced the door as quietly as he could. It splintered open with little resistance. Stürm readied his lasgun and stepped into the darkness beyond, waiting for his eyes to adjust.

He was in a narrow hallway. He made out doorways to his left and a wooden staircase ahead of him. Checking the downstairs rooms, he found an office and a parlour, both empty. He climbed the stairs, his eyes scouring the shadows that darkened his path. His stomach felt tight. The creak of every wooden step beneath his feet sounded like the screech of an alarm.

There were three more rooms upstairs. In the first of them, Stürm discerned the outlines of a bed with a chair alongside it – and a large, crumpled shape on the floor. His nostrils twitched at the mingled scents of gunpowder and blood. Fearing the worst, he crossed quickly to the window. He yanked its shutters open, flooding the room with reddish moonlight.

Guardsman Zoransky was dead.

Stürm turned the body over. Its armour-reinforced overcoat had been blasted to shreds. He teased a bullet out of the bloody mess of Zoransky's chest, aching with regret for having sent the big soldier to this fate. He took a deep breath, reining in his feelings. Feelings were the ruin of discipline, and Stürm had work to do. Of Sergeant Kramer, there was no sign. There was more blood on the bed, however, and its sheets were tangled and torn. His comrades had put up a fight.

He hissed into the comm-bead at his collar. 'Ven Eisen. Do you read me?'

A creaking floorboard behind him alerted him to danger. A man appeared in the doorway, well dressed and clean-shaven, with a pair of small, round spectacles. He was bringing a pistol to bear. Stürm snapped up his lasgun and fired first, shooting for the heart. The would-be assassin gasped and reeled backwards. He fired one bullet, at the ceiling – then crashed through a banister rail at the top of the stairs.

Stürm raced from the bedroom and descended the stairs four at a time, seeing no point in stealth now that the world had erupted into noise. He yelled Ven Eisen's name into his comm-bead, but there was no response. He had to get back to the tavern.

The assassin lay sprawled in the hallway. The elusive doktor, Stürm wondered? It hardly mattered. Broken bone protruded through the side of the corpse's neck. The shack door caught on its dead weight, and Stürm had to kick it out of his way.

He raced into the crisp night air, keeping his head down: a sensible precaution, as two more bullets thudded into the wall behind him. 'Hold it right there!' a gruff voice rang out, belatedly. Ignoring it, he dived behind a cluster of rainwater barrels and strafed the shadows around him with las-beams.

Suddenly, villagers were coming at him from every direction, some with pistols drawn, others wielding makeshift clubs or pitchforks or knives. Stürm loosed off five more shots into the advancing mass. He struck three men, maybe four, but the rest fell upon him, shouting and screaming and clawing and battering at him. Above their cries and the drumbeat of his own heart, he heard another voice, a familiar one:

'Don't shoot him. Do you hear me? If we take him alive, we buy ourselves another month.'

The crowd wrenched away his lasgun, punching and kicking until his grip on it was loosened. A dozen hands latched on to his uniform, hauling him to his feet. An old woman spat on him as they dragged him to meet the man who had called out.

Old Man Jerebeus stood straight-backed, eyes agleam with malice. He seemed perfectly sober now. 'You should have slept – you and your friend in there.' He nodded towards the physician's shack. 'We just wanted to get tonight over with and deal with the rest of you later, but you forced our–'

Stürm lunged at him, with a roar of effort. He took his captors by surprise, wrenching himself free of them. He knew for sure now that Jerebeus was the Emperor's enemy – and this would likely be his only chance to slay him.

His fingers almost reached the old man's throat. Then, something – a pistol butt, he would later assume – cracked the back of his skull, dislodging his cap. For a second, he deluded himself that willpower would keep him upright. Then a rain of fists drove him to the ground, and the stars above him seemed to pinwheel and explode.

The next thing his senses registered was the clanging of a heavy iron gate.

Stürm opened his eyes and instinctively lifted his head. A flash of pain blinded him and teased a groan out of his throat. His lasgun was gone, as was his combat knife. He felt a rush of shame, leavened with fear for his comrades, and he pushed himself up into a sitting position. Bedsprings creaked under his weight.

'I thought you'd be out for the night. I'm starting to wonder if you off-world types ever sleep at all.'

He was in a square cell that smelled faintly of cleaning agents. It was bordered by wooden walls on two sides and bars on the others. A crude symbol, meaningless to him, had been etched into the stone floor in blood. Someone had tried to scrub it away, but only partially succeeded. A tiny window above the bed was barred too. Stürm guessed that he was in the building he had seen before, beside the store. The gaolhouse. Through the bars to his left was a second cell, furnished like this one with a basic bunk and a chamber pot, otherwise empty.

Behind the bars in front of him was Magistrate Gideon Lymax. He was backlit by a candle sitting in a brass holder on a desk, casting his face into shadow. He had just locked the cell gate with a key: one of many, attached to a jangling ring. He tossed it casually to an older, grizzled man, who sat with his heels up on the desk.

'How long have I been unconscious?' asked Stürm.

Lymax shrugged. 'Not too long. Long enough.'

'Give me one hour,' he had said to Ven Eisen.

'Don't expect your friends to come rescue you,' said Lymax, as if he had read Stürm's mind. 'We had to take them prisoner too. You gave us no option, in the end. I thought it best to hold you separate from one another.'

'Those of us you haven't killed,' Stürm spat.

'The big fellow, you mean? Zoransky? That wasn't meant to... He should have known when to stop fighting. He should have known when he was beaten.'

'We are Mordian Iron Guard,' Stürm growled. 'We are never beaten.'

'Begging your pardon, that's not how it looks from over here.'

'What did you do to Sergeant Kramer? Where is he?'

Lymax's gaze dropped to his boots. It seemed he felt some shame for his actions, despite everything. 'He wouldn't have survived long, in any case. His wound was infected. We don't have the medicines to treat him.'

'What did you do to him?' Stürm demanded again.

'This village is more than our home,' said Lymax. 'Solace is our shelter. Here, we are protected. You've seen the monsters. You know what they can do. They're waiting for us out there, in the forest. For a hundred years, they have been waiting.'

He had ignored Stürm's question. Did that mean Kramer was dead? Stürm balled his fists, suppressing his righteous anger. It would do no good to scream at Lymax. As calmly as he could, his voice trembling a little, he asked, 'How are you protected?'

'They cannot reach us here,' said the magistrate.

'Why not? Some kind of weapon?'

'They can't set foot across the village limits.'

'What happens if they do?'

Lymax turned away, and Stürm thought he would say no more. In a hoarse voice, however, he confessed: 'I only saw it happen the one time. A female wood sprite. She made it as far as the tavern. We stepped out to meet her, those who could muster the nerve for it. We thought this was it, the final showdown. Only, then...'

His words ran dry. Stürm prompted him, impatiently. 'Then what?'

'Something, some force, set about her. I was standing just ten feet from her as she was pounded into the ground. I heard her bones snapping one by one. I couldn't see a damn thing, but I felt... My heart was pounding fit to burst out of my chest, and there were voices screaming in my ears, screaming for blood.'

Stürm swallowed down a rising tide of bile. '"Some force", you said.'

'Some invisible force.'

'You must know what you are describing.'

'That I do. Our protector. Our shield.'

'You must know what that–'

Lymax turned back to Stürm, and now his eyes were defiantly ablaze. 'The Emperor doesn't see us way out here, or chooses not to. Our ancestors faced slaughter. What choice had they? What choice have we, but to honour the deal they made?'

'You could choose to die with honour,' argued Stürm.

'At last count, this village houses one hundred and fourteen souls. My duty is to them. We have a deal – and it is a good deal, if hard to bear some days. We are protected in Solace – but yes, there is a price. There is always a price.'

Stürm had miscalculated. He had thought he could reason with the magistrate. He knew now that he was beyond reaching.

Lymax tipped his broad-brimmed hat, his old cordial self returning like a well-worn mask. 'Now, if you'll excuse me,' he drawled, 'I have business to attend to. I'll leave you in the hands of my trusted deputy here. Until the morning.'

He turned and strode out of the building. In the silence that followed, the deputy rocked back on his chair. He rummaged a bottle out of the desk and poured himself a drink, which he sucked through his ratty grey beard. He lit up a lho-leaf stick, filling the room with pungent smoke. He barely glanced at his prisoner at all. Stürm doubted there was much point in talking to him either.

He had to do something. He had a shrewd idea of what Lymax's 'business' must be, and he had to stop it. He levered himself to his feet, and was overcome by dizziness. He paced the cell to get his blood circulating again. He tore the threadbare sheets from his bed, and set about plaiting and knotting them together.

At this point, he imagined he had the deputy's attention. He kept his back to him, as he fashioned his sheets into a noose. He heard a scrape from the deputy's chair. He cast his makeshift rope over a ceiling rafter, as footsteps hurried up to the cell gate. He looped the rope around his bed frame and knotted it.

The deputy pounded his fist on the bars. 'What do you think you're doing?'

'I refuse to sit here waiting to die,' said Stürm. He stepped up onto the bed.

'But you aren't dying tonight. You could still have months yet. If you do as you're told and accept the way things are, you could even have a comfortable–'

'The Golden Throne I will,' spat Stürm, reaching for the dangling noose.

The deputy drew his pistol. 'Now, you step down from there.'

'Go ahead,' Stürm challenged him. 'Shoot me. That way, I die resisting the Emperor's enemies. That way, I die with honour – on my own terms, not on yours. My soul remains undefiled by whatever dark powers you have conjured here.' He slipped the noose over his head.

The deputy gave a start and fumbled with his jangling key ring. He thrust a key into the lock, cursing as it wouldn't turn.

Stürm tightened the noose around his own neck. As his gaoler found the right key at last, unlocked the gate and burst into the cell, he took a powerful leap from the bed. The slipknot he had tied around the frame unravelled. He cannoned into the deputy and sent him reeling backwards into the bars.

Stürm pressed his attack with two punches to the head, one more to the stomach. Dazed and winded, his victim slid gracelessly to the floor. Stürm snatched his weapon from him. He only wished there had been a more honourable way.

The deputy was conscious, though only just. 'Can't... stop them,' he groaned.

'How old are you?' asked Stürm. A few years younger than Old Man Jerebeus, he estimated. 'How long before your turn comes?' The deputy didn't answer him. His eyelids fluttered, and he slumped into unconsciousness. Stürm locked him in the cell and searched the outer room for his equipment, finding nothing.

He was left with the deputy's gun. Its operation seemed simple enough, similar to a stub pistol he had fired in training. It had no scope, just a notch at the end of the barrel to sight along. There were shells in each of its six chambers.

It wasn't much, but it was all the Emperor had granted him. It would have to be enough. Stürm heard a swell of excited voices. The crowd behind the gaolhouse was being whipped to fever pitch. He had no time to search for his imprisoned comrades. He hurried out of the building and plunged into the alleyway alongside it.

One hundred and fourteen souls, Lymax had said.

Almost all of them had assembled at Solace's heart. They filled an open square, at the centre of which had been erected a scaffold. The magistrate himself stood atop this, Old Man Jerebeus alongside him. Four younger men, between them, supported the limp, bound form of Sergeant Kramer.

Lymax was appealing for quiet. At length, the crowd

subsided enough for him to speak. Concealed in the mouth of the alleyway, behind their backs, Stürm watched and listened.

'This past month has been uncommonly kind to us,' said Lymax. 'Young Karib shook off his sickness to become a fine, strapping young man. Our hunting parties returned safe from the forest, having gathered all we need. We celebrated the arrival of a new member of our community.'

A smattering of applause greeted this pronouncement, as if childbirth were a rare event in Solace. It probably was.

'Even more crucially, no wood sprites dared enter our village. We were kept safe from the monsters that would slaughter us all in our beds. Our children were kept safe. We were protected. Now, it is the night of the Thanksgiving Moon once again, and time for us to show how we appreciate that protection.'

These words dampened the crowd's enthusiasm. Lymax continued, however: 'It pleases me to say that here too fortune has favoured us. Tonight, we were to say farewell to a long-time pillar of our community.' Old Man Jerebeus shuffled forward and took a half-bow. 'Thank you, my friend,' said Lymax, 'for what you were willing to do for all our sakes. It will not be forgotten. That sacrifice is no longer needed, however – because, tonight, five strangers came to Solace.'

Sergeant Kramer was dragged to the hanging frame. He was awake, but barely so. Stürm saw purple bruises on his face, even from this distance. Three of the young men lifted him, while the fourth looped a rope around his ankles. They were planning to hang Kramer upside down – like the aeldari out in the forest. Stürm felt anger overtaking him again, even as his stomach muscles cramped in disgust.

'They are not like us,' Lymax proclaimed. 'We know this

from hard-won experience. As city-dwellers, they live their lives protected by great walls and armies. They haven't endured what we have been forced to endure. They cannot comprehend our ways, and will never approve of them.'

The crowd rallied now. Many yelled out in anger – which made Stürm resent them all the more, because what did they have to be angry about? He sensed that proceedings were building to a climax. His every nerve screamed at him to act – but what could he do? Every man and woman here was armed as well as he was. Moonlight glinted off a blade in the magistrate's hand.

'The lives of these strangers will buy more life for all of us – their leader tonight, the others during the moons to come.'

Sergeant Kramer was hoisted by his ankles, the crowd hooting and jeering at him. Someone threw a bottle at him, which shattered on the hanging frame. For Stürm, it was the final straw. These people, every one of them, were traitors, consorting with the vilest forces imaginable. The thought of what they had done to Zoransky, what they were doing now, made his blood run hot in his veins. He wished he had killed the deputy at the gaolhouse. He wished he could kill every one of them.

'The appointed moment arrives once more,' Lymax intoned. He brandished his knife and stepped up to the hanging Kramer. He uttered an incantation in some arcane, blasphemous language. Stürm threw his hands to his ears, but couldn't quite blot out the terrible, painful words.

Then the crowd began to chant along with their magistrate: a grumbling undercurrent at first, but swelling to a resounding roar. They pounded their fists in the air. The moon was still full, the stars bright, but the sky seemed to have darkened. Stürm could feel the villagers' hyped-up emotions like a physical wave crashing over him, making his heart beat faster. The veins in his temple throbbed.

He had to force himself to breathe. He had to think clearly, now more than ever before. He raised his salvaged pistol. He could get off two shots, perhaps three, before the crowd saw where he was and fell upon him. He had to make them count.

He rested his sights upon Magistrate Lymax, whom he hated most of all. *Think clearly...* Would his death halt this unholy ceremony? Probably not. Someone else – Old Man Jerebeus or one of the younger men – would only take over from him.

'He wouldn't have survived long, in any case. His wound was infected.'

Stürm saw no way to save his comrade's life. He could save his soul, however. Vulfgang Kramer was a good man, a devout man. He deserved the Emperor's mercy. One bullet for him, then; one for the magistrate after. Stürm shifted his aim to his faithful comrade, his friend. He prayed for the fortitude to do his duty. He took a deep, steadying breath. His finger tightened on his trigger.

Then, with his peripheral vision, through the crowd, he saw her.

She was standing at the front, a hundred yards away from him. Her back was to him, but her vivid red tunic and flowing blonde hair were unmistakable.

Suddenly, Alyce's head snapped around. She couldn't have seen him in the shadows, not from that distance. It was impossible. While all other eyes were fixed upon the stage, however, her bright blue orbs stared directly at Guardsman Stürm.

His bullet ricocheted off the hanging frame. He cursed in

frustration. He had allowed himself to be distracted, and the strange weapon's recoil had surprised him. He re-aimed and fired again, hastily – even as Lymax dived for cover. Stürm was just in time to see his broad-brimmed hat dropping behind the scaffold.

The villagers turned on him, howling in indignation. He knew he had to run, lest he take Kramer's place. Then he realised that no one was moving towards him. The raging crowd parted, creating a channel from him to Alyce. She was skipping towards him, her eyes shining coldly, a smile pulling at her lips.

She raised a hand towards Stürm, and something struck him in the stomach. He doubled over with the force of the blow, which was followed by another and another. Invisible punches assailed him from every direction, filling him with pain, making him jerk like a broken puppet. His nostrils filled with the scent of blood, though he didn't think he had been cut. The faces of Solace's inhabitants leered before him, twisted into nightmare masks. Their raging voices filled his ears, building in intensity until he felt like his head would explode.

He recalled Lymax's tale of the aeldari that had penetrated the village, of the dark force that had destroyed it. In a moment of adrenaline-sharpened clarity, he knew that force had been the anger of the villagers themselves. A force that was killing him too. A force collected, directed, embodied – somehow, in some way that he couldn't understand and feared to try – by a blonde-haired, blue-eyed little girl.

Alyce had almost reached him. Stürm fell to his knees at her scuffed leather, open-toed shoes, tears and sweat blurring his vision. He gaped up at three images of her face with its fixed look of detached amusement. 'No,' he gasped. 'I am Mordian Iron Guard. No remorse, no mercy, no forgiveness.'

He had never encountered a psyker before. He had been trained to resist their malign mental influence, but had never imagined the effort would hurt so much. He felt as if his mind would shatter.

'Not a single step back, not a single moment of hesitation.' He recited the words of Colonel Drescher, when he had raised the legendary 18th Regiment – words that had been drilled into every Iron Guard recruit since.

'You will not... will not succumb to fear or... doubt...' His right arm was a dead weight, but he willed himself to raise it. The primitive pistol trembled in his grip. Three images of Alyce became hundreds, twisting and whirling in front of him as if he were looking at her through a cracked kaleidoscope.

'...and you will relent only after you have given your last moment for...'

Stürm screwed his eyes shut. He tried to focus past the pain that wracked his body, his mind and his soul. He tried to slow his breathing, which had become a series of tortured gasps, slicing into his lungs like icy blades. He couldn't see his enemy, couldn't hear her, but he knew where she was by the waves of hatred emanating from her.

'...for the Emperor!' he bellowed. And fired his pistol.

It felt like the world had stopped.

For one eternal moment, Stürm drifted in silent darkness and knew the Emperor's peace. Only gradually did he become aware of his surroundings again. He was still at the edge of the square, still on his knees. His pistol was still warm. It pinned his hand to the ground, as if it had become too heavy to bear.

Many members of the crowd were kneeling too. They might

have been praying – assuming they had anyone left to pray to. Their anger had drained out of them, leaving them spent. Someone let out a keening, despairing howl. It was Old Man Jerebeus, on the scaffold. Some followed his lead, while others wept self-pitying tears over Alyce's body or just into the dry, dusty soil.

Stürm had just shot a child. The thought made him feel nauseous. He would need to pray too, for forgiveness. Not now, though. The villagers appeared to have forgotten all about him. Doubtless they would pull themselves together soon and turn on the architect of their woes. Stürm knew he had to move – only he couldn't muster the energy to stand.

He saw a blur of movement, then another. He blinked, in case his vision was at fault. He witnessed an explosion of blood and gore in the crowd directly ahead of him, but couldn't see its cause. Momentarily, he glimpsed a milky-white face, silken black hair and mocking eyes. Then, there was more blood – and the screaming started.

There were aeldari in Solace. They must have been waiting all this time for their chance. As ever, there may only have been a handful of them; there may have been dozens. It was impossible to tell. Stürm only glimpsed them out of the corners of his eyes. He tracked them by their deadly wakes.

He saw the flashing of their slender blades. He saw one villager after another cut down before they could apprehend their peril. Some were just beginning to rally. Pistols were drawn and fired, their bullets striking more friends than foes.

Stürm pushed his way through them. He elbowed and punched them aside when they stumbled into his path. His duty, first and foremost, was to his endangered comrades. He reached the scaffold and pulled himself up onto it. He was too late.

Kramer was still hanging, inverted, from his ropes. His throat was slit. Old Man Jerebeus knelt beside him. Tears rolled down his ruddy cheeks. His hands dripped with the sergeant's blood. His clothes were plastered with it.

'I thought… I prayed, if I completed the sacrifice,' the old man bleated. He raised his head to the moon and cried out, 'Take me. Please. Take my body. My soul. Do with them as you wish. Just, please, do not desert us. We need you. My people. My family. Don't let the lives we have lived here count for–'

Stürm shot the old man in the head.

He heard the heavy double-clack of a cocking shotgun. He knew, before he turned, who he would find behind him. Lymax marched across the planking towards him, with both barrels levelled at Stürm's unprotected head. His pinhole eyes blazed with contempt. 'You did this,' he spluttered.

'I defended myself and my comrades from you.'

'From the moment we took you in here, you judged our way of life.'

'Your way of death.'

'We only defended ourselves too. We did what we had to, to survive.'

'But at a price.'

'A few lives – most of them close to ending, anyhow – in exchange for a hundred years of peace. Now, you have destroyed us.'

'Yes,' Stürm acknowledged, proudly. 'I have.' He straightened his back and puffed out his chest. Lymax could hardly miss him at this range, but he would die with honour. He had served the Emperor dutifully. His life was a price worth paying.

Suddenly, the magistrate stiffened. Blood trickled from one corner of his mouth and the shotgun slipped from his numbed fingers. It took Stürm a second to see the blade protruding from Lymax's chest. Then he noticed the shadow beside him. He fired at it, but the shadow, along with the blade, was gone. He whirled around, half expecting to find both looming behind him, but saw nothing.

Lymax's corpse hit the planking with a hefty, wet thud. Stürm was left alone on the scaffold at the eye of a maelstrom. He checked his gun: two bullets left. He decided to save them. He took a breath and leapt back into the heart of the melee.

He fought his way through it, through a writhing mass of anger and fear and despair, back the way he had come across the square. Some villagers yelled out as they saw him. Some even made hopeless grabs for him, but most were only concerned with themselves. Stürm saw no more aeldari, but he felt their presence in the spasms that wracked the crowd each time they struck.

He found himself trampling an increasing number of dead and dying. Hemmed in as he was, he was no less vulnerable than anyone else around him. He probably wouldn't even see the creature that slew him.

'Mordians don't run.' His own words returned to haunt him.

He fought his way along the alleyway between gaolhouse and store.

Beyond this, the crowd was dispersing. People streamed into their all-too-flimsy shacks, bolting doors behind them. One man, locked out of his home, hammered on the shutters, pleading with his family indoors. Seconds later, he lay dead on the ground, criss-crossed with livid red cuts. The aeldari were here too. *'They're faster than we are. They want the pleasure of hunting you down.'*

Stürm heard the cracks and whines of a pair of lasguns. He found the sound – something familiar, amid so much that was not – reassuring. Guardsmen Ven Eisen and Ludo stood back to back outside the tavern, ensuring that no one could sneak up behind either of them. Ven Eisen's posture was awkward, favouring his injured foot, while Ludo struggled to aim one-handed. They fought on, nevertheless.

Stürm hurried up to them. 'Where have you been?' Ven Eisen greeted him, breathlessly. He loosed another beam into the shadows, punching a hole through a barrel. 'What the Golden Throne is happening in Solace?'

'A long story,' said Stürm, 'best saved for our debriefing.'

'Armed men burst into our room. I was unarmed, and Ludo was sleeping. They held us captive. When the shouting started, one of them panicked and fled. We sprung on the other two and overpowered them.'

'We're leaving. Now,' said Stürm.

Ven Eisen gaped at him. 'What of Sergeant Kramer?'

Stürm shook his head. 'He's dead. Zoransky too. That leaves me in command of this squad, and I say we're leaving.'

How could he explain all he had witnessed here? Already, he questioned his own recollections, as if his mind knew they were too dangerous to retain. He felt as if he had just stumbled through a dream, and now reality's cold air had slapped him hard across the face. He only knew he had to get away from here.

He led his two surviving comrades out of the village, the same way they had entered it. The aeldari didn't bother them. By sheer good fortune or the Emperor's grace, he wondered? Perhaps they saw the villagers as the greater threat to them. Or they knew three Guardsmen wouldn't get far in the forest.

It was a few hours yet till dawn. 'My guess is, our compasses will lead us back to our campsite now,' said Stürm. He even half believed it himself.

They reached the branch from which the dead aeldari had hung. Someone had cut down the body and taken it away. From among the huddle of wooden buildings behind them, they heard a woman's scream, abruptly curtailed. Ven Eisen faltered. He had obeyed his orders, as any Mordian would. Now, however, he could hold his silence no longer. 'Shouldn't we fight for them? They are men, after all, facing the xenos scourge. Is it not our duty to protect them?'

Stürm shook his head emphatically. 'Not this time. Not these men. You haven't seen all I have seen. They have amply earned this fate. Our duty now is to survive to fight again – and choose a better battle, a worthier cause, next time.'

His comrades saw his grim expression and the shadows in his eyes, and they questioned him no more. They formed up and straightened their backs, adjusting their bright blue uniform greatcoats. As one, they stepped out into the dark, foreboding forest.

They shook the dust of Solace from their shoes to whatever fate now awaited them.

TIES OF BLOOD

Jamie Crisalli

As a lover of gritty melodrama and bloody combat, it seems fitting that debut author Jamie Crisalli chose to deliver us a tale of Slaaneshi cultists infiltrating a Khornate stronghold.

Armed with a sabre and swaggering self-assurance, Savrian and his allies undertake a daring heist on the Bastion of Red Dust in the hope of rescuing Savrian's long-lost son. But as a mortal descendent of Sarn the Everliving, Savrian should know that while blood may be thicker than water, the ties of family often mean naught to those who serve the Dark Gods.

The clouds shrouded the moon, and a thin knife of a ship slid over blood-tinged waters through a canyon of sandstone. Her oars sliced the water silently, her black sails lashed down. Out on the deck, Savrian, mortal descendant of Sarn the Everliving, pressed a scented silk cloth to his face to blot out the growing reek of blood.

Then the source of the dread stench hove into view. The Bastion of Red Dust, a mountain of basalt that loomed in the shattered canyon as if it had been hurled there from on high. Over time, the Sea of the Unwanted had filled the surrounding chasms and pooled at its feet, thick with the red dust that flowed off the fortress' flanks. Axe-wielding idols crusted its towers and watched over the blood-soaked arenas. Only those who bore Khorne's symbols could enter its singular gaping maw high above, to fight and die in the Blood God's name.

Savrian leaned against the rail, black plate creaking. Behind him, his slaves carried a tray of elixirs and powders, breathlessly waiting in case he had a need. They attached his sabre, Malisette, to his belt and wiped his black armour down with scented oils. Malisette had been impregnated with the narcotic tears of Blessed Ones at its forging, and caused a dreamy exhaustion in its victims, draining away their fighting spirit so they could be taken alive.

His second in command, Issaya, waited nearby, her dark-skinned face impassive, cutting her forearm with a small razor.

'Beloved, what is on your mind?'

Savrian started. He had not heard his wife, Cirine, approach. Suddenly he was aware of it all, the numbed skin, the near colourless vision, the aching joints, the muddled hearing. Beyond the damage from a lifetime of ecstatic devotion to Slaanesh, a near lethal poisoning by a rival seeking his crown had rendered him both decrepit and sterile. Fortunately his god-gifted beauty was untouched, his pale form still lean and graceful, his chiselled face still porcelain smooth, his hair still ink-black and lustrous. Yet, it was nothing more than a youthful shell over a worn and decaying carcass.

'Just regrets,' he said, though loath to admit it. 'I know I shouldn't. Regret implies fault.' He sighed. 'I should have realised Verigon was alive, that Chagorath took him. That Khornate wretch, he's had my son for years. I should have taken Verigon with me that day. He is the only other true-born alive.'

He looked at Cirine, his dark purple eyes gleaming. The eyes of Sarn, the eyes of the immortal. It was no trinket or title that marked his line, but rather Sarn's physical blessing that separated them from the masses.

'We will retrieve Verigon before dawn,' Cirine said, leaning against his shoulder. 'Your plan is perfect. A scalpel instead of a hammer. Your son is as good as saved.'

She touched his arm, her thin black claws teasing his skin. Beautiful and obscene, Cirine was everything he wanted in a mate. Clad in filmy silk that hid nothing from the eye, she oozed with a sensuality that she frequently denied him. She was cruel but never boring.

'You say that,' he said. 'But I do not have your confidence.'

He should. The plan was simple: infiltrate the fortress, retrieve Verigon, return the same way and then escape over the sea back to Sarn's Rest, their ancestral home. They knew their route and their enemy. It was no more complicated than sneaking into a forbidden harem.

A small bottle was pressed into his hand and he swallowed the bitter mouthful that lay inside. A warmth diffused through him. His breathing quickened. Colours enriched, sound sharpened. The aches and pains faded. Yet, this was no youth in a bottle. Before the poisoning, such a dosage would have left him in a fugue state lasting for days. Now it barely returned him to normality.

Cirine leaned forward and licked his lips, tasting the bitter concoction.

'What do you think of it, my love?' she whispered.

'I need something stronger,' he said. 'But it will do.'

The ship struck the craggy beach at the base of the fortress. Savrian leapt off the ship and offered Cirine his hand, which she grudgingly took as she stepped onto the beach. Issaya followed them, wary of threats.

Yeneya, his chief spy, joined them, a small slim woman still brushing at the red dust that marked her clothing. Of all the spies he had sent, only she had returned alive. 'Sire, there is the way in,' she said, pointing up.

High above them, small against the fortress' vast black bulk, was a crack, a wound that glowed orange in the darkness. It was like a gateway into a different world.

Once they had disembarked, the ship slipped away into the shadows of the canyon, all but invisible in the dark.

Then the four of them bounded up the cliff face, the challenge no match for their superior agility.

When Savrian reached the crack, the torchlight from within half blinded him. He listened for a long moment but no one seemed nearby. With a deep breath, he slithered through and dropped down a few feet. Landing lightly, his boots sank into fine red sand. He stood in an empty hallway, torches burning greasily. Skulls grinned at him from every surface. A scream echoed, plucking at his nerves.

'Yeneya, where are we?' Savrian said.

'Just underneath where Chagorath's reavers live,' Yeneya said as she slipped through.

'Live?' Savrian said. 'That's an exaggeration of prodigious proportions. For such savage souls, they repress themselves too much to call it living.'

Boots tramping through dust interrupted them. Savrian readied himself, his blood singing. It had been too long since he had been in battle.

A group of reavers rounded the corner down the hall. Clearly of common stock, the men wore blood-soaked rags, their bare torsos scarred, their faces bruised and noses crushed. Confusion flickered over their brute expressions for a moment, and then they barged forward.

Savrian charged in, whipping Malisette free from its sheath. Lightning quick, he cut open the closest reaver's throat, brilliant arterial splatter arcing through the air. With a graceful spin, Savrian turned and skewered another through the eye.

Savrian's companions fell on the rest with abandon, pulling their foes apart with sadistic glee. A shriek of pain burst out as Issaya slammed a blade through a man's chest. As the body fell into the dust, the echo rippled away from them, like a spirit seeking its master.

They froze, listening. Someone must have heard that scream. Long seconds passed, their senses straining. Water dripped, torches crackled, a rat skittered. Seconds turned into minutes and no one came.

They breathed out a sigh of relief.

Issaya's face flickered with disappointment. Her idea of perfection was very different from Savrian's. Martial prowess was the only worthy pursuit and she obsessed with frightening tenacity.

Savrian nudged a corpse with his foot, trying to imagine living with such ugly creatures. His son had been among such brutes for years. A stale, futile anger surfaced but he quashed it. In this place, his anger was dangerous, even blasphemous.

'We should move,' Issaya said, her voice toneless. 'Where to?'

'That way,' Yeneya said, nodding towards where the reavers had come from.

Yeneya led them through a maze of hallways and basalt stairs. Occasionally doors boomed open, men screamed and chains rattled. Each floor was seemingly a clone of its predecessors, just endless halls filled with red dust and ominous noises. At first, they were on edge, cautious and watchful. Then the itch of boredom grew, the sheer monotony of the place unsettling them.

The only relief was the occasional patrol of reavers, which they ambushed and dispatched with urgent speed. The need to take more time with their victims ate at them.

Savrian's mind sank into the abyss of wanton desire, an urge that screamed for bodies to use and souls to bless, for ecstatic screams and quivering flesh. Not this dull, inartistic murdering.

He had not seen any treasures or shrines, not a spot of gold in the entire place. Just this peculiar fiction of vigilance, with its warriors watching over nothing with ferocious jealousy.

Abruptly, Yeneya stopped, holding up a hand.

Ahead of them, a glowing firepit illuminated an unremarkable chamber. A man stood, turning a hunk of meat over the fire, while another lay snoring on the dirt floor. Barred oak doors lined the walls, jagged gashes etched into their planks. There was another entrance opposite where Savrian waited, a solid stone gate decorated with aged brass and leering skulls. Iron bars as thick as Savrian's wrist served as a ceiling, revealing the level above.

'The reavers are each kept in separate cells, I think so they don't kill each other,' Yeneya whispered.

'Did you hear something?' the reaver at the firepit said, clutching a large brass bell. The other curled up tighter, grumbling.

Savrian swore. This guard was annoyingly watchful.

The guard drew a crude short sword and looked cautiously around, sniffing the air.

Cirine stepped by Savrian and winked, her scent suddenly sweet and intoxicating. Issaya followed, her dark eyes flat as she tapped a long knife against her thigh. Pleasure coiled in his gut and Savrian retreated into the dark with Yeneya. This would be amusing.

The reaver gasped as Cirine stepped into the light, his eyes widening at her near nude form. The bell's clapper tapped the metal. Putting a finger to her lips, she closed on him, an intoxicating haze drifting in the air. The bell went still as she pulled it from his limp grasp. He took in more of her scent with every breath.

Utterly absorbed, the reaver touched her slim shoulder. Savrian repressed the urge to lop the filthy limb off.

Cirine ran a hand up his chest and her fingertips stopped at the hollow of his throat. Then she curled a finger, hooking a black talon into his flesh.

A thin rasp escaped the reaver as his muscles clenched tight. He choked, his veins puckering and blackening under his skin. Sweat beading, eyes bulging, he toppled into the dust. In a few quivering moments, the agonising bliss killed him.

Issaya crept up to the sleeper as he turned over, slapped a hand over his mouth and slashed open his throat. Gurgling, he sprawled in the dust, fumbling for his axe. Eyes widening in fascination, Issaya watched his life drain out.

Savrian smiled as he stepped by the reaver's contorted corpse. Cirine's venomous claws brought such ecstasy, a clash of pain and pleasure that Savrian knew well. It was a pity the poor thing died so quickly; he had enjoyed what Slaanesh offered for such a short time.

Cirine licked her fingertips.

'You let him touch you,' he said, with more spite than he intended.

She snickered. 'You're so beautiful when you're jealous.'

He reached for her but she swayed out of his reach. Savrian fumed. She might as well have slapped his hand away.

'Your son is in one of these cells,' Yeneya said. 'I don't know which one. And those aren't the only guards – stronger ones make the rounds up above.'

Cirine's games forgotten, Savrian looked around the identical doors. He scanned each, looking for some sign. Then he saw a crude symbol carved into the heavy bar across one of the doors. His son's name, barely legible.

'There you are,' he said.

'Hide!' Yeneya hissed.

They bolted into the shadows as two red-armoured warriors appeared on the level above them. Massive brutes with leathery skin and broken teeth, they gazed down with feral eyes.

'Sloppy like the others,' one growled.

'We must find them now,' the other said without enthusiasm. 'We can't have the rabble thinking ambushes outside the pits will be tolerated.'

They strode out of sight, hefting their bloody cleavers.

Now the Khornates were searching. How long did they have before those animals found them?

Savrian lifted the heavy bar free and jerked open the door to reveal Verigon's austere cell. Then he recoiled. It reeked of excrement, sweat and blood. Straw covered the dirt floor and the stone walls glistened with condensation. A man was sitting in a crude cot that was too small for him, groggily blinking away his sleep.

This was not the little boy Savrian remembered. He had gone from a scrawny, timid child to a powerful, scarred youth. His golden skin was tanned and his black hair stringy with old sweat. Yet, he had the deep purple eyes that marked Sarn's purest bloodline.

Savrian leapt back as Verigon lunged to his feet, snatching a broad-headed axe from a hanger on the wall. An expression of absolute rage twisted Verigon's face as he stalked forward, brandishing the weapon. Savrian stepped back, raising his empty hands. Verigon had to know who he was, didn't he? Would Savrian have to fight his own son?

'Verigon, stop,' Savrian said.

Verigon halted, his purple eyes narrowing.

'I am your father,' Savrian said, not a little relieved.

Verigon cocked his head and a peculiar expression flickered over his face.

'I have not heard that accent in a long time,' he replied. 'Why are you here?'

'I'm rescuing you,' Savrian said. 'Come, we need to go.'

'No.' Verigon tightened his grip on the axe.

Savrian froze. 'What?'

'I am a warrior of Khorne,' Verigon said. 'I will not leave.'

Savrian's heart stuttered. Of all the things he could have heard, that was the worst. Verigon had completely forgotten where he had come from.

'You are my son, the son of a king, a scion of Slaanesh,' Savrian said. 'This is no place for you. I keep my pack drevars in better accommodations.'

'Physical comfort is for the weak,' Verigon said. 'And to struggle is glorious.'

What kind of puritanical drivel was this? Savrian took a deep breath.

'Only Slaanesh knows true glory,' Savrian said.

'He does not see you,' Verigon said, though without malice. 'Who witnesses your deeds? Who is there to impress? My god can see me, yours cannot.'

Savrian clamped his jaw shut. What a bitter stroke it was. And it was true, that was the cruellest part about it. Every one of Slaanesh's followers knew the ache, the deep-down need that was worse than a widow's loneliness or a child's desire. Mortal tribes, daemon kindreds and sorcerous cabals scoured the realms in search of a glittering bauble, one shimmering hair or even just the echo of her divine voice. Deep in his soul, Savrian felt it too.

'It is true,' Savrian said, relaxing with false ease. 'She hides her face from us. I won't lie. It is a misery. I wouldn't wish it on my worst enemy. However, we are family under her and nothing is going to change that. Her being gone doesn't change that.' Somewhere beyond the cell a door opened. Savrian looked around, his ears perking up. 'You come from a dynasty that has stood for thousands of years. Daemons will bow to you on your name alone. Thousands of mortals owe you their allegiance. Whereas this path will reduce you to a common murderer, whether you kill dozens or thousands. You are worth more than that, especially to blessed Slaanesh. And to me. Please, my son, come with me.'

Some of it was truth, some of it was lies. However, once Verigon came back to Slaanesh, his family and his people, he would forgive Savrian for vastly exaggerating. He would understand that it was for his own good.

Verigon looked at him, then he lowered the axe, wracked with indecision.

'Highness, they're coming,' Issaya hissed, hovering around the exit with the others.

Savrian winced as the tramp of boots reached his ears. Now was the time for expediency. Cirine's venom would have to do the persuading. As Savrian gestured towards her, the central doors slammed open and the two brutes stepped into the chamber, with more behind. The first pair charged forward, their grotesquely muscular bodies rippling, hefting massive cleavers.

'Slaaneshi scum!' one roared, ferocity boiling off him in a red haze.

With a screaming roar, the first swung his cleaver at Savrian's head. Savrian ducked and slashed open his belly, guts falling free in a rush. Crouching under the blow aimed at his neck by the other, Savrian drove his sabre into the second's exposed armpit. The blade sheared through muscle and lung, and the brute dropped with a gurgle. Savrian planted his foot on the beast's shoulder and ripped out the blade.

He looked up, quivering with adrenaline.

A wall of red and brass hedged them in, blades gleaming. Yeneya, Issaya and Cirine were herded together as the warriors edged forward, preparing to charge.

'Wait,' a voice said, ugly and hard as slate.

A man the size of an ogor walked through the bristling wall, a bulwark of muscle and armour that dwarfed the room and everyone in it. An axe made from gore-soaked stone hung in his twitching hand. His head was bare, his face a featureless mask of scar tissue, teeth sharpened to points clacking together rhythmically, yellow eyes squinting with rage.

Chagorath: only he could command the wrath of such creatures.

Savrian's stale anger roared with new life. He never thought he would meet the man. Every sense heightened. Hate sharpened to a razor edge.

Aside from the creak of armour, no one made a sound.

'I remember the scent of you,' Chagorath said, pointing his axe at Yeneya.

He lunged forward and cleaved Yeneya's head with one swing of that brutal axe. A sound like a bird skull being crushed popped through the air. She was dead before she hit the ground.

'Spies,' Chagorath rasped. 'Tools of the weak.'

Then his gaze fell onto Verigon and dread coiled in Savrian's stomach.

'Verigon, why did you not kill this man?' Chagorath said. 'He is from your meaningless past.'

Wary, Verigon dropped to a defensive crouch, gripping his axe with two hands.

Chagorath's teeth clicked, the jaw working.

'Do not touch him,' Savrian snarled, pointing his bloody sabre at the hulking lord. He would not allow this animal to deny his desires and brutalise his betters. Chagorath gestured at him and dozens of grasping hands took Savrian down like a tentacled leviathan, pressing him to his knees.

Chagorath ignored him. With a sniff, he stalked forward, struck the axe out of Verigon's hands, snatched him by the throat and slammed him into a pillar. It was casually done, as if Chagorath were chastising a chattel slave. Verigon's feet kicked as he choked.

'Never let Slaaneshi talk,' Chagorath said.

Verigon punched Chagorath in the head but the massive man barely seemed to notice; he might as well have been punching a stone.

Chagorath looked back at Savrian and he grunted in comprehension.

'I see,' Chagorath said. 'Such sentimentality has no place under Khorne's gaze.' He dropped him and Verigon crumpled at his feet, gasping. 'Release the tribes into the highest arena. Let them see how strong Verigon is.'

His captors pinned Savrian and gagged him with a rag. A hundred doors boomed open and a great roar went up. Then they hauled him to his feet and dragged him out of the chamber through a sea of red warriors. Somewhere Cirine screamed, but he could not see her.

They entered a dark, close tunnel that reeked of urine and fear. The air was humid, the roar of a berserk crowd deafening. A maw-like portcullis clanked open in front of them, the teeth of it resembling Chagorath's snarl. Someone pressed Malisette into Savrian's hand and kicked him forward through the opening.

The ground squelched under his boots as he stumbled forward. He ripped the gag from his mouth, shuddering with disgust. Then he looked down and retched.

There was no earth under his feet, just a congealing soup of blood, bones and meat. A bloody fog hung in the air, moist like the inside of a heart. The eight-sided arena was cramped, built to force combatants into close proximity with each other. Above him, a barbarous audience roared in derision under furious stars. At the end of the arena, a crude idol loomed over them, more beast than man, an axe in each hand. Of all the places Savrian had imagined dying, this was not one.

Issaya and Cirine joined him, the latter revolted, the former impassive.

Savrian forced himself to breathe the disgusting air and gathered his dignity. As a civilised man, he would show them how to comport themselves. He swaggered into the centre, a smirk on his face, his arrogance armouring him as much as the steel that encased his body.

Chagorath appeared under the stone idol on a terrace and the crowd stilled.

Opposite them, a portcullis opened and Verigon stepped out, alone.

'Verigon, you have something to prove,' Chagorath growled, his voice carrying. 'Kill that man before the others do in equal combat. He is a degenerate, the feeble aesthete of a cowardly god. Prove that he is meaningless to you.'

The threat of death did not need to be spoken aloud.

Verigon looked up at Chagorath, then at the ground, hefting his axe. There was none of the feral instinct or the ferocity from before. Instead, he milled, his face working, his mind racing.

Then a flood of half-naked reavers leapt into the arena. Savrian lifted his sabre, disappointed in the calibre of his opposition. With a sigh, he leapt forward into the fray. They were no match for him, these squalling little murderers. He hewed off limbs and heads without effort. They rushed him in threes and fours, but it mattered not. His blade was a flickering wall. Elusive as smoke, he danced through them, and where he went, they died.

Those who tried their hand at Cirine and Issaya suffered similar fates. Cirine flitted about, her silks flowing, transfixing her enemies. When they reached for her, she sank her claws into their flesh, bringing them a spasmodic, depthless ecstasy they cursed and hated. Issaya killed painfully, cutting hamstrings, peeling away sheets of skin, crippling limbs with broken nerves. She left screaming bloody victims in her wake that died slowly.

Soon, only his son remained and Savrian approached him warily.

'Tell me, Verigon,' Savrian said, gesturing at the corpses, 'do you even remember their names?'

Verigon looked around him, his face revolted as if a sudden revelation had opened his eyes.

'It's nothing more than a cage, Verigon,' Savrian said. 'There are whole worlds beyond these walls. Do you really want to stay here?'

Verigon looked at him, his eyes steady. Then he seemed to make a decision.

'You cannot get us out,' Verigon said. 'Not from him.'

That was really why he stayed. Not anger but fear. Savrian looked at Chagorath. He was the key to the whole bloody wreck.

'I will not let him touch you ever again,' Savrian said. 'I swear it on Slaanesh's sacred eye. You are my son, the most precious thing to me in this dull world.'

Verigon took a deep breath. The axe drooped and his posture relaxed. His face softened, and Savrian recognised his child in that face. The sweet, curious child he had always known. These monsters had not managed to kill him.

Chagorath quivered and gasped with rage, his fist clenched on his axe. His feral eyes flicked back and forth between Verigon and Savrian. Savrian knew it was not intelligence or restraint that stayed the berserker. Rather he simply could not decide who to kill first.

Did Khorne watch his flailing vassal? Oh, if that blinkered god did and Savrian cast him down... Savrian's mind skittered to a halt. It was too perfect. If Chagorath died, his followers would fight for his position. Thousands of the wretched beasts would die in the mad fight for control while they escaped. And then Savrian and his kingdom would come in, mop up the weakened remains and turn the fortress towards a better, loftier purpose. He would succeed where his ancestors had failed so often in breaking this place.

Savrian pressed his fingers to his lips, a shuddering thrill rolling through his body. He threw back his head and laughed, the manic cackle spiralling through the still air. He knew he looked mad but this perfection of opportunity was too beautiful.

The only trick would be persuading Chagorath to cooperate in his own savage way.

'You know, I figured out what you are doing,' Savrian said. 'Collecting and offering all these skulls. Tell me, Chagorath, does Khorne know you're trying to buy his favour like a courtesan?'

Chagorath screamed, a wordless slavering howl. The brute leapt down into the arena, sweeping his axe from his belt and hefting it overhead. Savrian leapt away as the Khornate lord crashed in like a meteor, his mighty overhead blow splintering the stone beneath him, blood and gore flying.

Chagorath whirled around and charged, closing on him with shocking speed. Dropping into a crouch as Chagorath's axe whooshed overhead, Savrian grinned. Finally, someone worthy of his blade.

Springing aside as the brute's axe cleaved the air where he had just been standing, Savrian lashed out, whip-fast. Sparks flew from the warrior's red armour as Malisette bit deep. Chagorath bellowed, whirled around and swung his axe at Savrian's legs. Savrian vaulted over the whistling blade, spinning gracefully in the air.

Around them, more reavers and blood warriors rushed into the arena to try to kill the others. But Savrian could not protect them. He had his hands full.

Chagorath rushed after him, his strikes precise, while Savrian danced around him, every movement flowing like liquid, turning the duel into art. Chagorath's aggression curdled into frustration with every unrewarding swipe.

Gasping for the blood of his opponent, any at all, Chagorath reached a little farther, a little harder. Then Chagorath's form broke, his arm outstretched, and the gap between his breastplate and pauldron spread open to reveal pale, almost translucent, flesh.

Savrian sidestepped and whipped his blade into the gap. Blood flew. Chagorath's body hitched as soothing narcotics ran through his veins. Roaring, Chagorath spun around, his axe leading the movement. The blow whistled passed Savrian's face as he retreated.

The Khornate lord pursued him across the arena, slashing and howling, and Savrian was pushed back. With a boneless agility, he dodged around Chagorath's relentless attacks. He struck back where he could, his sabre lashing Chagorath's exposed flesh, but it was like trying to take down a rabid rhinox with a shaving razor. The brute bled from a dozen cuts but he never slowed, each wound another goad for his endless rage.

Savrian dropped into a low crouch, prowling around his bigger opponent like a frost sabre, Malisette held tight at his shoulder, the point following Chagorath. Indignation and ego boiled in him; Savrian hated being on the defensive. Yet, Chagorath was the bigger and taller man with reach and weight to match.

Maybe Savrian could use that. Yes. He could use that.

Savrian waited, watching for the shift in the brute's shoulder, in his hips, a twist in the torso. The muscles in his left thigh clenched as Chagorath shifted his weight. Another charge.

Chagorath barged in and Savrian spun away, allowing the axe to come close but not quite bite repeatedly. Allowing the stupid beast to feel like he was in control. Savrian watched his opponent's grunting, impatient face, waiting for just the right moment.

Then pain shot through Savrian's knee and he stumbled. Horrifyingly, the elixir was wearing off. The axe swooped in, the serrated edge ripping through Savrian's breastplate and slicing across his ribs. Pain seared through him, enlivening his dulling senses. He shuddered in ecstasy, staggering on weak legs.

'Cut me again,' Savrian breathed, steadying himself.

Stepping back, his scarred face etched with revulsion, Chagorath tightened his guard.

'Why not?' Savrian shouted, grinning manically.

He flicked his blade at Chagorath's face, a quick feint. Reflexively, not wanting to be touched, the beast snapped his axe up. Savrian sliced his blade down through Chagorath's weapon hand, sending fingers and axe spinning away. Roaring, Chagorath backhanded him with a meaty fist, catching Savrian full across the head.

Savrian crashed to the ground, Malisette disappearing into the ooze. The world wobbled and spun in a ruddy blur, his breathing too loud in his ears.

Chagorath crashed onto him and grabbed him by the throat with both hands, bloody nubs digging in.

'Die, you disgusting wretch,' Chagorath hissed.

Savrian flailed, scrabbling at the red bulk on top of him. The cartilage of his throat cracked. His lungs burned, his veins throbbed. Spots flickered over his vision, his skull straining as if it was going to burst. He tore at Chagorath's iron grip but it was like rock.

With a last gasp, Savrian rammed his thumb into Chagorath's glaring right eye. Jelly burst and the man howled, rearing back. His deadly grip loosened and Savrian sucked in the coppery air, made sweet by suffocation.

He slammed the heel of his hand into Chagorath's jaw, snapping his head back. Blood spurted as the beast bit through his tongue. A flicker caught Savrian's eye: Malisette. The Khornate lord toppled sideways like a felled tree and Savrian lunged towards his weapon. Chagorath grabbed his ankle, jerking him back bodily. Snarling, Savrian kicked him in the face, crushing his nose.

Chagorath released him. Weaving on his knees like a drunk, he struggled to rise.

Coughing painfully through a battered throat, Savrian staggered to his feet, his sabre in hand.

Loathing boiled in Savrian as he turned towards his weakened foe. This was the man who had ruined his life. A man who had slaughtered his first wife and all her court. The man who had stolen his son, brutalised him, told him his heritage was nothing. The man who had saddled Savrian with a mountain of regrets.

'You fought well,' Chagorath slurred.

'You did not,' Savrian said, his lip curling. 'Go to Slaanesh and feed her appetites as best you can.'

With a two-handed swing, Savrian cut up through Chagorath's skull, the ancient blade shearing through teeth and then bone. No skull for the skull throne. The god of commoners would receive nothing. The corpse crashed into the muck.

Savrian looked up at the silent crowd. Now was the moment of truth. Who did they hate more?

The Khornates did not look at him; instead they glowered sidelong at their neighbours. Fingers caressed hammers and axes. Lips curled into snarls. Soft growls rumbled in cracked throats. Armour clanked as barbarians shifted.

Someone screamed, a ragged, desperate cry. A man turned and slammed his axe into the guts of his neighbour. Blood flew. A towering brute with a flaming hammer smashed a man out of his way only to be beheaded in turn. The cry of 'Blood for the Blood God!' boomed.

With a great roar, the cultists ripped into each other with stunning ferocity, Savrian and his cohort forgotten. Savrian grinned in triumph: he had bet true.

Yet, out of the corner of his eye, Savrian thought he saw the great idol of Khorne smile.

'Verigon!' Savrian said, looking across the arena for his son.

The battle surged across the arena, a sea of blood-soaked

bodies thrashing through the gore. Savrian glimpsed Verigon before his son hurled himself into the melee with a roar. Cursing, Savrian slashed his way through the crowd, but it was like swimming against a tide. A painful hitch lodged itself in his right shoulder. He was losing his edge, but he could not leave.

A mass of armoured brutes coalesced around him and a throwing axe came whistling in.

Then Issaya bolted out of the crowd and slapped the throwing axe to the ground. She charged, her knives flickering. Agonised screams followed her as she crippled her foes. However, her thirst for pain led her deeper into the crowd and when Savrian ordered her to fall back, she ignored him. Savrian could only watch as axes hacked her down. Grinding his teeth in frustration, Savrian fought on. While they took his best followers, it seemed their numbers were endless.

'Husband, we should go,' Cirine said, flitting to him. Covered in gore, her gown in tatters, Cirine's eyes were wide with fear.

'I cannot find Verigon,' he said, barely glancing at her.

'But–' she said.

'My love, this will all be for nothing if we don't find him,' he said.

She pressed her lips together, as if possessed by some sudden doubt.

'What is it?' he asked, his voice hard with suspicion.

She opened her mouth to speak but at that moment, Savrian caught sight of Verigon.

'Verigon!' Savrian shouted, his sabre singing as he cut through the crowd.

The young man whirled about, his face snarling. He caught himself in mid-swing, pulling back the blow aimed at Savrian's head. Shuddering with adrenaline, his eyes hard as gems, Verigon glared at him.

'I was fine,' he growled.

'Of course you were,' Savrian said. 'It is time to leave.'

Verigon's eyes narrowed, as if making some calculation. Then he nodded.

'You're right,' he said. 'We should go.'

They fled from the arena, down into the guts of the complex. The battle thinned into isolated murderous brawlers and flocks of tattered slaves who scattered at the sight of them. All around, the cells were empty, the roar of battle echoing down to them through stone halls. Retracing the path back was easy and the three of them reached the open crack, where fresh air bled through and twilight broke out.

'Go on,' Savrian said. 'See that small beach?' Verigon nodded. 'That is where we are headed.'

Verigon slipped through and began the laborious climb down, his movements confident if lacking a certain grace. As Savrian prepared to go through himself, Cirine caught his arm.

'My love, I do not trust him,' she said.

Savrian paused, looking at her hand on his arm.

'He is my son,' Savrian said. 'He listens to me, he remembers me. I know he is not that promising now. But give me time. I can teach him.'

'He listens but does not hear,' she replied. 'He remembers but does not care. He does not want to be saved, my love. He is manipulating you and has been from the beginning.'

Cirine was a clever woman and deeply perceptive. Yet, what she suggested was preposterous, even paranoid. Then he recognised her true motive. It was jealousy, a scenario that had played out many times. While he had tolerated her possessiveness in the past because it amused him, this had to be ended now.

'Your desires do not trump mine,' Savrian growled, grabbing a fistful of her hair. 'My whims are absolute. I recommend that you get used to his presence. I desire that he returns to us, so he shall.'

'All I am saying is to be careful,' Cirine whispered.

'My sweet, I recommend you take your own advice,' Savrian hissed.

She looked away from him and Savrian knew he had won. He released her and then slipped out of the Bastion into the clean air. The climb down was much worse than the climb up. Savrian's joints ground together. His skin felt like that of a corpse, stretched dry over his bones. Colour faded, sound muddled. Once he reached the beach, bone-deep exhaustion dragged him down onto his knees. All the dreadful years fell back upon his shoulders.

'Father?' Verigon said, sounding concerned. He walked towards Savrian and then suddenly stopped, wary.

'It's nothing,' Savrian said, breathing hard. 'It will pass. We will go home, and I will teach you the joys of Slaanesh. Things I should have taught you years ago.'

Savrian took out a small silver flute on a chain around his neck. When he blew on it, there was no sound. However, the captain of his ship would hear it and come for them.

Savrian turned inward, drowning in his misery. Cirine crept over to him and hovered, her gaze fixed on Verigon.

Suddenly, sand churned and Cirine screamed. Savrian staggered, struggling to rise. An axe was stuck deep in Cirine's flesh. Some Khornate had found them, some brute lingered out here. Savrian froze.

Cirine fell, Verigon's axe buried deep in her chest. Verigon tore it free, a feral gleam in his purple eyes. With an adrenal shiver, he stepped over her corpse.

No. His son could not be doing this. He could not.

Savrian pushed the truth away even as his mind lurched for it. Verigon charged, teeth clenched, bloody axe swinging low. Sluggish, Savrian lunged back, his legs wobbling. The axe cleaved through the gash in his armour into vital organs.

The pain crushed him, obliterating every other sensation. The withdrawal blasted the sensation to unendurable highs. He rolled into the sand, unable to breathe, unable to think. A chill, cold as glacier-melt, filled his flesh. As he inhaled, the pain twisted his guts like a fist. Warmth bathed Savrian's side, and his hand came away red with blood.

Verigon looked down at him, muscles twitching in his face.

'I serve Khorne. Not Slaanesh. Never Slaanesh,' Verigon snarled.

'No one can reject her allure... She will not allow it,' Savrian gasped, struggling to his knees. 'You cannot be my son. Not the boy I raised. You are some fake. Some soul-dead counterfeit.'

'I am your son,' Verigon said, his voice quivering. 'I remember the towers and bathing pools, and the endless feasting and the vulgar rituals. I remember my mother. Her charms and venom did not save me. And you didn't either. You were off searching for a vanished god while we died. I've hated you ever since then.'

'I should have seen you for what you were – a wretched animal,' Savrian hissed, then he coughed and the pain flared.

'You did, and you ignored it,' Verigon said, circling around him. 'Because you are soft, like your useless, effete master.'

'Do not blame her for my decisions,' Savrian said. 'It's my fault you were taken. Slaanesh is perfect and cannot be blamed.'

'Perfect?' Verigon said, his voice full of venom. 'It was Khorne who kept me alive in the pits, who taught me to fight and set me free. You were right, the Bastion is a cage and Chagorath was a brainless fool for staying there. There are so many other ways I can please Khorne. Like turning the Kingdom of Sarn to a god that is actually worthy and not just a hole in the heart.'

Spite and hate and fury rose up in Savrian, desperate and clawing. It pushed him to his feet and helped him drag his sabre free of its sheath. Yet, he didn't have the strength to strike; the blood loss was too much.

'They will know your allegiance,' Savrian snarled. 'They will reject you.'

Verigon continued to stalk him, prowling just out of reach of Malisette.

'No, they won't,' Verigon said, smirking. 'They will see the purple eyes of Sarn's bloodline and love me as they were conditioned to. And they will follow me to Khorne's side like children.'

The horror of it crashed in. Savrian's dynasty was ending, the empire toppling, the work of a thousand ancestors burning away. His people's devotion to his bloodline would be the undoing of his house. And it was his fault.

'Slaanesh give me the strength to kill you,' Savrian whispered. 'I swear I'll have you dead. My ancestors will break your soul after they break your body. They'll–'

'You will see them before I do,' Verigon said. 'And if they're going to break anyone, it is you. If you desire vengeance, you should pray to Khorne.'

Verigon hefted the axe, encroaching on him.

Savrian recoiled, clutching his side. Malisette gleamed, outstretched in his other hand, but then his legs crumpled and he collapsed once more.

'No, I will not run from my goddess,' Savrian choked out. 'My devotion is true. Do not insult me, you heartless beast.'

Verigon stopped and stepped back then, his face dark with pity.

'You are pathetic,' Verigon said. 'You are so blinded by your sentimentality that you don't realise Slaanesh never cared about you. At least Khorne does not pretend to. I'll leave you to him, though I wonder if you even deserve that. Goodbye, father.'

Savrian tensed but the axe did not come. Verigon walked away, nothing more than an outline against the rising sun. Then he disappeared down the beach and Savrian was alone.

Darkness ate at Savrian's vision, his flesh clammy and cold. He could not feel anything. This was suffering, this long degeneration into the oubliette of one's own dying body. His thoughts slurred together, his memory turning to soup.

'Slaanesh, no, please,' Savrian said. 'Come to me, please. Beloved. Please. You cannot let him. Please, let me fix it. Let me…' Savrian's breath ran out as his life blood leaked from the mortal wound. His heart fluttered in his chest like a trapped bird. Savrian forced himself to inhale against the agony, but each breath became shallower and shallower as the abyss inside him grew.

He felt for some comfort, some presence as his soul loosened in its moorings. Just a hint of her. He would endure any soul-breaking torture just to see her. She could punish him in ways that would make a daemon wilt. All of that would be nothing if he could just see her. Just a glance. Just once.

'Beloved, where have you gone?' Savrian whispered.

He sank into a cold and endless abyss, his countless regrets whispering in the dark.

TURN OF THE ADDER

J C Stearns

Illinois-based author and drukhari enthusiast J C Stearns brings his zeal for all things dark and twisted to Inferno! for the first time.

When a treacherous wych cult affronts the Kabal of the Bladed Lotus by falling to Ynnead, the powerful Archon K'Shaic rallies his forces to wipe them from existence. But when K'Shaic attempts to sway the tide of battle by pitting his two sons against each other, the brothers reveal dastardly schemes of their own.

'The reward of treachery is victory.'

Thunderous cheers rolled through the drukhari fleet. Archon K'Shaic stood on the command dais of his battle-barque and held up a hand for silence. On hundreds of sleek-keeled Raiders, the archon's holographic image – projected from each transport's command relay or the hand-held unit of a dracon – towered over the kabalite foot-soldiers and gun crews. K'Shaic's image was repeated so frequently that even the countless hired mercenaries from lower Commorragh, soaring between the Raiders on jetbikes and skyboards, could hear his proclamations.

'The Dark City stands as an eternal monument to the power of betrayal!' Another cheer, loud enough to be heard over the screaming jets as the massive fleet barrelled through the webway. 'But,' the archon said, holding one interjectory finger aloft, 'what the Jade Labyrinth has done is no betrayal!'

All the fleet's members booed as one. They followed the

oratory lead of the great archon as surely as they followed the physical lead of his battle-barque. The triple-decked catamaran was larger even than the Razorwing jetfighters roaring overhead. Disintegrators and dark lances bristled along its long black decks. The graceful hull was the colour of oiled gunmetal, the sharp edges of its plates tinged violet, its sails boasting the insignia of the Bladed Lotus, in K'Shaic's colours of purple on steel. Evaeline, the barque's experienced pilot, commanded the ship from directly behind the command dais.

'Had the hekatarii of the Cult of the Jade Labyrinth merely turned upon us, they would be role models, not criminals. No, the Labyrinthae have done something far worse than betraying us – they have chosen subservience. They've made themselves willing slaves, whoring themselves for the false promise of a non-existent deity!'

Leaning against a railing on the barque, Naeddre and his brother Qeine watched their father rousing the bloodlust of his troops. K'Shaic, Archon of the Kabal of the Bladed Lotus, was in rare form. Naeddre didn't know how many slaves had been flayed to give his father such a youthful vigour, but the number had to be in the thousands. He'd never seen K'Shaic so energetic.

'I say, if these *Ynnari*,' K'Shaic snarled the word with undisguised contempt, 'if these wyches and whatever craftworld scum have lured them astray want to court death so badly, then let's give them exactly what they're asking for!'

The archon keyed his command dais. Across the fleet, his mighty holographic images vanished.

'Inspiring,' said Qeine. Tall and broad of shoulder, Qeine was a peak physical specimen of his kind. He wore ridged ghostplate armour to add to his profile, which made him tower over every warrior on the ship.

'Victory will give us our real inspiration,' said K'Shaic. Even without his holographic enhancements, he was an imposing figure. His own ghostplate armour was exquisite, a custom-built relic, its form the template for the armour of every kabalite soldier in his employ. His long flowing mane of ebony hair normally struck Naeddre as a token of vanity, out of place in his father's aging features. With the full glory of his youth restored, it suited the archon. His alabaster features could have been graven from purest marble, his cheekbones sharp enough to cut flesh. His ancient powerblade, the surgesabre, rested at his hip, silently hungering for murder.

'All the inspiration in the galaxy will do us little good if we're murdered from behind,' said Naeddre. Both his father and older brother fixed him with hateful glares, although he could see Qeine struggling to keep the edges of a smile out of his sneer.

Slender where his brother was muscular, short where Qeine was tall, Naeddre had always been seen as the lesser brother. Nearly everyone with whom they interacted seemed to take his reduced stature as evidence of a reduced character. Qeine boasted the best equipment, while Naeddre went to war in a studded flight vest befitting a wealthy heliarch. The thin material made it easier to manoeuvre on a skyboard, sacrificing none of the wearer's agility for added protection. In fact, while it looked as flimsy as the wychsuit of any hellion, it had been made by the same craftsmen as Qeine's ghostplate, and could easily deflect a bolt shell or Commorrite splinter shard.

'If you fear the forces at your back, then perhaps you're better suited to guarding the Amaranth Spire,' K'Shaic sneered.

'It's not our own forces that worry me,' said Naeddre.

'They're far more interested in murdering the Jade Labyrinth.' Which was true. When Kysthene and the wyches under her command had fled the Dark City, declaring allegiance to the Ynnari and seizing control of the Port of Widows, they'd done more than just betray their kabalite benefactors. They'd left the Bladed Lotus without their primary means of psychic sustenance. They'd cut off the kabal's access to the port that provided a great deal of its material wealth. Most importantly, they'd made the Kabal of the Bladed Lotus, and by extension every member of it, look foolish and weak. Their destruction was not only in compliance with Vect's edicts, but also a necessary step if the kabal was going to survive in the wake of Commorragh's recent upheavals.

'The garrisons?' Qeine guessed.

'The garrisons,' Naeddre confirmed.

Their father steepled his fingers, staring at his two sons. They needed no goading to know when he expected them to compete for his favour.

'Ignore them,' said Qeine. 'They're intended to reinforce the port in the event of sustained invasion, but the Port of Widows was never designed to repel invasion from the Commorragh side. We'll overwhelm them, put the Labyrinthae to death and surround whatever forces remain in the garrisons before they have time to assault our rear lines.' As ever, Qeine's plan was raw, naked aggression, designed to win through bravado and brute force.

'Take them one at a time,' Naeddre countered. 'We first overwhelm one of the rear garrisons, then the other, before moving on to the port itself. Let each enemy bastion that falls increase the terror of the next.'

'If the corsair fleets arrive at the Port of Widows, the wych cult will barter all the goods they've stolen from the kabal for passage away from our reach,' Qeine argued. 'We can't give them the time to escape.' He stood, looming over his brother. Naeddre wondered if his sibling truly believed they needed to act with such urgency, or if he just didn't want to return to the webway fortifications. Whenever K'Shaic wished to remove his sons from the Dark City, either as punishment or to curtail any sudden rises in influence, he often chose to send them to command the garrisons.

'No one's suggesting we do,' Naeddre countered. He dropped his arms to his side and returned his brother's aggressive posture, ignoring their height difference, their chests nearly touching, each close enough to feel the other's angry breath. 'The corsairs aren't due to arrive until tomorrow. By then, there won't even be a lock of wych hair remaining in the port.'

The brothers might have come to blows if Archon K'Shaic hadn't raised his voice.

'Enough,' he said, waving his hand. 'The kabal as a whole will bypass the garrisons entirely and assault the port. You'll each take your personal forces, the kabalites loyal to you and the mercenaries you've hired, and assault one of the garrisons. Naeddre will take the Viscerean Garrison, and Qeine the Weeping Garden. Waste no time in your conquest – once whatever commanders you find have been slain, join me with all due haste. Claim your glory in the main assault.' Their father gestured with his arm, and two of the Raiders flanking the barque drifted towards the rear. Each carried a trio of incubi, K'Shaic's customary 'gift' to protect his sons as well as to guard against treachery.

Naeddre and Qeine turned as one and stalked towards the aft of the barque. They needed no further instruction. Their father had turned the brothers upon one another, then taken the best part of each of their offerings and left them with only veiled threats. Each second that passed before they reached the Port of Widows would be another that saw their own personal contribution to the legend that K'Shaic was constructing diminish.

The brothers each boarded their own personal craft, Qeine astride the gleaming onyx bike he'd named *Razordirge*, and Naeddre atop a broad-winged skyboard of his own design.

'Watch your back, brother,' Qeine laughed before fitting his helm. At some point he'd had his teeth extracted and replaced with triangular neoferrium razors, giving him the look of a grinning predatory beast. 'I'd hate for one of your mercenary leaders to slay you for that fine toy of yours.'

Like all archons, each of the brothers was in charge of one of the kabal's commodities. Qeine, as a young officer, had taken troops loyal to him and captured a large chemical manufactory, giving him control of a great supply of quality ammunition for the poisoned weapons of the line in the Dark City. His forces were full of gunboats filled with kabal troops, outfitted with the finest weapons.

It was Naeddre's turn to laugh. 'No need,' he said. 'I've promised the heliarch who brings me the most plundered hekatarii knives a Moonfoe of his very own.' Naeddre's own commodity was more niche. Creating exquisite skyboards and jetbikes was a highly specific task, one that required specialised labour. It took slaves with a discerning enough ear to attune the acoustic crystal lattices as well as the manual dexterity to string them. It was no easy job, but decades of scouring the galaxy for the perfect servants to assist his work had paid off. His creations were the pride of the wych cults. Entire gangs of hellions would fight to the death, just so the last gang scum standing could receive one of Naeddre's cast-offs.

'Good,' said Qeine. He gunned *Razordirge*'s engine. 'You should be on your guard. This far from Commorragh, and with his pet wyches in open revolt, father is uncharacteristically vulnerable. One of his servants might take such an opportunity to remove him from his position.'

'How good of you to think of K'shaic in his time of need.' Naeddre snapped shut his own ghostplate helm, which was both his connection to the command network and his badge of office. He shivered as micro needles bit into his scalp, locking the helm securely. 'Take care to show the same caution with your own position.'

Qeine laughed, and his bike blazed away, leaving only a flare of pale energy behind him. This attack was what both brothers had been waiting decades for: an opportunity to assassinate their father while most of his forces were otherwise engaged. Which one of them took the mantle of leadership was open to speculation, but both of them would be willing to bleed that particular issue out after K'Shaic's fate had been settled. First, however, Naeddre had to take the garrison.

Following his orders, the soldiers loyal to him peeled away from the bulk of the attack fleet. Qeine had scores of Raiders at his command, enticed by the elder brother's legendary brutality, and flocks of scourges willing to follow him for the promise of his favour. Qeine was the preferred successor, and no small number of kabalites wanted to be able to claim that they had supported the new ruler before his ascension.

Naeddre's own forces were less prestigious. He had support from the kabal, to be sure, but the men and women who followed him did so because he had personally recruited them, because they had seen first hand the rewards of his leadership. Where Qeine had dozens of gunboats, a single squadron of Ravagers followed Naeddre's own force as they barrelled towards their target. No, Naeddre's forces consisted largely of Commorragh's dregs. For every Raider that Qeine could boast, Naeddre had a gang of hellions or pack of Reavers ready to murder at his command. They knew the arenas of the Jade Labyrinth would be inherited by someone, that a new wych cult would find themselves with the Bladed Lotus' patronage. The mass elevation of scores of low-born Commorrites was rare in the extreme, but circumstances had put just such a shining prize within their grasp, and every one of Naeddre's soldiers was determined to prove themselves worthy of such a reward. To show his solidarity with them, he even wielded a helglaive, albeit an exquisitely crafted one that had cost him an entire raid's worth of slaves.

The webway tunnel was massive, large enough to accommodate an entire battleship. The edges were so far away they were lost in the mists that clung to the borders of the passage. There was no wind within its confines, but so intense was their flight that they may as well have been flying into a hurricane gale.

Just as Naeddre finished concentrating on his gauntlet to bring the dark orb of his shadow field into existence, the oiled black metal of the Viscerean Garrison came distantly into view. A gleaming sphere of darkness, curving blades jutting from above and below, the fortress sported three decks, which ringed it like lines of longitude. All were empty. No picket line greeted them, no warning weapons fire harried them. No enemy aircraft hung above the fortification. Naeddre felt his heart begin to sink with the prospect that the enemy had left the stronghold undefended.

But then they began pouring forth. From both above and below, skyboards streamed into the air of the webway, and even at so great a distance, Naeddre could hear the shrieking war cries of the hellion gangs.

All around him, the low-born scum in his employ shrieked and cackled their own cries. Expletives, profanity, promises, curses and simple wordless screams of bloodlust: the desperate flock of murderers filled the air with a hateful chorus. Naeddre couldn't tell who opened fire first; the sound of splinter pods thrumming and the spitting of shards of toxin-laden death seemed to start simultaneously with the zipping hiss of glass needles shooting past. Neither side could hit a specific target, but that hardly mattered. The splinter pod wasn't a weapon of precision; it was intended to strafe, to keep the enemies' heads down long enough to close with agoniser and helglaive.

The cluster of hellions screaming towards them bore the colours of several rival gangs, all painted over with the looping knotwork designs of the Jade Labyrinth. There was no sign of any Ynnari banners or insignias. Naeddre crouched as the packs barrelled towards one another.

'Reavers, now,' said Naeddre. The gangs of jetbikers under his command leapt to obey. With a high-pitched whine of overcharged engines, the razored bikes careened ahead of the hellions and into the knotted mass of the enemy. With a speed that not even the hellions could match, they tore through flesh and skyboard alike.

The Reavers blazed through the masses of bodies, seeking targets with the most intricate skyboards, the greatest trophies dangling from their wychsuits. With grav-talons, envenomed blades and the shearing edges of the bikes themselves, the Reavers shredded the heliarchs where they found them, then shot away before the Labyrinthae could react.

Naeddre howled in joy as the lines smashed together. The

hiss and zip of traded splinter fire was gone, replaced by the clang of helglaives ringing from each other, the metallic sound of blade meeting flesh and the frustrated rage-filled shrieks of the dying.

For Naeddre, the battleground was an aerial slaughterhouse. The choking, repressive aura of his shadow field stole the momentum from any who came within its radius, slowing their reflexes and even the engines of their skyboards. His enemies came to him dulled, blinded and lethargic. He roared through the air, deflecting enemy blades aside and gutting foes with wanton abandon. Let Qeine and his father exalt in conquering enemies of equal skill; for Naeddre there was no greater thrill than killing his way, godlike, through an enemy force that stood helpless and weak before him. He was an obsidian cloud, blazing through the foe for his soldiers, casting a rain of riderless skyboards and dismembered body parts in his wake.

The pain of his victims was a wonderful thrill, so exquisite he could nearly taste it, but today something was wrong. Normally, the delightful rush of each victim's agony would be capped by the ultimate moment of fear and despair as they finally slipped away into death, but with each new kill, the climax remained absent. Naeddre frowned as he realised this. He lashed out with his helglaive and lopped the head from one of his own Reavers as the biker shot past. The pain was exquisite, sharp and solid like a pungent, aged funerary wine, but still the Reaver's life force slipped away without the final moment of despair.

'Soul drinkers,' he hissed. The revelation thrilled him and terrified him at the same time. Ever since the last disjunction, the archons and haemonculi had missed no opportunity to tell the populace of Commorragh about the falsehood of

Ynnead, that the god did not exist and that his followers were powerless.

Like all drukhari, he felt the pull of She-Who-Thirsts, the devouring addiction that eroded their souls with each passing moment. Each drop of fear and pain he inflicted fed the void of Her hunger by proxy, preserving his own spirit from consumption. However, since the flight of the first Ynnari and the shattering of Khaine's Gate, he had felt a second pull at his soul. Not the screaming, howling demand of his birthright, but a gentle, insistent call. He sometimes wondered how many other denizens of Commorragh listened to the wordless, whispered entreaty, and like him ignored it, all the while hoping no one would realise they heard the call of a god who wasn't supposed to exist.

Victorious cries echoed over the command net. The mob of hellions that had poured out to meet them were hopelessly outnumbered, their leaders surgically murdered by the arcing paths of the Reavers. The defenders were far from finished, though. The first wave of Labyrinthae was just a lure to bring the bulk of the Commorrites closer and keep them engaged. More hellions were swarming from the upper- and lower-most levels of the Viscerean Garrison now, manoeuvring to hit the attackers from above and below. The Venoms that had been conspicuously absent previously now hovered around from behind the fortress. A flock of scourges soared far overhead. The chatter and screams across the command network in Naeddre's helm announced a dozen new threats.

Naeddre glanced up to see incoming hellions, curling down like the leading edge of a great wave threatening to wash them out to sea. They had repainted the underside of their skyboards, each bearing a single part of a larger image, so that when they flew together, they formed a single picture: a jagged, stylised version of the rune of Ynnead. Even among his own battle-hardened and desperate troops, Naeddre could feel an undercurrent of fear at the sight of the image. He took a moment to savour the peppery spice of the terror rippling across the battlefield before responding.

'Raevij, this would be your moment.'

'Confirmed, your grace.'

The Ravagers that had trailed the attack force, creeping low and slow along the lowest edges of the massive webway tunnel, struck with the potency of a capricious, sadistic god. They rose from the mists, disintegrator arrays blazing. Coruscating streams of blue-white energy tore into the lower hellion pack. Boards and riders alike fell before the torrent, the superheated energies enough to utterly destroy anything they came into contact with.

'Reavers, tear their Venoms apart,' Naeddre commanded. 'All Raider crews, ignore the defenders. Land the damn troops, and *then* engage the Labyrinthae out here at will.' The scourge flock swooped in a great arcing glide, their haywire blasters raining down on the Ravagers below. 'Crimson Chains, break from orders and kill those winged bastards.' The Reaver gang swung away from the other bikers and fell into formation, rocketing towards the retreating scourges. 'As to the hellions, there's a second Moonfoe skyboard for whoever brings me the most scalps!'

The savages screamed loud enough to be heard over the roar of battle. Naeddre skimmed low beneath the melee in the sky, even as the reinforcements were crashing into them from above. He needed to end this battle quickly; something was out of place. The anguish of the dying was invigorating, but nowhere near as vitalising as it should have been. It was as if the lives of the dying were being extinguished before he and the other Commorrites could truly relish their suffering. If the rumours of the rebels were more than lies, then each death only empowered them, while denying the Commorrites a portion of their psychic spoils.

The first shot nearly tore his head from his shoulders. He had a moment to cast about looking for which direction it had come from before his shadow field collapsed, and only by a crazed drunken lurch was he able to keep his balance and avoid tumbling into the open air of the webway tunnel. Only the maddeningly expensive ghostplate helm kept the impact itself from killing him. The first was not the last, however: several more laser rounds slammed into him in rapid succession.

Righting himself, Naeddre stamped his foot and accelerated towards the garrison. The Moonfoe's manoeuvring jets screamed in protest as he cut a juddering, erratic path. Smoke poured from one of the board's jet vents. The laser bolts blazed in around him, close enough for him to feel the heat of their passing. Naeddre didn't need to see the rangers to recognise the product of their elegant weapons.

'Phaerl,' Naeddre signalled to the leader of the incubi his father had sent to accompany him, 'I've selected my breach point.' With one arm, Naeddre pointed his helglaive at the upper platform where the long rifles were being fired from. Let the cowards know he was coming; it made no difference.

'Noted, your grace. We will reinforce directly.'

The garrison loomed large. Naeddre leaned sharply, skimming along the outer wall of the structure. The rangers saw him coming, and unleashed a desperate hail of laser fire to prevent his assault.

Naeddre laughed, no longer trying to avoid the shots. The glancing injuries they could inflict were nothing compared to the vitality he was enjoying from the slaughter going on around him, even with the Ynnari stealing a portion of the suffering. One hit dug into the Moonfoe skyboard, making it waver uncertainly. Another tore into his shoulder, the impact sending waves of agony through his arm. He could think of no more perfect aperitif to the feast that was before him.

With a sadistic cackle, he released the control chain and fell away from the skyboard. He snapped his body with preternatural grace, rolling over in mid-air. With one foot, he kicked off the railing at the edge of the platform, with the other he kicked off the wall, and landed deftly on the walkway. The skyboard slammed into the rangers. The closest managed to duck low enough to avoid its bladed wings, but the two forming the rear rank were less fortunate. One was bisected, his head, neck and left arm severed from the rest of his body. The other took the full impact of the skyboard in his chest. The board, jets still firing, bucked skyward, rocketing away with enough force to pitch the ranger over the railing. Naeddre ignored it; he could recall the Moonfoe if necessary.

The remaining three rangers struggled to their feet, but Naeddre could feel their despair emanating from them. They stood no chance against him, and they knew it. The walkway was a firing platform, barely wide enough for three people abreast, and Naeddre was between them and the only entry to the garrison proper. Escape was as impossible as victory. Naeddre allowed them a cruel moment to appreciate their doom, then swung his helglaive in a broad spiral.

The blades hit the lead aeldari ranger three times in the first series of loops. Blood sprayed from a slash on his thigh, viscera poured forth from the rend across the youth's abdomen, and his gyrostatic arm soared away, severed completely at the shoulder. The ranger slumped to the ground, overwhelmed with pain. Naeddre stepped past him. The other two retreated, trying to bring their longrifles to bear. They knew that each razored blow could have been lethal if he'd so chosen. If he couldn't enjoy their deaths fully, then he'd just have to keep these poor unfortunate souls around for as long as possible, to maximise their suffering while they lived.

Naeddre lunged forward. The pain in his shoulder was gone, vanished amid the rush of his enemies' fear and pain. He flanked the two of them, smashing first one then the other with the blunt squared ends of his helglaive to drive them apart. He brought the glaive down in an overhead chop, cutting deep into the shoulder of the furthest. The second leaned back, bringing her longrifle up for a desperate shot. Sparing her only a sidelong glance, Naeddre slammed the helglaive backwards, hooked the longrifle and wrenched it from the ranger's grasp with a twisting forward yank.

The other aeldari, too injured to hold his rifle, pulled his shuriken pistol and fired. A monomolecular disc ricocheted off Naeddre's helm with a high-pitched *sping*. The ranger levelled his pistol for a second shot, unable to overcome his instinct to aim before firing, and in the moment of hesitation Naeddre struck. He smashed his helglaive's blunt end into the enemy's face, then flourished the same blade down with a curve of his wrist, slitting the Ynnari's throat.

Naeddre turned back to the female ranger. Her comrades still technically lived, their lifeblood pooling on the oily black metal, but she might as well have been alone. She glanced behind her, and Naeddre could see her realising that the entrance to the garrison was now open, if she could reach it before her drukhari attacker could overtake her.

'Run,' said Naeddre. 'Tell those within that I come for them, little herald.'

The ranger turned, her cloak fluttering like a frightened bird, and bolted for the door. Naeddre pulled his blast pistol from his side and shot her in the back. The darklight beam burst through her body, extinguishing her life in an instant. Naeddre flexed his shoulder. Beneath the burned edges of his vest, the flesh was whole and healthy. He holstered his pistol, looking forward to telling Qeine about the panicked battle with the rangers. He paused before heading deeper into the Viscerean Garrison to survey the battle.

The stronghold was too large for the Ynnari to defend properly. All along its platforms similar scenes were playing themselves out, with his attacking forces landing and seeing scattered or no defence. The rebels would be holed up inside, of course, at choke points and strategic nexuses.

Raevij had pulled her Ravagers back and gained altitude. They were beginning to tear into the enemy from above, although one of them appeared to have been damaged, only one of its guns still firing. The Venoms were now the largest threat remaining in the aerial battle, the raking passes of their splinter cannons scattering and felling the knots of hellions. Several smoking craters in the installation marked the termination of a Reaver's flight, the riders laid low by the toxic fusillade the attack craft could put out.

Acceptable losses, of course. While Naeddre needed to keep enough of his forces intact to contribute to the greater battle at the Port of Widows, he also recognised that each dead Commorrite was one fewer gang scum that he had to pay.

'Phaerl, do you intend to honour me with your presence any time in the near future?' Naeddre could see the Raider flying the banner of the Stalking Fiend Shrine. Two Venoms circled it in close arcs, their Labyrinthae boarding parties locked in combat with the incubi on deck.

'*Momentarily, your grace. We've run into a small bit of resistance.*'

Naeddre gave a great exaggerated sigh. 'If you're having too much trouble, ask my troops for some pointers. I'm sure you could find some gang scum willing to take you under their wing. Catch up whenever you get the time, Phaerl.'

Ignoring the incubus' hateful hiss, Naeddre held up his arm to stare into the *nishariel* crystal on his bracer. It took a mighty force of will to create and maintain a shadow field, and the crystal was the key to transforming intent into tangible effect. The moment he focused his attention on it, he felt the energies in the crystal rebel, attempting to scatter and diffuse his thoughts. He laughed arrogantly, allowing the last vestiges of agony from the rangers to buoy his willpower. He focused on the image of Phaerl's sputtering, indignant face, and as his hubris soared, his personal shadow field billowed back to life.

The halls of the garrison were empty, at first. They wound back and forth like a circular maze. There was little ornamentation, save for racks for splinter rifles and additional ammunition. He knew where to go, and the quickest path to get there. The years of monotonous service at the Viscerean Garrison had given him an intimate knowledge of its turns, paths and secrets. His movements were as sure and confident as a lover's touch.

The upper antechamber was where he would find resistance. It was where the elite soldiers, the commanders and favoured sybarites brought slaves for their cruel enjoyment, one of the only forms of entertainment to be had in the garrison. The room was large enough to amass a meaningful number of soldiers, and was the last such bulwark before reaching the command centre. He paused at the last junction before the antechamber, wondering if he should wait for Phaerl's assistance. His caution made the shadow field fluctuate, and that was all the chastisement he needed to storm around the corner.

The furniture in the antechamber had been formed into a makeshift barricade, torture tables and elegant reclining couches jammed together to form a single shoulder-high wall between the entrance and the archway to the command centre. A perfect firing position for desperate rebels trying to hold off a superior invading force coming through a choke point.

Naeddre was halfway across the room when he saw the grenades arcing over the wall. Half a dozen bronze orbs sailed into the antechamber, already billowing a putrid violet gas into the air. Phantasm grenades had been a smart decision, he admitted to himself. The fearful hallucinogens in the mist were no danger to him and the filter in his helm, but his eyes were no more able to pierce the fog than anyone else's.

The first sign of an attack was the silver of the knives flashing through the smoke. His enemies were like ghosts. They were silent, eerily silent. He'd never heard wyches before that weren't screaming battle cries or jabbering in drug-addled rage. The mute, focused wrath of the hekatarii was unsettling.

He fought back with fury. His helglaive whipped to and fro, tearing rifts through the smoke and cleaving through flesh. The rangers had just been sport. They had been children before an angry ursodon. The wyches had skill. They could strike and withdraw, leaving his counter-blows to slash in the air. In the final tally, however, they were still common rabble. He was the product of thousands of years of noble blood, tempered with the finest training and outfitted with the most masterful equipment that could be crafted, purchased or stolen.

Naeddre swept his helglaive in great arcs, keeping his enemies at as great a distance as possible. Their chemical-laden blood sprayed in broad fans across the walls of the antechamber with each hit. The discipline of the gladiatrixes broke at some point; he began to hear high-pitched screaming coming from all around him. The shadow field robbed the wyches' blows of real power. Still, it was only a matter of time before he felt a jab, a stinging sharpness in the broad meat of his left shoulder. The back of the same damn shoulder the ranger had shot. His arrogant bravado faltered for the briefest of moments, and with it the shadow field collapsed.

Nearly a dozen wyches lay dead at his feet. Phaerl and his compatriots had joined the fight somewhere along the line. In a straight fight, they might have been more evenly matched; both wyches and incubi were the peak of martial skill in the Dark City. The incubi had superior arms and armour, but the wyches had the advantage of speed, agility and numbers. Unfortunately for the Labyrinthae, it had not been a fair fight. Focused on the whirling, spinning form of the archon they'd surrounded, they'd been unprepared for the incubi to hit their line from behind.

Phaerl and his men moved through the carnage of the room, dispatching the wounded with cold, mechanical precision. The lead incubus gave a cry of protest when Naeddre skipped past him towards the command centre, but he ignored his father's lackey.

The command centre was a hollow icosahedron, carved from a single massive crystal, the nexus around which the entire garrison had been built. Floating images projected from each of its faces, showing the progress of the battle outside, which was grinding on towards an eventual victory for the Commorrites. Naeddre had been expecting a hekatrix, perhaps even a syren. The sight of an incubus was one he hadn't prepared for.

The rebel commander could never have been mistaken for one of the Stalking Fiends. Where their armour was the deep, sullen purple of a fresh, brutally swollen bruise, the Ynnari's was a pale, yellowish cream, like sun-dried bones, and trimmed with bright crimson. He wore a long red cape draped from his warsuit, bearing the same jagged sigil of Ynnead the hellions had flown.

'Hold and speak,' he said. 'We are all brothers and sisters here.'

Naeddre might have heard him out, but for Phaerl. At the entreaty to peace, the incubus let out a bellow, as if the Ynnari had personally befouled everything that Phaerl held dear. As one, the three incubi rushed their outcast brother.

'We have each performed this dance so many times,' the rebel commander said. He lashed the blade back and forth faster than a master heliarch could wield a much lighter, slimmer helglaive. It was as if it weighed nothing at all in his hands. 'Has its tune not grown dull to you? Its steps monotonous? Can you not hear the call of something different?'

The three incubi circled their quarry like khymerae, but his skill proved more than sufficient to hold their murderous pack at bay.

Naeddre leaned against the wall of the command centre and watched. If his father's bodyguards were so intent on proving themselves that they would attack without command, then they were welcome to do so alone.

'You can feel the pull,' the rebel incubus said again. 'The

Shrine of the Slit Throat heard it. You surely hear it, too.' He slashed his blade in a blinding series of cuts and swipes that drove all three of his attackers back a pace. 'Here, in this place, you can surely feel the souls of the fallen called to Ynnead's glory.'

Phaerl made a clicking sound in his throat, high and sharp. His brothers fell in beside him, their blades crossing over one another, forming a barrier of razored death.

'The Slit Throat are deluded soul drinkers,' Phaerl snarled. 'The Shrine of the Stalking Fiend shares neither their weakness, nor the rewards of their treachery.' He began stalking forward, his blade weaving through the air, over and under those of his brothers. The practised coordination of the blades left no gap, no weakness to exploit. They sacrificed personal glory for the surety of the kill. A tactic unnatural to the drukhari, of course, but utterly lethal when required.

'That's a shame,' said the rebel commander. He nodded.

The incubus at Phaerl's right hand stopped, his steps faltering. Phaerl spared a single glance towards his brother, whose arms had ceased their synchronised weaving. The hesitating drukhari dropped his klaive with a clatter. A moment later, his head tumbled from his shoulders, blood pumping furiously from the vacant neck stump. The corpse toppled to its knees, revealing the figure that had been hidden behind it.

No matter how many times Naeddre saw the Striking Scorpions in battle, they never ceased to amaze. Their segmented armour was as resilient as the wrist-thick plates of the giant gene-altered mon-keigh, but the brilliant green plates moved over one another silently. Every facet of them boasted of their skill. Bulky armour, rotating chainsword, even a mane of clacking beads streaming from their helms: each should have precluded the possibility of stealth, yet the Aspect Warriors went unheard and unseen, unless they wished otherwise.

To Phaerl's credit, he jerked away from the Striking Scorpion with lightning speed, a reflex that saved him from the flashing, whirring chainblade that slashed past his face a heartbeat later. The rebel incubus pressed the attack from the other side. The Commorrite incubi, on the offensive a moment ago, now found themselves fighting to retreat from the Ynnari.

'If you need some assistance, you had but to ask,' Naeddre said, peeling himself away from the wall. 'Don't fret, Phaerl – I'll rescue you.'

The stolid incubus couldn't contain a grunt of consternation as he desperately defended himself.

Naeddre leapt into the fight, his helglaive flashing. The Striking Scorpion turned on him, deflecting his blows defiantly. The Ynnari traitor swung his off hand to bring his shuriken pistol to bear. Naeddre cartwheeled to the side, letting the discs ping off the floor, trusting his spinning glaive to keep the ravenous teeth of the chainblade at bay.

With the fury of a hurricane, the Aspect Warrior moved from the younger drukhari to cross the room in a single bound and plunge his chainsword into the exposed back of Phaerl's other companion.

Phaerl kicked at the Striking Scorpion, who turned to meet Naeddre's furious rush.

'Shoulder to shoulder?' screamed Phaerl. Naeddre had spent decades taunting the temperamental incubus his father sent to watch him, but had never seen Phaerl so unhinged. Phaerl's klaive rose and fell in brutal, undisciplined hacks, his wrath stoked so greatly it threatened to burn them all. 'You stand shoulder to shoulder with the brood of Karandras? Does your dishonour have *no* limit?'

'It is you who dishonours yourself,' said the Ynnari incubus.

The Striking Scorpion pressed his assault against Naeddre, forcing the archon to spare his attention from the spectacle of Phaerl's meltdown. He gripped his helglaive close to the middle, closing as tightly as possible and weaving the ends like two separate weapons. Vicious little jolts from the Aspect Warrior's mandiblasters drove him away every time an opening presented itself.

'My friend seems quite perturbed,' Naeddre told the Striking Scorpion.

'That's because he feels the weight of his own shame,' said the craftworlder. 'He hears the call of the Whispering God, but his heart is too filled with fear to heed.'

The aeldari was masterful. His humming chainsword buzzed close enough to breathe across Naeddre's flesh, his pistol spat to hem the archon's movements one moment and blocked the haft of his glaive the next, and the stinging laser spikes of his mandiblasters forced the drukhari into contorting evasive twists and rolls. 'So he beats his breast and proclaims his greatness even as his soul slips away to feed She-Who-Thirsts.'

Naeddre ducked the chainsword and slashed in with a series of staccato hacks and chops, forcing the Striking Scorpion to back further and further away.

'When I win here,' Naeddre said, 'I'm going to drag you back to the Amaranth Spire, to fight over and over until I learn all these marvellous techniques of yours.'

The craftworlder didn't fight like a wych or a hellion; he never retreated. When he moved, it was to gain an advantageous position. When he withdrew, it was to goad his opponent into a mistake. Every one of Naeddre's blows was met not with a dodge or a weave, but with a bone-jarring parry.

'When this battle is concluded,' said the Striking Scorpion, 'you could command an army larger even than your father's.'

Naeddre was shocked, so shocked he faltered. He slashed at his opponent quickly, giving ground to regroup mentally.

'Kysthene tells us the Labyrinthae have always followed the Bladed Lotus in all things. Would it be less so among the Whispering God's warhost?' The Aspect Warrior jabbed at Naeddre again. The archon's mind reeled, trying to determine the craftworlder's angle. If the Striking Scorpion had wished, he could have torn Naeddre's throat open in the moment of his hesitation. He wasn't just trying to rattle Naeddre. But he couldn't be serious. Could he?

Behind him, he could hear the two incubi grunting in weary exertion. It seemed likely that they would fight until they died and withered away unless either he or the Aspect Warrior triumphed and came to their ally's aid.

'You've heard the whisper, haven't you?'

There was the question, out in the open. K'Shaic had not even dared to ask it of his sons. In the Dark City, no one dared ask. Colleague, compatriot, even brother – no one could tell who had felt the pull of Ynnead, who would be willing to follow his path. Since the disjunction, Naeddre's greatest fear, the one that squatted in the dark corners of his mind, lurking at the edges of his vision, was that someone would ask him directly if he had considered heeding the summons of the Ynnari.

For all his fear, there was no need. He didn't even have to answer aloud. The Striking Scorpion's shoulders relaxed a fraction; his guard remained up, but his blows were half-hearted, for show rather than to kill.

'If you answer the call, we would follow. We knew K'Shaic would send his sons to these garrisons. Right now your brother is hearing the same message – take up our banner, join our cause and we will follow you. We can fall upon your father like the vengeful storm, crush his forces between our fury and that of the Jade Labyrinth.' The Aspect Warrior holstered his pistol, holding his hand up as if to take Naeddre's. 'All you have to do is let go, to give in to the whisper you hear inside.'

The word 'yes' forced its way up Naeddre's throat. It nearly made it past his lips. But the sound choked in his mouth. He couldn't dare to speak it.

'I… cannot,' said Naeddre. 'That pull, that whisper… I've felt a pull all my life. Just as we all have. I have no way of knowing if this whisper is any different from the other.'

'And if you knew? If you knew that the Whispering God was not She-Who-Thirsts, that he would not tear you apart, but instead that he would put you back together?'

Naeddre had no words. He didn't need to speak. His silence was all the Striking Scorpion needed to know the truth, and all Naeddre needed to realise the truth himself: if he knew beyond a shadow of a doubt that the Ynnari spoke true, he would heed the whisper in a heartbeat, without hesitation.

'Then if you will not see, I will show you.' The Striking Scorpion reversed his chainsword, and plunged it through his own breast.

Naeddre felt the surge of agony as the teeth mangled the Aspect Warrior's heart and lungs to shreds. He could feel the pain the Ynnari felt, and for the first time since arriving, could feel the agony in its totality. He could feel the death rush. Then more. The dead aeldari gave his life force, not to Ynnead, but to *him*.

He reeled, the flood of sensation unlike anything he'd ever experienced.

He was a child, sprinting through the draping *keldora* ferns, laughing and chasing his cousin. He was too young to fully realise they were refugees, drifting through the stars on a craftworld that was as much their tomb as their home.

He was an aura painter. He stood before the artisans of Yme-Loc, presenting a floating, three-dimensional composition of photoluminens to the approval and emotional outpouring of his peers.

He was a Guardian, clad in grey-and-orange armour, shuriken catapult clutched to his chest. He stood knee-deep in corpses. For three days the humans in the long grey coats had hurled themselves at the eldar position, dying in droves, but never stopping in their relentless march. He wished beyond anything that he was back in his aura studio.

He was kneeling in the Shrine of the Veiled Threat. The Striking Scorpion Exarch Vakuna stood over him, asking him if he was ready to follow the footsteps and example of Karandras. He felt a great fear in his gut, but he knew that he would soon learn to summon the war mask, and that fear would be a thing of the past.

He was fighting again. Greenskins massing for a war against the aeldari. He stalked through their camps with his shrine brothers at his side. They slaughtered their enemies before they were seen, killed droves without a shot being fired. He still made art, but it was writ in blood and spilled viscera across a hundred warzones. He wasn't even sure he remembered how to paint.

He stood outside his shrine. Without the war mask upon him, he didn't know if he could bear donning the armour once again. Each time he fought the urge to lose himself to the path, each time he banished the war mask, he could feel a tiny piece of himself being cast aside. He had heard the whispered scream, the birth cry of a god, the whispering demand to open himself to it. He let go, not caring if his soul was obliterated. Anything would be better than an eternity of this torture.

He was fighting against a horde of daemons. The servants of Slaanesh swarmed the embattled Ynnari. His shrine brothers were dead. He slipped in a pool of gore, and fell. A squealing daemonette lunged over him, her scissoring claw raised for the killing blow. She vanished, cut down in a spray of ichor. A figure in a blood-red warsuit, a black cape draped over his shoulders, offered a hand to lift him back to his feet.

He was standing side by side with his long-lost spiritual brother, Jazao of the Shrine of the Slit Throat. They could hear the drukhari beyond the walls, see the Commorrites storming the Viscerean Garrison. The son of K'Shaic would arrive soon. He stepped back to blend into the shadows.

He was dying.

He opened his eyes.

Naeddre staggered, even as the body of the Striking Scorpion fell to the ground. He turned to see Phaerl still battling the other incubus. The two warriors had battled to exhaustion, and their blows had become slow and heavy. Before he could move to intervene, the Commorrite incubus brought his klaive down in a brutal overhand chop. Jazao blocked with his klaive in a two-handed grip, but the blow drove him low. Phaerl brought the sword down again, and then again. Each blow forced the other incubus down lower, first to a crouch, then to his knees.

Jazao caught Naeddre's dazed stare. He nodded, even as Phaerl smashed the klaive from his hands. The victorious incubus wiped the blood from his eyes and hefted his own klaive overhead.

'*Gashvat yandun*. Only I remain.' With a spat death curse, Phaerl struck Jazao's head from his shoulders.

Naeddre didn't just feel the rush as Jazao slipped away. He could feel the incubus, not snatched away to a warp fiend or a soul prison, but flowing through him to join the greater part of the aeldari people.

'Your father is waiting,' said Phaerl. The incubus had regained his composure for the most part, although Naeddre could see he was still breathing in great heaves.

'Did you hear any of that?' Naeddre asked.

'You mean the craftworlder wheedling you to join them? What of it?'

'Are you loyal to me?'

Naeddre's question went unanswered. The incubus cocked his head for a moment, then arrogantly turned his back to his ward and headed for the door, as if the query weren't of any merit.

'I am true to my shrine and my oaths,' Phaerl said. 'My loyalty has been paid for, and is unshakeable.'

Naeddre sighed. That's what he'd thought. He drew his blast pistol and shot Phaerl in the back. The warsuit had withstood wychblade and chainsword with ease, and even mitigated the slashing blows of the enemy klaive, but the lance of anti-light tore through it like it was mere slaveflesh. Naeddre felt the death rush, invigorating him and clearing his head. He paused to pull the red cloak, emblazoned with the drukhari version of Ynnead's rune, from Jazao's body. He draped it over his own shoulders, attaching the chain clips to his flight vest.

'Unfortunately,' he said as he stepped over Phaerl's smoking corpse, 'it was my father who paid you.'

* * *

Naeddre whistled as he exited the garrison. Dutifully, his Moonfoe skyboard heeded his call, wrenching itself loose from the wall and skittering to his side.

'Listen closely,' he said over the command net. All around him, aeldari tore one another apart, with blades and blasters and poisoned shards of glass. 'The archons in the highest spires of Commorragh have something in common with every one of you low-born gutterscum – every one of us, every single eldar, has heard the whispered invitation of Ynnead. We've just been too afraid to take it. We've seen what the birth of an eldar god heralds, and no matter how much we boast otherwise, we are terrified that this new god will finish what the first one started.'

The Moonfoe roared to life, trailing a thin stream of smoke but still capable of flight. The fighting had slowed, as gang leaders and dracons called for fire to be held, and each listened intently, many unable to believe what they were hearing.

'No more. We are the True Kin. We do not live in fear. If Ynnead draws the souls of the aeldari to himself, then the aeldari will answer. If K'Shaic and Vect and every other terrified old man in High Commorragh want to quaver in fear and ignore the call, then we will leave them behind with the orks and mon-keigh they've chosen to emulate.'

He shot through the ranks of troops, those bearing his colours, those in the green and black of the Jade Labyrinth and those daubed with the red of the Ynnari. The cloak fluttered behind him, a rallying banner that advertised the blood that united them and the blood that they would shed.

'The future belongs to the aeldari!'

He could have boarded a Raider and squeezed a tiny bit more speed from his advance, but there was strength in unity. He needed the hellions, and the full force of Reavers, when he impacted his father's lines. They swarmed behind him. Venoms and Raiders paused long enough to allow troops to board them, then roared to catch up with the skyboards and jetbikes already speeding to follow their archon.

The trip was brief. The garrisons had been designed to reinforce the port in the event of attack; it needed to be close. There wasn't even time to focus the nishariel crystal again before the webway artery curved and their destination was in sight.

The Port of Widows utterly dwarfed the garrison. It was huge, a maze of platforms and arched walkways, battlements and bunkers. Across its surface, the battle raged in full. Wyches matched blade with incubi. Hellions soared over clusters of gunmetal-armoured kabalite warriors, exchanging rattling, hissing volleys of splinter shard fire with each other. From a distance, the two sides couldn't even be discerned. Only a morass of aeldari, all fighting each other.

K'Shaic's battle-barque stood out as they drew closer. It was designed to: a massive banner daring the enemy to strike.

Corpses were strewn across all three decks of the barque, the remains of several assaults intended to decapitate the fleet's leadership. Half of the guns were silent, the gunners dead with no replacements available. Wych bodies had let forth a virtual river of blood, rent asunder by the klaives of K'Shaic's personal guard.

Most of the incubi had already died. Only one of them remained, a sullen, silent figure to whom Naeddre had never been introduced. Centuries of following his father's leadership could not evaporate in an instant. He wondered if he could speak to K'shaic, to convince him to heed the Whispering God.

K'shaic stood at his command dais, issuing instructions to his forces. At the metallic clank of Naeddre's booted feet on the grilled deck, he glanced up. He gave his son a jerk of his head: all the praise and reward he intended to give for Naeddre's performance.

The curt gesture sent cold fire coursing through Naeddre's body. Centuries of sacrificing his very soul upon the altar of his father's own hubris, for nothing more than a snide tilt of the head? His silver words turned to lead in his mouth. All thoughts of convincing his father to turn his banner evaporated. He drew his blast pistol and fired into his father's exposed back, turned to him with the same fatal arrogance Phaerl had shown.

The sole remaining incubus was a credit to his caste. He gave no indication of even looking at Naeddre, but when the blast pistol fired, he had already shoved his liege aside. The darklight instead bored a trough through the bodyguard's chest. He took a faltering step towards Naeddre, determined to protect K'Shaic to the end, but there was no more he could do. The drukhari collapsed.

K'shaic lunged at his son. He hadn't become the leader of one of Commorragh's greatest kabals by giving in to shock or sentiment. It was all Naeddre could do to get his helglaive up before his father's sabre gutted him. The surgesabre sent a cascade of sparks ringing off his weapon.

'Here?' his father bellowed, incredulous. 'Now? You couldn't wait?'

The surgesabre was lethally dangerous. It did not radiate energy or absorb light, or any of the fancy tricks that some archons desired in their weapons. It could, however, deliver an electrical charge that would kill a rampaging gnarloc. Naeddre had seen his father plunge the sword into an ork warboss, the furious energies holding the greenskin immobile while the power did its work, the warlord's mighty frame only able to twitch and spasm as its skin blackened and its eyes melted out of its skull. Even a glancing blow would stun him. A solid hit would mean death in an instant. He'd practised subjecting himself to shocks of increasing intensity so that he might one day be able to resist his father's weapon, but he had nowhere near the degree of tolerance he would need to survive a substantial blow from the surgesabre.

'Of course,' said Naeddre. 'How else can I make sure the Jade Labyrinth escapes your assault?'

He heard his words with a slight reverberation in his own helmet. His father's command dais was still on, still transmitting. Every dracon, solarite and klaivex could hear everything that happened on the command barge. Every pilot could see, in holographic miniature, the battle between father and son, playing out before their very eyes.

'The *rebels?*' K'shaic hissed. He wielded the surgesabre in his left hand, and a ghoulsteel knife, its grey-green metal inherently toxic to living flesh, in a backhand grip in his right. 'You join with the traitors?'

Naeddre didn't need to respond. The hellions, his hellions, were smashing into the Bladed Lotus forces.

'Why?' K'shaic drove his son backwards with his skill. His blades moved faster than any Naeddre had ever faced.

'For a better future,' Naeddre replied.

'Fantasies? You trade a seat at the right hand of greatness, the chance to steal the throne yourself, for a child's fairy tale?'

'A child's fairy tale?' It was Naeddre's turn to be furious. He'd never felt this sort of anger. 'Like the supremacy of Commorragh? How the galaxy lights torches because it is we who have made them fear the darkness?' His staccato back-and-forth attack pattern brought both blades to bear simultaneously, forcing his father to defend from both ends.

'We are supreme!' Never had the sentiment sounded so desperate before. Naeddre knew the truth now: his father spoke to convince himself. 'We take what we wish! We fear nothing, not even the Ancestral Enemy that the craftworlders shake and imprison their souls to avoid!'

Naeddre laughed in his father's face. The dam had broken, and he had centuries of disrespect built up.

'We are Her slaves!' he yelled. 'And She eats away at us, little by little.'

'And you think to break the cycle?' K'shaic sneered. 'Will you preach to me like one of the dirt-worshipping Exodites? Do you ignore the blood on your hands, Naeddre? The deeds you've committed?'

His father tried to vault off the command dais, but Naeddre's helglaive hooked the old archon's leg, tripping him. Before Naeddre could swing in to end the fight, K'Shaic had rolled to his feet.

'I did it all!' Naeddre laughed. His blows hammered away at K'Shaic, who was desperately defending himself from his son's ruthless onslaught. 'I slaughtered, and I killed. Millions wept. But I did what I did *because there wasn't another option*. I am a true son of Commorragh – if damnation is all that remains to me, I will drape it about myself like a cloak of regency, I will drink and savour it like a fine wine. But to choose damnation when salvation is not just an option, but freely offered? That's nothing more than the terrified cowardice of an old man too afraid of the future to unmire himself from a past that's eating him alive.' He stopped, allowing his father to gain a handful of steps between them.

'Go back to your Dark City,' Naeddre spat. 'Crawl back to

your Overlord. You can clutch each other together and cower in the darkness like frightened children.'

The battle was lit by a colossal explosion. Both combatants recoiled from a shock wave overhead, uncomfortably close. One of the Reapers that was the pride of K'Shaic's fleet burned in mid-air, its anti-gravity engines struggling to keep it aloft even as cobalt-blue flames engulfed its decks. Fighting had broken out between the crews, with the Reapers turning their massive vortex projectors on members of their own squadron.

'The future belongs to the aeldari!' The cry came over the command network. An unknown dracon, commanding his own men to turn on the loyalists. Throughout the fleet, those who had heard the whispered entreaty tugging at their hearts for weeks finally committed to its call.

For a moment, father and son stared at one another across the deck. The forces of the Bladed Lotus were in turmoil. Half of them floundered, unsure whether to attack Naeddre's forces or continue assaulting the Ynnari, not realising the two were now the same. A few dracons, believing a coordinated coup was underway, had chosen to support one of the sons rather than the father, and had struck K'Shaic's banner in favour of Naeddre or Qeine's colours instead. The Ynnari shared a much greater unity of purpose. The Commorrites who flew Naeddre's banner they largely left alone, turning their fury on those still bearing the purple-on-steel pennant of K'Shaic's Bladed Lotus.

The ancient archon crossed the dais in an instant, his blades scissoring at his son's neck. Naeddre gave ground, unable to do anything but defend against the feral attacks of his father. K'shaic's strength and savagery was born of desperation; he knew as well as Naeddre that whoever won their duel would win the loyalty of the majority of the kabal, and would carry the day.

Naeddre turned and ran straight for the prow of the barque, as though to hurl himself from the side. His father pursued, his wrath stoked to full blaze. Naeddre leapt, kicked off the highest point of the railing, and flipped backwards over his father's headlong charge. All it would take was a single kick to send his father tumbling into a fatal fall. As he flipped overhead, the surgesabre clipped his shoulder, slicing a slight nick in his flesh.

Naeddre crashed to the deck, skidding to the opposite rail. His limbs wouldn't work. All he could do was shake; every joint tried to clench and unclench at the same time. He could taste blood, ground his jaw hard enough to hear his teeth crack beneath the strain.

K'shaic stalked towards his son, pointing the blade at his wayward child. Naeddre's head, held aloft for all to see, would put the challenge of the Ynnari to rest with unambiguous finality.

The archon's chest burst apart, as a lance of black energy tore through him. K'shaic stared down in wrathful ignorance. Steaming, charred flesh ringed the wound. The archon turned to see Evaeline standing at the foot of the forecastle. She held Naeddre's blast pistol in a two-handed grip.

'The future belongs to the aeldari,' she said.

She didn't pause to help Naeddre up, returning instead to the pilot's console. Naeddre staggered to his feet and stumbled to the command dais. His limbs still twitched from the electrical fury the sabre had unleashed on him, but he fought through the tics and tremors with sheer willpower.

'The fortress belongs to the Ynnari,' he rasped, his voice harsh. Even his throat had suffered the ravages of K'shaic's sabre.

The proclamation was unnecessary. Many of the purple-on-steel banners were cut down, replaced by the pink-on-black of Naeddre's own banner. The Raiders, Venoms and Ravagers that had not struck the colours of K'Shaic's Bladed Lotus still fought, but for escape, not for victory. All that remained was to consolidate his forces.

Naeddre tapped the controls of the command dais, then stared in confusion. Qeine's forces were moving in the opposite direction. As if in answer to his confusion, his brother's voice cut over the communication network.

'K'Shaic is dead,' his brother said. *'Long live Archon Qeine, ruler of the Amaranth Spire and leader of the Kabal of the Bladed Lotus!'*

'Damn it,' said Naeddre, restricting the communication to Qeine alone. 'Brother, listen to me – there's a chance for something better. We don't have to do this.' No answer came back. Over the open network, he could still hear Qeine posturing and issuing orders.

'Excellency, what do we do?' Evaeline had brought the barque to a hovering halt.

'"Your grace" will still suffice,' Naeddre said.

'What do we do?' The barque pilot repeated. Long years of service to his father before him had taught Evaeline to be task-oriented and unfazed by threats, sarcasm or torrents of gunfire.

'We regroup,' said Naeddre. 'The corsairs of the Blackblood Nebula will be here tomorrow. We trade the goods in the port's holds to secure passage out of here.' He'd need to coordinate with Kysthene, if she still lived, to get the most out of the Labyrinthae. Eventually, he'd need a long-term plan. Raiding for supplies would be good, finding the bulk of the Ynnari would be better. Crusading to liberate more aeldari willing to fight for the future of their race, that seemed the most enticing.

Naeddre stood on the command dais, unmoving. The cowards who had fled for the Dark City were gone. The warriors, the Ynnari under his command, were rounding up the Commorrite loyalists they'd managed to capture. Many of the damaged ships could be repaired. Those who survived had their pick of equipment that could be scavenged from the dead. The hellion gangs were already scouring the wreckage far below, looking for weapons and other commodities to be bartered.

'Are you injured, your grace?'

'No,' said Naeddre, 'it's just quieter than I expected.'

Evaeline said nothing. Naeddre knew she'd piloted the barque for decades, and had witnessed the raucous aftermath of the Bladed Lotus' battles. She'd seen Naeddre and his brother boasting and threatening one another, laughing and lying as each recounted their own personal glories from the fight they'd just survived. They always claimed they were vying for K'Shaic's favour, but their braggadocious stories often continued long after the old archon had lost interest.

Naeddre gripped the railing, his legs still unsteady after the surgesabre's assault. There was an emptiness inside him. Not a devouring hole like the call of She-Who-Thirsts, or the gentle whisper of Ynnead. Just an emptiness. A pit where something had been lost, something that could never be replaced.

Still, it was the silence that hurt the worst.

NO HONOUR AMONG VERMIN

C L Werner

C L Werner *is known for his rip-roaring adventures in both the Mortal Realms and the World-That-Was. This time, Werner is commanding a murderous band of skaven as they undertake a near-impossible heist within enemy territory.*

Fylch Tattertail is part of a team tasked with stealing a Chaos cult's most prized possession – a daemon summoning bell. Now all he must do to succeed is survive a tide of blood-thirsty cultists, a scheming skaven warlock and crewmates whose daggers are never more than a whisker away from his turned back. If Fylch is lucky, he'll escape with his life... If he's really lucky, he might even get paid.

The pungent smell of incense was predominant, but there were underlying scents as well. Human scents. Odours of subjugation, anxiety and adoration. The stink of fear.

Fylch Tattertail's whiskers twitched as his nose instinctively tried to draw more information from the air. He knew it was a futile effort. The walls of the tunnel were much too thick and the alcove much too high to discern much by scent. It was by visual inspection that the truth would be revealed.

The brown-furred skaven pawed about in the pouches woven into the inside of his thread-bare tunic. Fylch pulled out a motley assortment of oddments. The skull of a weasel, the shiny carapace of a dried beetle, a rusty bolt of dubious importance, a gold coin badly scratched where it had been bitten, five buttons, a salted grot ear that looked a bit mouldy. Fylch let the litter of junk spill onto the tunnel floor. He didn't need any of it. What he wanted was… He stopped fumbling about his tunic when he removed the blackened bit of warpblend. Steel infused with trace amounts of warpstone, the three-inch rod was etched with Queekish symbols invoking the Horned One's protection. Fylch wasn't so sure he accepted the merchant's pitch about such divine defence, but he did know that the taste of warpblend on his tongue was a powerful stimulant, giving him a clarity and focus that was otherwise elusive.

Fylch scrambled up the last few steps to the top of the alcove. Slaves had spent several painstaking weeks excavating the secret stair and the little spy-perch at its top, working in absolute silence until their task was done. Fylch regretted it had been necessary to work them so hard – by the time the slaves were finished there hadn't been much meat left on their bones. And Skowl Scorchpaw had been counting on the slaves to supplement the meagre rations the expedition had brought along.

Fylch shook his head and bit down harder on the warpblend. He was letting himself get distracted. He had to focus on the job ahead.

At the top of the alcove, Fylch found the brass-rimmed eyepiece jutting from the wall. Just a twinge of fear coursed through him as he pressed his face to the lens. He knew what he should expect to see; his biggest concern was that he'd be too late. If things had gone too far and the skaven had to wait for the next moon... Well, there weren't any more slaves left to eat.

Peering through the lens, Fylch was afforded a bat's-eye view of the chamber on the other side of the wall. He didn't pretend to understand the complex arrangement of mirrors and mechanics that allowed the spy-scope to bring everything into view with such clarity. It was enough that the device worked the way it was supposed to work, something not always a certainty with Clan Skryre's inventions.

From high above the chamber, the scope brought the room into view, gathering up the fitful light from braziers and torches to throw a reddish cast across everything. To Fylch it was like looking at a reflection in a puddle of blood.

The chamber was vast, easily a hundred feet wide and thrice again as long. Parts of the walls and especially the ceiling looked raw and natural, but the floor had been smoothed and levelled. The wall sections that had been worked were likewise smoothed down and covered in a sort of plaster or limestone glaze. There were pictures and symbols painted on them, but some of those symbols made Fylch's glands clench and the less thought he gave to the murals the better.

Dominating the room, at its far end, was a broad altar of volcanic obsidian, its edges shining like mirrors. There were iron shackles set into the four corners of the altar, and Fylch could pick out the smell of dried blood rising from the shallow grooves cut into the top of the platform and the hound-faced basins resting on the floor beneath each one. Behind the altar, towering dozens of feet above it, was a monstrous statue. It had a roughly humanoid build, with broad shoulders and two powerful arms, but instead of legs it had a mass of serpentine bodies, their coils interlaced in grotesque patterns that defied the eye to follow them. There was no head; instead a bestial face jutted outwards from between the shoulders, its lips pulled back in a toothy snarl. One stony arm was held against the statue's side, a viciously crooked sword clutched in its hand. The other was outstretched, pointing one of its claws forwards.

Fylch held his breath when he saw that claw. There was a chain wrapped around it and at the end of the chain there was a hook. Normally that hook was unburdened, but now there was a huge bronze bell hanging from it. It looked as big around as an overfed duardin and was about as tall as a grot in boots. Fylch could make out the grisly runes cut into the sides of the bell. They almost seemed to glow with malice and precipitated a spurt of fear-musk from his glands as he looked upon them.

It wasn't just fear that Fylch felt. There was a brew of relief and eagerness that rushed through him as well. The bell was what they were after! It was the reason Skowl had brought them here. And despite his anxiety, Fylch knew that it wasn't too late. They still had time to steal the relic away from the humans.

He glanced across the robed figures that were seated on the floor facing the altar. They swayed in time to the angry cadence of a huge drum, their hooded heads sweeping across the ground. At an estimate, Fylch would have guessed there to be two hundred of them, but he found it hard to make an accurate assessment with their individual scents masked by the incense – he might be counting the same ones over and over. He was more certain about the dozen armoured guards who flanked the congregation, tall and imposing men locked inside heavy suits of bronze armour. Then of course, there was the masked priest standing underneath the statue, his visage locked behind the fanged skull of a monstrous hound. That was the man-thing to pay particular attention to, and Fylch gave him a scrutinising glower. The cultists were mindlessly obsessed with ritual and each ceremony was performed exactly like the ones before it. The priest would set the tempo, and from what Fylch could see there was still quite a bit of time before he'd be ready to start his mumbo jumbo and make an offering to the Blood God.

Fylch drew back from the eyepiece. If not for the warpblend bit in his mouth, he might have uttered a titter of triumph;

instead he simply lashed his forked tail from side to side in amusement. There was still time! Everything was ready and there was still time!

Fylch took the bit from his mouth and scurried back down the steps. He paused over the pile of junk he had dumped earlier. He picked through the rubbish, stuffing objects back into his pockets. It was a very pretty beetle husk, after all, and one never knew when even a mouldy salted grot ear might become appetising.

Fylch hurried down the narrow tunnel. He was reassured by its comforting confines, his whiskers brushing against solid walls to either side. All skaven preferred it when they knew nothing could go creeping around them and come at them from behind. When the tunnel opened into a wider corridor, Fylch's paw closed about the hilt of the sword tucked under his belt. It was an unthinking, instinctive motion, a reaction to the abrupt loss of the security offered by the tunnel.

It was also a mistake. Before Fylch could react, he was struck a powerful blow from the side. He crashed against the hard stone floor, the sword flying from his fingers as he slid across the ground. The tang of his own blood was on the air, and he could feel a sticky dampness under his tunic where he had been scratched by claws. His eyes darted to the creature who had struck him. No need to guess which of the five skaven in the corridor was to blame. Only the hulking Krick was licking blood from his claws.

Fylch bared his fangs and lashed his forked tail in fury. Krick glared back at him, showing his sharp teeth in a wicked grin. The big skaven was powerfully built, almost twice as massive as Fylch. His body was covered in woolly black fur, and the fur in turn was covered by metal armour and a hide cuirass. Krick absently wiped the rest of the blood on the hanging skirt of his cuirass and glanced at the sword Fylch was reaching for.

'Go. Take. Krick kill-bash Fylch fool-meat,' the big skaven snarled, fingers tightening about the spiked mace the brute carried.

A guttural snarl from one of the other skaven in the corridor caused Krick to drop down in a submissive posture, head turned and throat exposed in a gesture of contrition. 'Tattertail bring-carry sword-blade...' he stammered, trying to explain himself.

The skaven who had snarled at Krick gave the brute a menacing glower. He was a tall piebald ratman, lean and rangy in contrast to Krick's muscled bulk. He wore a voluminous leather robe-smock, its outer surface slick and shiny. A bewildering array of tool belts criss-crossed his waist and chest. Lashed across his side was a metal cylinder with a deranged assortment of hoses and wires streaming away from it. Many of these connected to the bulky metal glove that was strapped to his right hand. A sinister green glow pulsated from the cylindrical device... and from a reservoir on the back of the glove. Taken in whole, the device was a ghastly weapon and one that had given its inventor his name: Skowl Scorchpaw.

'Fylch too clever-smart to plot against me,' Skowl snapped, eyes straying from Krick to Fylch. They were ugly, bulging eyes, burned red by the chemical fumes of Clan Skryre's workshops, and it was a hard thing for any skaven to hold the warlock engineer's gaze for long.

'Yes-yes, mighty-great Skowl,' Fylch whined, his forked tail flicking across the ground. 'Fylch is loyal-true!'

Skowl held his crimson eyes on Fylch. 'And what has loyal Fylch spy-seen?'

'Man-things start rite,' Fylch said. 'Bell hang-swing from statue-beast.' Fylch looked across the other skaven in the corridor. 'Soon bring sacrifice-meat to altar-plate,' he declared.

One of the other skaven, a hunchbacked ratman with a scrapyard of weird tools and devices hooked to the basilisk-hide coat he wore, quickly fished a spherical instrument from one of his bags. He squinted at the crystal sphere and manipulated a dial on its underside. He bobbed his head in delight as the device blinked and whirred. 'Not-need fear-worry,' he squeaked. 'Cultists never start-slay without moon-time. Still time-chance for plan.' He jabbed a clawed finger at the sphere as though to prove his point.

Fylch ducked his head to hide his bared fangs. The tinker-rat was Teekritt Badscratch, as adept at creating new inventions as he was at stealing them from other skaven. Fylch wondered which category the strange lunar tracker belonged under. He almost hoped the thing wasn't working right just so he could watch Scorchpaw vent his displeasure on the arrogant Teekritt.

Skowl bruxed his fangs as he digested Teekritt's assurance. He turned to the other three skaven in the corridor. 'Know-remember what to do,' he said. 'Hide-find places. Wait-lurk.' His gaze roved across the three. The red eyes locked with that of a small, one-eyed ratman. 'Ragbrat send-show signal.'

Ragbrat's gloved paw caressed the barrel of the gun he carried. It was a massive warplock jezzail, its barrel etched with Queekish scratches and its stock carved from a gargant's tooth. There was a murderous twinkle in his eye. Fylch had heard it said the marksrat couldn't go to sleep unless he had shot something beforehand.

The two skaven who would be waiting for Ragbrat's signal were as different from each other as hot and cold.

Brakkik Gnash wore a smelly confusion of rathides and a big satchel slung across one shoulder. A long, hollow rod cobbled together from finger-bones was strapped to a loop that crossed his chest. On his shoulders and scampering about his feet were a pack of rats, each branded with a different Queekish glyph.

The other was Haak Blackear. From head to toe he was covered in a costume of heavy leather robes, gloves and boots. On his back he wore a heavy metal cylinder, hoses running from it connected to the long mask that, for the moment, was hanging against his neck. Slung at his side was a big ratskin basket containing a deadly profusion of poison gas bombs.

Skowl turned back to Teekritt. 'Prepare-ready box-casket,' he snarled, pointing a claw into the darkness. 'Wait-watch for Skowl return.' The inventor lost his arrogant confidence and dipped his head in a show of obedience. Licking his fangs, Teekritt scurried off into the shadows. Skowl watched him go, then turned to Ragbrat and gestured towards the concealed door that linked the skaven tunnels with the halls of the humans. 'Sneak-slink behind man-things. After priest-thing strike bell, Ragbrat give-send signal. Then Brakkik scare-scatter. Haak kill all-every brave-stupid man-things.' The marksrat and his companions hurried away to carry out their orders.

'Fylch, Krick, follow-stay,' Skowl announced. The warlock engineer mounted the steps leading up to the alcove.

Fylch started to follow, but a cuff from Krick sent him sprawling. The black-furred brute gave him a toothy grin as he stalked past. It was more than just a reminder of where Fylch stood in the pecking order. It was a promise that there would be an accounting between them when it was all finished.

Fylch had to repress a titter of amusement as he followed Krick. The verminous thug had no idea who it was he was dealing with if he thought he'd have a chance to settle scores.

Fylch was back in the hidden alcove above the cult temple. The tiny space was even more cramped now that Skowl and Krick were with him. He was thankful that the others were down below, creeping about the back of the temple. Trying to stuff six ratmen into the place wouldn't have left enough room to swing a dead mouse.

'Fylch! Watch-spy! Speak-squeak all that happens.' Skowl Scorchpaw gestured to the bat's-eye scope. Krick lashed his tail in annoyance when the other skaven walked to the top of the alcove.

Fylch wondered if Krick would feel so jealous if he understood why Skowl had bestowed this 'honour' on him. The warlock engineer had a trepidation about using any device he hadn't inspected beforehand. He had seen too many high-ranking skaven perish in unfortunate accidents – indeed had arranged several of them himself. With no time to extract the scope and examine it, he'd arrived at the pragmatic solution of letting Fylch take on the duty.

'Man-things still sit-pray,' Fylch reported as he gazed down at the cultists. The skull-masked priest was standing behind the altar, only now there was a bronze axe in his hands. Fylch knew it was just his imagination, but he fancied he could smell the blood caked onto the axe even through the heavy incense. The man-priest started to chant in a weird language that was unfamiliar to Fylch. It had a strange quality that he didn't think was purely human, more like the snarl of wolves or hungry dogs.

Suddenly the priest swung around and gestured with the

gore-caked axe, pointing it into the crowd. A cry of horror rose from one of the cultists. The worshippers to either side of him seized their companion and dragged him up with them as they stood. Fylch licked his fangs in grim anticipation as he watched the victim being led to the altar. 'Sacrifice-meat is chained to altar-plate,' he reported as the man was forced down onto the stone and bound by the shackles.

Now the man-priest reached down and tore open the front of the sacrifice's robe, laying bare his chest. The gore-crusted axe came into play, but instead of hewing the man asunder, the priest merely brought the weapon's edge to his victim's body, scraping bloody furrows in his skin. Fylch repeated what he saw to Skowl.

'Good,' the warlock engineer hissed. 'Soon they ring-strike bell.'

Fylch tried to control his glands when he heard Skowl speak. He knew what striking the bell would herald. Even so, he was compelled to keep watching the macabre tableau unfolding below.

The priest now turned from his victim and looked towards the dangling bell. With the man's blood still dripping off the axe, the cult leader brought the weapon smacking against the metal. A dolorous note rumbled through the cavernous chamber. From where he watched, Fylch could feel the sound throbbing through his bones. There was a power within it that went far beyond simple noise. It was an intonation to shiver the very soul.

A gruesome change overtook the hall below. The illumination grew notably darker even though the flames rising from the torches and braziers had risen to twice their previous height. Fylch could feel a clammy chill emanating from the room, coursing up through the scope. His gaze was fixated on the altar. There was another figure there now, something that had not been there an instant before. It was taller than the priest and far more powerfully built than even the armoured warriors who guarded the hall.

The dark shape surged towards the altar, moving with a grotesque undulating motion. Fylch gnashed his fangs to stifle the squeak of fright he wanted to utter. Moving out from under the shadow of the statue's arm, the daemon – for it could be nothing else – was revealed as a small simulacrum of the monstrous idol. Its flesh was slimy with fresh blood, its skin rippling as it moved. The eyes that glared from its hideous face were alight with a hellish fury, glowing with the kind of feverish intensity Fylch had seen only in warp-snuff addicts.

In stammering words, Fylch described what was happening to Skowl. Then the daemon swept to the man lashed to the altar and started to feed...

'Fool-meat!' Skowl growled as Fylch jerked away from the eyepiece. 'Watch-tell! Hurry-scurry!'

Krick pounced on Fylch and forced him back to his post. The brute's powerful arms were locked around his head, pressing his face against the eyepiece.

Down below, Fylch could see that the daemon had finished its meal. All that remained on the altar was a shambles of bone and shredded skin. Blood spilled from the gutters carved into the stone, filling the jars set beneath. The victim's head was missing and as the daemon slithered back under the idol's arm, Fylch could see the skull gripped in the beast's jaws.

The bell was still ringing from the blow the priest had struck, but now the reverberations stopped. Awed silence held the chamber, the cultists watching in fearful adoration as the murderous daemon they had called up vanished with the last echo of the bell's summons.

'Daemon-thing leave-gone,' Fylch told Skowl.

Skowl tittered with delight. 'Plan-plot start now!'

Fylch could see the man-priest standing behind the altar again. He brandished the axe above his head with both hands and began leading the cultists in another bestial chant. Then, above the roar of the crowd, a sharp boom cracked across the chamber. The wolf-skull mask of the priest was shattered, crumbling to the floor in ragged fragments. The priest fell back onto the coiled limbs of the statue, his face obliterated by the warpstone bullet that had struck him.

The cultists fell silent, stunned by the grisly death Ragbrat's shot had delivered from the back of the temple. Before they could gather their wits, cries of alarm sounded from the left flank of the congregation. Fire crackled against the wall, blazing away with ferocious violence. A second fire erupted from the right, soon to be followed by another and yet another.

Brakkik's work, or rather that of his trained rats. Keeping out of sight, the ratmaster was blowing specially scented pellets into the chamber. The smell of each pellet was prepared to entice the rat trained to seek it out. Only unlike the treats used to teach them, those Brakkik now used would start a pyrotechnic reaction when consumed by the rats, turning the rodents into living firebombs. Fylch had to concede that the scruffy skaven was creating a splendid distraction with his pets.

Thrown into panic by the fires, confused by the murder of their leader, the cultists lost all cohesion. They scattered in frantic flight. Only a few were devoted enough to remember the bell. Led by an under-priest and accompanied by a few armoured guards, a small group removed the bell from its hook and hurried through the swelling smoke and fire to a little door at the back of the chamber.

'Man-things take-fetch bell. Run-race through door.' Fylch dropped away from the eyepiece the instant he felt Krick release him. One paw darted for the sword he wore, but Fylch resisted the urge to stab his oppressor. It would be too easy to gut the vermin where he stood. Besides, Skowl wouldn't like it. Krick's part in the plan was just starting. The vault where the cultists secured the bell was only a few hundred yards down the tunnel from the alcove and the black-furred brute would be needed to help carry it away.

Skowl bruxed his fangs in delight. 'Yes-yes! Stupid-fool man-things! They do just what I want-need!' He gestured to Fylch and Krick, then pointed at the steps. 'Hurry-scurry! We find-fetch bell now!'

The three skaven scrambled back down the steps and into the tunnel. Fylch had lost count of how many times Skowl had forced them to practise this mad dash from the alcove, down the hidden tunnel to the secret door that opened into the cult's vault. This time, of course, they made the run in earnest and that urgency lent him more speed than he thought he could muster. He reached the door easily ahead of the others. In the thrill of the moment, he pushed against the stone portal, but it resisted his efforts. He had to wait for Krick to add his brute strength to the effort before the stone swung aside and exposed the cult strongroom.

The vault was a long, narrow room with a low ceiling and a rough floor of unworked stone. The walls were cut into little niches wherein the mouldering remains of coffins and human bones gave off a musty smell. There were other smells, too, that assailed Fylch's senses as Krick pushed him through the secret door. Blood was one. Evil was another, a brooding malice so potent that it conveyed itself to the skaven's sharp nose as a rank, desolate odour. It took Fylch only a heartbeat to detect where the smell was strongest – a huge obsidian sarcophagus that loomed at the far end of the vault.

The sarcophagus, Fylch knew, was where the cult kept the daemon-bell when it wasn't needed for their rituals. Arcane spells guarded the obsidian vessel and for more mundane purposes there were a series of complex locks that might have befuddled a duardin craftsman. Fylch was relieved to see the sarcophagus standing open. That meant they had beaten the humans to the vault and the bell hadn't been sealed away. It also meant Fylch would be able to skip the most dangerous role he would have played in Skowl's plan.

'Thieves! Ratkin desecraters!' The cry rang out through the vault. Fylch spun around to see the under-priest and his entourage entering through the vault's door. Four cultists bore the daemon-bell between them, and he could see the fanatical outrage that twisted their faces when their leader shouted. The armoured guards, however, were of far more immediate concern. They didn't simply glare at the skaven. They came charging towards Fylch with axes and swords. He glanced around for Skowl and Krick, but the other ratmen had ducked back inside the hidden passage.

Fylch cringed away from the guards as they rushed him. As the first swung at him with a bronze axe, the ratman whipped around, lashing out with his curved sword. Thinking the skaven cowed, the axeman was taken completely by surprise when Fylch's blade slashed across his arm and tore into his shoulder. The guard cried out as his useless limb lost its hold on the axe and the weight of the weapon dragged down his good arm. For an instant the man was exposed and vulnerable. It was all the opportunity the swift ratman needed. In a blur of fur and steel, Fylch stabbed the point of his sword into the warrior's throat. The man fell and thrashed on the floor while he choked on his own blood.

Fylch darted around as one of the other guards came at him with a sword. There was no question of parrying the man's blows. In a contest between human and skaven, the advantage of strength usually belonged to the man-thing. Even a comparative brute like Krick was merely able to hold his own against a human warrior. But the skaven had their own advantages over their enemies. If Fylch could not match the guard's strength, then the guard could not match his speed. While ducking around the warrior's blade, the ratman lashed out with his forked tail. Like a scaly whip it cracked against the man's leg, stinging the exposed skin of his thigh. The sudden and unexpected pain provided a moment of distraction, one that Fylch was quick to exploit. He dived in towards the guard, rolling across the floor and raking his sword across the man's side as he passed. The guard screamed in agony, a great gout of blood spilling from where the serrated edge of the skaven blade had ripped just above his hip, between the sections of his bronze armour.

Fylch darted a glance at the other cultists. Krick had finally rushed out from the tunnel. One guard was down with his head caved in while the other was trying to fend off the attentions of the spiked maul with his axe. The under-priest was shouting for help while at the same time forcing the cultists carrying the bell towards the obsidian sarcophagus. Fylch hissed a curse on the damnable humans. If they should make it...

One hand clutching his bleeding wound, the guard Fylch had injured chopped at him with his blade. Again, the wily skaven ducked the sweep of the sword and struck out with his own weapon. He had the satisfaction of feeling flesh rip under the steel, and saw a pair of fingers go bouncing across the floor. His hand maimed, the warrior staggered back, trying to recover his momentum. Fylch didn't give him the chance. Thrusting forwards, he stabbed his blade into the gap in his armour where pauldron joined cuirass. He felt bones crack under the blow and savoured the sharp tang of blood that sprayed from the man's torn flesh. Darting back from a desperate but unfocused sweep of the guard's sword, Fylch watched his foe crumple to the ground.

'The cult-men!' Skowl roared as he deigned to emerge from the tunnel. 'Stop-slay!'

Skowl acted on his own words; holding forth his metal glove he pointed the fingers at the cultists. Green energy crackled about the glove, sparks flying from the generator and the reservoir. Then streamers of jade lightning went shivering across the vault. Fylch threw himself to the ground as one of the green bolts hissed past his ears. Others smashed into the roof and walls, blasting little showers of pebbles from the stone.

Some of Skowl's erratic warp lightning seared into his intended targets. Anguished screams rose from the cultists as the green energy burned through them. Robes and hair burst into flames, flesh blackened and cracked as the humans were flash-boiled.

The immolated cultists fell, and as they fell the daemon-bell crashed to the floor. Again, the dolorous, shivering tone pulsed through the air and trembled through Fylch's bones.

The under-priest, half-cooked by Skowl's attack, lurched to his feet, his face ashen where it had not been burned, his eyes wide with terror. In a Herculean effort, he wrapped his arms around the bell and flung it into the sarcophagus. The lid slammed shut as the man collapsed beside it.

If the human had thought to save himself by locking away the bell, he was to be disappointed. Fylch could see the dark, monstrous shape that had suddenly manifested in the vault. He felt its ravenous, malevolent eyes sweep across him and the other skaven. The under-priest was closer to it, however, and it was the cultist it chose for its victim. In a rapid, undulating motion, the daemon surged over the prostrate priest. Fylch had thought the earlier ritual was ghastly, but now he was afforded a close-up view of the proceedings.

It was enough to gag a rat.

As before, once it had claimed its meal, the daemon evaporated with the same swiftness with which it had manifested. The only evidence of its advent was the gory litter it left behind.

Skowl was the first of the skaven to recover his wits once the daemon was gone. He glanced at his still glowing glove, then at the dead cultists, and finally at the sealed sarcophagus. His lips peeled back from his fangs and he lashed his tail angrily from side to side. Turning towards Fylch, he seized him and pulled him within inches of the exposed fangs.

'Fool-meat! Traitor-meat! Why Fylch not stop-slay man-things?' Skowl dumped Fylch to the floor and continued to glare at him. 'Now Fylch will open bell-box! Quick-quick!' He turned his head towards Krick, who was standing over the body of the last guard. 'Fail-falter and I will feed your spleen to Krick!' The proposition brought a grisly leer from the black-furred skaven.

'Yes-yes, bold-wise Skowl.' Fylch bobbed his head in an unctuous display. He didn't dare tell the warlock engineer that it was his fault the cultists had dropped the bell and

363

called the daemon back. A skaven quickly learned it wasn't smart to point out the mistakes of superiors.

Muttering curses under his breath, Fylch approached the sarcophagus. He was careful to keep away from the mangled mess that had been the under-priest. Closer to the obsidian vessel, he could feel the crackle of the protective wards cast upon it. The lid of the sarcophagus had been cut into the semblance of a human skeleton – a grim touch that he didn't appreciate under the circumstances. He wasn't certain what the wards would do to a thief and he wanted to keep things that way.

Fylch rummaged about the pouches sewn inside his tunic. He discarded a ball of twine, some rock-hard cheese, an empty moth cocoon, three azurite beads, a lizard fang... Finally his paws closed around the object he wanted. It was a long, smelly item: a severed skaven hand that had been pickled and then coated in paraffin. Each finger was upright with a little wick pinned to the claw. The mummer he had bought it from called it a 'paw of gory' and claimed the magics invested into it would counteract any spell that tried to foil a thief. Fylch had used it before, as two singed fingers attested, but never to steal anything that he was absolutely certain had some kind of arcane protection.

'Hurry-scurry! Quick-quick!' Skowl snapped. The warlock engineer didn't have much patience and what he did possess was wearing thin.

Gnashing his fangs and clenching his glands, Fylch set the paw of gory down on the floor. From another pocket he brought a duardin tinderbox and used it to light one of the wicks. He started to put it away, then reflected on the eerie sensation of the arcane wards. There was power here that might need more to oppose it. He hastily lit the other fingers so that all five were flickering with an ugly blue glow. Almost at once, he felt the uncanny crackle of the wards dissipate. As long as the wax-coated fingers burned, the arcane wards would be rendered impotent.

Fylch glanced back at Skowl and Krick, then swiftly set to work. There was no need to rummage around to find the intricate lock picks he carried. He kept them secure on his belt where they would always be in easy reach if he needed to get out of a tight spot quickly. Staring at the morbid sarcophagus, Fylch felt this was about as dangerous a place as he had ever been in.

With the paw of gory sputtering away, Fylch approached the mechanism the cult used to secure their relic. Previous inspection of it had convinced him it was going to be a tough bone to crack. Coupled with the wards, it was the reason he had persuaded Skowl that they should intercept the bell rather than try to steal it from the vault. Besides, the warlock engineer wanted to make sure the bell really summoned daemons before going through with the scheme.

Fylch now attacked the problem of the devilish locks. A pick gripped in each paw, two more clutched in the coils of his bifurcated tail, and a fifth clamped between his fangs, he set to work. Carefully, with the exacting caution only someone raised in the paranoid society of skaven could master, he manipulated the tumblers and teeth. There was a system to the mechanisms, forcing each to be opened in sequence before the whole would be overcome. Fylch experienced moments of panic as picks threatened to snap under the pressure of the teeth, and tumblers refused to budge. So intent was he on his task that he even ignored the demands and threats Skowl shouted at him. The locks would be finished when they were finished. Not before.

There was only one thing that could urge Fylch to reckless haste, and a chance glance back at the paw of gory provided it. Two of the fingers were already burned down to mere nubs while the others had less than half their length to go! Once they were all extinguished, whatever dread spell guarded the sarcophagus would be unleashed.

Fylch pried and prodded the locks with all five picks, juggling and jostling with abandon. Unable to think about what he was doing, he fell back to instinct and the innate sense of long experience. First one, then another of the locks sprang open. Soon it was Fylch's turn to demand haste.

'Fetch-take bell! Fast-quick!' He swung open the lid of the vessel, exposing the sinister bell.

Skowl now turned his impatient ire on Krick. 'Get-fetch! Help loyal-clever Fylch!' he snarled at the brute. Pointing the glowing warp-glove towards the skaven motivated him to be quick.

Fylch helped Krick lift the bell away from the sarcophagus, trying to ensure that the clapper didn't strike the sides. 'Quick-quick,' he hissed to the black-furred killer. He was watching the paw of gory burning down to its last knuckle. When it went out, the arcane wards would return.

'Lift-carry, tick-sniffer,' Krick cursed as he hefted the bell. Together the two ratmen managed to carry it away from the sarcophagus. Fylch felt the magical crackle of the restored wards as they scurried away. He was still happy not knowing what the spell would do to a thief.

'Rest later,' Skowl told them as they lugged the bell towards the tunnel. 'We find-seek Teekritt. Use his bell-box to take-leave cult-nest.'

Fylch and Krick both bobbed their heads in agreement. Right now, anything that let them set down the heavy bell sounded like a good idea. It seemed to grow heavier with each step they took, but knowing what would happen if they dropped it made them persist.

It wasn't particularly reassuring to Fylch to see Skowl keeping his distance as they trudged down the tunnels. If anything did happen, the warlock engineer was making sure it didn't happen to him.

Fylch's arms felt as though they were on fire by the time he and Krick finally reached the spot where Teekritt was waiting for them. Krick gave a happy squeak when he saw the cart and the big metal casket Teekritt had prepared to receive the bell. Fylch winced when he saw the ramshackle conveyance. It looked as if it would collapse under the bell's weight when they loaded it. Skowl had been so meticulous in all his plotting and scheming, but this minor detail appeared to have escaped his devious cunning.

'No-not drop-trip now!' Fylch warned the black skaven.

Krick bared his fangs. If his hands weren't around the bottom of the bell, he might have put them around Fylch's neck. 'If weasel-licking Fylch would hold-carry his end!' he growled.

Teekritt squeaked in horror when the two skaven took a final stumble towards the cart. The clapper swayed perilously close to the side of the bell. All three of the ratmen froze and didn't twitch so much as a whisker. Scrambling under the bell, Teekritt reached up and held the clapper still. Gesturing with his free paw he motioned the others forwards, keeping the bell silent while they pushed it onto the cart.

Fylch let out a deep breath once the bell was in place. 'Good-glad to put down bell.'

Krick grimaced at the rickety cart Teekritt had brought. A

spurt of fear musk wafted into the air. 'Need better-good way to carry-take bell,' he complained. He turned and looked at Skowl as the warlock engineer approached, finally deigning to join the others now that danger was no longer imminent. 'Cart make bell shake-ring.'

Skowl bruxed his fangs and gave Krick a sharp look. 'I already plan-plot. I need-want Krick carry bell. Now I need-want Krick keep bell quiet.'

Krick's ears were folded back in puzzlement as he heard Skowl speak. He still had that confused look when Fylch drove his sword into the ratman's back. Krick spun around, fangs bared, but Fylch's blow had been delivered with the murderous skill of an assassin. Death silenced Krick's fury before he could even raise a claw to his killer.

Skowl looked away from the corpse to Teekritt. 'Get to work,' he told the tinker-rat.

Teekritt scurried underneath the cart and dragged out a wooden skinning rack. In short order he had Krick's body stretched out and was peeling away the ratman's woolly hide with a flensing knife.

'Krick will muffle-quiet the bell,' Skowl declared. 'Let sleeping daemons sleep.' He turned to Fylch. 'Grey Seer Nezslik pay much-much for magic bell, but not enough for Krick-share.'

Fylch bobbed his head in agreement, while trying to keep any sign of agitation from his posture. 'Big-share better than little-share,' he said.

Skowl displayed his fangs in a gruesome grin. 'True-squeak,' he agreed. Before he could continue, the sound of something running down the tunnel brought all three skaven spinning around. Their agitation relaxed slightly when they saw that it was only Brakkik returning to join them. The ratmaster looked even more ragged than before, breathing heavily and without his entourage of trained rodents scurrying about his feet.

'Where are Haak and Ragbrat?' Skowl wanted to know.

Brakkik dipped his head in apology to the warlock engineer. 'Dead-die,' he reported, though there wasn't any regret in his tone. 'Ragbrat shoot-kill man-priest, then Brakkik's rats confuse-scare cult-things. Some cult-things see-find skaven. Chase-hunt! Ragbrat try to shoot-kill but jezzail-gun explode!' Brakkik made a violent gesture with his hand. 'Haak use Poison Wind globes to gas-kill, but poison get into mask!'

'Then they are all dead,' Skowl stated. He gave Fylch a knowing look.

Fylch fumbled among his pockets until he found the squirming bundle he wanted. He pulled out the rat, its back branded with the number four. A flick of his claws broke the tethers that bound its legs and jaws. He held the animal towards Brakkik. 'Lose-drop,' he said. 'Fylch find-save.'

As Fylch released the rat it went scampering straight for Brakkik. The ratmaster squeaked in horror, all too aware of what kind of treachery was afoot. He frantically patted his clothes, trying to find the scented treat that was drawing the number four rat to him. It was a futile effort, Fylch had hidden it with the same dexterity that had allowed him to steal it in the first place. Brakkik realised this and turned to flee down the tunnel, but even as he did, the rat reached him. It scurried up his back and down the neck of his coat. An instant later there was a hideous scream and a bright plume of fire as the vermin found its deadly treat and the resulting conflagration consumed its master.

'Then there were three,' Skowl stated. 'Clever-quick Fylch. Now we split all their shares.'

Fylch bobbed his head in agreement. Skowl watched as he

rummaged in one of his pockets and brought out the screw he had removed from Ragbrat's gun and the valve that had previously been attached to Haak's respirator. 'Skowl not need-want more?' Fylch asked, backing away from the warlock engineer.

'I did not need-want Brakkik and others,' Skowl said. 'They not-no useful. Clever-loyal Fylch is useful.' He looked aside to Teekritt as the tinker-rat was stuffing Krick's hide inside the bell to muffle its clapper. 'Teekritt clever-loyal too,' he added. 'Both clever-loyal skaven put bell inside bell-box now.'

Fylch scrambled up onto the cart beside Teekritt and helped the tinker-rat push the bell into the metal casket. Once it was inside, the lid was shut and Teekritt locked the casket with a small brass key.

Skowl held out his hand, waiting for Teekritt to give him the key. Fylch grabbed the tinker-rat and kept him from dropping down to join the warlock engineer. 'Wait-listen,' he hissed at Teekritt. 'Maybe share-three is too much for Skowl. Maybe share-twice is too much!'

'Doubt-question Skowl?' Teekritt tried to keep his voice level, his posture authoritative but not unduly threatening. His red eyes fixed on Fylch. 'Honest-clever Fylch learn-know Skowl is good-true. Pay much-much when Clan Skryre come to take-carry bell.'

Teekritt glanced at his weird timepiece. 'Yes-yes, Clan Skryre come soon-now.'

Skowl stroked his whiskers and bruxed his fangs. 'Pay Fylch much-much.'

'Same-like way Ragbrat and Haak and Brakkik and Krick pay much-much?' Fylch asked.

Skowl bared his fangs. He was tired of this slinking thief's impertinence. It didn't matter that Fylch was right and he'd be disposed of just like the others. That was simply what happened to underlings who were no longer useful.

'Traitor-Fylch!' Skowl roared. He raised his warp-glove, but then his eyes narrowed with vicious cunning. The bell was too close to risk using warp lightning. He glanced at Teekritt and saw the confusion in the half-crazed tinker-rat's eyes. There, at least, was an underling who was still useful. 'Teekritt! Kill-slay traitor-meat!'

The tinker-rat rounded on Fylch, but he was ready for him. Fylch's claws raked across Teekritt's face, then he dived against his foe and sent them both crashing down from the cart. The two skaven wrestled on the ground for a moment, then Fylch broke away and fled to the far side of the cart.

Skowl lifted his gloved hand, but again stayed himself because of the bell. His gaze drifted down to Teekritt. The tinker-rat didn't have the same shield to protect him. In a blast of green energy, Skowl immolated the hunchbacked rat-man. He leaned over the carcass and plucked the key from the charred claws.

'Only Fylch and Skowl now!' the warlock engineer snarled. He glared at the cart with his red eyes. 'Come out and die quick!'

For answer, an object came whistling out from the darkness. Skowl leapt back as it struck him. He expected to feel a stabbing pain; instead he felt an unpleasant warmth at his side. He stared down at the warp generator for his glove. A throwing star, similar to those employed by Clan Eshin, was buried in the device, causing it to spit sparks and green flame.

Frantically Skowl ripped away the straps that fastened the generator to his side. He pulled away the warp-glove and threw the whole apparatus far into the tunnel. He spun around and threw himself to the floor as the malfunctioning device exploded and sent metal shrapnel and bits of refined warpstone flying.

The explosion was still ringing in his ears when Skowl regained his feet. He glared at the darkness, trying to spot or scent Fylch. When he couldn't find the coward, a sneer of contempt curled his tail. Let the little thief run; once Skowl collected from the grey seer there wasn't anywhere in Skavendom Fylch could hide from him.

Skowl picked up Krick's maul and stood guard over the cart and the bell-box. He would not need to wait long. The conveyance he had arranged would be here soon to retrieve both himself and his prize.

Fylch watched from the shadows as the huge Clan Skryre digging machine burrowed its way into the tunnel. The crew helped Skowl aboard, then loaded the bell-box as well. Fylch held his breath while they carried the casket inside, but nothing happened. Then the digging machine was moving again, its huge drill gnawing away at the opposite wall while its wheels ground against the floor. In only a few moments, the huge machine was gone from sight.

Fylch dropped the woolly hide he had removed from the daemon-bell. He didn't need it any more. He also didn't need the key he had stolen from Teekritt. It was as useless to him now as the one he had replaced it with and which Skowl had taken with him. While the warlock engineer was getting rid of his warp generator, Fylch had used the real key to open the box and remove the muffling hide.

He crept down the tunnel to where the digging machine had gone. Fylch strained his ears in hope he would hear the faint tolling of a bell. He lashed his tail in amusement when he imagined the daemon appearing inside the machine to eat the crew. Even more amusing was the idea of Skowl trying to open the bell-box with the wrong key.

Grey Seer Nezslik would have to forget about adding this relic to his grisly collection. Skowl Scorchpaw had made a few too many enemies among his fellow warlock engineers. Enemies who had paid Fylch quite well to dispose of him in a manner that couldn't be traced back to them.

The problem Fylch had now was to make sure his employers paid him with money in his paw instead of a knife in his back. But that was an almost daily ordeal for any enterprising skaven. The fine balance between caution and ambition.

ABOUT THE AUTHORS

Guy Haley is the author of the Horus Heresy novels *Titandeath*, *Wolfsbane* and *Pharos*, the Primarchs novels *Corax: Lord of Shadows*, *Perturabo: The Hammer of Olympia*, and the Warhammer 40,000 novels *Dark Imperium*, *Dark Imperium: Plague War*, *The Devastation of Baal*, *Dante*, *Baneblade*, *Shadowsword*, *Valedor* and *Death of Integrity*. He has also written *Throneworld* and *The Beheading* for The Beast Arises series. His enthusiasm for all things greenskin has also led him to pen the eponymous Warhammer novel *Skarsnik*, as well as the End Times novel *The Rise of the Horned Rat*. He has also written stories set in the Age of Sigmar, included in *War Storm*, *Ghal Maraz* and *Call of Archaon*. He lives in Yorkshire with his wife and son.

Peter Fehervari is the author of the novels *Cult of the Spiral Dawn* and *Fire Caste*, featuring the Astra Militarum and T'au Empire, the novella *Fire and Ice* from the *Shas'o* anthology, and the T'au-themed short stories 'Out Caste' and 'A Sanctuary of Wyrms', the latter of which appeared in the anthology *Deathwatch: Xenos Hunters*. He also wrote the Space Marines short story 'Nightfall', which was in the *Heroes of the Space Marines* anthology, and 'The Crown of Thorns'. He lives and works in London.

Thomas Parrott is the kind of person who reads RPG rulebooks for fun. He fell in love with Warhammer 40,000 when he was fifteen and read the short story 'Apothecary's Honour' in the Dark Imperium anthology, and has never looked back. 'Spiritus In Machina' is his first story for Black Library.

Jaine Fenn is the award-winning author of the Hidden Empire series of space opera novels as well as numerous science fiction and fantasy short stories. After studying Linguistics and Astronomy at university she spent some years working in IT by day while writing, running and playing tabletop RPGs by night. She is now a full-time writer. Recently she has written for video-games such as *Halo Wars* and various games in the *Total War* franchise, including *Warhammer II*. She lives in Hampshire, with her husband and too many books. 'From the Deep' is her first story for Black Library.

Robert Charles' career as an author truly began when a senior colleague told him that he should under no circumstances seek a career as an author. Despite what people say, it's not true that Robert never leaves the house. While his body seldom strays far from a keyboard, his mind walks distant futures and forgotten pasts. That the better bits have a habit of finding their way onto the printed page is all to the good.

Miles A Drake is a professional bartender and aspiring author based in Amsterdam, Holland. His other work for Black Library includes the short story 'The Flesh Tithe'.

Steve Lyons' work in the Warhammer 40,000 universe includes the novellas *Engines of War* and *Angron's Monolith*, the Imperial Guard novels *Ice World* and *Dead Men Walking* – now collected in the omnibus *Honour Imperialis* – and the audio dramas *Waiting Death* and *The Madness Within*. He has also written numerous short stories and is currently working on more tales from the grim darkness of the far future.

'Ties of Blood' is the first Black Library story from **Jamie Crisalli**, who writes gritty melodrama and bloody combat. Fascinated with skulls, rivets and general gloominess, when she was introduced to the Warhammer universes, it was a natural fit. She has accumulated a frightful amount of monsters, ordnance and tiny soldiery over the years, not to mention books and role-playing games. Currently, she lives with her husband in a land of endless grey drizzle.

J C Stearns is an Illinois-based freelance author who has appeared in a range of science fiction publications. He is a keen Warhammer 40,000 player, with a sizable Dark Eldar army, and has also written the Black Library story 'Wraithbound'.

C L Werner's Black Library credits include the Age of Sigmar novels *Overlords of the Iron Dragon* and *The Tainted Heart*, the novella 'Scion of the Storm' in *Hammers of Sigmar*, the Warhammer novels *Deathblade, Mathias Thulmann: Witch Hunter, Runefang* and *Brunner the Bounty Hunter*, the Thanquol and Boneripper series and Time of Legends: The Black Plague series. For Warhammer 40,000 he has written the Space Marine Battles novel *The Siege of Castellax*. Currently living in the American south-west, he continues to write stories of mayhem and madness set in the Warhammer worlds.

YOUR NEXT READ

COMING FEBRUARY 2019

GODS & MORTALS

GUY HALEY ‡ JOSH REYNOLDS ‡ DAVID GUYMER
ROBBIE MACNIVEN ‡ DAVID ANNANDALE ‡ EVAN DICKEN
CL WERNER ‡ NICK HORTH ‡ ANDY CLARK

GODS & MORTALS
by Various Authors

The warriors of Sigmar's storm face the dark acolytes of Chaos across a host of stories telling tales of deeds noble and foul, the clash of heroes and villains – and the rise and fall of Gods and Mortals alike.

For these stories and more go to **blacklibrary.com, games-workshop.com**, Games Workshop and Warhammer stores, all good book stores or visit one of the thousands of independent retailers worldwide, which can be found at **games-workshop.com/storefinder**

An extract from
'Vault of Souls'
by Evan Dicken

Knight-Incantor Averon Stormsire scowled at the rows of listing colonnades that marked where the twisted, shadowy streets of Shadespire gave way to the mad architecture of the Nightvault. Like the shell of an Idoneth mollusk, the ancient prison necropolis spiralled deeper and deeper, its lower reaches lost to clinging darkness.

'At last.' Rastus' words boomed from behind his golden mask. The broad-shouldered Evocator cocked his head, hefting his heavy tempest blade with practised ease. 'But say the word, Knight-Incantor, and we shall drag Thalasar from his decrepit lair.'

'I doubt winnowing out the katophrane will be so easy.' Ammis spoke from behind Averon. Disliking how it restricted her vision, she had yet to don her high-crested helm, her attention fixed not on the entrance to the Nightvault, but on her tempest blade and stormstaff. Concentration cut deep grooves in her darkly tanned face, her lips pressed into a tight line as she checked and rechecked the network of arcane formulae that bound the glittering conduit of celestial energy to her weapons.

Averon held up a fist to silence his companions. It would not do to come so close to their prey only to have Thalasar slip away again. Anger and frustration burned in the Knight-Incantor's breast. There was no way of measuring time in the cursed half-light of Shadespire, but Averon and his Cursebreakers had spent far too long plumbing its maddening depths for the secrets of true immortality. Tasked by Sigmar himself, they sought a way to end the slow rasp of memory and soul that the Reforging process inflicted upon their fellow Stormcasts.

Closing his eyes, Averon reached out with his arcane senses, sifting through the fog of death energy for a hint of Thalasar's sorcery. He could feel the souls still trapped within the Nightvault, their struggles like candles guttering in the murk. In shaking the foundations of Shadespire, the Shyish necroquake had also breached the Nightvault, laying bare arcane knowledge locked away since before the cursed city was cast into shadow. It was the dark promise of these secrets that had drawn Averon and his Cursebreakers to the ancient prison, and to Thalasar.

A thin glimmer of gold threaded the necromantic gyre that shrouded the upper reaches of the Nightvault. Cloaked in shadow, it drew Averon on, just as it had captured his attention the first time he had sensed Thalasar's enchantments – so unlike that of his katophrane peers.

There was something different about it, something *familiar*. Averon had put a score of necromancers and unquiet shades to the question, and found that even among the most ancient katophranes, Thalasar's creations were spoken of with jealous awe. If anyone in Shadespire held the key to slipping the terrible loss of Reforging, it was Thalasar, Averon was sure of it.

'Knight-Incantor.' Ammis stood. She slipped on her helmet, gaze fixed on the gloom. 'Something moves in the darkness. I cannot see it, but I can feel its power.'

'I sense it, too.' Rastus interposed himself between his companions and the growing shadow, storm energy crackling around his weapons.

'Do you want to bring every gheist in a dozen miles down on us?' Averon shouldered past the tall Evocator, who lowered his blade and staff with a frustrated grunt. 'Douse those weapons and remain here until I call for you.'

'You are too hard on him.' Ammis stepped to Averon's side.

'I don't recall asking for your advice.' Averon picked up his pace. 'Or your company.'

She lengthened her stride, long legs easily keeping step. 'Rastus is young.'

'Rastus is a fool,' Averon snapped back. 'A boy who fancies himself a hero. His power is unrefined and uncontrolled, he overestimates his abilities.'

'As did we all, once.'

Averon grunted, brushing away her reply. Rastus' anger was understandable; unlike his companions, he had yet to be reforged. Like a fresh banner, his soul shone in the dark – bright, heroic and untattered in a way that Averon could hardly remember being himself.

Rather than respond, he studied the tides of death energy swirling around the Nightvault. Amidst strange, shadowy illusions that swathed the ancient prison, he noticed a thread of sorcery glimmering like a candle within the tides of dark energy.

It was Thalasar's work, of that he was sure.

Carefully, Averon sent a seeking spell after the glittering strand of arcane energy. A lesser mage would not have been able to tease the thread from the deathly morass swirling around the Nightvault, but Averon was a Knight-Incantor of the Sacrosanct Chamber, possessed of power and skill accrued over several lifetimes of study.

He caught the glittering thread, pulling ever so gently.

The shadows fell away to reveal a creature from Averon's nightmares.

Easily the size of a castle keep, the hulking undead monstrosity was supported by dozens of mismatched legs. Assembled from the mangled corpses of gargants, dracoliths, krakens and creatures Averon did not recognise, the construct lumbered along the upper levels of the Nightvault, its long, multi-jointed arms plucking struggling souls from among the rubble of the ancient prison. He and Ammis had drawn close enough not to see the jagged shards of shadeglass embedded in the monstrosity's quivering exterior. They glittered with reflected light each time a shrieking spirit was fed to the amethyst flames that burned deep within the thing's patchwork maw.